Loving Sarah

Sandy Raven

She's loved him all her life.

"Adventure runs in my blood," she began. "My family was establishing trade with countries around the world for hundreds of years before I was born. Because I was born a female I am told I cannot share in those adventures. I cannot sail the oceans and climb the highest peaks. I am allowed an education, but no venue to practice it. That is not the world I want to live in.

"I did leave a note so my family would not worry. And though you may think me spoiled, dancing and parties is not all I do." She was beginning to mellow now from the delicious wine. After taking another sip, she continued. "I'll have you know that I devote a great deal of time to volunteering at the children's hospital founded by my friend's mother and her aunt. I also assisted in the formation of a lending library in our village, and I currently teach children to read at Haldenwood, our family seat."

"Is this in between music and dancing lessons?"

"If you must know," she replied indignantly. "My lessons were over four years ago. I'm going to be twenty-one years of age in just two months."

"Hmmm. . . . So you're nearly a spinster, aren't you?"

Even with the thin veil of humor tinging his voice, she was offended by his comment. She knew that the clocked ticked louder for her to find a mate, having spent these past years more enjoying herself than finding a husband. She didn't need her captain to remind her of this. So she tossed the slim volume of poetry, which had been under her leg, at him. In return, he grabbed her ankle with a firm grip and yanked her forward until her bottom rested against his thigh. With her legs over his lap, the heat of him radiated through the thin woolen material of her baggy trousers, and she became very aware of his hard-muscled leg against her buttocks. Bare under the trousers she wore, her breath caught in her chest as one of his big, calloused hands slid up a pant leg, burning a painfully slow trail up her bare calf to rest on her knee, as the other held her in place.

There was no turning back now. This was what she'd led him to, what she'd wanted. And more than likely what he wanted too, as he could turn down this unspoken invitation to a brief affair. The fact that he didn't made her feel desirable and worthy of passion—yet aching inside with the fact that the love she desired probably wasn't on this man's agenda.

But at that moment she didn't care.

"Stop me, Sarah." The husky timber in his voice was pleading, almost begging.

His intent gaze held her mesmerized. She could hardly breathe, much less move away from him, but still she managed to shake her head as she mouthed, "No."

His bare hand rested on her knee while his thumb gently stroked the sensitive skin on the inside of it. Her other leg fell open, and Sarah felt his hardened manhood beneath her thigh. Shocked, she sucked in a breath. Yes. This was what she wanted. With the sensations his touch caused and the desire pooling at her core, how could she stop? The man was insane. Pressure was already building within her to hurry him along.

She wanted his engorged member inside her, claiming her and bringing her to the ecstasy purported to occur after he joined with her. She was ready for this.

"You're playing a dangerous game, my lady." His

voice was soft and raspy, yet filled with passion. "And with a man who has not had a woman in months." His fingers caressed the inside of her knee and up a few inches higher. She saw the determined look in his eye, and the tight curve to his lips. "Be sure this is what you want. Once I start, I won't stop until I'm satisfied."

She met his carnal stare with one of her own and wet her lips with the tip of her tongue. "I want…."

His large warm hand crept up her thigh slowly. Her breathing hitched. His look told her she had one last opportunity to stop him if she chose. But the aching void in the vicinity of her womb decided for her. "I want satisfaction…as well, Captain." His hand squeezed the flesh of her inner thigh, just below her moist curls, and a moan escaped her. If she never married, or if she did, this was the moment she would always remember. When Ian asked and she replied.

"I want you, Ian."

Loving Sarah

This book is a work of fiction. Names, characters, places, and incidents are the product of the author's imagination or are used fictitiously and are not to be construed as real. Any resemblance to actual persons, events, or organizations is entirely coincidental.

Copyright © 2014, Sandy Raven

All rights reserved. No part of this book may be used or reproduced in any manner whatsoever without written permission except in the case of brief quotations embodied in critical articles or reviews.

Cover design by The Killion Group, Inc
Formatting by Author E.M.S.
Editing by Gail Shelton
Proofreading by Editorial Inspirations

ISBN-13: 978-2-939359-06-3

Published in the United States of America

Dear Reader,

Loving Sarah is the third book in my series, The Caversham Chronicles, and I hope you enjoy Sarah and Ian's story too!

I fell in love with tall ships when I was growing up on the Texas Gulf Coast. I was fortunate enough to watch one being restored for several years while working in the building next to it. And almost from the time I could walk I remember loving hot tea (even in summer). As I grew into a voracious reader, I discovered this short period of time in the mid-1800s where they had tea races on tall ships from China to London, before the Suez Canal was built and steam engines made sailing obsolete. I fell in love with those stories and prints of famous paintings of tea clippers at full sail racing back to London with their hulls loaded with China's finest offerings for that year. I always knew I was a writer, even when I was forced to pass algebra, and it was inevitable that I would write a tea clipper story.

Loving Sarah and ***Lucky's Lady*** are the clipper stories I had to write.

Because the timing is off by ten to twelve years for it to be official tea races, my fictitious setup to those races is here, where Lucky and Ian race each other home. In the next book, there is mention of the number of boats participating in the race home from China increasing.

Though the *Ann McKim* did exist at the time, she obviously did not come from Ian's father's shipyard because it did not exist. I created Watkins Shipbuilding, and Harbor Village, in the area called Curtis Bay to serve my story.

Also, there have been many spellings for the Chinese port of Fuchow (Fuzhou and Foo Chow). I chose to use the version my editor selected, though I have seen all of the above spellings in ship logs and other documentations regarding the tea trade.

In the summer of 2014, be on the lookout for the fourth book in the series, ***Lucky's Lady***. It picks up right where ***Loving Sarah*** ends.

In his book, Lucky falls in love with an incredibly intelligent young woman who is a naval architect designing ships for her elderly husband who owns a shipyard that constructs the famous Baltimore clippers. Mary Michael Watkins is a young woman who desperately wants to conceive a child before her husband dies, and he wants her to have a child too because it's the one thing he could never give her. The man even goes so far as to help her choose Lucky as the perfect candidate for siring said child and facilitating their time alone. Knowing she's running out of time, and acknowledging there is more than just an ordinary attraction with the captain, Mary Michael accepts Lucky's flirtatious overtures knowing that once his business with her shipyard is over, he'll leave her and she'll hopefully have a child to raise—a son or daughter to inherit the shipyard and her husband's fortune.

What she doesn't count on is falling in love with a man to whom family, loyalty, and love mean everything.

I would love to hear from you! So, if you have any questions or comments,

I'm online at www.SandyRaven.com,
Facebook at www.Facebook.com/SandyRavenAuthor,
and www.Google.com/+SandyRavenAuthor.

Sincerely,
Sandy Raven

Acknowledgments

To the Beta Crew: Rosetta Boydston, Mary Mallini, Melinda Hicks, Janet Firestone, Gabriella Ortiz, and Donna Padilla. You ladies are awesome and I adore you. You don't gripe when I ask for a quick turnaround.

To my husband, mother-in-law, and both daughters: I love you more than you can ever know.

And a very special thank you to Michael.

CHAPTER ONE

Liverpool, June 1835

"What about her? She looks fast, doesn't she?"

"Hmmm...*Aurelia*," Ian Alexander Ross-Mackeever, grandson of the Earl Mackeever, mused as he strolled alongside his friend Lucky Gualtiero, brother of the Duchess of Caversham. "She may look fast, but she's not built the way I like. Something about her shape...too curvy if you ask me. It looks like she might fall apart before the ordeal is over."

"What about that one? *Evangeline*," his dark, olive-skinned friend asked.

Ian turned his gaze to where Lucky motioned. "Too top-heavy, and her bottom's too narrow to support her. She'll tip over in a stiff wind."

"What about that one?"

"Her bottom's too broad. She'll be too slow to tack."

"Well, you can't say the same about that one over there. She has a nice, well-proportioned hull. At least what I can see of it."

Ian didn't need to consider the vessel in question, for he knew her design well. He should, it was very similar to, if not exactly like, a design of his father's. "Yes. Nice curves, sturdily built, and I think I know her owner. If it is who I think, he has a load of money, but no skill at the wheel." He gazed at *Ann McKim* longingly. "She was launched five years ago from the very yard my father helped found and has already broken records for the fastest crossing times for the Atlantic and Pacific in both directions. But a ship like that could do far better with the right man at the wheel." Sighing, he turned to Lucky. "What that lady needs is a man with a knowledgeable, soft hand and the experience to coax her on when she wants to give up."

"So, do you think we stand a chance?" Lucky stopped and turned toward him.

Ian looked over the competition once more, and nodded. "Oh, I'd say the odds are very good. Next to McKim's lady out there, we've definitely got the best boats in this race. A little smaller, a little aged, but well broken in. More importantly, both of them are lovingly maintained and handled." They walked away from the dock and the preparations for the next day's ceremony. "I believe everything is ready for the morning. God willing, we'll have good wind."

"The weather will hold until we're well out," Lucky said as he scanned the sky and horizon around them. Ian didn't question him. He knew better. Like an old sailor, Lucky had an instinct for forecasting weather just by looking at the clouds. "Remember, my sister's throwing us a dinner party to see us off. Be at the house around seven."

"I'll be there. You know I wouldn't miss an opportunity for real food. Anything is better than the grub Old Will throws into a kettle," Ian said as they neared a waiting hackney.

"You need to find a better cook," Lucky replied. "So you stop trying to take mine."

Loving Sarah

The driver tipped his hat and opened the door for the gentlemen. "You go on without me. I'm just going to get cleaned up and make sure the watch is in place. I'll be right behind you."

"Fine." Lucky gave a quick nod to the man holding the door, then asked Ian if he needed the address again. Ian shook his head and simply asked the hackney driver to return for him after dropping off Lucky. "Then I'll see you soon."

The hackney door closed on Lucky. After the driver cued the horse to move on, Ian turned back to the dinghy tied below and rowed out to the *Revenge*, his best hope for victory in this race. Their supplies had been loaded earlier in the day, so he'd moved his boat away from the hustle and bustle of the dock. And any potential sabotage. Not that he suspected his fellow competitors of such underhanded behavior, but one could never be too careful when the stakes were this high. Tying off the dinghy, he climbed onto the deck and double-checked to make sure all was in readiness for the start of the race. Normally, he wouldn't have considered wasting their time entering a race, but the twenty-five-thousand-pound purse was far too large to ignore. More importantly, if he and Lucky were serious about succeeding in their joint venture, the newly chartered Empire Tea Importers, they needed more ships. Two retrofit Baltimore schooners, though a respectable beginning, wouldn't turn the kind of profits necessary to expand their business in the manner they wanted. The tea run they'd made last year left him with barely enough to live on after paying the note and their crew's salaries. Lucky might not need the money as much as Ian did, but he'd be damned if he'd let his partner pay their way until they could turn a profit. Lucky had done enough already by paying the shipyard bill for the retrofit of the two boats over the past winter.

His dream, and Lucky's too, was to have a fleet of at least a dozen clippers, preferably designed and built to their specifications. After carefully studying Colonel Beaufoy's publication, *Nautical and Hydraulic Experiments*, where Beaufoy tested and found Newton's hydraulics theory unlikely, Ian had begun drawing his own hull designs. To maximize hull space for valuable cargo, Ian's idea was first to streamline the design of the hull; next to make her longer and deeper in the keel; then, to eliminate the complete dependence on ballast and use lead plate on the keel in conjunction with minimal internal ballast for stabilization. He was excited and anxious to test his theory. If it worked, he knew it would forever change the way hulls were designed and built. And his father, wherever his soul rested, would be proud.

Having grown up with a university-educated naval architect for a father, a man who designed and built clipper hulls, Ian knew that shipyards in New York and Baltimore were willing to build experimental designs; whereas in Aberdeen and Halifax, they were more likely to insist the time-tested and proven designs they had been successfully building for the last twenty years were better. Ian knew his design held promise and so did his partner. So he would amuse Lucky and have the Aberdeen yards look at the designs, but Ian knew they would likely have to go back to America to have them built the way they wanted.

Ian made his way down to his small cabin, stopping to take a bucket of fresh water from the barrel near the companionway. He ladled some into the metal basin, set the bucket down near the washstand, then stripped. He dunked his head into the bowl and began washing. One day, he'd like to have a house with a proper bathing chamber. There would be no more tossing water out of portholes or over the railing and refilling wash basins. No more bathing with cold water, except when at sea. Worst of all were the times he had to bathe with salt water, because it always left him feeling sticky and itchy. For that reason, he understood why some of the crew went without baths during those times.

Life at sea wasn't the romantic, adventurous dream he'd imagined. But this had been his reality for the past five years since leaving university. He supposed he could have lived on credit and taken rooms somewhere, as did others in his financial situation. But Ian was too American for that, as Lucky reminded him on those rare occasions when Ian complained out loud. He might be the grandson of the Earl Mackeever, former commander in the King's Navy and a hero who was severely injured in the Siege of Charleston saving the lives of his sailors as his ship sank. But, he was still the American-born son of a Baltimore naval architect who'd designed ships for the Americans in their second war for independence— one of the two reasons his grandfather hated him and the old sod reminded him of it each time Ian had seen him. Of course, since *the incident*, Ian hadn't seen him at all.

Yes, the man with whom he shared blood despised him because of it. He never failed to remind Ian that his mother was a servant in his home and his father was a traitor to Great Britain and responsible for the deaths of many fine British sailors, perhaps even his uncle.

But there was another reason the old man hated him.

One so dark and so foul that Ian had never told a soul, not even his best friend. The secret existed only between him and his grandfather, and when the old bastard died, Ian would be free to live a normal life. Or, as normal as an American-born heir of a Scottish earl could live.

Coming to Britain as a child hadn't been easy. Some people, he'd learned over the years, had long memories, especially when they'd lost loved ones. And when your father was instrumental in expediting their dispatch to the next life, it was even more difficult to find a friendly face at school, and later university. Ian often felt he was the only unwelcome foreigner at school. It wasn't until Oxford, where he met Luchino Antonio Francesco Gualtiero, the Conte di Loretto, Lucky to all who knew him, that he'd found a kindred spirit. His new friend was just as much an outsider because of his swarthy, Mediterranean appearance as Ian was for his American blood. It was in that atmosphere, that he and Lucky had become fast friends and immediately after university, business partners.

Now, at age twenty-five, Ian had the entire world before him. And no place to call home except this ship. He wasn't British because he was born in America, but no longer American because nothing remained there for him, hadn't since his father died twelve years earlier, when Ian was thirteen. The last time Ian saw his father, Ian had been twelve years old and forced to board a ship to England to live with the grandfather and two aunts who would see to his proper education and preparation for him to take his place in society as his grandfather's heir. It had been something he'd fought against with all of his little boy might, to no avail.

Opening the cabinet, he remembered the cedar lining

still needed replacing as he took out his good clothing. Repairs inside his cabin had been low in priority during the renovations, but now as he looked over his best trousers to make sure they weren't moth-eaten or torn, he decided it needed to get moved up on the list. He checked the coat and linen shirt for tiny holes, saw none, and smiled. Lifting the only waistcoat he owned, he noticed the stitching at the edge of the wool where it met the satin was coming apart, but knew it would remain hidden by the coat.

If he ever did take his place in society, he would need to pay more attention to his dress. Ian owed it to his father's sisters not to be an embarrassment to them when he did, especially after all they'd done for him over the years, from taking him in when his father sent him over for his formal education to sponsoring his entrée into society. Events like this dinner with Lucky's family were sure to become more common as they became more successful. He had to think of tonight as an opportunity to polish his manners and become more accustomed with the world he'd not been born to but now found himself a reluctant part of.

Success would make his aunts, two dear old ladies he adored, proud. Until then, he had to stop wasting time worrying over his grandfather's hatred.

Lady Sarah Eileen Halden dropped her gaze as her brothers discussed the upcoming race, lest they see the delight in her eyes while her final plan started to form. The rented home in Liverpool the family had taken for the next several months was nowhere near as large or opulent as Caversham House or Haldenwood, but it had something that would serve her well this night. She'd spied it right after arriving and looking over her temporary bedroom. She had a balcony that was a mere ten or twelve feet above ground. Sarah could quite easily climb over the railing and ease herself down. The drop, after lowering herself as much as possible, wouldn't be much more than the jump from her favorite tree at home.

She saw it as a sign that she was meant to go with Lucky on this race.

"Ian and I have gone over the charts several times and already plotted our course." Lucky pointed to something on the map Sarah's brother Ren, the Duke of Caversham, had spread across the table in the drawing room where they'd all gathered while waiting for the last of their dinner guests to arrive. "Both crews have been with us at least a full year. They made the tea run with us, and they're all veteran sailors. Most have crossed the Atlantic at least once, some several times. So we're very confident in everyone's abilities."

"Good," Ren said, "I know this is an exciting challenge for you, but remember do not push your boat any harder than she can handle. Even if you don't win this race, you know I'll finance you."

"And I as well, Lucky," said Elise's husband Michael, the Earl Camden, and Sarah's brother-in-law.

"I appreciate your offer, Ren, truly. And yours too, Michael. But this is something I want to do on my own, and Ian feels the same."

The butler announced the arrival of Mr. Ian Ross-Mackeever, Lucky's business partner and long-time friend. When Sarah looked up and met his eyes, she could have sworn her heart skipped several beats and her mouth went dry. The man was far more handsome than she'd remembered. His greenish-brown gaze met hers, and she quickly turned away and took a sip of her sweet wine.

It had been almost a year since she'd last seen him, the night he'd come for dinner at Caversham House before leaving on their trip to China. It was just as the Little Season was getting underway, and she'd thought it was a shame he wouldn't be around to amuse her and her friends. After all, he was certainly good-looking enough then, but now he was a sun-kissed Adonis come to life. The time seemed to have made him even more ruggedly handsome. He'd become broader in the shoulders, and his face bore a healthy glow. His dark blond hair was liberally streaked with gold in a manner that could only have come from working in the sunshine on the open sea, like hers had when she was a girl sailing her little sloop around the pond at Haldenwood, pretending she was a great explorer.

Rugged and handsome. Those were the only words she could think of as she glanced at him again. Without a doubt, his Viking god-like looks were the cause of the tiny tremors that coursed through her body each time she looked at him. She felt perhaps, if given more time together, a plethora of emotions and feelings might have a chance to develop.

Sarah had to stop thinking of him this way. As attractive as the man was, she had no time for romance right now. She had a race to sail with Lucky. When it was over, she might indulge and see where a flirtation would lead.

From her position, half-turned from him, she covertly watched Ian greet some of the other guests as he made his way toward where she stood with her brother, Ren, her brother-in-law, Michael, and her brother-by-marriage, Lucky. As he did, she noticed his evening wear was somewhat outdated, but it did nothing to detract from his intense vitality. Before she embarrassed herself, she took her leave from Ren, Michael, and Lucky and sought her sister-in-law's company where she sat with a group of ladies.

Talk among the women soon turned to the goings-on in town now that the season was almost over. "My girls are still in town with their aunt," Lady Vance said, "and they were loathe to leave. Now that my two nieces are married, my sister is relishing taking my elder daughter through the season's events."

Sarah traveled in a different set than Miss Vance, the younger girl's friends being more the intellectual blue-stocking type. Just the same, she smiled politely, remembering how exciting her first season had been as well. She'd truly enjoyed her first and even her second season. Then her friends began to marry, leaving to start their own families. And with each season Sarah's tolerance for the superficiality that was the season grew thinner. In her head and heart, she was always elsewhere. Her friends knew it and the men she'd met sensed it, which was why she was twenty-one and still unwed, with no prospects on the horizon.

Sarah had long grown bored with her lot in life. She craved adventure. Longed to see the world. Growing up, she'd always questioned why men were respected when they successfully ventured outside the boundaries set for them by society, but never women. Why was a woman's reputation in tatters when she did something bold and adventurous, and not a man's?

The year before, she'd thought to stowaway with

Lucky to China, but had been afraid to actually dare it. That fear had been the only thing keeping her inside her comfy, gilded cage—the fear of not being accepted after returning from her grand adventure. But not this year.

With only a few weeks until the end of her third season, Sarah was beginning to feel her fate might lie in spinsterhood because of these desperate longings. She knew she was choosy, but wasn't about to compromise in her requirements for a husband. Not only did he have to desire adventure as much as she, but his kiss should leave her weak in the knees and curl her toes—something her sister and sister-in-law told her was how they knew their husbands were the ones for them.

So, unless and until she found that man, she wouldn't consider marriage. She'd rather remain the eccentric relative to her family. Because she would never compromise those two requirements.

Her decision made, she would turn her back on caution and grasp this opportunity.

"You're quiet little sister," Elise said as she sidled up to Sarah where she stood on the fringe of the group of ladies. "You have a wistful look about you. What are thinking about?"

"Wondering why I couldn't have been born a male. I envy Lucky."

Lia stifled a giggle. "You would have made a very effeminate male and not very attractive to the ladies I dare say."

Sarah shrugged. "You both know what I mean. I have to return to London and finish out the season. And I'll do so wishing the entire time I was racing with them."

"As ladies our rewards are in the home—in caring for our families, friends, and neighbors," Lia said. "Our legacy is the children we raise to carry on after we're gone. I never thought of it that way until after I had Isabel and needed to be a role model for her." Her sister-in-law turned her gaze on Sarah and studied her face. "I think next year we should concentrate more intently on finding you a match. We should talk to Ren about it after Lucky leaves. I think you're ready for that husband now that the social season holds no more charm for you."

Elise nodded. "Lia's right. And from my own experience, just as with a high-strung filly, a babe will settle that restless spirit of yours."

Sarah wanted to protest and remind her sisters of the stories she'd heard about Elise's own youth, but the dinner bell rang and all of the guests proceeded into the dining room, taking their seats. She discovered her dinner companion to her right was Lucky's partner, Mr. Ross-Mackeever. At first, having the handsome seafaring adventurer beside her caused her pulse to race. But it wasn't long before she knew it wasn't the fact that he'd sailed around the globe, but the man himself, that stirred her senses. The faint scent of cedar and citrus wafted from his direction, and she inhaled a shaky breath before looking his way.

She smiled. "So Mr. Ross-Mackeever, you must be excited. Lucky was when we spoke just before your arrival. And it must feel good to return to your home. Even if it is for only a day."

"The race is to New York. I wish I had time to visit Baltimore, but in all honesty, there is no reason for me to return there yet."

"Oh. Then you plan to eventually?"

"If we win this race, I will likely return to have my father's friend build our two new clippers. There is no finer shipyard on the eastern seaboard."

"You could have your ships built here. I'm sure His Grace can make the necessary introductions in Aberdeen. It's where his import company was based before he bought out his cousins and moved operations to London. I'm certain we have relatives who know a shipbuilder or two."

"That was one of the places we intended to query about building custom clippers."

Footmen began serving the soup, and Sarah listened as the men continued their pre-dinner discourse on the opportunities for trade and import now that the East India Company had lost its monopoly as sole importers of tea to Britain. Talk of finance, trade, and the importance of diversification floated about the table.

But not Sarah. Her entire being quivered in the presence of Lucky's partner. Or was it the excitement of the race? She was unsure. She pushed her fork around the plate as she listened to their conversation, trying to hide her anticipation. Sarah didn't know if her excitement came from her plan to stow aboard Lucky's clipper or her close proximity to this man who had a strange effect on her senses. She tried to make certain not to bump her arm into his, especially when she noted he was left-handed. But when she dropped her napkin she did, and he spilled soup on his cravat and waistcoat. Mortified, she met his gaze, wanting to disappear but at the same time to drown in his gold-flecked brown eyes. Or lick the warm and creamy onion soup from his chest.

Where had that thought come from?

"I'm so sorry. I...." Her face burned at the images racing through her head, and the entirety of the table staring their way. She immediately took her napkin and began to dab at his waistcoat until the footman hurried over to take care of it for her with a clean, damp linen. Mr. Ross-Mackeever waved the man away, blotting what little remained of the soup on his waistcoat himself.

"There wasn't much soup left, as I was nearly done." He showed her the bowl. "See? All is well, my lady," he said through a smile. "No harm done."

"Thank goodness," she whispered, "I'm not normally so clumsy, and I sincerely apologize."

Conversation resumed around them, and Mr. Ross-Mackeever spoke again. "Were you going to come out to the dockyards in the morning and watch the ships jockey for position at the starting line?"

Sarah kept her eyes cast downward, unwilling to have him see her excitement as she spooned up her soup. She took a deep breath to collect her emotions. "Yes, Mr. Ross-Mackeever. I wouldn't miss that for the world."

Her dinner partner was turning out to be very charming for an American. At first she'd thought him cocksure and a bit self-absorbed, she was fast coming to realize she was wrong. The man was gracious to everyone with whom he spoke.

"Your brother once said you and he are very much alike in that you are as adventuresome as he."

Sarah sighed, again regretting her gender. "Lucky is right. One would think we were true brother and sister, rather than joined by the marriage of our siblings."

"I'm fortunate to have your brother as a friend and partner. I've never met a more honest, intelligent, and unprejudiced man. I consider myself honored to call him friend."

Sarah smiled as she held another spoonful of the onion soup. "He can also be annoying and stubborn, but that's coming from a sisterly perspective."

"I never had a sibling to annoy, or I'm sure I would have been the same."

"Don't say so! It would ruin my image of you," she teased.

"Oh?" Mr. Ross-Mackeever laughed, the sound warm and pleasing. "What image is that?"

"One of a kind gentleman who is understanding and not as rigid and straight-laced as my older brother and Lucky."

They laughed and compared upbringings, and soon the next course was served and the topic changed to the two schooners, *Revenge* and *Avenger*. Mr. Ross-Mackeever described the remodeling done to the sister ships. It reaffirmed to Sarah that he and Lucky were obviously proud of the modifications made to their boats and felt they stood a solid chance of winning the race after sizing up most of their competition earlier that afternoon.

"On first glance," Lucky said, "the *Ann McKim* looks to be the best boat in the race, but looks can be deceiving. She's long and sleek all right. But without knowing how she carries her ballast, or the type of keel she has, there's really no knowing how well she'll do. She's a brand new design, built in Baltimore, at the very shipyard Ian's father helped found, and while the American owner will captain her, my opinion is he doesn't have half the experience necessary for an undertaking such as this."

An uneasy quiet came over the table as everyone realized that in such an endeavor as this not everyone survived. "Unfortunately," Ren said, "lives will be lost during this race. But I have every confidence in the two of you. In fact, were I twenty years younger, I might have entered myself. Not for the purse so much as the thrill of the adventure."

Sarah pushed the vegetables around on her plate and kept her eyes downcast, for that was the very reason she planned to stow away aboard Lucky's boat.

Sarah shoved the packed canvas bag she'd brought with her from London under her bed. She was going to be on that boat when it sailed in the morning. There was no way she was going to allow Lucky to have this adventure without her. She was tired of reading about everyone else's voyages and missing out on ones right before her.

She'd spent the last five years as the embodiment of a well-mannered young lady because that was what was expected of the sister of a duke. And for the past three seasons, she'd smiled and swallowed her envy as Lucky lived the adventures of which she could only dream. First he and his partner sailed to America to buy the two American-made schooners they required for their newly chartered import company. Then last year she forced herself to feign interest in the social season while Lucky prepared to sail to China on their tea run. And late last summer, she smiled and wished him well as he sailed away again, all the while wishing she were with them.

Well, the balls, musicales, dinner parties, morning calls, and rides through Hyde Park would still be there when she returned. She was not going to sit in her room and cry as he sailed away. Not this time. This was the chance of a lifetime, and she wasn't letting it pass her by.

By tomorrow night, she would feel the salty spray of the ocean on her face and the motion of the vessel under her feet. For some inexplicable reason she just knew her heart would soar as she heard the snapping of the sailcloth in the wind and the shouts of the men as they performed the tasks ordered by their captain. It would be just as Ren described when he'd told her of the adventures he had when she was a girl. Sarah smiled as she remembered forcing her brother to repeat each voyage every evening he was home.

When she was older, she read the journals and ship logs that lined the shelves of her brother's office, finding these far more stimulating reading than the historical or scientific tomes or romantic novels in the library. These were log books with descriptions written in the hand of her relatives, who had seen and witnessed each act and event she'd read.

It was those tales of adventure and the uncertainty of success that sparked this desire within her to travel and see the world. They were food to her adventurer's mind and soul.

Yes, without a doubt, Lucky would be angry with her when he discovered she'd stowed away, but he'd soon get over his anger when he realized he couldn't very well return her to dry land. Her older brother would be furious as well once he realized what she'd done. But by the time anyone noticed her missing, she'd already be somewhere in the Atlantic and there'd be nothing they could do. She'd write a note to Ren explaining what she'd done and leave it on the *secretaire*. They'd find it when they looked through her room for clues, though they should know she'd seize the opportunity to sail the Atlantic and see New York City when it presented itself. After all, she'd talked about her desire to see the Americas her entire life.

The devil take her, but she'd happily face Ren's anger upon her return for an adventure such as this!

A soft knock on her door preceded her maid, who'd come to help her undress for bed. While Trudy braided her thick mass of unruly waves, Sarah contemplated the timing of her escape. She had to leave well before breakfast and do so without calling attention to herself or setting up an alarm. Darkness was her ally.

With the mound of pillows on the bed, she would fashion a suitable form under the covers that hopefully upon first glance would appear human, thus indicating to her maid she still slept. Then once at the docks, she'd need someone to take her out to the boat. That was why she'd filled her coin purse and tossed it in the satchel. She didn't doubt that she'd find someone to take her. In her experience, when you offered someone enough money, they'd willingly do just about anything.

The summer she was ten years old, she'd mapped the entire estate over a period of five weeks while the rest of the family enjoyed their season in London. She had been studying geography at the time, and Ren had joked about her mapping the American continents one too many times. Sarah had wanted to prove her map-drawing skill to her brother and set out alone to accomplish the task.

Of course she was found out before she'd gone one hundred yards from the stables. Theo, the stable lad, had discovered what she was up to as she led her pony, loaded with all of her supplies, plus a rolled napkin with some pilfered crusty bread, fruit, and cheese from the kitchens. At first, he refused to keep quiet about her expedition, until she offered him her collection of Roman coins she'd dug up near the old church ruins.

And on her brother's birthday, she proudly presented

him with a rolled, charted map of Haldenwood, current up to that date, with boundaries and crude elevation changes. When asked how she'd accomplished the task, much to their appalled dismay, she proudly regaled to the entire family, her solo adventures in mapping.

She spent the next week writing a different essay each day on her irresponsible actions that could have led to her injury with no one knowing for hours that she was missing and the search for her that could have taken weeks on an estate the size of Haldenwood. Each essay had to be new and different. No duplicating what she'd written the day before.

Sarah waited until her maid had gone and smiled as she then opened the drawer to her desk and took out a sheet of vellum, quill, and ink.

My dearest family,

First, please do not be upset. Rest assured, I am safe with Lucky. And please, for pity's sake, do NOT interrupt the race because of my desire not to allow another adventure to pass me by!

I have decided that because it is highly doubtful that I shall ever marry, there are a few things I would like to do before I settle into my spinsterhood. One is seeing if the ocean really is as clear and blue as I've always heard; another is to see America.

Also, please do not fault Lucky in this. He knew nothing of my plans.

Love, and etc.,
Your Sister,
Sarah

With the note written, she placed it inside the old ship's journal she'd been reading, leaving it prominently placed on top of the *secretaire*. The only thing she waited for now was the house to go quiet for the night.

Slipping past the fire boy as he slept in the kitchen proved easier than she'd expected, and once outside, she made her way to the street, keeping to the shadows alongside the house as much as possible. She walked briskly and with intent toward the port a short distance away. She entered the area cordoned off for the morning ceremonies and began to look for someone to ferry her out to *Avenger*. Pulling the gray coarse-knit cap down lower over her brow, she took on a stooped posture and with the bag slung over her shoulder she looked very much like any other young sailor. She raised the collar of her coat, hiding her face and any trace of the waist-length braid tucked inside.

A scrawny lad sat with his feet dangling over the side of the dock. Glancing over the edge, she saw a dinghy tied below. Sarah dropped her voice, hoping she sounded masculine. "Can ye ferry me out to me boat, lad? I shoulda been on it hours ago and th' cap'n will be missin' me come sun-up."

The lad shook his head. "Can't do it. I'm waitin' on me own cap'n."

"There'll be coin in it for ye."

The boy looked more interested now that money was mentioned. "'Ow much ye got?"

Sarah fished two half sovereigns from her pocket and

showed him. The boy looked at the money in her hand, then around the darkened pier.

"Fine. But I gotta be quick, don't know when me cap'n's comin' back." Sarah tossed the bag into the dinghy and stepped down into it. Once the boy shoved away from the pier with the oar, he asked, "Which un's yer boat?"

"*Avenger.*"

"Aye. I knows where it is."

They rowed out about a hundred yards into the darkness with only the light of a cloud-covered sliver of moon. Gentle waves lapped the side of the tiny craft.

This was it. There was no turning back now. She was on her way to see the ocean and America. Well, at least one city in America. She told herself that she would return to see more of the country later. Perhaps once she found a traveling companion.

She trembled with anticipation when the lad brought the dinghy along-side Lucky's boat, near the rope ladder. "Are ye sure ye got the right boat?" she asked. "Don't want me cap'n lashin' me back."

"Aye, she's the right un. I'm right alongside ye on *Evangeline.*"

She handed the lad the two coins, tossed her satchel over her shoulder, and grabbed hold of the Jacob's ladder.

"Good luck to ye."

"Aye. And to you too," she replied as she began to climb up the port side.

She peered over the rail and saw no one about. Silently climbing onto the deck, Sarah wound her way toward the bow and prayed the hatch to the forward hold would be open. If so, she'd climb down and hide there.

If it wasn't, she knew she couldn't lift it easily or quietly. In that case, she'd have to find the lazarette, or dry goods storeroom, if there was one, and hide there.

Seeing the open hatch, she thanked God and knelt to look inside. It was dark out and even darker below in the hold. She'd just have to take her chances. She lowered her bag in and dropped it. It didn't make a sound so she assumed her landing, too, would be soft and silent. She sat in front of the hold, grabbing the lip of the hatch opposite, and scooted her bottom forward, then dropped herself feet first into the abyss.

As she'd suspected, she landed on folded canvas duck cloth. Yards and yards of the stuff. Spare sails, she thought. Wonderful. Moving to the far corner of the cavernous dark hold, she lay on the folded material and using her satchel as a pillow, forced her racing heart to calm and tried to sleep.

Grayish-pink light filtered into the forward hold from overhead. Day was breaking. Footsteps alerted her to at least one crewman awake above deck. The man drew closer to the bow, and her hideout. Sarah quickly lifted a fold of sailcloth and ducked under it, then remembered her bag and covered herself and it thoroughly. The hatch overhead slammed shut, echoing in the hold and reverberating through her body. Trapped. Truly shut-in. The time to cry off—if she were going to do such a thing—was now past.

She threw the stifling sail off her and thought about the adventure ahead. Soon, the race would be underway and Lucky wouldn't be able to send her ashore. That's when she would come out of hiding. There was no way she'd spend the entire voyage down here. She wanted to see the ocean teeming with fishes and feel the salty wind and sea spray as it whipped over her face and through her hair. She wanted to see no land, because she'd never sailed anywhere before where you couldn't see or swim to land nearby. She wanted to experience that sense of vulnerability that comes with being at the complete mercy of a force greater than any she'd ever known, that supreme force of nature described by her relatives and the other sea captains of whom she'd read. They were men who'd established trade with countries around the globe, men whose bravery and skills brought almost every boat and man home.

The darkened hold became stifling, the smell of pitch burning her lungs now that no air entered from the hatchway. Removing her coat, she clung to it, coughing into it for several minutes before tossing it to the side along with her hat and satchel. Sounds coming from above told her the crew was weighing anchor. The boat began to move, now free from its mooring. Sarah heard the excitement of the crew as the sails were raised and felt the vessel surge forward. The boat pitched hard to port as it turned, throwing Sarah into the bulkhead, where she struck her shoulder on a beam. After a muted scream of agony, she quickly scrambled under the folded sailcloth to keep from getting tossed about while she was down here. And even though it was more than a bit warm, the additional weight kept her relatively padded and safe from any abrupt movements.

She tried to get situated once again and settled in with the comforting rocking and rolling motion of a ship at full sail. Smiling in the inky blackness, she wondered if her maid had noticed her gone yet and if her brother had read her letter.

He was sure to be angry, but hopefully not so angry that he'd delay the start of the race to search Lucky's boat and haul her back home.

No, he wouldn't do that. That would cause a scandal. And if there was one thing the Duke of Caversham detested, it was the mere thought of the family name tangled up in a scandal.

Chapter Two

Sarah knew the precise moment they'd hit the open sea. The boat began to pitch unlike anything she'd ever known before. Of course, it didn't help being in the farthest front compartment as the bow sliced through the waves. Perhaps that was why people didn't sleep in the bow unless in a hammock and why only sails were stored here. Sails couldn't get beat up, like overconfident, impulsive ladies who didn't think before they got themselves locked in the forward hold.

Thankfully the sailcloth provided her some protection, but she was still tossed about the small compartment. Once she even hit the solid oak rafter of the deck above her. Sarah heard a voice issue orders above and the scurry of footsteps as the command was carried out.

This went on for quite a while, and Sarah contemplated banging on the hatch to have someone let her out. She was thirsty and hungry and needed to relieve herself. She had no idea how long she'd been down here, nor how far out of Liverpool they were. Another pitch and she felt weightless again, bracing herself for another hit against the rafter.

This was insane. She wanted adventure, not broken bones. When the boat turned hard over, Sarah flew into the right bulkhead. She vowed that the minute she heard footsteps above deck she would scream for the man to let her out. Having no idea how long the seas were going to be rough, or when anyone might open the hatch so she could get some fresh air, she decided she just could not wait any longer. Oh, what was she thinking? No one even knew she was down here. It was then she realized spare sails didn't need fresh air, just protection from water. If she didn't die from smashing her noggin on a beam, she'd surely suffocate.

It seemed an eternity before she heard voices and footsteps headed toward the bow. But as soon as she did, she let out with the loudest, longest scream she could muster.

Ian stood at the wheel with his eye on the fore-and-aft sail and foresail. Scanning the horizon once again, he caught sight of *Avenger* and knew Lucky followed his lead. He had an approximately six-minute lead out of the box, which meant nearly a mile separated the two vessels in this first ever Atlantic Crossing Challenge. Now, almost two hours into the race, ahead of him were one square-rigged vessel at full sail, and the *Ann McKim*. By luck of the draw, nineteen of the thirty-two boats entered in the competition left the starting box before him. Ian allowed himself a smile of satisfaction as he realized all that stood between him and the lead were the two vessels ahead, especially since the *Revenge* was a three-masted topsail schooner, which at first glance might not look nearly as fast as the *Ann McKim* with her long jibboom and four headsails, but was in fact much quicker.

LOVING SARAH

He knew a race such as this wasn't won on the number of sails or masts. A skilled captain was essential, but what some sailors tended to overlook was the one thing Ian considered most important. The hull and the keel. And these two boats had been retrofitted specifically to his design. If he was right and he won, then his entire fleet of schooners would be designed the same.

As he set a course to the next way point, Ian pondered the things he could do with that winning purse, the first being to hire a decent, reliable cook. It was during his musings that one of the crew shouted something to him from the bow. Looking out at the flying jib and seeing nothing awry, he motioned for the man to speak up.

"Cap'n, there's a lad stowed away in the sail locker!"

Ian handed the wheel over to his second and climbed down from his raised poop and strode the ninety-odd feet to the hatch in the bow. "Did I hear you correctly? You said there was a stow-away?"

"Right, Cap'n, sir. He's a hollerin' up a storm down there."

"Are you sure that's what you heard?" Ian asked as he held onto the railing on the side of the ship. Just then he heard it too, a voice, bellowing up from below.

"Get him out of there and ask him if he can cook. If he can't, lock him up. We'll turn him in when we return. He gets minimal ration, too. I'm not feeding some little whelp a full three squares if he's broken the law and stowed away."

"Aye-aye, Cap'n," the man said as Ian turned back to his post at the wheel.

A few minutes later, as Ian contemplated who was

going to cook now that Seamus was planning to plant some roots somewhere in the countryside for the remainder of his years, his crewman shoved a scrawny kid in front of him. His oil cloth slicker, two sizes too big, was buttoned to the chin and the knitted cap covered his head. "Cap'n, sir, he says he's your brother."

"I don't have a brother," Ian said without needing to look down at the scamp. "Lock him up in the lazarette. I'll deal with him later. And fetch Mr. Johnson for me."

"Where's Lucky?" the definitely female voice squeaked with fear.

Ian's gaze shot to the figure before him, and he looked down into the deepest sapphire-blue eyes, eyes he'd seen only twice before now. He didn't need to see the color of her hair or the slender feminine form that had plagued his dreams last night to know who it was. "Holy Mother of God," he swore, unable to take his gaze from hers. "What have you done?"

"Obviously stowed away onto the wrong boat," she replied, her determined little chin lifted and lips taut.

His crewman looked confused a moment, then quickly realized she wasn't a boy.

"Lock her in my cabin, instead," he ordered the crewman.

"I don't want to be locked anywhere, Mr…um, Captain." Lucky's sister said. "I want to see the ocean and feel the wind. It was rather stifling, not to mention dark and very dangerous down in the forward hold. I should have known the bow wasn't the best place to hide."

He shook his head. The last thing he needed right now was this added encumbrance. And she came with significant repercussions no matter what he did. "Get in my cabin. I'll deal with you later. Right now, I'm busy." Nodding to the crewman to take away their guest, he forced his gaze to the horizon and tried to concentrate on whether he should overtake the square-sail barquentine in front of him or turn back to Liverpool.

"Come, miss," the man beside her said as he took her elbow and led her toward the companionway. The only reason she followed him, Sarah told herself, was so she might find a chamber pot. And perhaps a meal. After having been closed in that darkened hold for who knew how many hours, she was not only in need of relief, but also immensely hungry.

"Well, that went better than I thought." She smiled at the young man escorting her. "Thankfully I remembered to call him *Captain*. It wouldn't do to disrespect the man, seeing as I'm aboard his ship. I really did mean to get on my brother's boat. The boy from the *Evangeline* said this was the *Avenger*. I paid him to bring me out to *her*."

"'E prob'ly couldn't read," the man replied with a chuckle.

She hadn't thought about that. And both boats did look very similar, if not identical, to each other. "You're more than likely correct, sir," she said. "I should have known better."

The crewman held open a door for her, and she entered the cabin. She set the satchel down on the table, then scanned the room, wondering where the chamber pot was hidden. After the man left, she locked the door and began to search for it. The tiny cabin held no furniture to speak of. What furnishings it had were either built into the bulkhead wall between the portholes or bolted to the deck. There was a chair, a four-drawer bureau, and a narrow clothes press with a string of hemp holding the doors shut. Sarah laughed to herself, because the doors looked as if they might burst if she removed the twine.

Remembering her mission, she began to lift the seats on the bench, which ran along one wall below the portholes, and found only clothing. Rain gear, boots, books, and tools were all jammed into the bins in a rather disorganized fashion. She pushed aside a mound of paperwork and more books from the corner seat. Finally finding the object of her most immediate necessity, she made use of it quickly, then spying an open porthole, she took the container and disposed of the contents and replaced the receptacle in its holder.

After unlocking the cabin door, Sarah took her cap off and unbuttoned her coat, tossing both onto the seat. Peering into the cloudy-looking glass over the bureau, she ran her hands over her horribly mussed and perpetually frizzed hair. If her maid could see this mess, she'd have a fit. She untied the leather binding holding the thick braid and ran her fingers through her hair, detangling it. She took the comb from her satchel, returned to the mirror, and began to smooth the mess out, then proceeded to re-braid it. The braid turned out crooked and fell over her right shoulder instead of straight down her back as it should. It would have to do, she thought, as she knelt on the bench in front of the open porthole and hung her head out, staring at the horizon and the Atlantic Ocean.

Sarah smiled. Her adventure was underway. She intended to experience and note every minute detail. She wished she had remembered to bring her journal. Then she could have written about it all, starting with how clear the water was and capturing the beauty of its dark, bluish-green tint. But more amazing than that was the absence of birds. She supposed it was too far from shore for land birds. Gulls and such might be able to rest on the waves, but she didn't even spy them. Large gray fish, porpoises likely, swam alongside the hull, and off in the distance, several jumped waves following the school and their boat.

It was an odd, almost eerie sensation, being way out on the great, wide ocean where the horizon held no shoreline. So very different from when she sailed her little twelve-footer around the tiny lake at home. Then, the sounds of birds were always off in the distance. You could almost always hear them, except perhaps when the wind whipped the waves into white caps.

But out here.... She looked left and right, taking in as much as she could of her surroundings, and she saw no land.

Resting her chin on her hands, she closed her eyes and smelled the unique salty tang. Unlike that in a coastal town where you had an overwhelming mixture of faint odors, this was pure, fresh, and salty. No smells of the city, nor that grass and fresh-turned earth scent of the country. It was so different and so amazing that she just wanted to savor it all while she had this opportunity.

Ian handed the wheel over to his first mate, Mr. Nigel Johnson, and made for his cabin. He was going to have to keep her in there, though he didn't know how he would accomplish that. His crew were tough men, not town dandies. Most were neither polite nor accustomed to dealing with the whims of well-bred ladies. He would explain this to her and hope she understood. If not, he'd lock her in for the duration. He had to. It was for her own safety.

He filled the wooden bucket with fresh water and climbed down the companionway. When he reached his cabin door, he stopped. Perhaps he should knock. She was a lady and he'd hate to embarrass her should he catch her indisposed. He knocked once, then twice. After getting no reply, he tested the lock, then opened the door.

The sight that greeted him was quite fetching indeed. Lady Sarah, her back to him, leaned out the open porthole, leaving her perfectly curved *derrière* clad only in boy's trousers exposed to his view. He knew then that her presence was sure to test his resolve to behave in a gentlemanly fashion. After he hung the bucket on the hook near the washstand, she still hadn't heard him, so he coughed, startling her. She bumped her head as she drew it back into the cabin, and her hand went immediately to the injured spot and rubbed. His tongue froze in place, thankfully behind his teeth, leaving him unable to speak.

It was already going to be a long few weeks until they reached New York, and with this tempting bit of fluff staring at him with those magnificent blue eyes, it was sure to be endless. Endless misery, as each moment in her presence would tempt him to beg for more time with her. He cleared his throat. "Are you all right?"

She lowered her hand and glanced at it to make sure she wasn't bleeding, then lifted her gaze to his. "Oh, yes." She smiled. "It was nothing."

"I brought fresh water," he said. "Unless you have a

taste for wine, it's all there is for a lady to drink."

"Thank you. I am quite thirsty."

He handed her a mug after he'd filled it. He took another for himself, sat on the bench, and held her gaze. "I need to know right now, does your brother know where you are?"

"I left him a note saying I was with Lucky. Why?"

"Because I must know whether or not to turn around and forfeit this race." His voice held an unexpected sharp edge he'd never used on a lady.

Her eyes grew wide with concern. "No! Don't do that. I know how important the race is to you and Lucky!"

"You're telling me the truth?" He tried to ascertain her honesty by staring hard into her gaze, but all it did was unsettle his libido further. "A part of me thinks I should run up a flag and slow my speed to hand you over to Lucky. Let you be his problem, except…I'd lose my lead." He shook his head, undecided as to what he should do. If he was going to run that flag to signal a problem to Lucky, now was the time. The farther they got from England, the longer she would be in his presence and the worse it would be for both of them. God alone knew he wasn't ready for a wife. And the duke would have every right to demand he marry her.

"Please, may I stay? I could be of use to you. I know how to sail, and I've never been sea sick a day in my life."

He had a hard enough time thinking clearly with her pleading azure eyes and her pouty lower lip glistening after she'd traced her tongue across it. The image of those lips beneath his as he lowered his head to hers caused an uncomfortable sensation in his breeks.

"I'll make the return trip with Lucky, and all will be

well. I promise!"

"I should say no." He rubbed his forehead and began to pace in the small cabin. "I should...refuse you, because I know women like you are nothing but trouble. But...." He stopped his nervous pacing and stared at her, hoping his features were enough to frighten her into submission. "But hear me well, my lady, if I learn, upon our return to Liverpool, that your family has been worried sick over your disappearance, I swear I will throttle you myself."

His stowaway appeared relieved. "Then you won't turn around?" She still sounded concerned, as though she didn't quite believe him.

"Every instinct in me says I should. But...no." He couldn't believe he was saying this. Damn her beautiful eyes, they had the power to suck a man in to her will. "Though when we reach New York, I *will* hand you over to Lucky."

His stowaway nodded and rewarded him with a dimpled smile, the simple act causing his mouth to suddenly become dry.

"Wonderful," she said, her excitement brimming over like a boiling pot.

She took another sip from her mug. Ian's gaze fixed on her braid. The way it had been twisted up into coils atop her head the night before had given no hint as to its length. Now he wondered how it would look fanned out on his pillow. Then another, even more indecent thought followed. She never should have come aboard his boat whether it was by accident or not. Ian was beginning to feel she was no safer from him than she was from his men.

He stood abruptly and went to the door. Her voice

caused him to turn around.

"May I come above deck and watch for a while?" She smiled wistfully.

"Absolutely not," he replied. "My crew is not accustomed to the presence of ladies of your station. They're all very experienced sailors, but still a rough lot of men."

"If you could just *not* think of me as a noblewoman, but as an ordinary girl, perhaps that would help."

He shook his head. "It won't help. In fact, it'll only make it worse. Your station is what protects you from those men. They are well aware of the laws concerning assault of a gentlewoman."

"They wouldn't bother me if they knew I had your protection," she reasoned.

She had a point. It was his damn boat, and he was captain.

"Please?"

The way she looked at him when she asked it, with her bright blue eyes wide and pleading, her lower lip trembling slightly, made him relent. He sighed. Of course, he'd regret it later. Hell, he'd more than likely regret not turning his boat around and depositing her back on the duke's doorstep. The only reason he didn't was that he had more at stake here than one silly chit's ruination. His ability to pay his own way, to be a true partner, lay in winning this race.

At the sight of her smile, a twisted, knotted feeling grew in the vicinity of his gut and his lungs felt as though his very breath was squeezed out of them. Obviously, she could tell she'd won, but he couldn't make her victory an easy one. He didn't want her to think she had free rein while she was on board. "You are not to interfere with my crew's duties."

She nodded eagerly.

"You will stay at my side at all times while I escort you. And do not begin to think that you have the freedom to come above whenever you wish. You must wait for me to bring you up each and every time. For the duration of the voyage. Understood?" Ian wanted to think he still had control of the situation, though he knew he'd lost it when their gazes first met above deck.

"I understand completely, Captain," she said through her wide, radiant smile.

"Put your coat back on and cover that hair. It won't do for you to have your charms exposed to men who will be without a woman until we return to Liverpool."

She buttoned her coat, her fingers nimbly flying from one to the next. "You seem to think that I have the ability to tempt men. I assure you, the men I've met thus far—and I'm coming out of my third season—don't see me in that manner. They have all commented on what a great friend I am. Never has one intimated that I am alluring or even the least bit pretty." She pulled her coarse-knit gray hat down over her ears. "Quite the contrary. Whenever I think a young man might be on the verge of showing a slight romantic interest in me, the very next day he's as cold as a fish. And try as I might, I have never been able to figure out why."

Ian shook his head. He didn't need to think why. He knew the answer, but didn't have the heart to tell her. With the Duke of Caversham as her brother, only the best possible match for her hand would be allowed her company. Her brother was doing his duty by weeding out the undesirables before any sensitive feeling could develop. It was quite simply the kind thing to do.

"Then they are not only fools, but blind as well, my lady." As she blushed, he held out his arm and led her up the companionway.

When they reached the deck, she inhaled a breath in awe. "I wish I were skilled with paints," she said. "Then I could translate the beauty of the open sea onto canvas."

"I'll bet you're better at it than you're leading me to believe," he mused, finding her unadulterated joy refreshing.

She laughed. "Remind me to show you one day some of my finer works."

"That bad, eh?"

"Stick figures in rather elementary landscapes." She smiled at him and something tripped in his gut. "And runny colors."

He nodded. "Well, that's to be expected when you're young."

She turned a mischievous gaze up to him, blue eyes sparkling with hints of gold in their depths. "I completed that painting about two months ago."

It was his turn to chuckle. "Surely you have other talents?"

She shook her head. "Not unless you count riding, swimming, and shooting. And those aren't talents so much as skills you learn." His unwanted guest smiled at his apparent confusion. "You know, the more you do them, the better you get."

At her mention of swimming, a vision of a very wet, very sensual water nymph, who appeared much like the lady at his side, popped into his head. Then he wondered what she wore when she swam. Did she, heaven forbid, swim in the nude as he did?

Stop. He couldn't allow himself to think such things,

or he'd wind up giving her another skill to practice to perfection. One she would practice only with him.

Ian thought about that possibility in earnest. It wouldn't be so bad, except that he had a very good reason not to marry anyone right now—at least while his grandfather lived. For the man had tried many times to ruin Ian's life since that day all those years ago. There was no doubt in his mind the man would try again.

He also did not want anyone saying he married this lady—or any other for that matter—for the woman's dowry. And it was sure to happen if *he* married her now, because he hadn't two shillings to spare and owed his soul to the bankers for their business venture.

"Don't you agree?" Sarah's voice cut through the fog in his brain.

"I'm sorry, my mind wandered. What did you ask?"

"I said the weather is quite nice."

"Yes. It is. But a good sailor knows that the weather can quickly turn against you and always keeps an eye on the sky." Like he should keep an eye on his self-control around this chit.

She nodded. "Did you know that Lucky forecasts weather by reading clouds? My Uncle Angus taught him. He tried to teach me, but I was a lost cause."

"I'd wondered how he learned to do that. It's eerie how accurate he can be." He looked behind him to see Lucky off in the distance. "For that reason, we stay within sight of his boat. In fact, we always remain within sight of each other. Though we may both be driven to make this venture of ours succeed, neither one of us is completely rash or impulsive. Our ships are only minimally gunned, and we count on our speed and maneuverability to outrun privateers, should we encounter any."

"I see."

He watched as his guest continued to scan the horizon all around them. The hours ticked by as one by one the other vessels faded out of their sight. Whether it was by choice due to the course they'd plotted or the wind separating them, there were soon just two boats—his and Lucky's—within his entire perimeter of vision.

He caught her glance as she looked up at him momentarily, then turned away. "Captain?" she asked rather sheepishly. "Would you happen to have something to eat on this boat? I haven't eaten since last night's dinner."

He continued staring off into the distance. "I remember how you pushed your food around your plate last night without eating much of it. Now I know why." She grasped the too-long sleeves of her jacket in her hands and slid her hands into the opposite sleeve. A nervous reaction, or was it to keep warm?

"Yes, I'll admit now I was too excited and afraid I wouldn't be able to keep any of my meal down if I over-ate."

He gave her a half-hearted grin. "I shall show you where the galley is on the way back to your cabin. Our cook, Seamus, is old, and his eyesight's not the best, but he boils a mean pot of water."

"Boiled water? Is that what I have to look forward to on this voyage?" Lady Sarah gave a curt laugh.

"I do not jest, my lady. Boiled water is the base of all gruel. You cannot add barley, oats, or corn meal unless the water is boiling. Of course, knowing what else to toss into the pot helps, but when it's all there is, then it's all we have."

"Well then," she said through a forced smile, "I've been meaning to drop some weight. I always gain it during the season and lose it once I return to Haldenwood."

Ian thought there was nothing wrong with her weight now. The women he knew were always complaining about something with regard to their looks. In his opinion, there was nothing wrong with Lady Sarah's figure or appearance, except maybe her clothing could use correcting. And when he thought of that bottom poking up as she hung out of that porthole.... He groaned and turned to lead her to the galley.

Later on the evening of their first night at sea, they ate their dinner of a beef and barley stew in the captain's cabin. It wasn't as bad as she'd been expecting. In fact, the fare was edible in Sarah's opinion, once she added a generous dash of salt. And she didn't complain about it at all.

She was afraid if she did, he might send her to the galley to cook and she didn't know the first thing about it, so it was truly for the continued good health of the entire crew that she not attempt to cook.

The cabin in which she was to sleep appeared to be the only cabin on board the ship. Sarah had to apologize for causing Ian any inconvenience. More importantly, she needed reassurance she wasn't inconveniencing him too much, seeing as she was his unplanned-for guest. She hated the thought of imposing on him, though she admitted to herself she would have had no qualms doing so to Lucky. Knowing no other way to find out except to bring the subject up first, she offered, "I'll sleep on the bench there, if you have a spare pillow and blanket."

"That's not necessary. I'll bunk in the crew's quarters

LOVING SARAH

with the men, forward from the galley. But you must keep your door locked at all times when I am not with you. I would hate to face your brother's anger should you become harmed in any way."

His meaning being quite clear, Sarah nodded in agreement. By now the entire crew knew who she was and what she'd done. Not one of the men she'd met was upset by her appearance, nor did they seem disturbed by their captain's diversion of attention earlier in the day. Everyone had a job to do, and each man did his with a precision and skill that any veteran captain would admire.

Sarah placed her plate and utensils on the tray, then went to a porthole to look at the night sky. The sliver of moon glowed over the tops of the waves and the inky black heavens sparkled with more stars than she'd seen in recent months, at least not since leaving Haldenwood for London. One rarely saw stars in the sky in town.

"I'll take this out for you," Ian said, "and return with more water so you can wash up if you'd like."

"Thank you. I'd appreciate that."

He left silently and was soon back with a full bucket of water. "Drink up while it's good. It gets mixed with rum after the second day. Also, there are towels under that seat and soap here in this drawer." He went to the door, and as if on a second thought, he turned back to her and reiterated, "Lock this behind me."

As Ian left the room, Sarah shut the door behind him and slid the bolt home. Only then did she hear his footsteps go up the companionway.

Chapter Three

The crashing noises echoing through the *Revenge*'s crew quarters brought Ian instantly alert. Not that he'd been in the hammock long, only about ten minutes, but he'd been so tired he quickly fell into that hovering state between sleep and wakefulness. He heard no screams, only a feminine voice—to his knowledge, the only female voice aboard his vessel—raised in anger. Sarah shouted threats of smashing some poor creature's head in and feeding it to the fishes.

"By Christ's blood, I swear I will—" a crash, more thumping, and muffled words, "—then toss your tiny arse out—" more unintelligible words, the likes of which he could only imagine, then, "—the sharks, you little rat."

Ian threw his legs over the side of the hammock and jammed his feet into his boots. Perhaps she needed help, though she sounded as though she had control of the situation. As he neared the cabin door, he heard more crashing and the sound of something being thrown, hitting the bulkhead with a solid thud.

Afraid she might have hit her head, he tried the latch and found it locked. He knocked, and when Lady Sarah didn't come immediately, he pounded on it. Finally, she threw the bolt and he pushed the door open.

"What in God's name is going on in here?" He surveyed the room and found books, boots, tools, the chamber pot—thankfully empty—and clothing all strewn about the floor. Lady Sarah stood in the middle of it all, an angry fire in her blue eyes and a boot in her raised hand ready to smash something.

Right then, even through his half-fogged, sleep-deprived brain, Ian knew what had disturbed her sleep.

"I'll go fetch the cat," he said before he noticed her captivating state of undress. "Ah, bolt the door until I return." He quickly shut the door before any other curious eyes came to see what the fuss was over. Ian didn't want anyone else seeing her dressed, or rather undressed, as she was.

Finding the ship's resident rodent exterminator curled up on the table in the galley, he lifted her and carried her back to his cabin. He pounded on the door again, and when she threw the bolt, he entered, making sure to close the door behind him.

"Here is Mouser." He set the cat down on the floor and petted her head. "She can sleep in here if the mice are a problem for you."

"Mice?" Sarah squeaked. "You mean there might be more than one?"

"I'd venture to guess that there are quite a few on board," he replied. *Do not look at her*, he told himself. *Not any part of her. Don't look at her bare feet and shapely calves. And most especially do not lift your eyes to that span of bare flesh just above those lovely knees.* To do so would be his undoing. He'd lose any restraint he still had.

"How can that be? You'd think out here on the water that they'd have a hard time getting aboard, having to swim and all. I didn't think mice *could* swim."

"They don't necessarily swim out to the boat and climb the hull. When we load cargo, they'll sometimes be hiding in the boxes. They also run along the mooring lines when we're docked. They're just a fact of life everyone has to deal with. Even out here."

As he said that, his gaze wandered, totally against his will, up those twin alabaster legs he was sure led to heaven. They were bare from midway down her thighs to her dainty little toes. She had fine, shapely legs, too. Knees, calves, ankles and feet, were all delicate, feminine and curvy. She was temptation incarnate. And every bit of her was perfectly proportioned for passion.

God help him, he wanted her.

Lucky would kill him. After, of course, her brother the duke killed him first.

He had to leave. Now. Or the increasing bulge in his trousers would give away his lust for her. If he acted on said lust, he'd be twice dead.

That would be very dead, he reminded himself as his feet still did not move. He couldn't seem to tear his eyes away from her slender form peeking at him through the worn material.

A groan rippled through him, and their eyes met, as the cat pounced on a moving creature in the corner behind him. It was enough to break the spell. "I'll leave you two to figure out the rodent situation." He reached for the brass handle. "Bolt this door," he said. Then almost as an afterthought, he added, "And whatever you do, do not open it for anyone." After she closed the door, he whispered, "Including me."

Loving Sarah

When Ian was gone again, Sarah reflected on what had just occurred. Earlier in the day, she'd wondered if there might be a connection between them, but now there was no doubt. He felt it just as she did. As she had from the moment they'd met the night before. Truth be told, she'd thought the year prior that he was handsome enough, but the past year had changed him in build and appearance. He'd grown more rugged-looking from an extra year of working outdoors. His dark blond hair was streaked with sun-kissed strands, and when he raked it with a nervous hand, it sent an odd sensation coursing through her innermost parts. Almost as though she were the one touching his hair, not he. She could imagine the feel of its texture and curl as the separate strands wove through her fingers. But she could not know this, as she'd never touched him in such an intimate manner. So, how could her body react in this way?

Now she was in a fine predicament. She had to spend the next several weeks in his company. How was she going to comport herself, knowing her attraction was likely reciprocated?

She certainly had not planned to have him catch her so scantily clad. The mouse did exist, as was evidenced by the cat in the corner toying with the thing. Glancing over at the stunned rodent, she reached for a stocking—one of his—and pushed her hand inside. Taking the stunned and paralyzed mouse by the tail, she held it as far from her person as possible, went to the porthole, and stuck her hand through. She opened her fingers, and the mouse dropped into the sea.

Turning to the cat, she said, "I'm sorry if that was your dinner, but you shall just have to wait until I let you out of here in the morning to eat. I'll not have rodent entrails on the floor in this room." The fat feline looked at her as though she'd lost her mind. Sarah realized that, quite possibly, she had—though long before the mouse made its appearance.

She began to clean the mess, seeing as she'd made it, and rearranged all the clutter until the room bore little resemblance to the cluttered cabin she'd entered earlier that day. Hopefully the captain would appreciate her organizing his belongings. While she put away his clothes, Sarah realized she was learning about him.

Captain Ian Alexander Ross-Mackeever lived aboard the *Revenge*. She knew this because there were personal belongings wrapped in sheets and stuffed in the bench seats that one would think he might leave in a treasured spot in a home. A framed portrait of a child with what she thought could be its parents—perhaps Ian with his mother and father? A silver-framed mirrored vanity tray with silver hair implements. An old perfume bottle. The contents were long gone, but when she pulled the stopper, it still held the faint scent of roses. An inexpensive feminine watch on a chain. Brass, she thought, from the looks of it.

She pushed the spring latch, and the lid popped open. The inscription inside read "*To my love, On our wedding day, March 5, 1805, HAR.*" Setting aside the watch, she then lifted the lid from a jeweler's box and drew in a breath when she saw the exquisite ring within.

On a bed of black velvet was a lady's gold band pinned to the insert. Mounted on the band was an enormous oval ruby solitaire, the quality of which was nearly as good as she'd ever seen. Why, it was nearly as perfect as the stone in her sister-in-law's pendant. Surely they had to be family heirlooms, ones the captain kept for sentimental reasons. Likely this magnificent ring was his mother's, as was the watch, and maybe one day he wanted to give them to his own bride. What other reason would someone hold on to a stone so valuable when he was in such need of funds for his business that he'd enter a race?

She removed the ring from the box, lifted it in the light, and put it on her ring finger. It was snug, but it fit. Holding her hand out, she admired the blood-red stone and setting, thinking it a divine symbol of eternal love. One day, hopefully, a man would place something similar on this same finger of this same left hand. She quickly chased the thought from her head. It was rather like putting the cart before the horse, as her governess had been so fond of saying. Before anyone ever placed something of this caliber on her hand, she had to first *find* that potential husband.

Sarah took the delicate band between two fingers and pulled, trying to remove it. The ring wouldn't budge. She made only a fraction of progress with twisting and tugging. The thing just did not want to go back over her knuckle. She couldn't let Ian find her with his mother's ring on her finger. He'd think her a most presumptuous and brazen wench, if not an outright thief.

Striding to the wash stand, she lifted the soap and ladled a scoop of water into the basin. She soaped her hands until they frothed with lather, then dipped her hands into the cold water and again attempted to remove the band. After a minute of twisting and pulling, she succeeded and heaved a deep sigh of relief. She rinsed the ring and dried it off, replaced it in the box, and put the box back in the wrapping, then placed the entire collection of family mementos in a safe place under the bench. Feeling a tad guilty for snooping, Sarah packed a blanket around Ian's treasures, cushioning them from the often jarring violence of the ocean waves. It wouldn't do to have any of them break.

She finished cleaning the mess she'd made while chasing the mouse. Then began to work on his clutter, putting things away for him. While she did, she would intermittently remind herself that she was doing Mr. Ross-Mackeever a service by organizing his cabin. She'd put all of the tools and books in nice, orderly sections and straightened his boots and shoes before climbing onto the big bed to attempt sleeping again.

Punching the pillow a few times to fluff the feathers, she pulled the cover over her body and resolved that in the morning she would tackle the drawers beneath the bed and his bureau and clothes press. She hadn't opened them, but surely they were in the same sorry condition as the contents of the bench seats.

She smiled into the darkened cabin. Before this journey was over, she'd have Mr. Ross-Mackeever's belongings, and quite obviously his home, all neatly arranged.

Sarah lifted an eyelid and peered into the glowing golden eyes of her feline cabin mate as it sat on her stomach. Daybreak had begun to permeate the room with an eerie glow, barely enough to warrant getting out of bed. Had she been at home, she most definitely would still be sleeping. The tabby began to knead her chest through the covers.

Ignoring the irritating creature, she dislodged it as she rolled onto her side and pulled the blanket up over her head. The determined cat climbed back on top of her and continued.

"What do you want? The sun's not even up yet." Pushing the animal off the bed, she threw the covers back and stood. It was obvious that Mouser was not going to let her sleep any longer and wanted out of the cabin. Sarah went to the door and remembered the captain's warning.

But the cat, who now sat in front of the room's only safe exit, obviously wanted out. Not hearing any voices on the other side, she decided if she were quick about it, she wouldn't get caught by the captain while opening the door to release the feline. She quickly threw the bolt back and pulled the door open just enough to let that cat through, then just as fast shut it and slid the bolt back in place.

Climbing back onto the raised bed, she thought to sleep longer, but more and more footsteps started shuffling about above deck and in the companionway. She heard bells, then voices talk about breaking fast, and her stomach started rumbling, reminding her of its empty state.

She wondered if she should wait for Ian to come get her or if she should venture forth to fetch her own meal. After dressing and waiting for what seemed an eternity, as always when one was hungry, she took the initiative and went in search of food. Entering the tiny galley, Sarah noticed two things. First, there was no chocolate. Second, there was no choice in what to eat.

Breakfast was soupy porridge, not even appetizing-looking porridge with fruit slices or berries on top as cook would do for her when she was in town. Just this plain bowl of watery, lumpy mush.

"Can I scoop ye a bowl, m'lady?" A stooped-over, gray-bearded grizzled old man smiled at her, revealing a mouthful of rotten-appearing black teeth. Perhaps that was why they were eating cereal cooked to mush, she thought. Likely the rest of the crew had teeth in similar condition. She decided to take the bowl and eat the stuff seeing as it looked to be the only thing available and she was very hungry.

"Yes, please." She took the bowl after the man had filled it. "Thank you, sir." Two men entered the galley behind her, one taking a seat on the bench against the wall. Deciding not to eat in the galley, she had turned to leave when she saw a stack of crates against the wall. One of them contained oranges. She motioned to the fruit, looking back at the old cook. "May I have one, please?"

"Aye. Eat one of those every day and ye'll not come down wit' the scurvy."

"Thank you. Though I'm not sure what the malady you mentioned is, I will be sure to eat one of these every morning."

"That's a good lassie," the cook replied in an almost a fatherly tone.

She nodded to him and returned his smile, then left the galley to go back to her room. Her first friend. As her brother always said, it can be very beneficial to have an ally when in unfamiliar territory. And this sailor, because he was responsible for the food they ate, would make a very beneficial ally, she told herself as she walked through the men breaking their fast on deck. Because this was going to be a long voyage, and she needed more than just the one friend, she nodded a greeting to them, introducing herself as Lucky's sister-by-marriage, who truly did land aboard their vessel by accident.

She didn't run into Ian while walking back to the cabin and was glad for it. He'd made it clear the day before that he didn't want her roaming about unless she was with him. If he knew she'd already ventured into the galley he might become angry, though really it was just a matter of time before he learned of it.

By the time she'd finished her breakfast, she still hadn't seen him, though she'd heard his voice booming orders above deck. Nearly two hours passed before she deduced he was avoiding her. And as she knelt on the bench before the open port hole, watching the monotonous watery horizon pass by, she thought about this attraction she felt for him. More importantly, she considered what she would do about it.

Sarah sensed her captain felt something as well. It wasn't until after he'd left the room last night that she realized she never should have opened the door for him without first pulling her trousers on. But in the excitement of the moment with the mouse running about in the cabin, she hadn't given a thought to what she was wearing. All she'd wanted was to get that disgusting rodent out of the room she was supposed to *sleep* in.

But she noticed he looked at her in a…different way. Unlike the many beau she'd met during her three years out, Captain Ross-Mackeever's gaze had raked over her body in an almost carnal manner, which warmed her even now, twelve hours later.

And she'd bet her last shilling that was why he avoided her this morning. After spending three years on the marriage mart where she'd met no one who attracted her as this man did, Sarah had an odd sensation that Mr.

Ian Alexander Ross-Mackeever might be someone with whom she could be happy. First, he was handsome above all reason, and the attraction was undeniable on her part, and almost certainly on his. Also, he was a proud, determined, entrepreneur, much like every man in her family, likely a reason why he got along so well with her brother and brothers-in-law. It also helps that he was the grandson and heir to an earldom. That alone would make him worthy in her brother's eyes, whether he had wealth or not. If they married, he would gain wealth upon their marriage.

If he said he cared for her even a little, she'd ask her brother to consider Ian as a possible husband for her. After all, this captain set her senses on edge and made her feel like both a giddy, silly school girl and a primal, sensual woman.

Sarah shivered in the cabin, and not from the comfortable temperatures. Let him avoid her for now. Eventually he would have to confront his emotion, if he had any for her at all.

Sarah decided she could continue to ponder the strange sensation she felt whenever he was near while working on those drawers beneath the bed. She pulled the first of the two out and spread the contents on the bed covers so as to rearrange them in a neat and orderly fashion.

As she sat on the floor, she organized the books into stacks by subject. There were financial ledgers, which she did *not* open, even though her natural curiosity begged her to. He had a few classic historical tomes, a book on warfare and strategy, and several on maritime business, astronomy, and physics. Even a thin volume of poetry. They were all ordinary books. Books you might assume belonged to an educated man.

But one book stood out from the rest. It had a simple black leather cover, worn along the edge as though read many times. The faded gold leaf embossing was illegible, and her curiosity roused. She turned it to the light to better see the title. It was difficult to decipher and when she did she was flabbergasted to read: *A Modern Gentleman's Practical Guide to Seduction and the Act of Love*.

Sitting there on the floor, she opened the book and fanned the pages, finding not only text but also drawings and color plates. She'd never seen anything like it in her life and sat with open-mouthed wonder as she realized what the couples in those drawings were doing. The book very graphically depicted what should be a private, intimate act between a man and his wife.

Heat coursed through her as her entire body blushed while she turned page after page. In all her nearly twenty-one years, she'd never imagined the acts she saw portrayed within the covers of the book she held on her lap. Sarah was no innocent. She had witnessed the mating of animals. But then, animals did it only one way, whereas according to this book, the innumerable and varying positions that a man and woman could possibly copulate boggled her mind. She had to put her hand over her mouth to keep from squealing in shock as each one appeared more and more inconceivable.

It was all surprisingly erotic. She felt curious, and something else, titillated perhaps, just looking at them. Some of the poses she was certain were physically impossible. Surely a woman could not bend her body in such positions. They must be a figment of the artist's imagination.

Sarah flipped through the book, stopping frequently to study the drawings. She set it aside, eager to read it as soon as she was finished with her self-imposed task of righting the room. Though there were a great number of drawings and several color plates, the chapters of text appeared enlightening to someone such as herself, uneducated in matters pertaining to the marriage bed.

She finished rearranging that drawer and started on the other. When she'd finished those, she quickly did the same to the clothes press and bureau. Two hours after she'd begun, and just as she finished her chore, someone knocked on the door.

Grabbing the book, she stuffed it under the pillow and smoothed flat the bed cover, before moving to the door. "Yes?"

"I was wondering if you needed anything," the captain said.

Sarah slid the bolt open and allowed him in, unable to look him in the eye after seeing the outrageous depictions in the book. Her imagination began to take hold of her conscious thought, and images of her and this captain flitted through her mind, causing her to flush with embarrassment.

His eyebrows arched as he noticed the difference in the room. He seemed pleased that she'd righted the space after having torn it asunder the night before in search of the unwanted visitor.

"The cabin looks better than it did when last I saw it."

Sarah nodded, her gaze scanning to room, trying to imagine it as he saw it. "I felt it only right that I clean the mess I'd made. And I've taken to reorganizing your bins beneath the benches and the drawers beneath the bed.

Also your dresser and clothes press." With her shoulders back and chin high, she was proud of the job she'd done. "Everything is neat and orderly now," she added.

"Did you not think that I might find your interference an invasion of my privacy?"

"Not at all. I cannot think clearly with clutter up to my eyeballs, as it was. And I don't know how you do."

"I knew where everything was."

"And you will relearn where everything is now." At his look she wanted to laugh but held back not wanting to raise his ire. "It's all in the same general vicinity of where you placed them…. Just organized now."

"And Mouser? Did she bother you during the night? She can be as much a pest as a mouse, especially when she wants attention."

"We reached an impasse. While I did sleep better knowing the cat was in here with me, she was not allowed to walk across my face during the night."

"Good. If you'd like, you can keep her with you at night then."

"I would appreciate that. Thank you."

"Did she eat it?"

"The mouse?" She shook her head sorrowfully. "Unfortunately for her, I could not allow that. I tossed it out the port hole. Afterward, she appeared vexed with me."

"I'm sure she was. You threw her dinner away."

Her gaze finally met and held his, and a thousand erotic images flashed through her mind. She envisioned herself and the captain performing the acts depicted in the drawings and her body began to tingle all over.

He broke the spell when he went to the bureau, took some toiletries out, and wrapped them in a towel as though he meant to wash up elsewhere. Then he took a fresh set of clothing and folded it over his arm. "When I return, I'll take you on deck for a stroll and some fresh air."

"Thank you," she replied. "I look forward to it."

He nodded and left the room, but not before reminding her to throw the bolt behind him. As soon as she'd locked the door, she ran back to the book and took it from its hiding space, went to the bench beneath the porthole window and began to read. Again.

Ian splashed cold water on his face, then dunked his head into the bucket. What he needed was a cold bath. Sarah might be impulsive and imprudent, he thought, but at least she had the good sense to be embarrassed by the state of her undress last night—even if it did come after the fact. He *must* quit thinking about the way she looked in the dim light of the cabin, wearing nothing but a boy's shirt with her blond curls loose over her shoulders and falling down her back. But even more painful than that was remembering the curve of bare thigh that had peeked out from under the hem of that shirt. *That* vision had caused him to lose sleep, making him admittedly grumpy earlier.

The gentleman in him realized he should have done the polite thing and escorted her to the galley, but he didn't think he could have done so without snapping at her. And while asking her for a stroll about the deck perhaps wasn't the wisest decision—because he remembered exactly how fetching she looked without trousers—he reasoned he couldn't very well keep her locked away for the duration of the voyage. No, if he planned to return her to her brother untouched, he simply needed to avoid scenes like last night's until they reached New York. Then he'd hand her over to Lucky and let him deal with her.

He also considered having one of his crew escort her so she could take in the fresh air, but couldn't think of an appropriate man. When staffing his ships, he sought the best, most experienced seamen available for their maritime experience and sailing skills, not escorts for ladies. The men on his ships weren't refined gentlemen. They were coarse and unused to entertaining ladies. Well, ladies of *her* caliber.

Come to think of it, neither was he.

Lifting the razor, he tilted his head and carefully began to remove the two days' growth shadowing his face. The yellowed looking-glass over the wash stand in the crew's quarters wasn't as good as his, but it would have to do. A wave hit the lee side of the boat, and he lurched forward, banging his head into a beam. Thankfully, he didn't have the razor to this neck, or he might have mortally injured himself.

This was why most sailors grew beards on their voyages. They didn't want to slice their own throats while attempting to shave. But he'd committed himself after the first stroke of the razor and couldn't very well stop, so he continued, albeit very cautiously.

Then he thought of the reason he had the blade to his throat while skating swells and troughs in the mid-Atlantic. The blue-eyed temptress now occupying his cabin. That uninvited, very enticing bit of fluff had played a big role in his dreams the past two nights.

He simply *had* to stop thinking about her. Either in his bed or undressed. To do so only made him realize how long he'd been without a woman. He'd be hard pressed to refuse her if she invited him to share his quarters with her. Not that *that* was likely to happen. He doubted she'd ever even kissed a man, being unwed, and more importantly the *unmarried* sister of the Duke of Caversham, her brother. That man impressed him as a fierce protector of his family. A man no one wanted to cross swords with.

Another reason to avoid the lady altogether: his intentions were as dishonorable as his grandfather thought he was.

But even with every reason in the world not to socialize with her, minutes later, freshly shaved, he found himself with his hand poised to knock on her door, to ask her to stroll in the mid-day sun. What madness had overcome him? Why had he promised her a stroll? And now that he had, it wasn't as though he had to keep the promise. He could back out, say an important matter needed his attention and strolling with her would take him away from the work at hand. It sounded like a perfectly reasonable excuse to him for canceling.

Still, he knocked.

He heard her shuffling, and she soon opened the door with a charming blush on her cheeks. What had she been doing, or more likely thinking of, to have such an alluring look about her? Perhaps she was still embarrassed? No. If she were, she wouldn't have that soft smile curving her lips or that veiled look to her sapphire-colored eyes.

"Ready for some sunshine?"

She smoothed her hands on her trouser legs and nodded, then reached for her coat and hat. After she'd put both on, he held the door for her. Once above deck, he offered his arm and they strolled for a minute in silence. He spoke to a crewman coiling a line, and another as he performed his duties. When they were alone on the quarter deck, he said, "If it would ease your embarrassment, no one knows you allowed me entrance into the cabin while you were…inappropriately attired."

She turned an adorable shade of pink as she turned her blue eyes to him and said, "Thank you." They watched his crewmen at their various tasks for a few minutes, and he explained some of what they were doing. "I have wanted to come above and sit in the sunshine and watch as you work," she said during a lull in the conversation. "If I promise not to get in the way, may I?"

"One day when the weather is calm, certainly." She needed more fresh air and sunshine. It was good for a person. Besides, she had this healthy glow about her that told him she was accustomed to it, so he didn't fear for her health if she were to spend some time with him on deck.

"You know I've read everything in your library except your mechanical arts and engineering tomes, ocean charts, and financial ledgers. You also need to keep better ship's logs. I found them incomplete for starters, and what entries there were lacked excitement and adventure."

Ian chuckled. "The entries missing are from this race only, and that's because you are in my cabin. As for exciting tales, you're looking for a journal, and I don't journal. Usually, when I go to my cabin at night, I'm so tired I barely have the energy to make an entry into the log."

"As a child, the logs from Ren's grandfather, his uncle, and cousins stirred my imagination. Captain, you must keep a journal of your travels for future generations. Just think, one day your grandchildren will come across them and find them fascinating and think you dashing and brave." She turned that damn adorable smile up to him and added, "Especially if you mention a pirate ship or two."

"He wasn't your grandfather also?"

"No. Ren and Elise have a different mother. She died after Elise was born. Our father married my mother, also a confirmed spinster, many years later. I was born shortly after their wedding."

She exhaled, visibly relaxing at the same time. "I wish I'd thought to bring a dress or two. I know that wearing boy's clothes isn't proper, but I needed it to get onto the ship, and it is all I have with me." She glanced at him then looked away again. "At the time I packed my satchel, I didn't think morning dresses would be suitable for a voyage of this nature."

"You're right, they wouldn't be. But then *ladies* wouldn't normally be on a clipper of this size and sort. If a *lady* wished to cross the Atlantic, she'd be on a much larger vessel, one equipped for passengers."

His guest looked at him, meeting his gaze with a determined tilt to her chin. "Captain, you are attempting to make me feel guilty for having stowed away aboard your boat, and I will not be made to feel so. Granted, I landed on the wrong ship, but I had to make this journey. Not only because I've always dreamed of seeing America, but also because I am tired of everyone around me having grand adventures when I cannot. You have no idea what it is like to always be aware of the rules of society and appropriate behavior for a lady of my station. It's been drilled into my head since I was a child that ladies must behave in a certain manner and to go outside those boundaries will bring censure, perhaps even scandal to one's family. "Well, I'm tired of living inside the gilded cage. For once in my life I want to fly away." Her mood changed from bold and assertive to wistful sadness when she added, "Even if eventually I must return."

"Yes, but when you return, will you still be able to enjoy the benefits of the life to which you were born? Or will you be shunned by polite society for having been in the company of a crew of men without the benefit of a chaperone?"

She turned away, he thought because she realized the hardened truth of his words. "I care not what others think of me. Those who love me will believe in me and know the truth."

"What if you find that your friends' parents will not allow them in your company because to do so might taint *their daughter* with *your* stained reputation? What then, my lady?"

"Please, can we change the topic?" She gave him a pleading gaze, but for some reason it was important to him that she understand the severity of the possible consequences of her actions.

"Avoiding the subject will not resolve the issue. I would think you'd want to be prepared for the possibility that you might have fewer willing companions when you return to Town. It seems to me you haven't thought your way through this to the inevitable outcome."

Ian could tell his words were hitting their intended mark, as she appeared more and more remorseful as he went on. Then she stiffened her spine and turned to climb down the stairs to the main deck.

"Where are you going?"

"I really don't feel like hearing a lecture on my behavior. You obviously do not understand my desire…no, my *need* to taste freedom before settling into a dismal life of confined comfort." She stopped at the entrance to the companionway and turned back to face him. "So, I believe I shall return to the cabin now. Thank you for the stroll in the sunshine."

He hadn't meant for the conversation to turn out that way. It had started out nicely and had quickly changed when he began to chastise. The look on her face told him he'd hurt her feelings, and he wondered if perhaps he should apologize.

Then he thought not. It was more than likely long past time someone showed the chit what repercussions her actions would have. She needed to be taught to think before she acted.

If only she hadn't had that wounded-doe look. Too, he could have sworn her lower lip trembled as she thanked him for taking her out in the fresh air.

In the end, it was the look on her face that made him feel like a blackguard of the first order. He decided to follow her down to the cabin and apologize.

Chapter Four

Sarah locked the door, threw the hat and coat onto the bench, and plopped herself onto the bed. She refused to cry even though she felt that familiar knot in her throat that preceded the tears. Hardly knowing him, the man had the ability to make her feel like a foolish six-year-old who'd been caught with her hand in the cookie jar.

She was no child, but a woman fully grown. A woman who knew her mind and her heart. A woman who longed for adventure and had the confidence to take it when the opportunity arose. She absently toyed with the ribbon holding her braid and tugged, pulling it free. Children wore their hair braided, not women. She walked to the mirror and fingered her too-thick messy curls, beginning to untangle them with her comb, when a knock sounded.

If the man meant to continue his tirade in the privacy of her room, she would have to make it clear to him that she would take no more.

Throwing back the bolt, she yanked open the door, prepared to vent her anger at him when he pushed past her. The sound of the latch sliding home and the strange emotion in his gold-flecked hazel eyes were more titillating than fear-inducing.

"If you've come to continue lecturing me, you can save your breath because I will not hear it." She turned her back to him and continued combing her hair, trying to ignore his proximity in the confines of the small room.

"I thought to apologize. But…."

"Apology accepted. Now, please…," her voice cracked. "Please go." She didn't look at him.

His voice carried growing frustration as he spoke, his tone becoming more aggressive. "This is *my* ship, and I'll leave when *I* damn well choose."

Startled, she met his steely gaze in the mirror. Her parched throat closed, and she stood frozen in place, trembling now that she'd forced him to anger.

"I didn't have to let you stay in here," he stated. "I could have had you locked in the lazarette below as a common prisoner."

She held his direct, scathing stare in the mirror and refused to cower.

"With no light and only a blanket and one meal a day. Remember, *you* stole aboard *my* vessel of your own volition and that makes you no better than a common criminal. Because of who you are, I felt it my responsibility to care for your well-being. But your attitude at my hospitality could use some adjustment."

He came to stand directly behind her, so close she felt the warmth radiating off his body, felt his breath in her tangled curls. She saw in the mirror that his gaze caressed her tumbledown mess of hair. Even in her fear, she wanted to feel his touch. She knew that if he touched her, she would melt before him.

"So let me clarify something to you, *my lady*. You are under *my* protection, and as a friend to Lucky, you will hear what I have to say regarding your imprudent actions, especially as they will likely affect me in some way. His Grace will surely question me thoroughly."

She felt the heat of his hands a fraction of an inch away from her body as though he wanted to touch her, to feel her, but would not. Without making contact, they roved over her form, causing her skin beneath her linen shirt and trousers to flame as though he stroked her naked body. Now she knew. He felt it, too. The attraction she felt for him *was* returned; it wasn't her imagination.

"You never should have come here," his husky voice whispered.

If she moved at all, even to take a deep breath, his palms would be on her, and if that happened, she didn't know where they'd go from there.

The drawings in that book came to mind, and she groaned silently.

"I am not your brother that you can behave with that haughty demeanor of yours and get away with it. And you can give me your excuses and expect all to be well. I am not easily pacified."

His hands fell to his side, and he stepped away, leaving Sarah wondering what might have happened if she had taken a step back into his arms.

"Consider yourself warned, my lady." He turned and left the room.

The comb fell to the floor, and she sat on the bench staring at the door, shaken with the knowledge that if he'd simply touched her, she would have melted into him. Would have given him anything he'd wanted because, God help her, it was what she wanted as well. She wasn't sure why, but something inside her wanted a relationship with this man, telling her that no other man would do. It wasn't just because of that titillating little book either. Her body had been attracted to Mr. Ross-Mackeever from the moment he walked into the drawing room at the rented house in Liverpool the night before the race. Of course, she didn't know what this feeling was then. But now, with the help of that erotic book, she concluded this feeling was what the author described as *chemistry*.

When the bell signaling the noon meal rang, Sarah quickly donned her hat and coat again and went to the galley. Thankfully, Ian was nowhere in sight. After greeting a few of her new friends, she returned to her room alone and ate the bland but filling fare with gusto.

Ian didn't come to the cabin that evening or the next morning or the morning after that, which gave her plenty of time to read and re-read *The Modern Gentleman's Guide to Seduction and the Act of Love*. She read late into the night, finding the text, along with the graphic plates and drawings, most informative and inspiring. The whole book was enlightening, especially to a curious young woman with no prior knowledge of the physical act as it pertained to humans. Though according to this book, it wasn't so much an act as it was an art.

She'd heard whispers of a woman's wifely duty, but never details. It was never openly discussed among her friends, even the married ones. But according to this very enlightening book, presumably an instructional text, this *duty* was really no duty at all, but entirely pleasurable for both parties if done correctly. Sarah gathered from what she'd been reading that the gratification derived came from the mechanics of the act itself and the sensations would be heightened if there was a certain chemistry between the parties involved. Most especially from the man's perspective, which, once she thought about it, made complete sense. After all, the book was written by men for men. There had been an entire chapter on what they called foreplay, instructing the male in the use of flowery phrases and words of love, and the timing of using such expressions for maximum effect.

Parts of the text angered her because the authors depicted all women as easily swayed and impressed with a man's knowledge of poetry and skill at music and art—not things she necessarily sought in a man—which was probably why she was so attracted to her captain. Somehow she didn't see Ian as the type to woo with sweet words, romantic poetry, or music. He was too direct and honest. And as she'd listened to his calls to his crew the past few days, she could say with certainty that her captain was entirely too gruff.

Scandalous though it was, she had to admit the book was arousing, causing her to squirm in her seat as she read the descriptions of acts and the benefits to performing them in that particular manner. After falling asleep that first night and each night afterward, her dreams had been of herself and Ian. Perhaps inspired by his last visit to her room when he'd nearly touched her. Sarah would have done nothing to stop him. In fact, she'd desired his touch that day. And she wanted it even more now. Because now she understood the emotion she felt.

Lust.

She wanted him in all of the intimate, physical ways

depicted in this book. Just thinking about it made her wet between her legs—and intensified a needy, hollow feeling low in her belly.

But how did a single, young woman like herself, especially one from her station, go about embarking on a liaison without giving up any and all hope for a suitable marriage? Because once given away, her lack of virtue would be noticed by a future husband. And that would not make for a good start to a marriage. Not that anyone had singled her out as yet. Quite the contrary, it seemed no one was interested in marrying her.

Thus after three seasons out without once falling in love, or even meeting anyone with whom she cared to share her life, she was just about to concede the fact that there might be something wrong with her and that she might be doomed to a life on the shelf. It almost made her feel as though she were a failure in her family, with both her sister and brother making very successful love matches.

So she made her decision right then and there.

If spinsterhood was to be her lot in life, she was going to taste the pleasures of the flesh before going on reserve. The ever-curious adventurer in her wanted to know what she would be missing by not marrying.

And who better than to taste those sinful delights with than her captain? Surely he could be persuaded to accommodate her in her quest for knowledge and experience. But he couldn't know she planned to use him to satisfy her curiosity. She sensed if he knew this he would never agree to satisfy her simply because of *who* she was.

So she had to come up with a plan of sorts. A plan for seducing her captain.

Loving Sarah

Another two full days passed without her crossing his path. It seemed they both made an effort to avoid each other. Of course, Sarah went only to the galley and back, and as a result, the cabin felt smaller with each hour that passed. Ian, for his part avoided her by taking the wheel of the ship at night, while she slept.

The thirty crewmen on the boat had become accustomed to her presence as they followed the cook's lead and greeted her when she entered the galley at mealtimes. Even though she knew most by name now, she never ate among the men because she feared raising her captain's ire. Too she noticed that when she was in the presence of Ian's crewmen, they seemed somewhat restrained. Oh, they were pleasant enough to her, but the animated dialogue she heard every day from above deck through the open porthole or echoing through the companionway always ceased when she stepped through her door.

She supposed their captain had warned them about their behavior in her presence, and she was both thankful he'd done so as he was looking out for her sensibilities, yet sorry that the men were having to repress their natural tendencies toward informal conversation with each other. The last thing she'd considered when she started out on her adventure was to inconvenience the crew, thus provoking any resentment.

That was one of the reasons she'd chosen to hermit in the cabin, another was her desire to study that fascinating book.

But there was one even more important than angering the captain and studying the book.

She had to control the erotic visions she'd been having lately. Visions of her and Ian in the varying positions portrayed in the plates and drawings. Until she could do so, she would never be able to look him in the eyes and would continue to feel this quivering embarrassment in his presence.

After a few days below deck, the walls were closing in on her and she needed to breathe, so she headed topside. She bundled up against the North Atlantic winds and donned her hat and coat. The thought of going above without his escort had become less and less frightening. She didn't worry about getting attacked now that she'd met almost all of the crew. Yes, she might incur Mr. Ross-Mackeever's wrath, but decided that any anger from her captain was worth the few moments in the sun and brisk air.

Grasping the handrails, she climbed the steep stairs to the main deck where she paused at the top, relishing the warmth of sunlight on her face. In contrast, the crisp and cool wind whipped some stray tendrils that refused to remain under the hat onto her face. She inhaled the scent of the ocean—a salty-tangy combination that was strangely comforting and oddly arousing. Moving to the rail, she leaned against it as she scanned the horizon to the lee-side. She saw nothing but water and one ship far off into the distance ahead of them. Spray washed up and wet her face as the hull sliced through a wave. Thankfully, she'd buttoned up her oil-cloth slicker, or she'd be soaked.

Suddenly, she felt the fine hairs along the back of her neck rise to attention and she knew without looking that her captain stood behind her.

"I'm sorry, but I couldn't stay below any longer," she

said without turning. "I needed fresh air, sunshine, and a change of scenery."

His arms came around her and held the rail on each side of her, imprisoning her. "Then you should have sent word, and I would have brought you out before this. As I am now back to my normal hours, I can bring you above again." His breath stirred the wisps of hair near her ear. His voice was rough, as though he held his displeasure in check. "But right now is not a good time for you to be up here."

"Why?" With the rise of the bow, she fell back into his chest. He absorbed the shock and just as quickly as she'd fallen, she righted herself, grabbing onto the polished brass rail of the upper deck again.

"Because we're moving into rough weather ahead. Can't you tell?"

"Of course. The waves are growing larger, and the boat in front of us has disappeared into a curtain of rain, even though the sun is shining on us. Our wind is coming from the northeast, and that system seems to be moving toward us from the southwest. It doesn't bode well, does it? Perhaps we should take a northerly tack and skirt around the storm."

"Very good, my lady. Well done. That's Lucky in front of us. He overtook us two days ago. I'm trusting his sense in this. If I'm not mistaken, he believes skirting to the north would diminish any lead we may have. He also doesn't believe this storm to be of any significance. I concur with that assessment, but only because of the disorganized formation of the clouds. So it appears to me to be merely a storm front and nothing worse."

"Fine, so it may rain and the seas might get a little rough. Why must I go below again?" She turned in his arms and faced him. He was unshaven, with several days' growth of a dark-blond beard on his handsome face.

Having never seen a man with a beard up close, she acted on impulse and reached up to touch his jaw, laying her hand flat against the stubble. The dark blond hair was coarse and somewhat prickly, giving his face a roughened appearance, but in no way did it mar his rugged good looks. Quite the contrary, she found it appealing. As she stared at his firm, wide lips, she dropped her hand away, her palm scorched from the heat between them.

Sarah realized now was the perfect time to begin the seduction of her captain. She turned her face up to him with a limpid-eyed look she'd used frequently on Ren as a child to get her way. It was the same look she'd perfected in the mirror in her room during those interminable bouts of punishment. The look worked for a while, until he caught her teaching his daughter, Isabel, the same trick. She hoped the look would work again now.

"It's lonely down there," she began in a practiced tone, just short of a whine, but one that worked amazingly on men for some reason. "I've been cooped up in that room for days with no one to talk to. If you continue to confine me, I will go mad." Sarah straightened her spine and gave him what she hoped was a repentant, pleading look. "I am more than ready to apologize for whatever my transgressions were."

He stepped back out of her reach. "You would be safer below during this weather. If you get wet, you might catch a chill. Or worse."

Another wave hit the side of the boat and pitched her forward, straight into his arms, which he wrapped around her protectively. She couldn't have asked for a better lead in to her seduction. Looking up at his face, she realized if she stood on her toes she could place a kiss on his lips from this position. Of course, if she did and he was not as attracted to her as she to him, he would think her a desperate lady, rightfully on her way to Spinster's Corner.

"Come," he said with a gravelly voice. His moist, warm breath on her ear sent rivulets of arousal coursing through her.

All it would take is one kiss, she told herself. Just one, and she would be in his arms just as the women in that book of his...experiencing the passion she hoped he'd learned from reading it as well. She wanted that so desperately now.

"Let's get you below before you get hurt," he said as he led her to the companionway. "Get in the cabin and lock the door. I'll return after we clear this weather. It shouldn't take too long."

Sarah nodded and after he left, she smiled to the empty room. She would be ready for him when he returned. A part of her realized, even before she'd left the cozy confines of the rented house in Liverpool, that by joining this race she would likely take the direct route to spinsterhood—meaning no further seasons—and likely a hasty marriage to someone who would have her after her escapade ended. Someone likely in need of her fortune and a connection with her family.

And if that was her future, then by damn she was going to enjoy the present.

Ian reclaimed his position at the wheel. Instinct took over as he issued commands to his crewmen and steered his vessel into the rain. As he fought to stay on course, his mind wandered to the woman safely tucked away below in his cabin.

Her touch still burned where it had lingered on his jaw. Why had she done that? Surely she'd seen an unshaven man before landing aboard his ship. If she hadn't, she'd have to get used to it, because after that potentially lethal fiasco while attempting to shave for her benefit that first day out, he'd decided to do as he usually did while at sea and let his beard grow.

He'd been right about leaving her alone for a few days. It never seemed to fail him how solitary confinement worked to make a person more cooperative. So now that he had her cooperation, what was it exactly he wanted her cooperation with?

Admittedly, he'd be happy if they just didn't argue. But he didn't see that happening. He wanted her to be aware of what was likely to happen on their return to England. It was impossible to imagine that she could escape the societal repercussions that were sure to await her upon her return home. More likely than not, His Grace would demand a marriage.

They came from polar opposite backgrounds. Yes, he was the grandson of an earl and out of some weird twist of fate next in line to that old man's fortune-less title. And Ian had no wealth of his own yet, though he was working on bettering his condition. He also wasn't born in her country. He was an American, the son of a naval architect who'd designed the very ships that decimated the British Navy twenty-five years earlier. Lady Sarah was born the daughter of a duke and had grown up with all of the amenities inherent to her birth.

That position, though providing opportunities and

conveniences he'd never been fortunate enough to experience, also came with restrictions, even more so because of her sex. As long as she understood the repercussions at the end of this journey were not his doing, he was fine carrying her to New York. If her name was ruined, it was her own fault. Though having her return to England in the company of her brother Lucky would only benefit his self-control, it might cause even more problems for her in the long run because Lucky was not her blood brother.

Ian had to get control of his over-eager cock, which sprang to attention each time she was near. He had to focus on the race and not the desire to have her legs wrapped around his waist or her lithe frame on top of him, riding him to the finish. Frankly, he didn't need her type of complication in his life just yet, and that's what she'd be. A complication.

But it seemed the fates had spoken the night before the race when she landed aboard his boat.

The winds shifted, and the rain started to fall as they entered into the edge of the storm's boundary. His crew worked seamlessly, without requiring instruction and with the second officer making the calls to reef the sails. They knew their jobs, and most of these veteran sailors knew the sea and sky as well as any university professor knew his subject. Tacking the sails appropriately to minimize luff, they held a steady course roughly four to six minutes behind Lucky, not that they could see *Avenger* through the driving rain, but Ian knew she was there ahead of him.

The hull of *Revenge* dipped and rose as her bow sliced through wave after wave. After what seemed an eternity, they emerged on the other side of the front to find sunshine, smooth sea, and a cooler temperature. As he predicted, Lucky was still there, though his lead had lessened to approximately one minute. When Ian's ship drew closer, he saw the reason for their loss of lead. The crew of *Avenger* was raising a main lower topsail, causing Ian to look over his canvas carefully.

And as he did so, he had a fleeting thought—one that caused a twist in his gut. He should do the right thing and run up the flag to signal Lucky to stop so he could send Sarah over to *Avenger* while he had the chance. He'd had the opportunity two days ago when *Avenger* had taken the lead, but Ian had let that opportunity pass. While he struggled with himself, trying to justify keeping her with him, the crew on the other boat worked quickly and efficiently to get that new sail up. And once it was catching the wind like all the others, Ian knew the opportunity to hand his guest over to her brother was gone.

Seeing nothing out of line with his own sails, and with the weather conditions much improved, Ian handed over the wheel to his first officer, Nigel Johnson, for the night, and headed below.

Sarah replaced the book as soon as they'd broke through the rough seas, anticipating Ian's knock at any moment. Even though she'd read and re-read the entire text over the past days, she still went back and read the section on seduction again. Loosely following the instructions in chapter two—after all they were written for a male audience—she'd come up with a plan. Then began to put in in motion when she prepared herself for his visit by washing up, which was no easy task in the rough seas. She went one step further and removed her demi-corset and drawers, redressed in the trousers and shirt, then unbraided and combed out her hair. If she wanted to seduce her captain, she'd need to be as alluring as she could manage and let him see she was agreeable to being invited to his bed.

He desired her. This she knew for a fact. She also sensed he fought that emotion for reasons she was sure had to do with her being his friend's sister. Well, tonight she wanted him to see her as a woman, not Lucky's sister or a member of the *ton*. But as an enticing, willing woman. A woman he could not resist.

She unlocked the door, picked up the book of poetry she'd taken out earlier, and went to sit on the bench under an open porthole. Reclining back against the bulkhead, she arranged her hair, bringing it over one shoulder to run down the front of her shirt. Barefoot, she stretched one leg out before her and bent the other in what she hoped was a fetching position, then propped the open book of poetry up on a knee, holding the page open while she daydreamed. As if on cue, there was a knock on the door. Drawing a deep breath to bolster her courage, she lifted her head and bid him enter.

Ian came in carrying a bottle and two glasses. Her eyes met his, and in the diminishing light of the cabin, she saw something—desire perhaps—flicker in them. She hoped so. It would make this entire seduction easier if he wanted her as much as she did him. Placing her bookmark between the pages, she closed the book and set it down, then stood to help him with the glasses he held.

"Seamus, our...cook, is still preparing dinner, so I asked him to bring us a tray when he was done." He pulled the cork from the bottle and poured the wine. "In the meantime, I brought us something to drink as he didn't have an opportunity to make grog this afternoon because of the weather."

"Wine will do, though I was wondering earlier if you had tea. I've discovered I'm not fond of the grog. Even the weakest stuff is horrible."

"I'll ask Seamus to see that you have tea when you would like. Although, you're likely to have to wait until the fire is available."

"Thank you, Captain." She lifted her gaze to his while she sipped from the contents of her glass. His eyes were such a fathomless shade of green and golden-brown, she just wanted to lose herself in them.

"What are you reading?"

"I found a collection of Byron's and didn't think you would mind. I had to do something to keep me occupied these past few days. So I've been reading."

He nodded, then brought the flame up in both hanging lanterns; the room was beginning to grow dimmer with the setting of the sun. His eyes roved up and down her length, and she felt her body burn as his gaze traveled over her. When it settled on her breasts, her nipples tightened, intentionally bare for him under the fine cotton. She saw the knot in his throat bob as he swallowed, then again as he sipped from his glass once more. Lifting her glass, she did the same as she boldly held his gaze.

"Why enter the race? Is it for the excitement? Or the glory and accolades that go with being the winners?" She would have guessed he was in it for the excitement. He seemed the type, which was why his next words surprised her.

"I don't come from the same circumstance as you. The winning purse for this race will fund my portion of our business venture, so it's imperative I, or Lucky, wins. He is in this race to help me."

"He can be very sweet at times." She forced herself to turn away and looked down at her glass. "How long do you think it will take us to reach New York?" She reached out and wrapped a lock of her blond curls around her fingers and unconsciously began to twirl it.

"About three more weeks, give or take a few days. I would love to do it in two and a half, but that isn't likely on an uphill passage, even if I were to lay on all the sail the masts could hold."

"Uphill?" Sarah frowned. "But isn't the sea flat? How can it be uphill?"

Ian grinned at her. Heaven help her, but he had a beautiful smile. "When you're traveling west across the Atlantic," he explained, "there are prevailing winds and currents that push toward the east. We fight them constantly as we sail westward. Such as the front we went through today. Thus the term *uphill*."

"Now on the return, or *downhill* passage, those currents and winds are in our favor, and we can get back to Liverpool in almost half the time. It's as though the wind and currents carry us home."

"I remember reading about a boat once that returned in fifteen days. This was back when I was a child." She sipped from her glass again. "It was in the newspaper."

"You read the newspapers? As a child?"

He sounded surprised to learn that she cared about something other than ribbons and lace. Sarah wished Seamus would hurry with their dinner. She was afraid he might not remain as interested in her sexually if she had to continue discussing her education.

"Of course. My sister-in-law oversaw our education. Lucky and I had the best tutors. When he went to Eton, she hired a governess for me who conversed in five languages. Fluently. You will find I am not lacking in a comparable education to yours, Captain. I just choose not to flaunt it."

She returned to her seat in the corner and faced him, propping her chin on her drawn up knees. He took a seat further down from her, but if she stretched her legs out, her bare feet just might reach his thigh. Maybe she should try. Lifting her glass, she took another sip of wine and felt the warming effects of the liquid start to wend its way through her veins, relaxing her. "I am looking forward to seeing America. I've never been, you know."

"I'm not sure how much you think you're going to see." His gaze followed her foot as she began to slowly stretch her leg down the seat. Interesting. Did that mean her seduction was working? "We're only staying one night. All boats must stay twenty-four hours, as it's a mandatory hold to re-supply the vessel and rest. We are unable to leave before our twenty-four hours is up."

"Surely if we're going to stay the night anyway, we can go ashore." She could barely think about what she was saying as they both watched her toes touch the trouser-covered outer edge of his right thigh. "Perhaps spend the night at an inn and take advantage of a real tub of hot water."

"Maybe you should not have left the comforts of home in search of a non-adventure." His gaze still watched as her foot rubbed along the length of his thigh.

At first, the look on his face was daring her to touch him. Now she was afraid if she removed her foot he would grasp it and bring it back to him. "Oh, but this *is* an adventure for me. You see, I've never been anywhere exciting."

"London isn't exciting enough for you?"

"Not at all." She shook her head for emphasis. "Quite the contrary. It's tedious and boring. With all the same people at all the same events, each night in a different location. Over and over, night after night."

"Isn't that what young ladies such as yourself are supposed to do during the season? Socialize and meet young men from whom to select a prospective husband?"

She wiggled her toes as he watched, then stretched her right leg out to join the other and wiggled all ten toes against his thigh. "Yes. And I have," Sarah said, just before she heard a hitch in his breathing. "But there are no prospects I wish to have as a husband."

"What's wrong with the current crop of fops and dandies?"

When she placed her feet on the outside of his thigh, Sarah felt a shiver move through him, and she knew without a doubt he was as eager for this as she. "They're just that. Fops and dandies. Most of them have no purpose in life save to socialize and marry well."

"But isn't that what the ladies of your set are encouraged to do as well?"

Sarah nodded. "We're expected to latch onto a man with the most noble title and largest income available and convince him to marry us." Then her voice lowered and she held his gaze boldly. "But that's not what I want. You see, I already have both."

She knew her life would take a drastic turn upon her return to Liverpool, and she had no idea what exactly that future held for her. But for tonight, she wanted this man to love her in the same manner as all of the depictions in that erotic little book. And while she might long for this type of attraction and arousal in a future husband, she doubted that would happen for someone like her because she could never be happy locked away in the country doing these things with someone she held no physical attraction for. Someone she had no chemistry with. Someone she didn't desire.

She could very easily be persuaded to do this with Mr. Ross-Mackeever, her captain, on a nightly *and* daily basis. Oh, yes. This man she *would* marry if he'd ask. And she would give him as many children as he wished because suddenly she wanted them. With him.

Breaking her gaze, he tossed back his wine, swallowing hard. "What is it you want, my lady?"

She thought about it a moment, then replied honestly. "I want a man who wants *me*, not my dowry and inheritance or a political connection. I want a man who has dreams and ambitions, because I want to be a partner in his endeavors and dream along with him." What she couldn't tell him was more than all of that, she wanted love. Love such as that found by Lia and Elise.

But something so intense was sure to scare away most men.

Both her brother and brother-in-law had killed men for injuring their women because their love was so deep they could not imagine a life without their wives. From what she'd seen of *ton* marriages thus far, that type of devotion wasn't common. Her friends' marriages were lukewarm at best according to the gossips. Each one was a political or financial match with the men benefiting from the union far more than her friends. That was why she was still single. She wanted more than that.

"And here I thought you were merely a spoiled, inconsiderate, young...adventuress."

"I can see why you'd think I deserve that." She took another sip of the sweet wine. "Though I should like to defend myself, if I may."

Sarah didn't know why she bothered with an explanation to this man, except that for some reason she didn't want him to think her vapid and empty-headed. That she didn't always seek out adventure irresponsibly. And that she was also a well-educated lady who gave back to her community in ways that she could derive satisfaction, by teaching and patronizing causes.

"Please do." He held up his glass in a sort of wave, as though giving permission to continue.

"Adventure runs in my blood," she began. "My family was establishing trade with countries around the world for hundreds of years before I was born. Because I was born a female I am told I cannot share in those adventures. I cannot sail the oceans and climb the highest peaks. I am allowed an education, but no venue to practice it. That is not the world I want to live in.

"I did leave a note so my family would not worry. And though you may think me spoiled, dancing and parties is not all I do." She was beginning to mellow now from the delicious wine. After taking another sip, she continued. "I'll have you know that I devote a great deal of time to volunteering at the children's hospital founded by my friend's mother and her aunt. I also assisted in the formation of a lending library in our village, and I currently teach children to read at Haldenwood, our family seat."

"Is this in between music and dancing lessons?"

"If you must know," she replied indignantly. "My lessons were over four years ago. I'm going to be twenty-one years of age in just two months."

"Hmmm.... So you're nearly a spinster, aren't you?"

Even with the thin veil of humor tinging his voice, she was offended by his comment. She knew that the clocked ticked louder for her to find a mate, having spent these past years more enjoying herself than finding a husband. She didn't need her captain to remind her of this. So she tossed the slim volume of poetry, which had been under her leg, at him. In return, he grabbed her ankle with a firm grip and yanked her forward until her bottom rested against his thigh. With her legs over his lap, the heat of him radiated through the thin woolen material of her baggy trousers, and she became very aware of his hard-muscled leg against her buttocks. Bare under the trousers she wore, her breath caught in her chest as one of his big, calloused hands slid up a pant leg, burning a painfully slow trail up her bare calf to rest on her knee, as the other held her in place.

There was no turning back now. This was what she'd led him to, what she'd wanted. And more than likely what he wanted too, as he could turn down this unspoken invitation to a brief affair. The fact that he didn't made her feel desirable and worthy of passion— yet aching inside with the fact that the love she desired probably wasn't on this man's agenda.

But at that moment she didn't care.

"Stop me, Sarah." The husky timber in his voice was pleading, almost begging.

His intent gaze held her mesmerized. She could hardly breathe, much less move away from him, but still she managed to shake her head as she mouthed, "No."

His bare hand rested on her knee while his thumb gently stroked the sensitive skin on the inside of it. Her other leg fell open, and Sarah felt his hardened manhood beneath her thigh. Shocked, she sucked in a breath. Yes. This was what she wanted. With the sensations his touch caused and the desire pooling at her core, how could she stop? The man was insane. Pressure was already building within her to hurry him along.

She wanted his engorged member inside her, claiming her and bringing her to the ecstasy purported to occur after he joined with her. She was ready for this.

"You're playing a dangerous game, my lady." His voice was soft and raspy, yet filled with passion. "And with a man who has not had a woman in months." His fingers caressed the inside of her knee and up a few inches higher. She saw the determined look in his eye, and the tight curve to his lips. "Be sure this is what you want. Once I start, I won't stop until I'm satisfied."

She met his carnal stare with one of her own and wet her lips with the tip of her tongue. "I want…."

His large warm hand crept up her thigh slowly. Her breathing hitched. His look told her she had one last opportunity to stop him if she chose. But the aching void in the vicinity of her womb decided for her. "I want satisfaction…as well, Captain." His hand squeezed the flesh of her inner thigh, just below her moist curls, and a moan escaped her. If she never married, or if she did, this was the moment she would always remember. When Ian asked and she replied.

"I want you, Ian."

Chapter Five

Ian slid his hand up her soft, curved inner thigh until he reached the downy curls he sought. The trousers she wore prevented him from cupping her and feeling her the way he wanted, but his fingers still found what he was looking for.

She was wet and ready for him.

Bringing his hand back down and out of her pant leg, he laid his palm over her soft, flat belly, before unbuttoning several of her trouser fastenings.

A knock on the door broke the spell cast over them, and he barked out, "What?"

"Cap'n, I got yer dinner tray," Cook said.

"Bring it back in an hour." Ian's gaze never left her hungry, ocean-blue eyes.

"It'll get cold, Cap'n."

It was his own fault that he'd forgotten that he'd asked the man to bring him the tray, though at the time he'd spoken to Seamus, he didn't think Sarah would be in his cabin, setting the scene for an evening of carnal pleasures. And right now his cock told him food could wait. "Bring it in one hour, I said!"

"Aye, Cap'n." The old salt walked away from the door.

With a slow hand, he grasped her waistband and

began to slide the trousers down her hips and off over her bare feet. As he did so, he savored the beauty of her smooth alabaster skin. Pale and nearly naked, Sarah lay there on the bench next to him, wearing only the softly worn white linen shirt and a seductive smile.

"Are you certain this is what you wish?" He had to give her one last opportunity to back out of this game she played, but she never flinched.

Her next word caused his cock to stiffen uncomfortably in his breeks. "Very," she replied in a husky voice that held no quaver. It wasn't just her looks that aroused him, it was also her initiative to take what she wanted. She was no meek lamb, this woman. She was an adventurer at heart, willing to brave the night to stow away on his ship, and a beautiful seductress, inviting him to her bed. And only a fool would say no to her.

Before this very moment, he would have made the assumption she was an untried virgin, but no virgin he knew could allure and fascinate a man such as this one did him. Sarah impressed him as a woman who knew what she wanted and needed. And she wanted and needed relief as much as he.

His fingers went back to her mound to explore more deeply. Her legs parted for him, allowing him access to her silky-wet inner depths, and he dipped inside her to find her slick and tight. She made encouraging little mewling sounds while his thumb played over her sensitive nub, her inner muscles clenched, drawing him in further, and she moaned deeply as her thighs quivered. She gave a keening little cry as she arched into his hand, just as the brink of her first climax of the night came upon her. Within seconds she shattered, flooding his fingers with more of her sweet juices.

God, it had been so long since he'd had a woman. He had to get inside her and relieve his need quickly, then he could fuck her properly after dinner. Standing, he pushed aside her corn silk-colored curls at her temple, as he looked onto her ethereally beautiful face. She smiled that sleepy, satisfied grin one feels after experiencing an orgasm, and he did the same knowing he was about to join her. Ian turned away from her for a moment to yank the blanket back on the bed before taking Sarah's hand and lifting her to her feet before him.

"Raise your arms," he said so he could remove the boy's shirt from her. Once that was gone, he brought his lips down on hers and reached down and lifted her, placing her onto the bed before stepping away to gaze down onto her nakedness. He couldn't breathe, couldn't turn away from her. She was like a mythical goddess come to life to render him senseless. Slender and curvy with high small breasts coming to hard, dark-rosy peaks.

She boldly watched him undress, making his cock even harder, if that were possible. She slid one hand down to cover her woman's curls, and the other up to cover her breasts. He wondered at her sudden shyness. He'd just fingered her depths to orgasm, and now she covers herself?

"Don't hide yourself from me," he whispered as he hurriedly shucked off his shirt.

"I'm not accustomed to being so…naked," she whispered, and Ian realized he'd never seen this side of her before. The Sarah he'd met the week before was nothing if not bold and adventurous. Yet just now, something—a look in her eyes or the way she tilted her head as her smile faded—told him she was, at the heart of it all, a shy, uncertain young woman. One who'd never had a lover with the candles lit.

LOVING SARAH

Finally as naked as she, he slid onto the bed next to her, his eyes never leaving hers. Reaching out with a finger, he brushed a stray strand of hair off her face. Something compelled him to ask again—whether it was his relationship with her brother, Lucky, or a well-honed instinct that told him when something was too good to be true and about to go so wrong. "You're sure?"

"I am very sure, Captain."

The taut tips of her breasts begged to be suckled, Ian ran his tongue over first one rosy peak, then the other before drawing one into his mouth. Releasing the tip, he slid over her and traced a path down the valley of her abdomen with his tongue, until he reached the wet core his fingers had ministered to just moments ago. He parted her nether lips, he swiped his tongue over her tight nub, and she bucked under him.

"Oh, yes," she whispered on a breath. "Don't stop."

He didn't. Spreading her thighs wide, he feasted until she cried out as another release quickly came over her. He raised up to stand at the edge of the bed, then hooking his arms under her knees, he pulled her until her buttocks met his thighs at the edge of the mattress. As he guided his cock to her very slick, very wet entrance, her gaze widened.

Ian chuckled. "You're not worried are you? Though it may have been a few months, I haven't forgotten how. You'll be truly satisfied before the night's over."

"I'm not worried," she said. "You're just...a bit larger than I've seen before."

He rubbed himself up and down over her slit and chuckled. It wasn't the first time he'd gotten that response from a woman. Strange, but he somehow felt proud she approved of him. She was incredibly beautiful and uncommonly original, stimulating him in more ways than just sex. At another time in his life, she might have been someone he would have considered as a possible wife. "I assure you I'll fit and you will be pleased."

"It's just…I've never…."

His heart stopped, afraid she was about to say the words that would prevent him from consummating the act. He looked down at her with a narrowed, suspicious gaze. "You've never what, my lady?"

Sarah thought a moment before replying, not wanting to reveal the truth of her inexperience, because he would surely stop. And she didn't want that. Not now that she's had a sample of his loving. A slight smile curved her lips, and she said, "I've never seen one so big."

His face relaxed and he grinned. Sarah watched as he held his own shaft and slid it up and down over her slick flesh. The image was more erotic than reading that handy little tome she'd found. Just knowing that at any moment he would put that inside of her was both exciting and a little frightening. The book mentioned pain upon first entry, but she'd felt none when his fingers were inside her. She watched the glistening tip of his shaft as he rubbed it over her nub, the sensation causing her to moan with anticipation.

His voice sounded hoarse and uncertain. "And you've seen many, then?"

"A few." The lie rolled off her tongue so easily it frightened her. She couldn't tell him the male members she'd seen were all in books—either his own book on seducing women or educational compendiums of art—and that the drawings didn't do his exemplary specimen justice. She shivered—no, *trembled* was more like it—with a mixture of anticipation and desire. A part of her feared she hadn't studied sufficiently the things the book said a man found pleasing, though she knew she had several weeks yet in his company to read and practice everything the book suggested.

The height of the raised bed, because of the storage drawers beneath, put her at the perfect height for him to enter her while standing. This position was depicted in the book, and she remembered the caption beneath relating that this was effective for deep penetration and extremely pleasurable for both the man and the woman. It also said from the standing position, the man could see the woman's face, and pleasure her breasts and sensitive nub if he chose, all while inside of her.

"I need release soon, else I will burst," he whispered.

He stroked his tip up and down over her nub once more before placing it at her entrance. When he pushed forward slightly, it stretched her painfully, and he groaned with pleasure. A tremor coursed through her, and she bit her tongue. He would never believe her if she told him now she'd never lain with a man. Perhaps she was wrong in thinking she could handle everything all at once, but she was committed now. She wanted to experience the rest of this exquisite act because these may be the only times she'd ever experience anything so erotic and titillating for the rest of her life—especially if she was forced to endure this glorious act under any man she was not attracted to.

"Oh, yes," Sarah moaned, wanting him to continue with whatever it was he was doing, giving him everything he wanted because she realized she wanted and needed it as well. The twinge of pain was quickly gone, and she began to understand what the authors of that book meant. Relaxation certainly helped with the initial invasion. Ian's member filled her completely, and she wasn't sure how he was going to move as she'd read he must do to achieve his satisfaction.

"Sarah," he uttered in a hoarse whisper that sounded more like a prayer than an exclamation of her name. He withdrew from her, and she felt vacant and desirous of so much more. She opened her eyes to meet his greenish-brown gaze, and he said, "After I climax once, I promise I will love you more slowly later. I just need this right now, so desperately." With that, he plunged his hips forward, impaling her.

Sarah stifled a scream, biting her lower lip as burning pain ripped through her. Tears welled in her eyes, and she squeezed them shut so he wouldn't see them. Bringing her hand to her mouth, she bit her fingers, as his curses filled the room. Damn. She didn't think the pain could get any worse until he rammed into her with all of his might. Nowhere in that book did it say he had to do it like *that*. She controlled her breathing as the book had suggested by taking slow, deep breaths. And as she did, she felt a new sensation, not pain, but pure pleasure. He was now deeper than he'd been with his fingers, deeper than he'd ventured just moments ago. He was so deep inside her that she felt him touch her womb.

He held still, deeply embedded within. "What game do you play?" The tone of his voice told her his anger was barely contained. She'd managed to infuriate him thoroughly this time. Hopefully he wouldn't be so angry he'd pull out, because her body was already adjusting to his size and she found it increasingly pleasurable.

"None, I swear it," she replied, her voice sounding strained even to her own ears. His hands held her tight at the waist, keeping her still. Her legs rested over the crook of his elbows, and she was effectively trapped. Unable to pull away, she felt every slow grinding deep pulse of his member inside her.

"Then why didn't you tell me?" His head was thrown back as he nearly yelled his words. "I gave you several chances to tell me, and you didn't. Why?"

"Because I wanted this," she said softly, honestly. "Wanted it with you."

"Well, you got it. The deed is done now." He took a deep breath, began to pull out then stopped himself, pressing deep again. "Damn it to hell!"

"Please don't stop," she begged. "I know there's more and I want it." She wanted that orgasmic pleasure mentioned in the book—the sensation of floating among the stars and soaring over mountains and valleys that the gentlemen authors said *both* parties experience at the climax of the act. But Sarah couldn't tell him she'd found his book, then he'd know she'd been snooping.

"*How* do you know?"

She met his icy gaze, with a pleading one, "I just do. I've heard and read about it. Please, please don't stop. The discomfort has already eased." She traced her hands down his forearms, then rested them on his hands. Her voice dropped to barely a whisper. "Please Ian. I want it all."

"I don't think I could stop now if I wanted to," he confessed as he pushed into her again.

When she winced, he said, "Let's change position."

He then withdrew and climbed onto the bed and moved Sarah to the center. She was so thankful he was going to complete the act. She wanted to feel what the authors called a man's orgasm. A smile came over her as she thought about the memories of this affair and how they would satisfy and console her during her spinsterhood. This man would forever be her adventure in sexual initiation.

Lying next to her, he returned his hand to her mons. His fingers parted her again and began to slide over her sensitive bud, dipping inside to draw forth more of her lubricating wetness. Something tightened deep within, and she knew it was the stirring of another climax as it built. He positioned himself over her and lifted her legs, "Wrap them around me when I enter you." This time when he entered, she experienced only a minor twinge at her entrance. But as he moved, the discomfort disappeared, replaced by a ravenous need to reach something inexplicable. She met his rapid thrusts because it seemed the only way to achieve what her body craved.

In a matter of minutes, she shattered into a profusion of tiny pieces, held together only by his strong arms wrapped around her. She had only a moment to savor her climax as she sucked in a shaky breath. And just as her body began to relax, he continued his driving into her, and he raced to his own release. When he reached it, he drove into her a last time, and she felt him tense as he filled her with his seed.

His breathing was deep and ragged, matching her own as their sweat-covered bodies began to cool in the night air. Sarah wasn't sure how much time had passed because she lay quiet and sated in Ian's arms. She stirred when a knock came at the door. Ian rose, threw the blanket over her and put his trousers on to answer it. She heard him throw the bolt and place the tray on the table. Opening her eyes, she rose onto her elbow and pushed her hair from her face.

"Dinner has arrived." Ignoring the tray, he turned the chair around and sat on it, with his chin resting on his folded hands on the chair back, his gaze shot daggers at her. It unsettled her to be under such scrutiny, and she knew she now had questions to answer.

"May I have my shirt?" She held the blanket with one hand and caught the shirt when he tossed it her way. When she stood, she winced at the tenderness between her legs. Then she looked down to see the stain of her irreclaimable maidenhead and their lovemaking on the sheet.

He must have seen it as well. "We need to talk." His voice was clipped and taut.

She climbed back onto the bed and sat under the covers. "The food will grow cold," she offered.

"I don't give a damn about the food!" The depth of anger in his voice sent a tremor of fear through her. "Do you know what you just did? You basically signed our marriage license with that act! I am not ready for a wife and family, and you.... Why? For the love of God, why?"

She didn't know what it was that stopped his tirade—likely the fear in her expression—but she stopped him when she spoke. "I am not expecting anything from you." He stared at her as though she'd sprouted two heads.

"It doesn't matter what you expect!" He slapped his thighs in frustration. "What just happened seals our fate, unless by some miracle you can magically get us out of a forced marriage. I have nothing to offer a bride yet. Getting married is not in my plan for several years yet!"

"And I never said I wanted to get married, did I? Besides, if ever I do marry, I would settle for nothing less than a man whom I love and who loves me in return."

"Love has nothing to do with what just happened. That was lust. Pure and simple."

It was lust, as he'd said, but it hurt to hear him say that he didn't want to marry her. Even though she felt an attraction toward him, he didn't even think enough of her to offer. Obviously he didn't care about her in that manner, and it *hurt*. She didn't think she was *that* plain, and she certainly had the connections and dowry necessary to attract a man. So why not the man she was attracted to?

She wanted to cry, but not in front of him. She never thought he would react in this way. This entire fiasco tonight was her plan, her idea, she wanted it, and she had to live with his reaction and the consequences. And it was best that he not know the things he made her feel when he was near—how her heart raced and her body tingled and grew warm and how with just a touch her core tingled, becoming wet and ready for him.

No, Sarah felt it would be far worse to live in a loveless marriage where resentment would build to anger than to live the life of an eccentric, adventurous aunt, who chaperoned her nieces on a tour of the continent or America.

"I'll never marry," she reiterated, "anyone, Captain." Sarah avoided his eyes. It wouldn't do to have him see that his words hurt. She wanted to feel wanted. He obviously didn't feel anything toward her but lust. Where her thoughts ran a little deeper than that, she wasn't sure she was in love with him. What she felt was just infatuation and lust—almost a primal sexual urge in need of satisfying. She took a lock of hair between her fingers and began to twist it.

LOVING SARAH

"You cannot imagine there will be no penalty for what we've done. Your brother will force us to wed, and rightfully so. Hell, I would do the same if I had a sister!" For some reason, his ire had lessened somewhat, almost as though he'd resigned himself to a noose, much like the horse to a saddle. He exhaled slowly and shook his tousled sandy blond hair. "Why did you do it? What on earth possessed you?" At her continued silence, he added, "Dear God, did you trap me?"

"Never!" She felt her eyes well with tears, and she wiped them with the sheet. "I swear it was never my intent to trap you at all, Ian," she said as she met his gaze to prove to him her honesty in this. "I never intended to land on your ship. I swear it! Leave my family to me. You'll not face the heinous sentence of marriage to me."

"You haven't answered me," he said. "I want to know why. What reason was there to do what you did?"

Sarah wiped her eyes again. There was no need to tell him about the book and the curiosity it stirred in a woman who was already attracted to him. She was truthful with him earlier when she'd said that she was planning for a life as a spinster. "No reason." She shrugged her shoulders. "I wanted this experience before going on that proverbial shelf." She stood, taking the sheet with her to hide her nudity from him, and began to look for her trousers, she didn't want to meet his accusing stare any longer so she feigned interest in getting dressed. "Again, I apologize, and I swear to you, you shall not be forced to marry me. Because I have a plan too, Captain. I will not marry anyone unless I love the man and he loves me. Since we don't, we won't." She spied her stockings and shoes and made busy to pick them up. Her voice sounded more resolved than she felt inside. "Marry, that is." She cleared her throat of some imagined irritant. "We will not marry."

"We have no choice now, much as I wish it were not so."

With that, he shoved his arms in his shirt and his feet in his boots and left the room. Her stomach growled when she realized he'd left the tureen with the stew. Half afraid he would return, she waited a few minutes before going to the table and lifting the lid. Taking a spoon, she fished out a piece of the meat and tasted it. Returning it, she decided she could go without tonight, having suddenly lost her appetite.

She didn't think he'd be quite so upset and honestly thought he'd accept what she would have proposed had he not erupted with anger—an affair for the duration of the trip to New York. For a man who admitted to feeling an attraction to her, why wouldn't he want to pursue a possible future with her? She might not be a *ton* beauty, but was not entirely unattractive, and she was descended from the best families in England. And Ian, merely because of his bloodline, would make a good choice of husband for her.

...much as I wish it were not so. Except he didn't want her, and that hurt most. If she had not invited him to sin, he likely would never have pursued the physical attraction he felt for her.

Sarah opened the door to the cat's scratches and bolted it after she'd entered, then boxed in the tureen on the table so the congealing contents wouldn't spill. She doubted Ian would return, so she stripped down to her shirt again and climbed into bed. He was beyond unwilling to forgive her for her actions, even though she had apologized and admitted trapping him was not her intent. She just hadn't thought her plan through and had now made an even bigger muddle of things. Only this type of muddle caused permanent, life-long changes to both of their lives.

Damn her for getting aroused by that silly book, and damn Ian for breaking her heart! How was it he had the ability to make her desire the one thing she swore to herself she would not seek with him? Where had the sudden desire to hear him say sweet words of love come from?

She had a romantic heart, like most other women. Except after three years on the market and receiving not one, *not a single one*, offer for her hand, she thought perhaps there was something wrong with her, which was why she wanted to have this sexual experience with Ian now before she took herself off the market. She hadn't planned on coming aboard his ship. Had not planned on finding that book either. But secretly, she was glad she had and happy to have experienced the sex act with him. Now she knew what it could be like when someone felt that type of passion.

She wiped her eyes with the sheet again, determined to push aside this sudden turn of emotion and remain honest with herself, keeping in mind that when she embarked upon this seduction of her host, she'd known exactly what she wanted. None of which included a marriage proposal or any vow of everlasting love. She'd wanted sex. Just sex. With him.

Which was exactly what she got.

Ian went above to check the ship's progress. The

second crew was on, and they were sailing quickly through the night, on course and blessedly ahead of schedule if his calculations were correct.

Thinking back over the past hour, he couldn't believe what had just happened. Couldn't believe she'd done that. When he left the room, he'd been in an anger-filled daze. Though it might have since diminished a bit, but he was still left asking himself what on earth would possess a young woman to do something so shocking, so irresponsible, so desperate, so...so damn selfish! He'd never have taken her in such a manner had he known she was a virgin.

If he was honest with himself, he knew from the moment he recognized who she was, that her actions—whether intended or not—forever changed his future. Whether he'd bedded her or not, his plans changed the moment she boarded his ship. He reasoned he could either be angry about experiencing one of the most satisfying sexual encounters of his life or he could be angry with the lad who'd left her on the wrong damn boat.

He had to reconcile himself to the fact that he didn't stop upon discovering her maidenhead either. Oh no. Damn his horny hide. He went on and completed the act to both their satisfaction. There was now the possibility of a child. Whether the thought of fatherhood frightened him or not, whether he was ready for marriage or not, both were now in his future.

He mentally counted the weeks until they returned home. If he never touched her again during the rest of the voyage, she should know before reaching Liverpool if she carried a babe.

Then again, if he was going to marry her anyway,

sharing his bed and their bodies would be accepted.

Since the night of the mouse in the cabin, whenever he was in her presence he got nervous inside. Tonight was no different. He was actually glad she'd never been with a man because she stirred feelings inside him no other had ever made him feel before she stepped onto this boat.

Now he had to reevaluate his plans, because marriage hadn't been a part of them for years yet. He had nothing but this boat. Where would they live? How would he support a family?

And there was his grandfather.... The bastard was one of the reasons he wanted to wait to take a bride. He didn't want his grandfather's disgusting vitriol to touch her or her family. The old bastard hated him—especially since that day in the study—and he didn't want to imagine the words the old earl would have for him if he found out he'd married Caversham's sister. He'd remind Ian once again that he was not fit to wipe his dead uncle's boots and that he was not a true Brit because he was born of a servant in that heathen-filled country across the sea. Each accusation he'd heard before, and all things he'd wanted to protect any wife of his from experiencing. But it was the other accusation that kept them both quiet, and for how much longer he didn't know. The only freedom would come when the man died.

As he scanned the horizon once more before seeking a hammock for the night, the old sailmaker and makeshift cook Seamus came up behind him.

"Ye ken she's the Duke's sister, don't ye?" he said, his nearly rotted-toothed grin obscured by the shadows of night.

"I know who she is."

"Then ye'd best do the right thing by her."

"Not that it's any of your business old man, but I'll do what's right for the lady," Ian said. The veteran sailor had been with Ian since he and Lucky had started sailing these boats four years earlier. He'd come highly recommended by his previous captains, having sailed on the duke's ships for many years. As a result, the man was familiar with the Caversham family dynamics. If it weren't for that fact, and that he was excellent with a needle as a sailmaker—if someone threaded it for him—and a tolerable cook, the man would not now be on his boat.

"Ah, that's a good lad," the old salt said as he walked away. And as he did, Ian swore he heard him mutter something about dancing a jig at his wedding, or on his grave, it was his choice which.

The quarter-moon shone down on the water, reflecting off the surface, and he looked ahead at *Avenger*. He didn't want to think about Lucky's anger at learning his sister-by-marriage was with him. Not only that she was on his boat, but that he had also bedded her. Ian knew that if he had a sister, he'd be angry with his friend if Lucky had so thoroughly ruined her. But would he kill him? Probably not. Not if the woman in question was of age and a willing participant in the liaison. Both of which Sarah was.

He had no idea how he would manage an explanation to both Lucky and the duke, but he'd have to for both of their sakes.

But for right now, he had to get over this feeling of being caught in a snare. If he was honest with himself, it that helpless feeling of being trapped with no way out that frightened and angered him most. That his whole future was decided for him because of the imprudent actions of one spoiled little chit.

Chapter Six

Two days after she'd served herself up to the captain, Sarah hovered in that blissful reverie that she often felt before becoming fully conscious, a clap of thunder so loud as to reverberate through the beams of the ship jolted her awake. Rolling out of bed with some measure of difficulty because the boat was pitching about on a choppy sea, she went to the portholes and without needing to open them, she could tell the rain was coming down in sheets. She scrambled back up onto the safety of the bed with the cat, wrapped the blanket tighter about her, and wondered where Ian was and if he was safe.

He had not come to see her since he'd stormed out the other night. Thus, Sarah had come to a satisfied conclusion regarding the events of that night. She was going to deny they happened if anyone asked. She didn't think Ian would admit to her family that they'd been intimate. And as she'd been to the galley several times to get her meals, she could say with some certainty that none of the crew looked at her differently. Not even Seamus, who knew what had taken place because he had taken the linens from the room, had mentioned it to anyone.

The boat rocked hard starboard, and she heard her captain's voice over the sounds of the rain and wind and knew he was struggling against the worsening storm.

Ian cursed as the fore upper topsail tore away from the crewman trying to hang it. The winds were blowing hard out of the north-northwest, and with the tight, dark cloud formations, rising swells, and murky water, he knew they were in for a worsening storm within a matter of hours. Perhaps he shouldn't have ordered the changing of that sail. It had begun to show wear, and he'd thought to replace it before the storm, rather than lose it during, possibly killing a man putting the replacement up.

Glancing down from the foremast after the crewman regained control of the line, he saw a flash of long golden braid over a gunmetal gray slicker standing at the rail. Foolish woman! Didn't she know her safety was in jeopardy with the conditions as they were? All he needed was to have her fall and slide overboard through a scupper. She wasn't tied off to the lifeline as the rest of the crew was during this type of weather.

He wanted her back in the safety of his cabin, but when he called out for her, his voice was drowned in the howling of the wind. So he did the only thing he could do. He motioned toward her to a crewman standing on the quarter-deck, and the man went to fetch her.

"What are you doing up here? Get back in the cabin," he shouted.

"I wanted to see what was happening and check on the weather conditions."

"We're on the edge of a storm. I won't be able to protect you and my crew at the same time. Please, go back to the cabin and sit tight. I'm not sure how long we're going to be in this thing."

She was completely ignoring him, scanning the horizon. "Where's Lucky? I don't see him."

"He's out there somewhere. I promise you, he's fine. Now, go below." When she made no move to leave, he added sternly, "I am not asking you, Sarah. I'm commanding you." He nodded to the man next to her. The man offered his arm and led her to the companionway.

When she opened the door to the cabin, the cat scrambled back in with her, seeking a hiding place from the storm no doubt. Sarah went to the bed and lay upon it, the cat jumping up to lie with her, and as she cuddled the cat, she prayed that they would all make it through the storm unharmed.

As the hours passed, the rain, wind, and lightning grew more intense. The rolling and dipping motion of the vessel became more violent, prompting her to pray harder. Not for herself, but for each of the men on both boats, and most especially those who had wives and children back home. She learned early in her volunteering that widows and children were the ones to suffer most when their husbands and fathers died.

Hours later, as night fell, she decided to forego lighting the lantern for fear of breaking it and perhaps causing a fire. So she lay there on the bed, in the dark, holding the cat, and trying desperately to rest, even knowing that sleep would never come because of her worries. She had confidence in Ian. She did. He'd been to China twice already with Lucky, and she remembered hearing that he'd sailed as a child, just as Lucky had, so he was as comparably skilled a sailor as Lucky. And she was sure he had no desire to die in the middle of the Atlantic, so surely he would do everything in his power to see them through.

At least that was what she told herself while she prayed for their safe exit from this horrible weather.

This storm was larger and more dangerous than the one a few days earlier. Several times the ship pitched so steeply, it nearly rolled her out of the bed. If she'd managed to catch any sleep, she might have fallen out. Moments after a particularly hard pitch, she heard voices on deck crying out "man overboard." Fear gripped her, for she'd come to know every man aboard the boat. She wanted to know who to pray for and if Ian was well after all this. She wouldn't go on deck, but she had to see what the conditions were. She'd go no further than to stand at the top of the stairs in the companionway. She had to go. Had to see for herself if everything was being done to rescue the man. Even knowing she'd have to face Ian's wrath if he saw her, she opened the door and climbed up the stairs. She reached the main deck just in time to witness him jumping off the side of the boat into the angry ocean.

Sarah screamed as she fell back into the companionway with another pitch of the boat.

When she awoke, it was to find the cook, Seamus, standing over her in the dim lantern-light of the cabin as she lay on the bed with a cold, wet rag on her head. Why? What was she doing—Ian! He'd gone over the side of the ship. Where was he? Was he alive? She had to find him. Sarah attempted to sit up so she could go above and find him.

She had to know if he had lived or died. Ian had gone over the side. He didn't fall. He jumped over the rail. He'd risked his own life to try to save that of another. She didn't think it was possible that the two of them had made it back on the boat. Not with the ocean as violent as it was when she saw him dive into it. How long had it been? She couldn't tell. The only light came from the lantern, and the room was not pitching as violently as before.

She should go find him. She tried to rise and fell back onto the bed. God her head throbbed. "Ian?"

"No, lassie. 'Tis me, Seamus."

"Of course I know who you are." Good God, her head was splitting! "Where's Ian?" She groaned as she sat up. "Did I hit my head?"

"Cap'n's 'pon deck, m'lady, at the helm. And ye got a right big goose egg on the back of yer head, ye do."

"I saw him go over." She tried to remember exactly what it was she did see before she'd fallen. "I thought he...."

"He did go after that scrawny kid Bartholomew. The daft lad fell off the fore mast when he was checking on that sail he hung. If'n he'd hung it right the first time, there'd never been need for 'im to go up a second time during the height of the storm."

"Ian's safe?" she asked, astounded he'd made it back. "What about young Bartholomew?"

"E's back, too." Seamus grinned, revealing an uneven set of blackened teeth in his leathery face just before another violent pitch sent the hull nearly over. The grizzled old sailor clung to the support beam steadying the light so the thing wouldn't smash against the roof.

Knowing he was safe, she reclined back onto the pillow and said a prayer of thanks for the crew's lives and their good fortune to see the storm through. "I never thought someone could make it out of the water when the seas were that rough."

"In weather likes this, we tie off to the rail or a mast, m'lady. We might go over, but we're dangling alongside until someone brings us up. In Bart's case, he was tied at the mast and was hanging unconscious off the side of the hull. He smashed his noggin' pretty good. He'll be a'right though. The cap'n got him and he's recuperatin' in 'is hammock."

"Does the captain know I fell?"

"No. I figured he's got enough ta worry over without worryin' over you."

"Thank you. Please don't tell him about this. As you said, it'll only cause him undue concern." She gave the veteran sailor a wan smile.

"You're a good lass." The man handed her a mug with wine from the bottle on Ian's bookcase. "Now drink some of this, and ye'll be feelin' better in no time."

"Thank you." Sarah accepted the mug from the grizzled old man and sipped from the same bottle of wine she'd had the other night. Another flash of light in the darkened afternoon sky and the immediate clap of thunder told them both that the storm was still not over. The ship and all of her crew were still at risk. Her head throbbed, and she leaned back against the headboard. "Are you certain the captain is well? Perhaps he needs some help?"

"He's just fine, m'lady." Seamus made himself comfortable on the bench seat with a pillow to rest his head upon as he leaned into the corner. "We all went through worse than this last year roundin' the cape comin' back from China. Both cap'n's are fine sailors and knows what their boats can handle."

Sarah sipped from her mug, the sweet wine warming

her from the inside. She said nothing as the old veteran sailor droned on. She wasn't sure if he talked to relieve her fears or because the noise drowned out some of the sounds from above deck. "I spent me whole life at sea, m'lady, most of it in service to me country. Then I sailed with Cap'n Cully for a while. I was there as he taught a young Lucky how to tie knots on the voyage from Italy.

"The young cap'ns have a good head for this business," he added. "Both are strong sailors. They remind me of the brothers, Cully and Flynn. And that makes it easy for a man to sign onto a ship when the captain knows what he's doin' and isn't afraid to get his hands dirty alongside his crew."

"Or jump into the ocean to save one of his crewmen," she muttered.

"Aye. That too," the grizzled old salt agreed.

"I knew he was special from the moment we met, and...I ruined his life, his plans, everything, and he...hates me now. But...I...." How could she explain the odd feeling she had to their captain. The attraction and desire she felt?

"Have ye told the lad how ye feel?"

She shook her head and sighed. "No. He is not very happy with me and has made that quite clear."

"So, when we return home ye'll be partin' ways, then?"

Sarah nodded. "Before that." She swallowed past the lump forming hard in her throat. "In New York. I return with Lucky." She swiped at a tear, likely her exhausted state from worrying over the crew during the storm causing this unwanted release of emotion. "You know, none of this would have happened if that silly boy had rowed me out to the right boat," she choked. "We might have had a different beginning, with a happier ending."

Sarah began to feel as though she needed sleep. She yawned and caught herself as her head fell forward. She frowned her suspicion as Seamus. "Did you put something in that wine?"

The old cook shook his head. "It's from the cap'n's bottle right there. I ain't touched it." The man smiled. "Well, I tasted a bit o' it to make sure it hadn't gone to vinegar, y'see. Can't have His Grace's sister drinkin' bad wine."

Sarah wanted to ask him if the rest of the crew knew who she was but was already beginning to drift into slumber. She nodded and slunk down on the mattress, too tired to be angry with him. "If I sleep, will I get tossed from the bed?"

"Seein' as this bed ain't got a fiddle rail, I'll tuck ye in right tight, lassie. And I won't be leavin' the cabin, unless they need me topside."

"Thank you, Seamus." Sarah grabbed Ian's pillow and hugged it tight, wishing it were him she was holding. Wishing she could start over from the moment she landed on this ship. There were so many things she would do over.

So many things.

Ian entered the cabin several hours later, once they'd cleared the storm, and found Seamus lying on the bench, snoring. The old man's eyes opened when he heard him come in, and he sat up and rubbed his eyes.

"The lass fell down the steps when she saw ye jump in after the lad. She didna want me to tell ye, but I thought ye might need ta know, Cap'n."

Loving Sarah

Concern for Sarah quickened his step, and he went to the bed. He turned a questioning glance to Seamus. "Did she hit her head?" He turned back to look as her slumbering form. Not only would he have to explain a hasty marriage in the New York harbor to her brother, now he had to explain her injury as well.

And marry her he would. The last couple of days he'd resigned himself to the fact that the right thing to do was marry her, no matter what his plans had been. There was no way he could avoid it. It angered him that these circumstances were forced upon him, but if he were honest with himself he'd known this was the case before she'd offered herself up to him. And he'd resolved to talk to her about it tonight before they came upon the storm.

He kept replaying the events of the other night. Before he'd gotten angry and accusatory with her. Each time, he remembered that amazing hour of carnal sex unlike any he'd ever experienced before, he wondered what it might be like to marry her and be done with the courtesans.

Sarah was eager, adventurous, curious, and willing. She wasn't unattractive. He actually enjoyed looking at her, especially naked. From the moment he'd sat next to her at the dinner the night before the race, he'd felt more than a little pull toward her. All in all, he could do much worse than a beautiful, intelligent, well-connected lady for a wife.

She'd be the perfect countess for him one day when that wicked old bastard cocked up his toes and became fertilizer for some churchyard. He thought about how to go forward from here. First he had to apologize for his actions from two nights ago and discuss what might possibly lie ahead for them.

"She's got a knot on the back o' her skull, Cap'n. We spoke a while, and she seemed fine te me, an' I reassured her ye was a'right. Then I gave her a bit o' wine to help her sleep through the rest o' the storm."

Ian met the old salt's gaze.

"It was just wine," the old sailor said again. "She was worried for ye."

"I'm sure you told her I could handle myself out there," Ian replied.

"I did." Seamus stood and made great theatrics of stretching his back while groaning. "Y'know, the lass thinks ye hate her, and I know she's not been 'erself these past few days."

"My anger is more at the circumstances that forced us together, than at the lady herself," Ian said before turning his attention back to the sleeping Sarah. "I don't hate her." He brushed a lock of hair from her forehead and she sighed. "Far from it," he whispered. "I'll be forever indebted to you for saving the next Countess Mackeever."

The grizzled old salt nodded as he shuffled from the cabin and quietly shut the door behind him. Ian slid the bolt, then removed his wet clothing, replacing them with a dry shirt and drawers. His mind whirled over the day's events and the revelations he'd settled himself into before the storm. He lay next to her on the bed to get a few hours of sleep, both his mind and body physically exhausted.

Sarah slowly came awake to the soft snoring of a man near her ear, and her heart raced. Why had Ian come to sleep in here? With his arm loosely draped over her waist, she noticed he'd removed her trousers and demi-corset, and if he'd done *that* what else had he done while she was sleeping? Her bladder would burst if she didn't get behind the screen soon. She closed her eyes and took a deep breath, praying she didn't wake him. When she rolled away, she tried her best to avoid stirring him as she slid off the bed.

Her entire body ached from the tumble she took the day before, and she had to bite her tongue to keep from groaning out loud with the stiffness in her back. Her shoulder and entire left side felt as though she'd been trampled by a team of horses. She stood in front of the room's only mirror, cursing the fact that it was nowhere near large enough to show her much beyond her head and shoulders. And to make matters worse, the thing was mounted to the wall where she could only see the top of her head, which was fine if she was combing and braiding her hair, but if she wanted to see anything more she'd have to stand on the chair. And she'd be damned if she was going to stand on a chair and undress in front of Ian.

She crept behind the screen and noted his clothing from the day before draped over the top to dry. After removing her shirt and making use of the pot, she stood behind the screen, twisting and turning to get a good look at the dreadful coloring of her skin on her entire left side from knee to shoulder. Blue, purple, eggplant, and greens blended to form a kaleidoscope of sorts from the good bruising she got thanks to her fall. And she never would have fallen if she hadn't worried about the crewmen at the cry of man overboard, Ian in particular. That moment had played in her dreams all night long, and each time she relived what had happened as she stood at the top of the steps.

She remembered finding the hatch closed, and she had to push it open to see on deck. As she held it against the wind, the very first thing she saw was Ian jumping over the side of the ship, and her mind froze. She didn't remember if he'd had a tether—hadn't seen one through the driving rain. But instinct took over and she leaped forward screaming his name as she let go of the hatch, which then came down on the top of her head, sending her falling back into the companionway.

Ian. She swiped a tear when she thought about her actions. She covered her face with her shirt, wishing she'd done things differently. No doubt what she'd done was wrong, using him to satisfy her curiosity as she did, but she'd enjoyed it so much that when she relived the hour of foreplay and sensual pleasure her core began to tingle and she grew wet again. And each time she imagined doing the act again, it was always Ian's face that came to mind as her lover.

Except her captain wanted nothing more to do with her. He'd made himself clear three nights ago when he left this very room in a rage and never returned.

Until last night.

Sarah thought she'd be happy if they could just have peace between them. He didn't have to get on bended knee and propose marriage because she wouldn't marry him now anyway after the horrible accusations. But she didn't want to stay cooped up in the cabin, punished for her actions.

Slipping her shirt over her head, she turned to find the object of her desire and disaffection staring around the corner of the screen.

"Why are you in here, Captain?"

"Your bruising is severe. Are you in pain?"

"Nothing I can't handle, I assure you." She met his hazel-eyed stare with one of her own. "Why are you here?"

"Because this is my cabin, and that is my bed. After a grueling day of fighting that storm, I wanted a warm, soft bed to stretch out upon, not a narrow hammock to squeeze myself into."

She humphed. "You are rather...large." She moved past him and into the room and found her trousers and stockings and went to the bench where she redressed. Moving to the mirror, she picked up her comb and raised her arms to comb her hair and winced at the pain in her left shoulder.

As she braided her hair, he made use of the pot. He reappeared and took the chair from against the bench and moved it to the center of the room. He watched her, studied her as she dressed, without saying a word, and it was disconcerting to her. When her coat was buttoned and her braid was tied, she turned back to him to tell him she was leaving the room, but he stopped her.

"When we reach New York, we will marry and...."

She closed her eyes, knowing this was what she'd dreamed, but saw his expression from the other night when he asked, *"Did you trap me?"* To cover her pain, Sarah barked out in laughter. "I will never marry you, Captain, so you may as well get that into your thick skull."

"You'll marry me." He sounded so certain it irritated her. "And because we will marry, I've decided I'm moving back to my bed."

For a fraction of a moment, a thrill ran through her at the thought of them once again exploring bodies and finding satisfaction in each other's arms. Then she remembered, he was only doing this because of her brother and Lucky. He didn't care for her at all. She had to set him straight, as she was not giving up her life of independence and adventure. "Listen, Ian, my only wish is that for the duration of this journey, we not yell, throw unfounded accusations, or walk off without finishing our discussions." She wanted him to understand she was serious about not marrying him.

"I will work on that, as it is a weakness I have."

"Great. Work on it now, and perfect that part of your personality before you find some lovely young lady to marry—when your plan allows." She grabbed the tureen from the night before to take to the galley. "Especially the part about hurling accusations. It will make for a much more peaceful life."

"Sarah, I apologize for raising my voice with you. I'm not accustomed to dealing with ladies of your caliber. And though I made accusations in the heat of the argument, those *were* my feelings at the time." He sighed as though he was feeling those emotions again. "I was feeling trapped."

"The last thing I want to do is trap you, which is why I do not want to marry you. It was never my intent, Captain."

"What was your intent, if I might be so bold as to ask?"

"I was curious, Captain. That is all. And you've now satisfied my curiosity." Taking the tureen, she left him in the room and went to get her breakfast. And this time, for the first time since leaving Liverpool, she ate her breakfast in the galley under Seamus's watchful eye to give her captain time to leave the cabin.

After luncheon, Ian stood at the door to the cabin, hand raised, ready to knock. He debated with himself about taking her above to walk a time or two about the main deck. She'd said earlier that she was bored and had read some of his books, and he knew there was not much in the way of romantic novels or poetry in his collection, which led him to believe she might like a walk in the fresh air.

Knowing he needed to apologize, and they needed a fresh start if there was to be any harmony with her at all, he stood at the door, feeling somewhat green and nervous. If he didn't think there was a chance for some happiness, he wouldn't have been there. He could just as easily have said they would marry, deposit her in England afterward, and go on about his life.

Except for the need for an heir one day.

And the strong desire for that luscious body of hers.

He rapped twice.

He heard shuffling, and in a moment she stood before him, her braid falling down her back and the loose tendrils around her face curling loose and free. He wanted to touch them but restrained himself.

"Yes, Captain," she said, a curious tilt to her head.

"I thought in the interest of restoration of harmony, I might escort you on a walk in the sun for a bit."

"Though I would love a walk in the open air, I'd rather do it on my own and not with you, Captain."

"I'm sorry, my lady, but the only way you will have freedom to walk the decks is with my escort."

She went back into the room, and he followed. When he looked at the mussed bed covers and the arranged pillows he realized why he heard the shuffling. "I'm sorry. Did I disturb your rest?"

"Not really. I cannot seem to find a comfortable position for longer than ten minutes."

"Perhaps if you got up and moved around it might help," he offered.

"But that would mean I'd have to go up with you, and I'd rather not."

"Are you afraid you might fall under my spell?"

"You're forgetting. I'm the manipulative one, I don't fall under spells. I weave them to the demise of all men I wish to ruin."

Ian knew after the things he'd said the other night, he'd not have an easy time of making peace with her. Still, she had to know he wasn't backing down.

"Sarah, I'll be sleeping in this bed tonight and every other night. You can lie to yourself all you want and think we will not marry, but the fact is our fate was sealed from the moment you climbed out of that forward sail locker. And you might want to think on this…had you actually made it on board *Avenger,* you would have been in worse situation than you are now."

"Impossible," she argued.

"Oh, yes," he replied. "You would have been ruined, even more had you landed on Lucky's boat. Your family would have had to scramble to find someone to marry you quickly to save your reputation because Lucky is not your brother by blood. And I know he would never marry someone he considers a sister, and neither could you marry someone you loved as a brother.

"So any acceptable match would be considered. It easily could have been someone beneath your status who needed your money. Or an overweight old man willing to look the other way at the situation you found yourself in for the opportunity to beget his heirs on you." She lowered herself onto the bench, and he could see she knew he spoke the truth because she had no argument. "I can assure you it would not have been me taking your hand, because as I said the other night I was not prepared for a bride. I'm *still* not. But I have resigned myself to the fact." He didn't have to explain to her the arguments, both for and against, like he'd had with himself while he sailed through the storm. His inner struggles were his own. And for as long as he could, he'd shield her from the bastard in Edinburgh.

"How many times are you going to make me apologize for being curious the other night?"

He chuckled slightly, and her complexion turned deep pink. "My lady, that was beyond curious."

She stared at the ceiling, and Ian could see, even through her closed eyes, she fought tears. "You should have refused me. Told me…."

He walked over to where she sat and stood before her. Her hair blew out of her braid because of the breeze coming in the open porthole behind her. Reaching out a finger, he touched her face, intending to push the curls behind her ear, and her red-rimmed blue eyes opened. "I felt something too. That's why I think there might be a chance for some middle ground here. I'll not protest a marriage, because it was decided for us before we shared my bed."

She turned her cheek away. "As much as I accept your apology for your words the other night, I still do not wish to marry anyone. And that includes you, Captain." Sarah would be damned before she settled for a man *resigned* to marrying her. He either wanted her or she wouldn't marry him.

He walked over to her jacket and handed it to her, then offered her his hand to help her stand. "Think on it for the next few weeks. It would easier on both of us if we married in New York and returned home happily wed."

She managed to get her arm in one sleeve, but had difficulty with the other. He assisted her, then helped her with her buttons.

"Come. A walk in the sunshine will do you some good."

That night, Sarah decided her aches and bruising were at its peak. From what she could tell not having a pier glass, she looked like a giant walking eggplant. She truly was bruised from knee to shoulder and across her back. She was just thankful to the high heavens there were no broken bones and that her clothing covered all of the bruising. The bump on her head had already begun to diminish, and her head hurt less and less as the day had gone on. Ian brought her to the cabin hours ago and returned to his position for the remainder of his shift, and while he was gone, she had time to think about his idea.

As much as she would have liked to marry someone as stimulating as he, she couldn't do it. He didn't want her. He'd bluntly admitted he was *resigned* to marrying her. And as if that wasn't painful enough, she still relived his words from that night, the painful accusation of intentionally trapping him and his explanation from this morning when he admitted those really were his feelings at that time.

"Well, he can keep his feelings," she said aloud to the

room's feline occupant. "And I shall keep mine." She heard the dinner bell and decided to fetch her dinner quickly and eat it, thus avoiding Ian if he thought to walk her to the galley now that he thought was going to marry her.

She'd made it through the line to get her meal with everyone else and thankfully never saw Ian. He was likely above, letting his crew have a turn at the food first. She'd noticed that about him since she'd been on his boat. Sarah, though, preferred to eat first because she noticed there was more beans, meat, or grain in the food if you got in the line earlier. She couldn't wait to get back to Caversham House or Haldenwood and dine on the cook's delicate turtle soup and roasted leg of lamb with potatoes and gravy.

As she walked to the cabin and looked down into the carved wood bowl of tasteless stew, she decided she'd pretend the meal she was about to eat was anything but what it was and hope that it made the food go down easier. When she opened the door to the cabin, she knew a peaceful evening was not in the cards for her.

"I brought dinner for two, but I see you've gotten yours already."

She glanced at him and nodded, then slid behind the table onto the bench. "I didn't know what your plans were. You'd never mentioned them."

His voice was patient when he replied. "I did, you just didn't hear me."

"I'm sorry," she said with feigned interest in his words. "I've been eating on my own since my arrival on this ship. Why would I think tonight was any different?

"Every night will be different now," he said, and something in his tone and manner reminded her of her brother when he was on the verge of anger.

"How so?" she squeaked, while she stirred the unappealing slop in her bowl, unable to meet his gaze.

He studied her intently, his gaze making her uncomfortable in her seat. Remembering she was no insect under a magnifying lens, she straightened and gave him her attention.

"Is it an act? Is that how you do it?"

She tilted her chin and stared at him. "Is what an act?" It only served to anger him more.

"This...this...pretending," he ground out. "You heard me clearly earlier today when I said I would now be staying in my cabin, and now you act as though you did not." His menacing voice dropped to a whisper as his fiery gaze scorched her. "As much as you want it to be so, you cannot wish away what happened the other night. We both knew what we were doing. And because of *what* we did, there might now be a child we are responsible for."

Her spoon slipped from her hand, and she quickly retrieved it, her mind in a whirl.

"Surely you had to know?"

How could she tell him she did, but forgot? Because it was the truth. The adventure of it, the experience and sensations of the act were what she'd been focused on, not any potential outcome. And a child would be a wonderful outcome if she were wed, but she wasn't, nor was she planning to marry him.

She'd just have to pray his seed didn't take, because she was not going to offer herself up as a holiday sweet to this man again. There would be no more adventures of the sexual sort with him. Ever.

"I can see you didn't even consider it." He chuckled. "Funny thing is, I knew and chose to ignore the voice in my head warning me." He pushed his bowl away. "So who is more at fault here, you or me?"

Sarah shook her head, and the knot on the back of her head chose just this moment to grow painful again. She raised a hand to cover it, saying, "I...I didn't even consider it, and I should have."

"Because we were both rash and irresponsible, the right thing to do is marry. And the best time to do it, is in New York. This will minimize the rumor and innuendo sure to be on everyone's tongues as we sit here."

"No. I'm sure my sisters have thought of that and are telling only those necessary what they want them to know. Believe me, it's how things are done in my family."

"There's no covering up something like this, especially if you return with child." He backed his chair away, obviously done even though his bowl was still half-full. "I'm tired of sleeping in a hammock on my own boat, and I see no need to continue to do so since we're getting married." He went to the door. "Do not lock me out or the lock will be removed. I will be back later to sleep."

Sarah emptied the contents of the bowls out the porthole and gathered everything to return to the galley. When she got back to the cabin, she locked the door, sat under the open port hole and began to cry.

Why did he have to be right? What caused her to be so reckless as to not consider the possibility of a child? She knew better! Now she had this added worry, all because of her recklessness.

She had wanted children one day, but didn't think she'd ever marry so she'd resigned herself to the possibility of never having any. And now it looked like she was going to be forced to wed someone who didn't want her, because he feared her brother and Lucky. Of course, there was the one hour of hedonistic intercourse that she would never forget, but how could she marry him knowing how he felt?

Before the room grew dark, she lit one lantern and readied herself for bed. She didn't want him in the bed with her, but didn't think she could ask him to sleep elsewhere. And there was no place else for her to go.

So she quickly unbolted the door when she heard his heavy-booted footfall leave the steering deck over her head and scrambled onto the far-side of the bed under the covers. When he entered the room, she feigned sleep when he asked if she were awake.

The following morning, realizing her ploy had worked, she went about her day, same as the one before. She ignored him when he came to bed, pretending to be asleep, and did it again the following night, and the one after that.

Eventually he caught on to her game, because on the fifth night, he woke her up.

Chapter Seven

Ian climbed into the bed thinking she was asleep, as she'd been the past few nights. But when he heard the hitch in her breath, as though she'd been crying, he reached out toward her.

"Why the tears?" he asked, thinking to comfort her. Instead she pushed him away and scrambled from the bed to go to the wash basin and get a cool rag from the bowl.

"No reason. I'm a woman. Can I not shed a tear every so often without it being for a specific reason?"

"There's always a reason," he replied, trying to sound sympathetic. His eyes followed her in the moonlit room as she sat on the chair and placed her compress over her eyes.

"Well, I have none except that" —she removed the compress and faced him— "we will be in New York soon, and…you will think this is selfish beyond measure, but…I would like some soap and a bath in a real tub and perhaps a dress or two. Because" —she paused for a breath— "I am so tired of these clothes. I want to feel like a lady again. Maybe then…."

He gave her a moment to finish, but when she didn't he asked, "Maybe then, what?"

She put her head back, and she replaced the compress

to her eyes. "Nothing," she whispered. "Nothing."

"Are you afraid of what Lucky will say or do? If that is the case, you will not be alone facing him or even your brother when we return."

"I'm not afraid," she said. The hitch in her voice before she replied told him he'd hit the root of her problem.

"Where's the bravado from two weeks ago? You said, 'leave my family to me,' and now you're worried. I would like to know why?"

"You presume much, Captain."

Ian noticed her shirt had risen up her thighs as she held her head back with the compress over her eyes. With her arms raised, he could see the curve of her bare thigh and the faint shadow of bruising visible in the dark room. He knew she was still sore from her fall, but he thought her vulnerable and pretending to be strong in the light of what was about to happen when they reached New York.

Ian threw the covers back and stood, moving to stand before her. He lifted the compress. "There will be no time to go ashore, but I can add a few things to the list of stores we need restocked." He read the disappointment on her face in the moment before the shutters closed on her blue eyes. "And you will never have to fear your family's reaction because I will be there."

He thought he saw a tear fall from one of her eyes, and he wiped it with a thumb. He lifted her hand and raised her to stand. She looked so vulnerable, and for some reason, he wanted to hold her, give her some of his strength. Then his cock stirred to life. What a lecherous bastard he was for wanting her now, while she was scared and vulnerable. He wanted her right then as much as he did that night he'd first taken her, and just as much as he did every night in between.

There would be no more evasion. He wanted her. If they married in New York Harbor, she wouldn't have to face her brother alone.

He took her into his arms and lowered his head to hers, taking her lips in a long, deep kiss that sent tiny tremors through him. He hadn't expected to feel these things for her. At least not yet. And this revelation was starting to unnerve him. He wasn't any more ready for home and hearth today as he was when they met. And he had a grandfather who couldn't die fast enough, so until he did, Ian planned to sail the seas to build the business he'd started with Lucky.

Grasping her bare bottom, he lifted her against him and slid his tongue into her mouth when she gasped at the evidence of his arousal. He broke the kiss to remove her shirt, then lifting her so as not to hurt her side, he set her gently on the bed. He stepped away to remove his own clothing and returned to stand next to her where he drank in her moon-lit beauty, marred only slightly by the bruising. She sucked the breath right from him, not just with her looks, but with her naïve eagerness for everything in her life. Sarah was so unlike any other woman he'd known.

She pushed back the hair that had fallen over her face, and he slid onto the bed next to her, taking the hard peak of a breast into his mouth while he toyed with the other between his thumb and fingers. God, she tasted so good. He never wanted to leave the bed as long as she was in it. With one hand supporting his weight, he let the other trail down from her right breast to cup her warm, moist apex. His fingers parted her and delved into her, moving in and out, mimicking his shaft. She was so tight and wet; he was about to burst with wanting her.

He withdrew his slick fingers and toyed with her swollen nub.

"I want you, Sarah."

"Do you really?" Her voice held no surprise, but rather was throaty and seductive, sending his blood rushing straight to his cock.

"Yes." He slid down her body, trailing kisses down to her navel, then lower still. Parting her inner folds, he brought his mouth down on her and gently held her sensitive core with his teeth while he rubbed it with his tongue. Her moans told him she was enjoying his attention as did the way she grabbed onto his head and held him in place with her fingers entwined in his hair.

When she began to quiver at the onset of her climax, he pushed two fingers into her narrow, silken sheath and felt her muscles first accept, then clench around them as she cried out in pleasure. She fell back onto the pillows, and he withdrew his hand as he raised over her and drove home. He took her lips again and moved deeply and rhythmically, seeking his own release now.

He didn't know what it was about this woman, something more than her physical appearance…but something made him *want* to please her. Maybe it was her willingness to have someone like him or the glimpses of shyness he saw in her face at times, but she was definitely made to fit him perfectly in more than just a sexual way.

She was so tight and slick with her own moisture that it didn't take long before he felt his climax come upon him, building quickly. Her whispered sighs drove him on, and when her hands burned a trail down to grasp his buttocks, it was his undoing. She cried out his name, and when he felt her tighten her silken muscles and draw him in further, he gave her his seed. He pressed kisses on her flushed face and swollen lips, then rolled off, bringing her with him.

He held her as she fell asleep in his arms, and in the dim light of a cloudless night on the water, he thought he just might be the luckiest man in the world.

Sarah almost gave her true feelings away. As she lay next to him in the bed, listening to the creaking of the timbers as the ship moved through the water, she realized she'd almost told Ian what she was really crying about.

She'd almost confessed her desire to be wanted by him, not just in the erotic and sensual manner they had already shared, but rather in a romantic sense. Not one man in all the years she'd been on the market had offered for her, nor had any even come close to showing interest in her.

Except as a friend. She was always someone's friend. Her sister, Elise, told her that she should use this time to get to know people and that a man would come along one day that was worthy of her.

In her mind, it had been three years already, and if she hadn't found this man yet, he likely didn't exist among those available in her social realm. She'd heard stories of spinsters marrying late—her own mother was one—but they were the rare exceptions. More often than not, women past a certain age weren't so lucky. She knew a marriage to Ian would have been full of adventure. They could have sailed the seas together.

Except he didn't really want her, and because of that she would never marry him. She could never marry a man who accused her of trapping him.

Ten days later, Sarah held onto the brightwork railing beneath the quarter deck, watching as they sailed parallel to the American coast. This was the first land she'd seen in three weeks, two days, and six hours. It wasn't as though Sarah intended to count them, but she had. Knowing Ian believed she had trapped him, and that he had to *resolve* himself to marriage, she knew she could never marry him. He didn't want her. That was his way of telling her this.

So she planned her quiet exit from *Revenge*, deciding to disappear into town with Seamus and Goran when they went to fetch supplies. As soon as she took care of her needs, she'd go to Lucky. Ian thought she feared her family. She had never feared the ones who loved her. Lucky might be angry when he realized what she'd done, but would understand her need for adventure and not force her to something so horrible as a marriage to a man who didn't want her.

As Ian predicted, the northern course across the Atlantic had, indeed, proven the quickest route. It may have been harder sailing, as evidenced by the number of times Seamus was called away from the galley to help repair torn sails, but the winds were steady, and with the fore-and-aft rigging, they'd been able to make use of even the slightest variable breeze.

The chatter among the men was full of relief and excitement. Of course, their position wouldn't be known until they sailed into New York Harbor, but the crew was very optimistic about their time. All said they'd never crossed the Atlantic so quickly. Then they started betting amongst themselves about what place they were currently in, and with the *Avenger* barely visible ahead of them, it was presumed that they were in at least second place. No one could know whether the boats crossing on a more southerly route had made it in already and were now headed back to Liverpool after the requisite twenty-four-hour hold.

Even with the air all around her charged with anticipation, each time she thought of separating from Ian, Sarah felt as though her soul was being ripped from her body. As a result, she'd spent the past two days on the verge of tears every time she thought of the return trip without Ian at the helm or by her side at night.

Standing on the main deck near the steps up to the steering deck, Sarah watched the lushly forested and rocky coastline slowly grow closer. She turned to look up at Ian as he stood on the steering deck talking to his helmsman as he was about to hand over the wheel. A moment later, he stood beside her. He'd kept his dark blond beard neatly trimmed with scissors and thus was not as offensive as she'd originally thought. She thought back to how wonderful he looked when she last saw him shaved, then wanted to cry at knowing she'd never see him that way again.

His sun-kissed locks hung straight just past his shirt collar, and though unfashionable, Sarah found it entirely too appealing. She'd adored running her fingers through it when they were in the intimate quarters of their cabin.

She drank in the sight of him as he offered a smile to her, his sparkling hazel eyes shining with mirth. These were the memories she would hold onto after she left him later that very day. Forcing herself to return his smile, she reached out and took his hand, bringing it to her cheek and resting it there. Sarah closed her eyes before he could see her heart in them.

"How much longer before we are in New York harbor?"

"Within four hours we will have the anchor dropped." While there was a hint of excitement in his voice, he looked at her with an expression she could only describe as regret mixed with remorse. It was yet another reason not to marry him. He didn't want her complicating his plans—he'd told her that immediately upon discovering her on his boat.

Exactly as he predicted, several hours later, at one-seventeen in the afternoon, they crossed the line set by buoy markers and were soon anchored in the harbor under a cloudy and drizzly sky. Sarah took his book and packed it in her satchel with her clothing, then closed the drawer under the bed, after leaving a note for Ian inside his ledger. She knew Ian would get it when she was long gone from his ship.

She was doing the right thing in leaving the note. Hopefully when he saw it, he would be less angry with her. In the letter, she'd poured out her heart and told him what he meant to her and the reasons why she would never want to trap him. To trap him would be like caging a bird that needed the sky or a fish who needed sea.

Sarah wiped the last of her tears shortly before leaving the cabin and reached the deck just as the crew dropped the anchors. Ian commented that he didn't think any of the boats in the harbor were race participants but Lucky's. "When I return from reporting to the race steward, I will take you over to *Avenger*, and we can speak with Lucky."

She nodded. "Until then I will try to be helpful in the galley."

Sarah knew she had a narrow window in which to escape, and she waited until Ian and three men left in one of the gigs. She and Seamus climbed into the second gig with Goran and the others who were charged with replenishing the stores. No one had known of her plans to leave except Seamus, who reluctantly agreed to come along as her protector when she threatened to leave without him.

Goran and the other men gave looks of surprise as they took their seat in this gig when the one that left minutes earlier had much more room.

"Does the captain know yer leavin'?" Goran asked.

"I didn't decide until the captain left that I wanted to go into the town," she lied. "I'd been thinking of it, and even mentioned it to him, but wasn't certain until just now." She gave the men what she hoped was her most convincing smile. "Believe me, he'll be happy I went when he realizes I don't look and smell like the rest of you. You see, I plan to purchase scented soaps and a few dresses."

There a few grumbles about the captain not knowing, and one man commented on the captain's anger when he learned of her trip into town.

"I'll be fine, gentlemen. Don't worry," she assured them with a grin. "Seamus will be with me to carry all of my packages and boxes."

Sarah was adorable when she stuck out her bottom lip and pouted. It made Ian want to do all manner of erotic things with that mouth of hers. Beginning with a sweet, nibble of a kiss and ending with....

He growled in frustration. Were all women such frustrating contradictions? He wanted her so badly, he ached every moment of every day. Yet he wished he was better able to read her. Women had always confounded him, and Sarah was no different. Except with Sarah, he was learning, his exasperation was often triggered when she expected to have her girlish whims catered to. And those whims usually arose when he had work to do.

There were times when he thought he could perhaps be a bit more understanding of her situation, and it was when those ideas entered his mind that he reminded himself he did not invite her aboard. So he felt no remorse for not granting her every impulse and fancy.

Except in bed. There he did grant her every wish because more often than not, they were what he wanted as well. He had lived the past nearly four weeks in a perpetual state of arousal. No sooner had he finished loving her than he felt himself needing her again.

Sarah had proven she was not a typical woman. How many of those same ladies had the courage and spirit to do what she had done to feed her need for adventure? Not many, he'd wager. Sarah volunteered to help Seamus cook and serve meals to the entire crew of salty veteran sailors. She never feared a single one of them, called most of the men by name, and remembered the names of their families at home.

Truth be told, he'd never met anyone like her. She was often assertive, initiating their sexual play, though he knew for a fact that she'd never been with another. Sarah was everything a man wanted in a woman—desirable and willing, virtuous and wanton. Surely, no man could be luckier than he.

Of course none of that changed the fact that he was not yet prepared to support a wife and family, but he had no choice in the matter. She was a lady of noble birth, and by her actions and the mistake of the lad who'd brought her to his ship, Ian now found himself saddled with a wife and quite possibly a family in the near future.

He would marry her right away so she would not have to face the ostracism of society for her reckless behavior. And he reminded himself once again that this was for her own good. He was doing this because he cared for her and wanted the best for her.

So she wanted to see New York. It wouldn't hurt to take a little time and bring her to a mercantile to let her purchase some necessities before taking her to meet her brother aboard *Avenger*.

Chapter Eight

Sarah had never seen anything like this in her life. This bustling port of New York was enormous, stretching for as far as one could see in all directions. A forest of masts bobbed gently around them as the gig rowed closer to the pier. Brick and stone facade buildings, which appeared newly built, lined the docks, and the wharves teemed with laborers. And that pungent aroma of tar and dead fish, those scents distinctive to a busy, working port of call, was the same as in London and Liverpool. The cry of seagulls begging for any scrap of food was almost as constant as the wind. The heat was not something she'd counted on, though she wore her jacket for modesty's sake. The warm weather and humid air made her uncomfortably sticky with perspiration.

Seeing Lucky's boat nearby, Sarah smiled. She took in everything around her, the sights, odors, hustle and bustle of the hundreds of people on the wharf moving about in their daily jobs. It was like home, but it wasn't. For though it didn't look or smell much different than the ports of London or Liverpool, this was America. She was in New York harbor. *America.*

She could now tell her grandchildren one day, should she be so fortunate, that she had actually been to a country other than England or Scotland.

Loving Sarah

Their gig tied off to the pier, Seamus exited first and extended his hand to her. He assisted her to the lower platform. He then looked down into the gig at the two men who rowed them out.

"Meet us back here in three hours," Seamus said. The other men nodded.

He then turned a piercing dark gaze at Sarah and said again, "Ye have three hours."

She nodded and they went up the steps and onto the dock where Seamus hired a hack on the bustling wharf. It took a great deal of pleading with the old salt to get him to agree to this excursion before taking her over to the *Avenger*. The entire ride into the city, the old man swore over and over that if Ian and Lucky didn't string him up, the duke would flay him alive.

"Ye know how protective his grace is of his family," Seamus said. "The man would skin me alive if I let anything happen to ye. So it'd be in my best interest to make sure ye get what yer wantin' within reason and get ye safely over to Cap'n Lucky.

The hack rolled to a stop in front of a row of shops. "I know my brother well," Sarah said, "and I'm willing to bet my entire inheritance that he'll be so happy upon my safe return that he'll not flay anyone, especially you, Seamus. Though I cannot say I'm as positive about Ian's safety. Ren will be upset if he learns of some details. But I shall take the blame, for truly it was not Ian's fault. I…It's all my fault. Everything that occurred between us was my doing. All of it."

The driver held open the door for them as they disembarked, and Seamus paid the man to wait for them as they shopped. She dropped her voice to a whisper as they walked toward the door of the shop. "And for that I am willing to accept my fate."

Seamus waited outside near the door as Sarah went in the establishment. Once inside, she found she needed more than just the two or three items she originally intended to purchase, and when the shopkeeper gave her the total, she paid the woman. Before she could lift the tied package, a boy appeared and carried it to Seamus, who tucked it under his arm and escorted her to the hack.

She asked the driver to then take them to a dressmaker who might have a few ready-made dresses and other lady's clothing. Minutes later, they rolled to a stop in front of a shop, and she entered alone while Seamus and their driver waited outside.

After first enduring the stares and whispers of the *modiste* and her staff, she was sure due to her outlandish and unladylike garb, Sarah left nearly an hour later with enough purchases to make the women regret their original opinion of her. When they'd asked her to please come back again, she promised she would indeed visit them again if she ever returned to America. One of the younger seamstresses went out to fetch Seamus so he could carry her packages. Then the young woman recommended the cobbler next door for a pair of well-made boots.

Two pairs of practical shoes and one pair of boots later, she'd finally had everything she thought she would need, then discovered she needed a trunk to carry it all. So the cobbler recommended a shop down the street, and Sarah purchased an embossed leather trunk with polished brass accents.

"Americans really are an accommodating lot," she commented to her companion. "Everyone here has been very pleasant and helpful" She smiled at the cab driver.

"They're bound to be pleasant and helpful, as ye say," Seamus muttered, "when ye spend a small fortune in each shop ye go into."

Sarah pretended to be taken aback. "You mean they're only after my coin?"

"Aye lassie," her protector replied. "You're not having some bloke billed for your purchases, so they likely think you're a member of the oldest profession having a really good week."

She felt the heat rise to her cheeks. "Surely they don't think that I…that I…?"

"Oh, I'm sure they do. But it doesna matter, does it? They don't know who ye are."

She exhaled a deep sigh. "You have a point. It doesn't matter."

They returned to the waiting hack, and Sarah asked the driver to carry them to a respectable, clean hotel. Preferably a very nice one, as the food was sure to be better there. After arriving, Seamus procured a room for her, then tipped an attendant to carry her packages and trunk up. The first thing she did was order a hot bath to be sent up, then she and Seamus waited in the public room, feasting on fall-apart-tender roasted ham, fresh warm bread, and plates piled high with summer vegetables.

"Please do not take offense, Seamus," Sarah said through a full mouth, "but this surpasses anything you've made on the boat. I wonder if I could hire this cook for the return voyage."

"When cookin' on board a boat, lassie" —he stressed his pet name for her, obviously insulted— "it's not the talent o' the cook that makes the meal—though it doesn't hurt ta have a skilled cook. It's the supplies ye have on hand and the limited use of fire. Ye know there's only the one flame. So naturally the biscuits will be cold before the main course is done. And that, too, is why yer meals are usually slopped into a bowl and eaten wit' a spoon."

Just then a maid entered the dining parlor of the main floor in the hotel, informing the lady that her bath was ready. Sarah smiled as she stood, eager to get clean. "I will see you in a bit, as I plan to make up for a month without a tub."

She followed the maid to her room and bolted the door, then spent the next hour soaking in the most luxurious hot bath she'd ever had in her life.

Well, at least since she left London.

Ian stepped onto the dock surveying the boxes of foodstuffs and crates of marine supplies being loaded onto his longboats for delivery to *Revenge*. Out of the corner of his eye, he spotted Lucky heading his way.

His friend obviously hadn't heard yet about Sarah or he wouldn't be wearing a smile. Ian had planned to go over to *Avenger* with Sarah as soon as the items on this dock made it onto *Revenge*. And if he were honest with himself, he almost expected Lucky to have heard something from the crew gossip as the men congregated on the dock while working on transferring goods and materials. He didn't want to speak in such a public place, so he motioned for Lucky to follow him off to the side a few feet away from the working men.

"Do you have everything you requested?" Lucky asked.

"Aye," Ian replied. "Though once this boat is loaded,

you should come with me to *Revenge*. We had an incident that you should be aware of."

"What happened?" His friend's expression grew sober and intent. "Is everyone well? Did anyone get injured during the storm?"

"Everyone is well," he replied. "We had a stowaway that no one discovered until we were miles from home."

"Hopefully you put the lad to work," Lucky said with a chuckle. "I'd make him earn those three meals."

"Umm…. You will need to come with me. This guest is not your average stow away."

Lucky looked at him rather oddly, his face then going pale. Ian knew him so well, he could see his friend's thought process, and it was as though he knew at heart, but didn't want to believe. "Tell me" —Lucky ground out, his voice so deep and threatening Ian actually feared for Sarah— "it is not who I think it is, and if it is tell me she is alive and in once piece so I can throttle her."

"She has occupied my cabin the entire trip," Ian said, right before a flood of curses in both English and Italian poured from his friend.

"Impossible! Sarah's here?" Lucky hissed, not wanting to yell in front of his sailors. "How on earth…? No, I know how. When I get my hands on her, I'll wring her scrawny neck."

Ian's voice took an uncharacteristically hard edge when he replied, "She's a lady, and you'll not be harming a lady, sister or not." At Lucky's look of surprise, he added, "Much as I have wanted to over the past month, I've managed to restrain myself. I think you can as well."

"Ren's going to be furious! And Lia's probably beside herself with worry."

"Sarah assures me she left them a note telling them what she's done."

"How on earth did she come to be with you?"

Ian explained the story as she told it to him, and Lucky couldn't help but laugh. Their laughter died down at the sight of a young lad running toward their pier.

"Anyone here from the *Revenge?*" A group of his crewmen verified, and Ian stepped forward.

"I'm her captain. What's the message?"

"Do ya have a dollar coin?" The lad looked from Ian to Lucky and back. "Well do ya? I was told when I delivered the message that I'd get a whole dollar."

Both men searched their pockets for an appropriate equivalent, and each handed one to the lad. "What's the message?"

"Seamus said the lady finished her shopping and is safe in a room, but she's takin' a bath and it's keeping him from making it back on time."

"I'm going to put her over my knee and—" Ian muttered. Then he started with a panic. "Where in hell are they?"

The towheaded lad looked barely ten summers and was likely accustomed to hearing the foul language of the docks because he didn't even flinch. "At the new Continental Arms, on Merchant Street," he said as he inspected the coins to see if they were real. Presuming they were, he smiled at the two men and continued. "The fire last winter burnt the old one to the ground, but the new one is right nice I hear. And made o' brick and stone too, so it can't burn like the last one did."

Before the boy was even finished talking, Lucky and Ian were searching for officers to leave in charge of the loading. Then Ian took the steps up to the dock and immediately hired a hack. He jumped in front of the driver's perch. "The Continental Arms on Merchant Street," he said just as Lucky jumped in.

"Faster if you can please," Lucky added as he tapped his fingers on his knee.

"I told her not to leave the boat. That I would take her to you," Ian said.

"She has never listened to reason when reason interfered with her wishes. Now she's ruined any chance of ever having a decent marriage. And Ren will have to find someone willing to take her...."

"I'm going to marry her."

"You don't have to do that." Lucky must have thought Ian was being helpful by sacrificing himself for the sake of the family reputation when, in fact, it was the opposite. He needed Sarah.

"No, I *want* to," Ian said, trying to hide the fear rising in his gut about her safety.

"She does come with a sizable dowry and an inheritance. It will make getting funding for those new clippers a great deal easier...."

"I don't want her money."

"It's your money if you marry her."

"I don't want her money," he repeated. "And I don't want to be known as a fortune-hunter. Any success we achieve will be because of our hard work and determination."

"I'll not argue with you." Lucky was silent for a brief moment as the hack moved through the congested traffic on Merchant Street. "You're certain she left a note?" he asked Ian again.

Ian nodded, praying she was truthful in this, because

if he found out otherwise, he'd throttle her—for real this time.

"I don't know why you want to marry her, Ian. She'll vex you for the rest of your life, man. Do you know what you're saying?"

"Of course, I do," Ian said. "Sarah will fight this marriage tooth and nail. But the sooner we get it over with, the better for her. We can marry in England, though it might be wiser to do it now."

His friend gave him a look that was both curious and disbelieving as he asked, "Why *wiser?*"

Ian just gave him a level-eyed stare—one his friend understood.

Sarah dried her wrinkled and water-logged skin with the towels the maid provided. She should never have fallen asleep in the tub, but the water was so warm and clean that she'd forgotten she wasn't in London and relaxed perhaps a bit too much.

The maid knocked at the door, and Sarah called out for her to enter, and the petite brunette crossed the room and said, "Ma'am, there's two gents in the parlor downstairs and they said you had better hurry."

"Young men? What happened to Seamus?"

"If you're meanin' the old salt, they told him to get back to his boat."

Sarah shook her head. "Well, it seems I am found out." She turned around and asked the maid, "How are you at the duties of a lady's maid?"

"I'm not a maid to the likes of soiled doves! I clean rooms thank you very much. That's honest work, it is." The girl got down on her hands and knees and began to wipe the spilled water on the floor as she continued her diatribe. "I'm trying to work my way *up* not down! The fires of hell await those who succumb to the pleasures of the flesh outside wedlock. And you with two men...you're long past redemption!"

Sarah laughed. "Fine then, think what you will," she said as she disappeared behind the screen and reappeared with her petticoat and drawers. "One of those two men downstairs is my brother, you ninny, and the other is his friend." She looked at the maid, cleaning the room and readying it for the next customer. Just then it dawned on Sarah what type of establishment she'd rested in, and she giggled. "Oh, my! You think...that I'm...." She took in the decor earlier and thought it bold, but not particularly bawdy. "I understand now why you think as you do, but I assure you...you're...." Sarah blushed. She couldn't even think clearly. That the girl thought she was a light skirt was rather embarrassingly funny. "Well, you're wrong in your judgment, but I don't care at this point. We have to leave in a few hours for the second leg of the race. Now, there's a coin in it for you if you help me with my demi-corset and dress. And if you can do something with my hair, I'll double that coin."

Different barmaids kept coming into the parlor trying to attract the attention of Ian and Lucky while they waited for Sarah to reappear. The room's fringed decorations looked straight from a Parisian brothel, and why Seamus brought Sarah here, Ian would never know.

The crushed red velvet walls and lounges were all the latest fashion—if this were a bawdy house. Scarlet and black, trimmed with gold leaf on the carved crown molding and wainscoting, was unlike anything he'd ever seen before. Ian kept his eye on the door and saw a woman enter the room in a smart yellow dress and did a double-take. Even without her boy's clothing he'd grown accustomed to seeing her wear, he instantly recognized Sarah.

Lucky rushed toward her and hugged her, then backed away and began giving her the scolding she deserved. Ian met Sarah's gaze when she looked past Lucky to where he stood near the cold hearth.

"Do you know how angry Ren will be? How frightened Lia must be?" Lucky droned on and on about all the possible repercussions facing Sarah upon her return, and Lucky finally mentioned the only way out of the social shunning she should expect upon her return to London.

"You'll have to marry quickly," Lucky said, then he went on to add, "Ian has volunteered to marry you, and it's ideal actually…."

"Never," Sarah said.

"What?" her brother asked.

Ian stepped forward, finally finding his tongue as he watched her, a vision in yellow, tell her brother she would not marry him. He'd let her argue, play her hand if you will, for now. But he still held the trump card.

She tilted her stubborn chin up, determination in her expression as she looked at Lucky. "I will not marry, Ian. He does not love me, nor does he *want* to marry me. I'll not let him sacrifice himself because I didn't hire a boy who could read to bring me to the right boat." She looked to Ian for support, but she'd get none from him. Either they married here or in England, especially when her brother found out she wasn't with Lucky during the first leg of the race.

"Sarah, whether you want to or not is beyond the point now," he said.

"Never," she said, then started to cry. Lucky was a sucker for woman's tears, and his sister surely knew this.

"Fine, we can discuss this later. Let's get you back to the boat."

"Can I return with you, Lucky? I don't want to go back with Ian. I've interfered in his life enough." Lucky looked over Sarah's head with a questioning gaze. All he could do was shrug. Turning his back to them, Ian went to the lobby and asked for the lady's trunk and a handsome cab to return them all to the docks.

Chapter Nine

He didn't love her. He didn't want her. He'd *resigned* himself to a marriage with her.

Sarah had to remind herself of the fact for at least the one-hundredth time. She swiped her eyes angrily as she tied the trunk handles to the foot of Lucky's bed to keep the thing from sliding about the room once they made the open sea.

The entire time she'd been selecting dresses that afternoon, she chose each one with Ian in mind. He'd said once that he thought she would look good in yellow, so she chose a yellow gingham with white rosettes on the puffed sleeves. Another time, he'd said sapphires and diamonds would look beautiful on her, so she chose a deep blue day dress with silver piping. And there were more yellow and blue dresses, and the silver pelisse with white satin trim.

Of course, Ian would never see her in them. He hadn't asked her to remain with him. She would have, had he asked. She didn't hold out hope for love. But if he just said he wanted her to stay with him she would have. She wiped her eyes again, the tears falling with greater frequency. She'd thought to swallow her pride and beg *him* to allow her to stay, but she just couldn't. Her pride wouldn't let her.

And she didn't think Lucky suspected anything sexual between them, or he would have condemned her to marriage immediately. It was best that Lucky not learn of their affair. He might pressure Ian into something he was not prepared for. And she'd already resolved not to do that.

She thought about what she would do after she returned to London. Somehow falling back into her previous life, attending the social events she had in the past, seemed trivial. Meaningless, even. Thankfully, the season would be over by the time they got back, for her heart would not be up for round after round of musicals and balls, teas and dinner parties. Especially now with a majority of her friends all newly married or planning weddings, she was certainly the odd one among her set. What she wanted was solitude, and the only place she knew to get it was Haldenwood.

And if by some miracle she discovered she carried Ian's babe, she might need to go to The Box for a while until she figured out what to do next. If she wasn't with child, then she'd go home to Haldenwood and decide later what her future held. If she threw herself into her volunteer work, then maybe her heart wouldn't hurt so much and she wouldn't think of Ian every moment of the day.

She pulled the pins from her hair and with her new brush began untangling the frizzy mess. Ian had told her once he'd loved her hair. If he loved her hair, her eyes, and other various parts of her body, why couldn't he love her? Was the person on the inside unlovable?

Damn the tears! Why wouldn't they stop? She swiped at them again. She should hate him, but could not. For in truth, this was all her own fault. Hers and the author of that silly little book for men.

The hair snagged on a tangle, and Sarah pulled the knot apart with a viciousness her maid would scold her for. *"You make your hair look ratty when ye mistreat it like that."* It looked ratty without Sarah's help, so she didn't think she made it any worse.

It seemed that for almost her entire life she never did anything right. She couldn't be a lady a man wanted, nor a lover a man needed.

"Gentleman's Guide," she whispered in the silence of the cabin. "Ha! My big toe!" The only thing that book did was make her crave a sexual experience. "I certainly got that!"

With only the sounds of water lapping beneath the open port holes and the muted murmurs of the few men still above deck, Sarah thought about her actions. The last week and a half, she'd been nothing more than a temporary bed-warmer to him. She knew this each time she welcomed him into her body.

She didn't expect Ian to say he loved her, but she also didn't expect him to remind her that he was sacrificing himself because of her actions at least once each day. He'd told her he would marry her out of friendship to Lucky. He'd all but said as much after he accused her of trying to trap him in a marriage that first night.

She was such a fool for falling in love with a man who would never return her affection.

Yes, she had been curious and had offered herself to him initially, but she had recently tried to show him through her actions that she'd grown to care for him and the people and things he cared for. And he, obtuse man that he was, could not—or would not—see it. Not only that, he repeatedly told her that he was unprepared for a wife and family.

Ugh! She hated the man! She wished she could get the letter out of the drawer before he found it. In that letter, she'd poured her heart out to him. Those feelings no longer existed. The letter was no longer an accurate reflection of her sentiments. She no longer meant any of it.

As she brushed, her mind wandered, showing her Ian at the wheel. She saw Ian again go over the side of the boat to save the young lad who'd fallen over. Ian smiling at her through his smoky-green hazel eyes when he'd realized that her desires mirrored his. Oh, who was she trying to fool? She still meant each and every word in that letter. For who could turn off an emotion such as this, whether it was love or just lust, as easily as a snap of the finger?

The voices of several men, including Lucky, came through the open portholes with the minimal breeze. They sounded as though they'd had a good dinner and were all a bit in their cups. Heavy footfalls of the men grew closer, and before she could lift her brush again, a knock sounded at the door of Lucky's cabin. She stood and opened it. The brush fell from her hand at the sight that greeted her.

Five men lined the short companionway, and one by one, they entered the small cabin, Ian pushed forward by Lucky. The smell of liquor immediately filled the room, and Sarah wondered what they intended. Fear clawed at her heart as she looked at Seamus, who averted his gaze, then to the two strangers. She'd told Ian repeatedly that she would never marry him and made certain he understood how she felt. Lucky promised her just hours ago that he would not force her to marry Ian.

"Sarah," Lucky said solemnly, "Ian's is going to marry you now."

"What?" She held her voice to just short of a screech as her head exploded and her stomach clenched. "Get out, all of you! I'll marry no one! Not this night, nor any other." She didn't want to live in a marriage where her husband would come to resent her for forcing his hand. That was worse than being in a loveless union. She could see their future now, Ian accusing her of keeping him from achieving his dreams because she'd trapped him.

"Never." She turned pleading eyes to the two strangers. "Who are you?" She didn't even wait for them to answer, but rushed on with her questions, pleading for their assistance. "Can you help me? Because this is under duress. There must be laws against a forced marriage in this country."

"Told you so," the hazel-eyed, golden-haired object of her misery stated flatly. She noticed his whisker-less face and trimmed hair. His clothes were new and his grin devilish. He was going to force her into this because of some archaic laws regarding taking a woman's maidenhead then thinking she was thenceforth his possession. Except *he* didn't want her! Why didn't he fight this more? She didn't understand.

Seamus came to her side, obviously as drunk as her brother and Ian. "Lass, I was wit' ye aboart that boat. I know ye have feelin's for the lad, so let's just make this short and sweet and we can all get some sleep. The mornin's jest a few hours away."

"All of you are either drunk or demented." She looked from one to the other of the men in the cabin. Returning Lucky's stare, she said without emotion, "You can't force me to marry a man who doesn't want a wife."

At this, Ian gave an inebriated chuckle. "I told 'em you weren't agreeable to marriage," he slurred. "But they wouldn't listen to me." He shook his head for emphasis. "Nooo."

If Sarah could have thrown the proverbial daggers at him with her gaze, she would have. By the dozens. She could not let them actually marry her to Ian. At one time, she thought they could have made a decent go of a relationship, but after learning how he really felt about her, she couldn't do it. She'd ruin both of their lives. "Stuff a sock in that trap of yours, you drunken lout. You're more drunk than the rest of them."

He gave her a boyish grin. "That's 'cause I got started earlier than they did."

She stomped her foot, so angry she wished she could kick someone—preferably Ian, though Lucky was a suitable target as well—then glared at the two strangers. "And just who *are* the two of you?" she asked again.

The elder of the two motioned to the gentleman standing next to him. "This is Mr. Joshua Stevens, a clerk of the Court for the City of New York, and I am Reverend Archibald Humphrey, St. Peter's Episcopal Church."

"Well, Mr. Stevens, Reverend Humphrey, I'm afraid there has been a grave mistake made this evening. I apologize on behalf of my inebriated relative and this" —she flapped a hand toward Ian— "drunken oaf for disrupting your evening. They brought you both out here for nothing."

Lucky came forward and whispered into her ear. "Sarah, you're marrying Ian now or after we return to England. One or the other." He exhaled an alcohol-infused breath that caused her stomach to roil. "And did you stop to think that there's already a chance you might carry his babe? Do you really want people to count back the months after the babe's born then whisper behind your back when they realize exactly what you were up to on this voyage?"

Sarah felt the blood leave her face.

"I see you get my meaning, sister dear," Lucky said.

"Be a good lass and sign the license the nice clerk's brung wit' him," Seamus said, "and let the minister do his job."

She turned to her brother by marriage—the only one in the family who understood her love for the sea and her desire to see the world. "You cannot ask this of me, Lucky. Ian doesn't want to marry me." Swallowing hard so that no tear rose in her eye, she tried desperately one last time to convince him. "He told me he didn't want to marry me. People already think I'm odd, so a trip such as this would be no more than they expect!"

Lucky stood resolute, his expression never changing, which angered her.

"Ren would never force this on me."

"If Ren were here, he'd be right with us."

She shot him a hardened glare. "He would not. My big brother would never force me to marry a man that didn't want me for his wife. He's told me that I could marry for love and I will." What she could never reveal to these drunken oafs was that she was already half in love with Ian and had been for weeks now. But she couldn't give in yet, because Ian didn't want *her*.

Seamus drew closer, his voice lowered to just a hair above a whisper. "Ye love the lad and ye know it."

"I do not," she hissed at the old man. "You're light in

the noggin," she argued as she calculated if she could make it through the door—desperate for a way out.

"Ye do, else you wouldn't have been pourin' out the tears like ye were earlier this very morning as we sailed inte this harbor."

Frustrated that her emotions had been found out, Sarah began to tremble. They were really going to force her into this, and Ian would hate her for the rest of her life. She would have no choice but to go through with it, yet she shook her head, fighting to the last.

"I swear," Lucky scowled at her, "I've never seen a girl so stubborn in all my life."

She looked from one man to the next, then at the one she was expected to wed. "You will be ruining our lives by forcing me to marry him," she told her brother through lips so tense they never parted.

Lucky shook his head. "You cannot see it now through your anger, but I'm doing the right thing as the only male relative you have here, which makes me your temporary guardian." He glanced over his shoulder at Ian and nodded.

Clenching her fists into tight balls, she wished Ian's chest was before her so she could pummel him into the harbor. He could put a stop to this and chose not to. He left it all up to her to fight against the marriage. Sarah snapped her head toward the clerk. "Give me that worthless piece of paper, and let's get this farce over with. I'm tired and would like to go to sleep."

Sarah thought she saw a strange look, relief perhaps, compassion maybe, cross Ian's brow. She didn't understand it, because she knew he had no desire to wed her. She thought she was giving him what he wanted by fighting against Lucky's demand. "Let's get this over with so we can seek our *separate* beds."

"Aye, let's get it done." Ian slurred his words, then gave her an impish smile.

Her heart froze inside her breast when he said the words. Along with his accusation and resignation, it was yet one more thing she would never forget, because it too cut her to the core.

She never wanted to fall under the spell of his charm again. She'd made that mistake once, and now had an indifferent bridegroom who only enjoyed their recreational activities in bed.

Taking the pen offered to her, her hand trembled as she signed her name on the license and handed the writing implement over to Ian. She watched as he confidently signed his name to the certificate. For as fearful as she was about his future resentment, she noticed he didn't fight the idea of marriage. In fact, he'd never once said a word publicly against taking her to wife.

But she knew, because she remembered the words. *"...Much as I wish it weren't so,"* and *"I have resigned myself..."* They'd pierced her heart and were forever, indelibly carved onto her soul. He felt she'd trapped him when he was not ready for a wife or family. Never once did he say he wanted her outside the bed they shared. And now he was settling for this marriage because it was expected of them after what she'd done.

Her heart wanted so much more. It wanted to be loved. It wanted adventure, excitement, and travel. She wanted to see the Americas, Africa, India, and China, though now traveling was not likely to ever happen.

The minister took out his prayer book, read a scripture passage, and within minutes, she and Ian were husband and wife. "You may kiss your bride," the cleric said. Sarah lowered her gaze, not unwilling for a kiss, but not anticipating one either. It would have spoken volumes to her as to how he intended for the marriage to go forward. But Ian turned away from her first, moving to the door, ready to leave. There was no kiss, and that told the occupants of the room exactly what he'd thought of his marriage to her. Sarah found herself fighting tears, partly from the obvious, painful rejection and abhorrence he felt toward her, but also because she'd just proven to the other men in the cabin that she was right. Her new husband didn't want her.

One by one the men disappeared, leaving Sarah alone in the room. Before she gave into the tears that were pooling in her eyes, she had to smile. God help her, but he *was* handsome. Just being in the same room with him did tingly things to her whole body. Made her want his arms around her, desire his kisses, and everything that came after. While he might not have wanted a marriage with her, he had no objections to them using each other's body for release.

Tears slipped off her lower lashes, and she swiped them away. Why did she have to fall in love with a man who would never love her? There could never be hope for a happy future because he would resent this night for the rest of his life. He would blame her for his every misery, even if she wasn't on the same continent.

Sarah lifted her nightdress and wiped her eyes, and just as she was about to slip behind the screen to prepare for bed, someone knocked softly at the door.

"Lucky?" she asked, before unlocking the bolt. Heaven forbid it was that cranky American captain she had just married.

"Yes. May I come in?"

Sarah opened the door and closed it behind him. "Was there something else?" She looked at the man who was her brother just as much as Ren was and saw sympathy on his brow. It was the only reason she was willing to tolerate his semi-drunken state and what were sure to be nonsensical ramblings.

"Please listen to what I have to say," he said softly, "and if, at the end, you still wish to remain with me, I will not force you to return with Ian."

She sniffled and wiped her eyes again. "You cannot tell me that what just happened was the right thing for us to do."

"Yes. I can, Sarah." Several crewmen walked through the companionway toward the midship steps to the main deck, making sounds of revelry. "It's the right thing because of the circumstance. Even if you had landed here, Ren would have had to scramble to find a husband to accept you or send you away for a while until things died down. Something this scandalous could take years for the gossips to forget about." He took a breath and smiled. "But this marriage is perfect. He may be a bit rough around the edges, but Ian *is* an acceptable match for you. And the fact that there is already some attraction between you should make getting along much easier."

She blushed, and Lucky began to laugh. Then she started to laugh and relax a bit, especially knowing he wasn't angry.

"I have to say, I never saw *that* coming," Lucky said.

"I did, from the moment he walked into the drawing room in Liverpool. Only I thought it would happen after the race, because I'd planned to sail both legs of it with you," she confessed. "And it doesn't change the fact that he thinks I've ruined his plans for his future. He told me this, Lucky."

Lucky mumbled something about plans that she couldn't hear because she was busy wiping her eyes again. "Sarah, I know Ian. He's been my friend for over ten years. From the conversation we just had at dinner, I am *certain* he cares about you because he couldn't stop talking about you. When the topic among every other sailor in that tavern is the race, and our two boats leading the pack, you would think we'd have talked about strategy for the return leg in between all the congratulatory toasts." With a barely perceptible shake of his head, and a sympathetic look in his brown eyes, he said, "No. Sarah, the entire conversation was you. That's why I know he cares more than he will ever say.

"Now if you wish to return to Liverpool with me, you certainly may. But" —Lucky tipped her chin to face him and he smiled at her— "I think you'd rather be with Ian. Am I right?"

One hour later, with her trunk now tied securely to the foot of Ian's bed, Sarah began to undress. She didn't know how he would react to finding her in his cabin, especially after he'd abandoned her on Lucky's boat minutes after marrying her, but she knew one thing about her new husband. Ian enjoyed sex with her. When he arrived back to his cabin, he'd find her waiting for him in his bed.

He could either tell her to leave or allow her to stay.

Granted this wasn't the way she'd wanted things to happen. She should never have read that book. Even though she found it titillating and bold, luring Ian into a sexual liaison merely to satisfy her curiosity was likely the biggest mistake she'd ever made. But there was no crying over it now because it was done. She simply had to make the best of the circumstances now.

But Sarah didn't think their future was entirely dim. She had funds, so he didn't have to feel as driven as he had to turn a profit to support a family. Her fortune, and the estate in Surrey, would take care of them for the entirety of their lives. That should certainly be a relief to him.

She just hoped he could get over the notion that she'd planned this from the onset because for him to think she'd trapped him into a marriage was what upset her most. Sometimes when she thought about that night, she remembered him asking her repeatedly if she wanted to halt their lovemaking. In hindsight, she probably should have said yes.

After checking her appearance one more time, Sarah noted the absence of any discoloration from the bruising on her leg and side. Smiling to herself, she then climbed into the bed and pulled the sheet and blanket over her and settled in for a nap while she waited for her husband.

Ian returned to *Revenge* after escorting the two men to their respective homes in the city. He felt responsible for their safe return to their families, seeing as he and Lucky had taken the men from their evening meals.

Rowing back out to his boat with three of his crew who'd been in a nearby tavern waiting for his return and celebrating, Ian sat quietly and relived the brief marriage ceremony that took place in Lucky's cabin. Sarah wasn't as mad with them as he'd thought she'd be. Oh, she was upset at having her hand forced, yes. But Ian read more fear and sadness in her eyes than anger.

He'd told her there was nothing to fear, promised her

he'd be with her to face her family, and what did he do? He abandoned her. It was the single-most cowardly thing he'd ever done. He wanted to go to the other boat and fetch her, then thought of the hour and decided he'd get her at first sun.

If she refused to come with him, he'd throw her over his shoulder and take her by force. She was his wife now. Her place was by his side.

So why couldn't he tell her the things he wanted to? Why did he always push her away or anger her so she left him?

When the minister told him to kiss his bride, he saw a glimmer of hope in her eyes that he would, then the window shut, and he turned away without making a move toward her. Why did he hesitate?

He desired her. He was, in fact, glad to be married to her.

She was attractive and of proper background as to be a good match for him. So why then was he feeling as though she'd cornered him? Was it because she'd taken the initiative and started the affair, taking the control of the relationship from the onset? Is that what bothered him? That she'd taken the courtship and seduction out of his hands?

Did he feel less of a man because of that? He wasn't sure.

As she fought against the marriage in the confines of the cabin, with five men surrounding her, overwhelming her with force, he realized it was pain, not fear, he saw in her eyes. His Sarah didn't fear him. She didn't fear anyone. She was hurting. And now he had to figure out what it was he'd done and make up for it. Only he couldn't get her until morning.

Knowing he could do nothing until then, he grunted to the crew as they tied the gig to the side of the boat, then he climbed the ladder to make for his own bed. When Ian reached his cabin, he slid the latch and found the door bolted from within. He jiggled the handle in case it was stuck, and it wouldn't give. He muttered an oath, and wondered who among his crew was skinny enough to go through a porthole, because he could think of no other way he was going to get into his room. Right as he was about to find someone small, he heard her voice.

"One minute," Sarah's voice called out through the door.

He felt a jolt of excitement stir his cock. "Sarah? What are you doing here? I thought...."

When the door opened, his tongue nearly dropped from his mouth and his eyes from their sockets. His new wife wore one of his shirts and nothing else. Her loose curls cascaded over her shoulders and past the peaks of her breasts, hiding them from his view. His gaze lowered along her white-linen-clad form to where the shirt ended just above her bare knees and calves and farther, to her dainty, bare feet.

She had to know what wearing something like that would do to a man.

The cat skittered out of the room, and he entered quickly, before any of his crew might happen by. He slid the bolt home, then turned to face her.

"Sarah." The word came out on a sigh, and even to his own ears it sounded weak and vulnerable to her presence.

"I want to return with you Ian. And...." She paused, as though considering her words carefully, then took a fortifying breath, pushing her breasts against the linen shirt. He swallowed past the dry knot in his throat and forced his cock to settle down. "And I want more than anything to make this marriage work."

"Oh, Sarah-mine, I have been a fool," he whispered as he claimed her lips in the kiss he longed to give her a few hours earlier—the one that made her his.

"You'll have to explain. I...don't understand," Sarah said early the next morning as they lay under a mound of covers on the bed, Ian facing her and their legs entwined. Fresh from her morning toilette, she climbed back into bed unwilling to be parted from him for a moment now that they'd reached this comfortable intimacy. "Where would...it...go?" she asked sheepishly as she looked up at him as he rested on his elbow gazing down at her.

Ian offered her another sip from his glass of wine he'd poured just moments before returning to her side under the covers. She shook her head too interested in what he said. Her new husband dipped two of his fingers in the glass, then finished the contents with two gulps and set the glass on the floor next to the bed. "My dear, naive seductress, there are other ways for a woman to be with men without her losing her virginity."

"How so?" She was curious now that her husband intimated of ways other than those they'd done and from those she'd seen in the book.

He tipped her chin up to face him, and he slid the two fingers into her mouth. "Imagine this was my shaft," he whispered.

She'd read about this act, fellatio, in his book, and

swirled her tongue around his fingers, before taking them in deep, suckling as she did. He groaned and took his fingers from between her lips and closed his eyes. She could tell he tried to control his breathing and wondered if that were something he desired. When she lifted her gaze back to his, she gave him a shy smile and asked, "Did I do it right?"

He nodded, the barely restrained passion in his hazel eyes telling her where this was heading. "You did it right, wife." His green-brown gaze told her how right she had performed that little trick. "But there is also one other place…." His voice trailed off because he knew it would rouse her curiosity.

She gave him what she hoped was a seductive look as she quirked a brow in curiosity. "What is that?"

He motioned for her to roll onto her side, away from him, and he slid closer to her, spooning her, and warming her chilly body with his massive warm one as he snuggled close behind her. Sarah felt his rigid shaft rest between her upper thighs. She sighed as his hand came around her waist to cover her mons. He worked his fingers between her lips and began to tease her nub again.

"Some men also enjoy this other hole," he said fingering her moistness and moving it up to her rear entrance, where she clenched instinctively.

"Really?" she squeaked.

He chuckled softly into her ear. "Really."

Pressing his erection against the groove of her buttocks, he continued to play with her nub, driving her even more insane with need. He spread her wetness up and down the split, then ran the tip of a finger around the slick, tightened entrance.

LOVING SARAH

She tried to pull away from him, but he held her fast with his arm around her waist. "Surely you don't mean...."

With the hand in front, he continued to rub her very sensitive nub, driving her insane with desire to have him fill her again, but with his other hand on her behind, he dipped into her slick wetness and drew forth more of her natural lubrication and laved her other, tighter entrance with her own juices. "Some men find this a pleasurable diversion from the norm. And from what I've heard, there are some women who enjoy it as well."

"I don't think I am one of them," she stated, trying unsuccessfully to scoot out of his reach. "It sounds rather perverse, and I would rather do it the way we have been. It feels so much better."

"Trust me, Sarah-mine," he whispered into her ear as he held her. "Now, lift your leg for me." He then took her leg and moved it over his, making his access easier.

His palms caressed her nakedness, stirring heat within her traitorous body. "Ian, even with my great desire to learn and experience all that I can in order to please you, I assure you I do not want to try that."

"Shhh, Sarah," he whispered. "Trust me." He placed the tip of his engorged rod at her entrance, thankfully not *that* entrance, and slid in easily.

"I do, Ian," she said as she surrendered to him, and more importantly, wanting him to remain in the orifice he'd entered. "I trust you."

Then he plunged into her from behind, spooning her as he thrust deeply and thoroughly, filling her until she felt him touching her soul. "I'm glad you trust me, Sarah-mine," he took a deep breath and began to move slowly, steadily. "Because I don't particularly enjoy *that* manner of lovemaking either."

"Thank goodness," she said as she heaved a sigh of relief and began to relax and enjoy his slow thrusts.

Soon they began to move as one, and he carried her back to the pinnacle of all sensation and desire. To that special place where only release would ease the torturous need building within her. And after he gave her what she sought so desperately, he found his own completion.

A t one-seventeen p.m., exactly twenty-four hours after their arrival in New York harbor, Ian skillfully maneuvered his three-masted Baltimore clipper through the buoys set as the start line for the start of the second leg of their race.

"Which boat comes out of the box next?" Sarah asked. Because she'd gone into the town to shop, she didn't see which boats came in behind them. When she'd returned after her expedition to the hotel for a bath, she'd noticed two other competitors dropping anchor and another sailing into the harbor, but didn't catch the names.

"*Evangeline* comes out next, then the *Mirage* and *Solent*. In that order. *Ann McKim* came in overnight, but she's not one to discount yet. She's set records crossing the Pacific and Atlantic each year since she was launched."

Sarah saw the look of sadness or longing cross his face for a brief moment and wanted to delve into his life and upbringing, but knew she had to wait for the right time. She'd tried once before, and he closed up like a box, keeping his secrets inside, unwilling to share yet what she thought to be his pain.

"When I look at her, I see the mark of my father's

influence in her design, though he's long been dead. The architect on record is M. Michael Watkins, and I believe he may be the son of my father's partner, though I don't remember the man having a wife, much less children."

They sat in silence a few minutes as he pointed his bowsprit in the center of the two buoys. "How far ahead is Lucky?"

Ian nodded. "His departure is eleven minutes ahead of us."

"Hang all the sail you can on those yardarms, Captain," she said to her husband. "We have a race to win."

"Competitive, wife?"

"I've been losing to Lucky in most competitive endeavors my whole life. Just once, I'd love to beat him at *something*!"

"It doesn't matter which of us wins, we're applying the purse to the purchase of the new ships." Ian looked at her and smiled, warming her all over, yet sending shivers of delight through her. "Besides," he leaned toward her and said just loudly enough for her to hear, "I've already won."

The entire crew stood on deck to watch as they crossed the start line. When they did, the men cheered, their voices echoing through the harbor as they began the second leg of their journey.

"What drives you?" Sarah asked Ian several days later, as she sat behind him on the steering deck as he held his course through the warm, summer day. Sailing conditions had been optimal for them thus far, and the assisting currents he'd once mentioned were doing exactly as he'd said and pushing them home. Sarah had long ago taken the hat off and turned her face to the sun to feel its kiss on her cheeks.

"A desire to succeed," he replied, looking at her with curious gaze. "Isn't that what drives most men?" His tousled blond locks blew in the breeze, giving him a boyish quality that she found irresistible on him. It made her want to run her hands through it.

"Perhaps," she squinted up at him, shielding the sun with a hand. "But you aren't most men. I've never met anyone your age who has the drive you do. Your ambition is unmatched, and I want to know the reasons behind it, because I sense you are much more complex than you appear."

He looked at her with a soft-eyed hazel gaze. "I didn't have the life you had, Sarah. The man whose title I will inherit hated my father and, by my blood, me. If not for my two aunts, I don't know what would have happened to me."

"Ren's godmothers are a delight," she said.

Ian nodded as he smiled. "They are dear to me, but my grandfather.... The man is vindictive and mean. He basically cut off any support to them the year I went to Oxford. They are the only two people in the world who care about him, and he cuts them off. Not just financially. He refused to see them for years." Ian scanned the horizon around them and managed the wheel in silence as he appeared to contemplate his next words. Sarah knew he struggled with what he was about to say, so she let him form his thoughts with no prodding from her. "He recently called them to his side saying he's on his deathbed, but it's been months and the bastard still won't die.

"He lives in this world inside his head where he thinks he's more important than he really is. Do you know how he became the first Earl Mackeever? It is because he was crippled in service to the crown. He commanded a ship in Charleston harbor during the siege. As his ship went down, he rescued as many men as he could until he was shot in the leg. The story goes that the bullet went clean through and he tied a tourniquet and continued releasing his men who'd been imprisoned below as the ship was sinking. He lost five men in all that day and later the leg to infection. I will never dispute the fact that the man was a hero."

"Then why your hatred of him?"

"It's a very long story, and he is a very bitter and evil man. I pray with every voyage I take that he is dead upon my return—and not because I inherit his title. I would be just as happy, if not more so, to not have it."

Sarah was surprised to hear him wish a relative dead and even more shocked to think there was such an act that would warrant those feelings. *Family is the treasure in life*, Lia always said. So to hear this come from the man she had married and was growing to love was quite shocking. "I don't understand Ian. He is your grandfather, your elder. You should honor and respect him with your words and actions."

"You don't know him, and I pray you never will."

She scoffed at the notion of an old man harming her in any way. "He cannot hurt us, Ian. My God, he is a sickly old man! And near death from what you and your aunts have said."

"It is my belief that he has tried to have me killed from the moment I discovered his secret," Ian whispered. "He is a dangerous man. And I believe he would harm anyone I care for to get even with me. That is one of the reasons why I wanted to wait to marry. Not only did I not want him to hurt you, I didn't want him to breathe the same air as you."

"What on earth did you discover that warranted him wanting you dead?" Sarah was desperate for a reason her husband feared an old, nearly dead war hero.

"It's so vile, that if the admiralty knew what I knew of him, he would be stripped of his title and medals. He'd be a hero no more, and he could no longer live the revered life he does. And he knows…he knows, Sarah, that if something were to happen to me, while he still lived, I have ensured the whole country would know of his secret. Threatening him is the only way I can protect myself. That, and sailing. Because being out here is as far as I can get from him."

Sarah stood, went behind Ian and wrapped her arms around his waist. "At first, I was curious what he'd done, but now…I don't believe I *want* to know."

"You would be safer not."

Chapter Ten

Late in the afternoon of July seventeenth, everyone, herself included, instinctively knew home was within a day's sail. Sarah smelled the land. Others said they knew because of the color of the water. And still other sailors said they knew because of the currents. Either way, the excitement aboard the boat made concentration on their assigned tasks difficult.

For Sarah, a tiny cloud of fear had settled over her. She worried about what her brother would do or say, not just to her but also to Ian. More than she wanted Ren's forgiveness for running after adventure as she did, she needed his acceptance of her marriage. While she might not have initially wanted to marry Ian because of what he'd said, she was wed now. They seemed to have reached a comfortable place in their union, and there was no going back and undoing the act.

And, in all honesty, she didn't want to, not now. Sarah hugged herself in the empty cabin, happy that she and Ian had settled into their relationship, especially as she was fairly certain she carried her captain's child. She was late with her menses, but also as she prepared for bed her stomach grew upset, causing her to become ill for the first time in years.

At first she wondered if her stomach was upset from

the worry over her brother's reaction to her return, the lack of fresh food, or a babe. She finally decided it was likely a combination of all three. Certainly all were weighing heavily on her mind. She crawled into the bed with the cat after Ian left the room, then said a prayer that Ren wouldn't be too upset with her. She could only say the words he'd told her often enough—what is done is done, learn from it and move on.

The following morning, the crew lined the rail as Ian brought *Revenge* across the finish line at eleven thirty-nine—three weeks and one day after leaving New York. Their soaring spirits and cheers were contagious, serving to drown out her anxiety, for His Grace was sure to be at the dock awaiting her return. She feared her brother's reaction, not only to her escapade, but also to her marriage. It worried her so much that she'd been unable to eat breakfast.

Right before crossing between the two marked buoys, Ian motioned for her to stand next to him. When she did, he moved her between him and the wheel as they crossed the finish line to the cheers and huzzahs of his crew. He cheered along with his men and began thanking each one as they came up to the steering deck as they coasted into the harbor. It was at this moment she knew she'd fallen completely in love with him.

But she feared telling him, unsure of how he'd react to her confession. Her husband had never mentioned love to her. Oh, he was polite, kind, and thoughtful toward her. He was affectionate and desirous of her as well.

Still, it was difficult to let go of the fact that he'd originally felt she trapped him into marriage and that he clearly stated those were, in fact, his feelings at that time. Sarah believed, with all her heart, that his feeling toward her was different now. Though he'd never said so, he did behave differently toward her, and she felt this emotion in his caring actions toward her. So, if he didn't say he loved her, did it really matter?

She shivered in his embrace, and he wrapped his slicker, which blocked the wind, around her, enveloping her in his great warmth. "You won't have to face him alone," he said, thinking she feared her brother's reaction.

Sarah wasn't completely honest when, in her reply, she let Ian continue to believe she feared Ren. It was that other realization, the one that portend ten fingers and ten toes, that she feared a little more than meeting with her brother. "Thank you." She said as she stared into his eyes, the elated expression on his face was contagious, but her fear kept her from sharing fully in Ian's exuberance. "I'm afraid my brother will be more than just a little miffed."

She relished the heat his broad body offered her, and she snuggled closer. "We're married now," Ian said. "It wasn't what we planned, but it happened, and we did the right thing to minimize gossip."

"I'm afraid he will be angry that I left to begin with." She inhaled deeply of the salty-sandalwood-cedar scent that was Ian's slicker. If she could, she would stay with him like this forever. But if her suspicions were correct, she would have to stay ashore for the next eight months.

"You said you left a note where it would be easily found. So why are you worried?" Ian asked.

"I don't know. I've never been afraid of him before. Then again, I've never done anything quite *this* impulsive either. I honestly intended to make this voyage with Lucky, and I didn't believe doing so would have such life-altering consequences, but...." She shrugged as she wiped the tears that again began to fall. "I am such a watering can of tears. It must be because we're home," Sarah said, hoping he didn't catch on to her suspicions.

"Must be," her husband offered, changing the subject back to the race. Sarah dried her eyes. She knew Ian was uncomfortable with her tears. "We know Lucky is behind us by just over an hour. What we do not know is if anyone arrived before us. None of us on our boat ever saw another ship on the horizon, other than Lucky's. I just pray we're the first in because that purse will help us build our fleet."

Sarah's heart swelled with pride for Ian when she realized they might have actually won this race, even if it meant her brother would lose. And though Ian had declined her dowry, Sarah was now determined to find a way to get it into his accounts. She just had to figure out a way to do it without him learning of it because his American pride might take a bruising knowing she'd gone against his wishes.

One hour later, just as she'd surmised, Ren was waiting at the dock when their gig rowed up—as were Lia, Elise, and Michael, and some of their older children. It was more than she'd been prepared to face at first, but the family never did anything without the support and consent of the others. It made sense they'd be together for the arrival of Lucky and Ian's boats—and Sarah's return.

No sooner had they tied the gig to the steps, than Ian was immediately surrounded by the race steward and harbor master. They climbed up to the dock, and even with the realization they had won the first ever Atlantic Crossing Challenge, Sarah nervously scanned the ever-growing crowd for Ren's face. Once she found him, she saw no anger there, only relief. The same held true for Lia, Elise, and Michael.

Lia was the first to come forward and hug her. Sarah returned her embrace, hugging her tightly. Lia whispered in her ear, "Why are you with Mr. Ross-Mackeever and not Lucky?"

"It's a very long story," Sarah replied, returning her whisper. "As you can guess, we are now married. Lucky insisted on it in New York harbor."

Her sister-in-law did the thing that made her so special: she did not pass judgment nor did she over-react to the news. Lia just hugged her tight. "We are all relieved that you have returned safe and sound. No matter what your brother and sister will say, I am happy you are home." Sarah whispered her thanks, and just before Lia released her, she added, "And you've brought me another brother!"

She didn't have time to react as Michael came to her side. "Did you have your grand adventure, my lady?" he said as he came forward to hug her.

"I did, my lord," she replied as he released her. Her eyes sought Ren and found him standing next to Ian, waiting for him to finish signing papers shoved in his direction as soon as he had two feet on the dock. She turned back to Michael. "Please believe me when I say I am so very thankful to be home again."

No one could imagine how much she meant those words. Sarah couldn't wait to eat anything cooked by Nettie, their family cook, and soak in a hot bath infused with lavender and chamomile oils. She wanted to wash her hair and brush it dry in front of a fire. She wanted to sleep in a bed and room that didn't rock. She wanted to experience the sound of silence again, something that was impossible on the ocean.

Her niece Charlotte, Michael and Elise's eldest, came forward to stand next to her father. She was just blossoming from her lanky, youthful figure at thirteen and was filling out nicely. Her dark hair and fair skin gave promise to her developing beauty. It was already anticipated that when she came out, she'd be her season's diamond. Right now though, the starry-eyed romantic seemed eager to learn of Sarah's adventure. Knowing how Elise felt, Sarah knew she had to proceed with caution and not give the older girls the idea they should consider anything so outlandish or dangerous as what she'd just done.

"Aunt Sarah," Charlotte said, her blue-gray eyes wide with excitement, "was it as wonderful as it sounded? Stowing away and sailing to America?"

Elise rolled her eyes. "Do you see what a monster you have created? I have had to listen to nothing else but how 'exciting it must be,' 'how romantic it is,' and 'how brave you are,' for the past two months. One day you will have children, Sarah, and if they are daughters, you will see how difficult it is to keep them from doing things that could harm their reputations."

"I am sorry, sister, for any inappropriate example I have given to both young ladies." She turned a dire gaze to Ren and Lia's only daughter, Isabel, who was the same age as Charlotte and her cousin's closest friend. Isabel's golden-brown eyes, mahogany tresses, and petite frame hid the fact that she was a serious thinker. Intelligent beyond imagination, she hid her genius behind a facade of pleasant cheerfulness. Sarah thought the girl smiled so often so no one would know she was deep in thought, and thus mistake her for a bluestocking. For even though she professed to enjoy being different, on the most basic level Isabel wanted to be like other girls. She wanted attention from boys, but she'd already learned that boys were intimidated by smart girls.

Sarah held the gazes of both young ladies. "That was more adventure than I bargained for. I give you all my word, I'll never do anything so imprudent and foolish again. I promise. Why, there were times I even feared for my life!"

"From savages, Aunt Sarah?" This was from ten-year-old Jonathan, Elise and Michael's oldest son. Their youngest, Andrew, at six years of age, was likely back at the house with his nanny, as well as Ren and Lia's youngest, four-year-old Christopher.

"No, Jonathan. It was the storms that nearly did us in. The one going to New York wasn't nearly as frightening as the one coming back. I feared the boat capsizing several times!"

"Ah, that's nothing. I can swim. It's the savages I want to see. Did you see any at all?"

"Not a one, Jonathan. I'm sorry."

"See, told you so," fifteen-year-old Marcus said as he nudged his younger cousin. As Ren and Lia's oldest, he designated himself the authority on all things. "New York is civilized, you dolt. If you want to see savages nowadays, you must go west and cross the Mississippi River. That's where you'll really see the wilds of North America," he said with a certainty that only comes from being the eldest child in the family.

Out of the corner of her eye, Sarah saw that Ian and Ren had come closer to their group and were now in deep conversation with a race official. Ian came to her side and held her hand as he announced that after checking with the race steward and harbor master he could confirm what he and his crew suspected. They'd won.

Congratulations and huzzahs were said all around the dock, from the crewmen of *Revenge* to the crowd of strangers gathering on the dock. The winning purse, he said, was to be awarded in a ceremony one week from the day of their arrival. This was to allow all of the remaining boats time to return.

Sarah looked out just beyond the harbor toward the horizon and wondered how much farther Lucky was. When last she'd seen his flags, it was through Ian's spyglass, and he was about an hour behind them. She said a quick, silent prayer of thanks that the crews of both ships would make it home safe and sound.

His Grace, the Duke of Caversham, came to stand by Ian's side when he reached the dock. As he half-listened to the details the race steward said, an uneasy sensation settled over Ian. The portly man, a representative of the group of men sponsoring the Atlantic Cup Challenge, droned on, officially congratulating him on his safe return, then informed him of his time, and finally proclaimed him the winner of the first annual race. All the while, Ian felt his new brother-in-law simmered with unasked questions, and he knew why. His previously unmarried sister returned home in the company of a man not Lucky, and he wanted an explanation. Now.

LOVING SARAH

Ian wasn't going to argue with him. What was done was done. He hadn't caused the predicament he found himself in, and even though he wasn't born a gentleman in this country, he'd done the right thing and married her.

He smiled while several of the men from his ship joined him on the dock. Everyone clapped his back and shook his hand while his eyes searched the crowd forming around him for Sarah. He saw her blond curls, pulled back in a simple ribbon, as she spoke to her family. Her back was to him, and he wondered what she was saying, what the expression on her face was, and if she feared her brother.

He'd promised her he'd stand by her, that she wouldn't have to face His Grace alone. He intended to keep that promise no matter what his new brother-in-law had to say regarding their marriage.

Ian took the first opportunity he could to step away from the crowd of well-wishers, and he returned to Sarah's brother, the Duke of Caversham—a man several on his crew knew and respected outside of the man's social realm, as His Grace had sailed for years before he married and settled with his wife and in his ducal duties.

Ian spoke first, hopefully the act would convey to the duke that he was in accord with what happened and was happy with the arrangement.

"She landed on my boat by accident the night before the race began. I knew nothing of her existence until after I'd rounded Anglesey, and she has been safe with me the entire time."

"I thank you for caring for my sister, but…."

Ian interrupted him. "We married in New York harbor. I have the license and certificate."

The duke, equal to him in height, though not in breadth, eyed him intently. "Was she willing?" he whispered.

Ian almost got the impression the older man would help his sister if she were unhappy with the situation, and he knew better than to lie to the man. "Not at first, but we didn't give her a choice." Ian turned his head and glanced her way again. Their gazes met. He smiled at his wife. "She balked a while, until she had to be reminded of a few things."

"I take it that all is well now?" the duke asked.

"It is." His new brother-in-law clapped him on the back. "Well then. I suppose congratulations are in order for this as well."

"Thank you." Ian turned to face the duke. "There are still things we need to work out. I was not prepared for a wife yet. You know I own no land, have no home except that ship out there, and am estranged from my grandfather whose title I will inherit."

"Everything will work out in the end as long as you're willing to listen and compromise," His Grace said. "Always remember that. Listen and compromise."

Ian agreed and watched as Sarah spoke with her nieces and nephews. The glimpse he'd had of her face, and knowing the way she usually carried herself, told him she was tired. He went to her side, the duke following him. He slipped in beside his wife and took her small, cold hand in his.

A group of his crewmen who waited closer to the bulkhead began to cheer, and Ian knew then his friend was coming into view. He leaned over and whispered to her, "You're tired and cold." He looked around for a place for her to sit and rest. The ducal coach stood nearby. "Would you like to rest in the coach a while? It could be forty minutes or more before he steps ashore."

All of a sudden a ruckus arose among the sailors as they realized two boats were coming into view. Lucky's colors were clearly visible on the first. The second was as yet indistinguishable. From their vantage on the wharf, and the distance and angle of the finish line, everyone knew both boats could easily have been in the second place position.

Ian squinted his eyes and within moments recognized the *Ann McKim*. God, he wanted one like her. Sleek and fast. That boat had arrived in New York after dark, some nine hours behind him. A part of Ian wondered how on earth she managed to recover the distance between them. The other part of him knew. She was a true Baltimore clipper. Made for speed. And it looked like she was about to take second place from Lucky's grasp.

"It's hard to tell, isn't it?" Sarah moved to stand before him near the bulkhead, and Ian removed his coat and wrapped it around her to keep her warm as they all watched the two ships closely. "I see Lucky's colors, but from here I can't tell if he's ahead or not."

"He is, but just barely," Ian assured everyone nearby. He had his hands over his eyes, shielding the sun as he squinted and watched the two boats near the buoy markers. The crowd with them grew silent. Then suddenly, a cheer rang out collectively. The sister to *Revenge* had crossed the finish line with what appeared barely a jib's length between the two boats. Surely no race could ever end closer than that.

Sarah jumped up and down for joy, as did all of her younger relatives, while the Duchess and the Countess stood clapping next to their husbands. This was an awkward sensation, one Ian had never experienced before, as he hadn't had the kind of family who showed support for his efforts.

He looked around at the crowd and recognized the two women he loved as mothers were nowhere around. Again. He knew if they'd been able to come, they would be here. So he stepped toward the duchess.

"Your Grace, how are my aunts? Are they well?"

"They are well, Mr. Ross-Mackeever," the duchess replied, her green eyes growing sober with sympathy. "They are again at your grandfather's bedside, as it seems he may be nearing his time."

He choked back a laugh, and the duchess gave him a surprised look. "Your Grace, forgive me for saying what is sure to sound disrespectful regarding my grandfather's condition, but he's done this before, several times in fact. I'll believe he's dead when my aunts tell me they've seen his casket nailed shut with his body inside."

"Far be in from me to say whether your grandfather is, or is not, deserving of your affection as I do not know the relationship you have with him," the dark-haired duchess said for his ears alone. "But I have learned in my short life that sometimes our elders react in anger when they cannot express their pain."

"You may be right, Your Grace. But I see no scenario in which we shall ever be in each other's favor. As it is, I do not know a life in which he is in any way repentant or civil to anyone."

"Your aunts have previously confided that their father was not a kind man," Her Grace said as she looked at the two ships sailing toward the harbor, sails furling to slow their speed as the crowd around them still cheered the crew of Lucky's boat. "They say he is changed now that his end is near. I've often felt that if we tried to understand where

LOVING SARAH

his pain comes from, we might better understand him. Not that you should forgive him or even love him."

Ian didn't want to tell her that he never gave the old man the time of day, and if it weren't for his missing aunts, he'd never have asked about his grandfather. "You are right," he said. "And I shall think on it, though I can make no promise where he is concerned."

"I can ask no more than that, can I?" She smiled and went to stand next to her husband, who leaned down and whispered to her the news of his and Sarah's wedding. She turned back at him and smiled, then leaned over to whisper to the Countess Camden, who then came to hug Sarah. Ian watched as His Grace and Lord Camden spoke privately while the two men looked off into the harbor.

So now they all knew—all except for the children, and they were sure to learn of it soon enough.

Everyone waited for Lucky's arrival, and when he and the captain of the *Ann McKim* both came ashore, the two men confirmed what the race steward was fairly sure they'd all seen. Lucky had taken second place.

He shook hands with the captain of the Baltimore clipper and congratulated the man for sailing a good race. And within an hour of Lucky's return, Ian was waving to Sarah as she left for the rented house with her family to rest while he and Lucky made arrangements to sail to their home port in London within the week.

"They will have questions, I'm sure," Lucky said. "But my brother-in-law and Michael are good men, and they care for Sarah's well-being and happiness."

He just nodded as he climbed down to the landing, ready to step into the gig with several of his men and Lucky.

"As do I now," Ian replied. "Though I am no closer to being ready for a wife and family as I was before I left Liverpool at the start of this race. I had a plan and wanted to accomplish certain things before I took on the responsibilities of...." He sighed as he rowed. No use lamenting what he could do nothing about now.

"That just goes to show that sometimes when we make plans God finds humor in them," Lucky said as he rowed alongside him. "Which is why I never make a plan beyond right now. Life is too short to worry about what we're going to do in five years' time."

The gig coasted alongside the hull of Ian's *Revenge*, and Ian handed over the oar to a crewman, stood, and grasped the rope ladder as the boat slipped alongside, never coming to a complete stop. "I'll see you this evening. What time was dinner again?"

"I'll come back to get you. Be ready in about an hour," his friend shouted as the men began to row again. "I'm certain there will be questions, so bring the license and certificate with you."

Once he had both feet over the rail, Ian called for Goran to boil a pot of water and come help him trim his hair and give him a shave. "I have dinner at the duke's residence this evening and must hurry. It wouldn't do to appear like a shaggy dog, would it?" Goran laughed as he headed back to the galley.

The man had the steadiest hand on his entire ship, so if Ian needed a shave he wanted the best hand he knew to do the job. While he waited, he washed as best he could from head to toe so as to make a suitable impression on Sarah's family. Goran arrived twenty minutes later with the razor tray and a bowl of steaming water.

He supposed one day he would need to groom on a regular basis, and he'd likely have to hire a valet for the job. But those were things he'd need when he settled down, and it wasn't likely to happen in the near future. And that was something he'd have to prepare Sarah for, because he wasn't ready to remain grounded. Since they'd never spoke of what would happen upon their return, he didn't know if she wanted to return to her old life, or did she want to remain aboard *Revenge* with him?

He had to admit he'd grown used to her presence in his bed and enjoyed sex with her, but he didn't think living aboard a boat was for a lady, and Ian was nowhere near ready to be landed. Even if his grandfather was toes-up in his casket, Ian was not ready for a life completely on land yet. His business still needed his full attention as it was about to expand significantly over the next few years. It was in his and Lucky's plans.

Thinking on it, though he was glad to be married to her now, being married hadn't been in his plans for at least a few more years, and Sarah knew this. To save her from disgrace, he'd married her, but as he'd already bedded her, it wasn't as though he didn't expect it eventually. He'd just taken the initiative and did it sooner rather than later.

As he saw it, their best option was for her to continue living with her family for the next few years, and he would return to stay with her as frequently as possible, because he did care for her. He cared a great deal. Now he just had to convince her that this was the best arrangement for both of them.

Chapter Eleven

Hours later, after seeing Lucky safely ashore, Sarah sat in a refreshing, hot bath with her favorite lavender-scented soap and rested her eyes as she planned what she'd say to Ren, who was in his office at that very moment questioning Ian and Lucky, and likely examining their marriage certificate Ian brought from New York.

Sarah tried to plan her reaction to each scenario that might play out once she entered her brother's office. She didn't think he would demand an annulment or divorce, as they were wed by a minister, but more importantly because of the scandal either would cause. As for bloodlines, Ian would be considered a superb match for her. That he was rough around the edges could be attributed to his lack of exposure to the gentler sex, and in her opinion, that made him very attractive.

As she saw it, the man needed her to help refine him and find his way socially. It was something she was quite proficient at, and as a married woman, it was her duty to make for him a comfortable home and bear his children.

She sunk lower into the tub, allowing the warm water to rise to her chin. She grinned as she wondered if he would be happy about the babe she was almost certain she carried. They both found fulfillment in their lovemaking, surely her new husband would enjoy the product of their loving. What man didn't wish for sons and daughters? Heirs to carry on the familial legacy?

Sarah also wondered *when* she should tell him. He and Lucky planned to leave in a matter of weeks for China. Because she was never very regular with her monthly course, it was difficult to say for certain she *was* carrying, having only been late this one month. She'd felt fine once she returned to dry land and had been able to have tea and cakes before her bath with no upset stomach. So likely it was the food on the boat that had finally gotten to her.

Her maid helped her rinse and handed her a towel when she stood. As she pat herself dry, she noticed it. Upon wiping her thighs there were faint streaks of blood. She stood in shocked silence before calling for Trudy to bring her the proper undergarments.

Sarah wanted to shout in anger, needed to cry in sadness, but could do neither at that moment. Then suddenly a vice-like grip on her heart wrenched a silent scream from her just as she began to weep for her loss. She'd wanted so desperately to be with child, had even begun to feel the new life in her very soul.

A babe. A son or daughter. She'd wanted it so very much. Sarah had wanted to give her husband an heir, and now it would be many months before he returned from China and she'd have an opportunity to conceive again. Her heart burst with sadness, and even a little shame for her inability to do what all wives wished to do.

Sarah sent a note to Lia that she was feeling unwell and would remain in her room this evening. She then wrapped herself in a bathrobe and sat at her dressing table while

Trudy began to remove the tangles from her wet hair.

She opened her eyes at a knock on the door and bid the person enter. Her sister-in-law came in, a sympathetic smile on her face. It was almost enough to bring Sarah to tears—yet again. She dismissed her maid. "I'll finish brushing it dry. Thank you, Trudy."

"I've put your night dress and robe across the chaise, my lady. It's just over there," she pointed to the soft linen sleep dress before leaving the room.

Lia took up the brush and began to work a small section of Sarah's hair. "I used to love doing this when you were younger," Lia said, "and I think you enjoyed it as well. I know Isabel still likes for me to brush her hair at times, and she's at that impossible age."

"There's something soothing about having someone you love brush your hair," Sarah whispered as she choked on her tears. "I'd so wanted to do the same with a child of my own. But that won't be happening any time soon."

Lia wrapped her arms around her from behind and met her gaze in the mirror. "It will eventually. It sometimes takes years to conceive a babe. You have nothing to fear, as long as you're comfortable and he's kind," her sister-in-law said sympathetically.

"He is very kind, and we…are comfortable." She sniffled and blew her nose yet again. "But Ian hadn't wanted marriage yet but was forced into it because of what I'd done."

Lia was silent a moment, as though she contemplated everything Sarah had just said. When she spoke, she had but one statement. "You love him."

Through her tears, she replied honestly, "I fell in love with him, yes."

"It's interesting that you are both taking blame for your newly married state," Lia said. "Ren believes Ian is as taken with you as I think you are with him."

Sarah frowned, feeling the tears rising. "No. He tolerates me at best." She cried as she related her tale from the fateful ride out to the wrong vessel, to standing a few moments earlier in the tub and realizing she didn't carry her husband's child.

Lia continued combing the tangles from Sarah's curly hair. "Did you know that your captain *twice* had the opportunity to hand you over to Lucky before you reached New York and he chose to remain silent and keep you with him? That tells me he wanted you as well."

She shook her head. "No. If anything he has resigned himself to our marriage. He said as much, making it very clear it wasn't what he wanted. He did not want to get married to anyone yet. And I don't want Ren to punish Ian for something he had no part in. He knew nothing of my plan to go with Lucky. It truly was an unfortunate accident that I landed on his boat. It wasn't his fault."

"He's not punishing your new husband, Sarah. While he is not happy with how it all began, your brother is not angry with Ian. In fact, the four men are in his study, toasting Ian with brandy, and it smells as though they're smoking cigars."

Pensive silence stretched between them. When she spoke, Sarah asked, "I should like to remain in my room for the night. I cannot imagine celebrating with the way I am feeling."

"Ren has asked to speak with you," Lia said. "Shall I call him up rather than you go below?"

Sarah nodded. There was no getting around facing

her brother. It was the one interview she was not looking forward to. "You're certain he is not planning my departure for The Box?"

Lia smiled. "He's not planning to send you away. Though The Box is a wonderful place to go on a wedding trip. You should convince your husband to take you next summer before he goes to China again."

"I'm not sure how Ian will feel about returning to Scotland," Sarah said. "He said he hasn't been in many years. I assume it is because of the tension with the old earl. Though if his grandfather has passed, I don't see why he wouldn't want to go."

"It was never my intent to sail forever. Only until my predecessor cocked up his toes and I could be free to settle in one location. Then perhaps marry one day." Ian sipped the smooth liquor and contemplated his future with Sarah. His main priority now was to protect her from his grandfather. The man might use her against him.

The duke tapped the ash from his cigar in a dish and reclined in his deep-cushioned leather chair. "You must explain to me how a harmless old man has kept you from taking root somewhere? Your grandfather frequented my club when he used to come to Town." His new brother-in-law looked at him curiously, then at Camden sitting next to him on the settee, with Lucky across from Caversham in a matching, dark-leather wing-back. "I know the man. He is an honorable sort—a bit gruff at times—but always straightforward."

Ian puffed on his cigar and stared into his glass. Memories of what he'd witnessed that afternoon when he'd walked in on his grandfather and his friend flooded his mind. Ian knew his grandfather's friend as a fellow survivor of the Siege at Charleston, a junior officer at the time of the battle that sank their ship. Though he could not forget the scene he'd stumbled upon, Ian had never spoken of it. He wasn't even sure he could now, except that he wanted to protect Sarah.

The last time he saw his grandfather, it was for his forced annual visit, the month before his seventeenth birthday, and just weeks before the start of his first term at Oxford. For the first few years of his life in England, one or the other of his aunts would accompany him on these visits north. On this particular visit, Ian made the trip on his own. The ship upon which he'd traveled had arrived several hours earlier than the appointed time, and Ian was happy because he hoped to be done with the annual tirade in time to catch that return packet to London the very same evening, eliminating an overnight stay in the man's home.

His grandfather's house was surprisingly understaffed when he arrived, and he initially attributed it to the servants' day off. In hindsight, he should have known the man was deep in debt because his aunts had dropped hints at just that very thing during his most recent visit to see them. Ian let himself into the unlocked house after knocking several times and strode into his grandfather's office, knowing if he were home, that was where the man would be. He was, but the commander was not alone.

Shock unlike anything he'd ever experienced registered in his brain, freezing him momentarily to the spot. It took a moment to comprehend what exactly he was witnessing, but there was no mistaking it. Ian was certain the expression on their faces was very much like his. It seemed his grandfather had not been expecting him to arrive early.

In his stupefied stillness, Ian watched as the old man—wearing his full commander's uniform sans trousers and with his wooden leg strapped around his upper thigh—sodomized the man Ian knew was the old man's friend. In his grandfather's favor, if such a thing could be said, this other man didn't appear to be putting up a fight. And though he might have thought the situation abhorrent, he knew such things existed. The lads at school spoke of such vulgar behaviors with little to no surprise. He just didn't think someone as strict, disciplined, and militaristic as the old man would have been one to partake of that particular peccadillo.

He found it shocking and unnatural. Perhaps it was because he'd come from a conservative upbringing that he was shocked by the sight. It didn't matter. The moment he recognized what was happening, Ian fled the house with the speed of a hare chased by a fox, returned the rented horse, and ran toward the docks, where he bought passage on the first ship leaving no matter the destination. As it turned out, he wound up sailing north to Aberdeen, then taking another packet the next day headed south back to London.

He started classes at the beginning of the term, and within several weeks discovered his grandfather had sent two thugs to follow him. Who knew what they would have done had they caught him? He was always watching his back, trying to stay one step ahead of the two. During his first term break, he'd gone to Lucky's home, attempting to hide from the thugs. When classes resumed, he stayed with Lucky at his apartment rather than return to his student housing.

LOVING SARAH

He had to confide some of the events of that day to Lucky when Ian asked to sleep on his couch for an undetermined amount of time, but he could never share all of the details.

He later learned that should the admiralty discover his grandfather's affinity for sodomy, the admiralty could have his grandfather's title and all of his accolades and medals stripped from him and be thrown in prison. He'd no longer be the hero the entire nation believed him to be.

Ian exhaled the smoke from his cigar, and with it all memories of that time in his life. He then gave his new brother-in-law the reply he hoped would placate him. "The Commander was desperate at one time," Ian began, "but I believe we are at an impasse with regard to that threat. He was cruel, not just to me, but to his own daughters. Once a year, I was forced as a child to listen to his hate-filled orations about how my uncle, who died during our second war for independence, had such promise, a military hero, handsome and charming, and I would never compare as an heir. As a young boy, I could handle that. But when he attacked my parents, I could take no more. He called my father a traitor to the crown because he'd fought for his new country, and my mother a whore because she was the daughter of one of his servants. I could take no more. After Rugby, I'd decided I'd had enough of his vitriol and chose to never visit him again. He ceased paying my school fees and expenses. My aunts paid for all three years at Oxford, an expense neither could afford. At the time I promised to repay them, last year I did."

"Do you feel he will harm my sister?" the duke asked.

Ian shook his head. "No, I don't fear that. My thought

is to spare Sarah his wild, hate-filled rants. They were upsetting enough to me as a young man. But to a lady...." Ian trailed off, unsure of how to convey his concern for his wife's safety without telling the other three men what he knew. He stared into the contents of his snifter as he swirled it about. "He has an added reason to want to get even with me, because I know things—dark things—about him. I was witness to it, and I'm afraid he'd use Sarah to get to me."

The other three men in the room shared uneasy glances, and Lucky nodded having lived through it with him.

"We shall do our best then," Michael said.

"Thank you," Ian said, hoping they'd understand his next request. "To protect Sarah, I wish to keep this marriage a private matter between us for the time being. We can place notices in papers and such after the old man dies."

"A sister of duke marries the elusive heir to a much-loved national hero, and you wish to keep *that* a secret?" Lucky chuckled. "Good luck, old boy."

Ian glanced from Ren to Michael, ignoring Lucky.

Michael spoke first. "It might be a little late. I think there was mention of your marriage on the dock earlier today."

"And newspaper writers from London were there reporting on the race," Ren added.

Ian just nodded, trying to figure out what he would do now, as the door opened and a footman handed the duke a note. His grace snuffed out his cigar, rose, and tugged at his starched cuffs and waistcoat before buttoning his coat. "If you will excuse me gentlemen, my wife has called for me."

Loving Sarah

Sarah waited in her sister-in-law's sitting room with Lia at her side for a meeting with her brother. He'd wanted to speak with her separately before she joined the rest of the family below. Both women stood when Ren entered the room, and Sarah clutched her sister-in-law's hand as her brother approached them.

His gray eyes always had a way of frightening her when he was angry. They took on a much darker tone, as they did now. His features seemed relaxed, though Sarah thought she saw a muscle twitch near the corner of his lips. She hadn't noticed earlier, but in the two months she'd been gone, it seemed he'd aged ten years. For that she was sorry.

"You look well," he said. Though calm, his voice had the merest trace of a hardened undertone, one she hadn't heard in a while, but instantly caused her to tremble.

"Thank you, I am."

"Husband, be kind," Lia cautioned.

"Kind?" His voice held an ominous edge that warned he was not to be deterred in his chastisement of her. "Was she kind to have left as she did? Scaring me to death?"

"I left a note." Sarah focused on the thin golden rope fringe dangling from the tieback on the berry-colored velvet curtains behind her brother, unable to look into his eyes. Remorse ate at her for causing her entire family to be upset, truly it did. But at the time she didn't think about anything but not letting the opportunity pass her by.

"Any number of things could have happened to you," he countered, that edge becoming sharper, deadlier. "Do you care?"

Unable to speak, she swallowed past a painful lump forming in her throat and nodded. She would not cry. "I am sorry," she offered as she dropped her gaze to the floor. She truly was too, but she still couldn't meet his gaze, knowing she'd caused them both such fear and worry.

Her brother sighed before relaxing his stance. Only then did Sarah cautiously lift her gaze to see his lips soften into a sliver of a smile.

"I realize there is much to be done now with regard to notices to the papers and such, but Ian has asked that we not notify the papers as of yet," Ren said. "He doesn't want his grandfather to know of your marriage for some reason that is important to him."

"Are you saying we must keep their marriage a secret?" her sister-in-law asked.

"For the time being, yes," her brother replied. "Though if we do not hear about the earl's passing soon, I shall make inquiries as to his condition.

"But first I must ask you this," her brother's voice was soft and non-threatening. She looked at him again. "Are you happy, Sarah? Is remaining married to Ian what you wish?"

"If he will have me, yes."

"Then come downstairs for dinner," Lia said.

After dinner, Ian asked Sarah's maid to have a footman bring them a decanter of wine and two glasses, telling the woman she could retire for the night once she'd done that. He followed Sarah to her small sitting area in the corner of the room, lit another candle, then sat in one of the two chairs. She'd been different tonight than she was from that very morning when she was excited and cheering them across the finish line. She was more subdued and distracted than he'd ever remembered seeing her. He wondered what was causing her to be upset and how he could draw her from it.

He started their conversation with, "It will be very different for me to sleep in a room that is not moving."

"It is," she said softly. "I haven't been on the water as long as you have, so I'm sure you will find it more difficult than I to fall asleep. One thing I noticed immediately was that I missed the sound of the ocean moving beneath the open window." She gave him a shy smile, unlike her normal exuberant self. "It was odd to hear the birds as I was attempting to nap earlier."

It was almost as though she feared something, but he didn't know what that could be. Certainly she didn't fear him. Her brother and the rest of the family were satisfied with their marriage. Did she perhaps fear the future? As he had no home, could it be she felt he would bring her to sea with him? Whatever it was, she had changed significantly from that very morning.

A footman brought a tray with a decanter of red wine and two glasses and was quickly gone. Ian poured and offered the first glass to Sarah, then took another for himself. She took two sips then placed her glass on the fragile-looking table between the two chairs. He would never get used to delicate furniture after years of sailing on a ship and having everything built into the walls and floor. He felt overly large and out of place on pieces such as this, almost as though the spindly legs would collapse under him.

He had to quit avoiding the conversation, but didn't

know where to start. In the end, she broke the ice for them.

"I'm sure you've noticed that I haven't been feeling well this afternoon," she whispered as she looked at her folded hands in her lap. Her subdued countenance began to concern him, because she wasn't quite this upset below stairs in the drawing room after dinner while he and Lucky spoke of their race.

He thought perhaps something or someone was pressuring her to end the marriage before anyone other than the family knew of it. "Sarah, do you regret our marriage now that we are home?"

"Never," she assured him. "Please do not think that. It's just…I…." She stuttered on her reply, and a sadness came over her. Her blue eyes looked darker in the candlelight, and they began to fill with tears. He went to her and knelt at her side.

"What is it, Sarah-mine? Did I forget something? Do, or say, something to cause you to be upset during dinner?"

"No. I realized this afternoon that I'm not" —she began to cry in earnest now— "carrying…a child, and I wanted one very much."

He sat back on his heels and heaved a great sigh. "Oh Sarah," he began to chuckle slightly, relief flowing through him. "Is that all? You had me terrified you were regretting the marriage. But not carrying a child? For us, right now, not having a child is a good thing. According to my plan, I will not be home for a great majority of the year, and a child now would be a burden on you." He took her hand in his and kissed it. "Be thankful."

She stared at him quizzically, as though he was in the

process of sprouting a third eye as she witnessed it. "I don't understand. I thought all men wanted children. Do you want them at all?"

"Perhaps one day," he replied. "Though in all honesty, if I have none, I shall be just as happy."

She didn't give him time to clarify his statement before she came back with disapproving, almost accusatory questions. "How can you say such a thing, Ian? Why get married if not to have children?"

"If you'll remember, I wasn't given much of a choice on marriage. That was inevitable from the minute you threw a leg over my railing."

Her eyes grew round and large, red-rimmed from crying. She looked as though she'd been slapped. Her mouth opened and closed a few times before she formed her reply. "You are right. I…I'm…so very sorry, Ian, that I disturbed your well-planned life. This is all my fault, and I apologize." She stood and tugged at the bell pull behind her. "If you will excuse me. As I said, I am not feeling well and would have my maid help me dress for bed."

"You don't need her," he said. "I'll help you as I did on the boat."

"No, please. I would rather you leave. Perhaps we can talk again when I am not quite so tired, and feel better." She went to her washstand and dipped her cloth into the clean, cool water, then wiped her face.

He didn't know much about women, but what he did know from hearing other men talk was that when they were upset at this time of the month, it was best to leave them alone. "Fine. I will return to my boat. When you're feeling better, send for me. Until then," he said and bowed to her and took his leave.

He made for the back staircase and found himself next to the kitchen, and he slipped out the door without seeing any other family and went directly to his boat. Once there, Ian found himself pacing his cabin and wishing he hadn't left. Glancing around his quarters, he noticed her clothing and belongings she'd purchased in New York were gone, all sent to the rented Liverpool house.

When the next day ended and she had not sent a note for him to come back to her side, he thought to give her time to get over her emotions. Lucky stopped by, and the two of them watched several other ships entered in the race return from his steering deck over a bottle of wine. He had no idea what to ask with regard to Sarah, as he'd never had a wife before and didn't know how to deal with someone who cried for no particular reason.

When another day passed with still no word from Sarah, he asked Lucky how she was feeling, all his friend could say was that Sarah was still at the house and that he rarely saw her as she was keeping to her rooms with an unexplained malady.

They both mused that it was likely a good idea to keep a distance for a few days, as they had no idea if she was contagious or had eaten something that didn't agree with her.

"What the lass needs is a bit of me porridge," Seamus said as he moved the sail he was working on, looking for another tear to repair. The man had been on the other side of the railing quietly doing his job and listening in on the conversation.

"That's not likely to help," Ian said as he leaned back against the railing of the steps up to the anchor deck and tossed back the ale in his mug. "I think it was your slop that sickened her."

"If ye really have no idea why your wife is feeling under the weather, then perhaps you're not as smart as you think ye are," Seamus muttered, never looking up at him as he pulled his needle through the canvas and tied off the thread to begin another seam. "And you with that university education."

"Ugh," Ian groaned. "Don't you have a family somewhere you can visit, that you have to remain on the boat at all times?" Ian carried his empty mug down to the galley on the way to his quarters. He decided he would pay his wife a visit to find out what was really wrong with her. But first he needed to clean up.

The water in her bath was growing cool, and so was the bathing chamber, as Sarah realized the fire had dwindled down to barely glowing coals. Unlike her room in their home in London, or at Haldenwood, this house had only two bathing chambers for the entire home, fitted into out-of-the-way cupboards on the below ground-floor level of the home. The fireplace in the tiny room helped to keep it warm, which made bathing down here tolerable, but she'd rather be at Haldenwood where she could bathe in her own bathing chamber.

She sighed, feeling somewhat better now that her monthly had run its course. This was the shortest and lightest flux she'd remembered having—three days— and she now felt better than she had in a while. A part of her was still angry that Ian hadn't come to see how she was doing. Try as she might, she couldn't remember the evening he left. It was the evening of the day they'd returned from the race. She'd been tired, feeling sick to her stomach, and wanted nothing more than to crawl into her bed to sleep it off.

One thing she clearly remembered hearing him say was that he was thankful she wasn't carrying a child. That revelation was surprising, especially after the comfortable intimacy they'd reached during the return leg of the race. He'd never said he wanted no children. Ever. But this, and the fact that he'd initially thought she'd forced his hand in marriage, both hurt deeper than she could express. She'd cried into her pillow each night after Trudy had gone to bed, then woke the next morning with red, puffy eyes and a splitting headache as wide as the Thames.

How could she tell her family that she might have made a mistake in marrying him? Lia and Elise knew how much she loved children. She'd always wanted a great many of them, and until she met Ian she thought she might have a chance to have them. But the way things stood right now that was not likely. And it tore at her soul. It cut at the very reason for being a woman. Why else would a woman suffer these blasted courses each month if not for the promise of a child when she married?

She needed to speak with Ian and find out if this was something he felt strongly about. A part of her doubted it, because he'd used no protection, and she'd heard there were things that could prevent this, though they were not mentioned in that erotic book of his.

If he never wanted children, then they needed to seek an annulment of their marriage.

She rose and wrapped a towel around her hair and began to pat herself dry. Trudy arrived and helped her dress in a comfortable pale peach day dress, and she climbed the servant's stairs to the floor where her room was, then had her maid brush her hair dry before the fire.

While Trudy was coiling and pinning her hair, Lia knocked and entered. When she drew closer, she said, "Ian has arrived and would like to know if you are well enough for visitors?"

She met Lia's gaze in the mirror. "What is his mood?"

"Pleasant, I believe," her sister-in-law replied. "He's never been anything less than amiable."

"Could he come up here, so we may speak privately?"

"Of course, he is your husband, Sarah."

"Fine, then send him up." She turned to her fresh-faced maid and said, "We can leave the hair for now and pin it before dinner." As the woman turned to go, Sarah remembered, "Can you ask for a tea tray too, please Trudy?"

The maid nodded, then bobbed a curtsy and was off, leaving her in the room with Lia.

"I am feeling more myself now that I've had some rest and good food," she said. "There are a great many things I think I need some clarity on with my husband before we can proceed in this marriage."

The duchess nodded and said, "Then do not settle for anything less than what you want for your marriage. You are half this union. He should respect *your* voice for *your* desires for *your* union."

"I agree. There is no turning back on the marriage, and I would like a normal husband-wife…," she scanned the room to make sure no servants had entered. "I want a normal marriage bed! Not one where my husband is praying I don't conceive."

"Well, there is only one way not to conceive, and

unless he plans to never take you to his bed again, there will always be the possibility no matter which preventive manner he chooses to practice."

"I agree." Sarah rose and smoothed her pink morning dress. "Will you send him up, please? I am ready to take on my husband."

"Remember to be kind," her sister-in-law added. "You will attract more flies with honey than with vinegar."

She was glad she'd worn this dress. She felt the shade of pastel peach helped her cheeks appear healthier than if she'd worn any another color. And with the natural light coming in from the windows with the curtains pulled open, she hoped she looked better than she did three days ago.

Sarah recognized his booted footfall as he strode with determination down the carpeted hallway. She noticed it was something he always did wherever he went. Suddenly, her door opened and Ian's frame filled the doorway. It was a comical sight actually, one she had no memory of seeing when he came several days earlier. Her husband had to duck his head to enter the room, and his broad shoulders nearly touched the edges to each side. Funny thing, she never thought the doorway particularly narrow or short, but to see *him* come through made her reconsider that.

"You look well again," Ian said.

Why couldn't he greet her as a man who'd missed his wife? Or tell her she looked beautiful? Was she less than what he'd desired? They might have been forced to marry because of her impulsive actions, but couldn't he like her even a little outside of the bed?

Sarah had to stop thinking this way—feeling sorry

for herself. She raised her shoulders and straightened her back. "Thank you, I do feel much better."

He shifted uncomfortably, and she offered him a seat on one of the two chairs near her windows. She watched as he unbuttoned his coat and sat in one of them. The tea cart arrived, and Sarah poured for them both and took the seat opposite him.

"I am glad you have recovered," he said, just before an uneasy silence fell between them. She sipped her tea, and he the same.

She wanted to ask him what had taken him so long and why did he come now. But she felt both questions might sound more accusatory than she would intend for them to be, so they went unspoken. "As am I." Sarah didn't know what else to say in the space between them. She went back to staring at the contents of her tea cup, wondering how she would tell him all of the things she needed to say to him, having reached the decision as she had while bathing just over an hour ago.

"We need to talk," he began

"Where have you…?" She stopped and motioned for him to continue.

He cleared his throat first before speaking. "If you were going to ask where I have been, you had to know I've been on *Revenge*." When she nodded, he offered her a slight smile. "Lucky says your family is returning to Haldenwood from here, as the season is over." She nodded and his facial features became serious. "There is something that we must discuss before I leave for London, then China."

"You are right," she replied, then took the lead asking the first question. "The other night you said you were thankful I had not conceived during the race."

He set the cup on the tea table. "I've spent the last three

days regretting that I upset you," he said. "I think my words may not have come out as I intended Sarah, and I feel the need to clarify."

"Please do," she said. "Because if you cannot make me see your reasoning, then…there can be no future for us." Sarah forced back the tears, refusing to give in to them just yet. "We are done. I want children, Ian."

He pulled at his collar to loosen it some, then ran his hand over his forehead to pinch the bridge of his nose. Sarah could tell these were his nervous actions, things he likely didn't think she knew about him.

"I did not have the idyllic upbringing you had, Sarah. My father sent me away when I was old enough to attend school in England because I had to succeed my grandfather. There is much I did not understand as a child, and there are no letters, no journals, nothing…nothing to help me understand why my father was so willing to part with me. I idolized him and he sent me away."

Her husband stood and began to pace the tiny area between the hearth and where she sat near the window. "When I arrived, my grandfather did not want me in his home. He said that I wasn't fit to wipe mud from his boots. He called my mother a common whore and my father a traitor to the crown. I was sent to Rugby School and on my breaks lived with my aunts, except for that annual meeting I was forced to make to my grandfather. After…." He stopped at the window and looked out on to the back garden. "Well, when I reached a certain age, I never went back to visit him. The man detested me, a child, without knowing me. As soon as I became old enough to refuse to see him, I quit torturing us both."

Sarah watched his back as he struggled with his inner

demons. "Why didn't you go back to Baltimore? Didn't you have friends there?"

He shook his head and Sarah felt sorry for him. "There was nothing left for me in Harbor Village, where I'm from. No one. My mother died when I was a child, I had no siblings, and my father was dead within a year of my leaving."

Her attitude softened, but she still wanted to know why he'd never mentioned this lack of desire for children until now. She wanted children very much. It would devastate her to remain in a marriage with a man she was growing to love if he did not love children as much as she.

Ian turned to face her as he leaned against the window frame. "Obviously, there was plenty of opportunity for you to conceive during the race, and if you had I would have…." He gave her a sheepish shrug of the shoulders. "I guess I would have welcomed a child." He came to her side. "I know you are sad because you did not conceive, but in all honesty, I am happy to not have the added worries and responsibilities of a child at this time. That's not to say I will never…. Sarah?"

She heard loud roaring of water whooshing to the beat of her heart, and it drowned out anything more he was saying. She made out snippets, as bile began to rise in her throat, burning its way out. Running to the chamber pot, she made it just in time.

"I thought you were feeling better," he said, concern evident in his voice. "Shall I ring for your maid?"

Sarah rested back on her heels and nodded. After wiping her mouth, she met his concerned gaze, fully intending to call him out on not sharing this idea of his. "I understand you had a less than loving upbringing, and

I sympathize with that. But...*welcomed?* You *guess* you would have *welcomed* a child?" She was simply astonished at his attitude. "As though it was a visitor and you had a choice? And at any time, did it *ever* cross your mind that I might want to know of this...this...lack of desire for a child?" He turned away. "Perhaps you should go, Ian. I would hate for you to get sick before leaving for China."

"I...." Sarah never heard what else he said because she had to turn her head to the chamber pot again.

"I'm sorry. Please, just leave, Ian."

He stood on the other side of her privacy screen, listening to her heaving the emptiness from her stomach. "I shall return, Sarah," he said. "Before I leave for London. I will come back to make sure you are well."

"Don't bother, Ian. Really, I'll be fine as soon as I get over this upset stomach." She sounded far braver than she felt. And her husband must have understood her loud and clear because he turned and left the room without a glance back.

As soon as he shut the door, she burst into tears.

Chapter Twelve

Summer soon gave way to fall. The miserable wet, cold season had always been Sarah's least favorite time of year. And this autumn was no different. Hearing through family conversations, because she would never ask directly, she learned that Ian and Lucky had gone to the Chinese port of Fuchow to load their ships with crates of tea for England.

Every man on board those two vessels—from the old salts to the young boys—had earned her respect and admiration for the work they did, so she prayed nightly for their safe journey and that all the men she met on both ships would return to their loved ones, including Ian.

Yes, she prayed daily—several times a day, actually—that he would realize she loved him and that he might grow to love her in return. Oh, she was certain he had some sentiment for her. He'd said he missed her, and she held on to that delicate thread, hoping that was his meaning, hoping he was growing to love her as well.

Sarah sat in her bedroom window seat that dreary afternoon in October, watching as a light rain fell. She stared out at the vast, masterfully tended lawn of Haldenwood, the grass beginning to turn its autumnal green-golden color. A light wind blew the first of the dead leaves from the trees, and they began to line the macadam drive in the distance. Nearly the entire length of the drive was lined with oaks planted centuries before her birth, and the duchess's garden designs hadn't changed from the days her grandmother had placed each shrub and bush into the earth when Sarah was a babe. According to Lia, they would not change for as long as she was the duchess, because to look at them, she'd said, reminded her of a woman she loved and respected during the short time they knew one another.

She saw the light carriage come down the drive and knew it was time to ask an enormous favor of Ian's aunts. Sarah prayed they didn't refuse her. She didn't see why they should, as they were her aunts now too. And they would be relieved to know that her brother had given his blessing to the plan, but only after she agreed to his concessions.

She caressed her expanding belly lovingly and thought of her child's future. Ian might be furious when he returned, especially when he learned of the entirety of her doings. But this was her babe, and she was doing what was right for her child and her family's future. Hopefully, her husband would one day see it this way too.

She rest her palms on her belly, feeling the light fluttering of life within. If anything should happen to her during or after the birth, she prayed that when Ian learned of his son or daughter he would be pleased.

Her maid entered the room, notifying her that Ian's aunts had arrived and that she was invited to meet the duchess and the guests in the yellow salon.

"Thank you, Trudy," she said. After checking her appearance in the tall pier glass, she smoothed her skirts and went below. As she entered the salon, she smiled at the two elderly women seated across from Lia. Ian's aunts were about to learn of her changed condition.

"There you are, dear," one elderly twin said.

"Yes, how lovely to see you again," said the other.

Two silver heads bobbed in unison as they commented on her healthful looks. Sarah didn't have to imagine their thoughts at her appearance, because she knew she'd gained weight. They discussed the earl's degrading health and his tenacity to cling to life even when certain death was imminent.

"He is the strongest, most invincible, man we know," said one twin.

The other's turbaned head bobbed. "Oh, yes. He will not pass from this earth until he is ready."

"I am very happy he is doing well and have prayed for him daily. I know that Ian has said he wanted no relationship with the man, but I feel that if his lordship would just make an overture toward peace, surely I can get my husband to speak with him. They need to put this behind them both."

"We agree, dear," replied Lady Stone. "But it's not likely to ever happen."

The room fell silent a moment until Lia said the reason she'd invited the ladies on this afternoon. "I have asked the Ladies Royce and Stone to visit and mentioned that we have a proposition for them."

Sarah nodded. Ian's aunts had learned of their wedding while in Edinburgh as they read the newspaper one morning. And after the earl had once again made an amazing recovery with this latest bout with his bad heart, the ladies returned to Haldenwood to gush over how they were both thrilled with the union. They then confided a deep concern over the rift between their father and their nephew. She couldn't speak of it yet as her plans were not final, but if all went as Sarah was planning, next summer the earl would be at their home for a visit while her husband bounced their child on his knee. Then perhaps Ian and his grandfather would finally make amends or come to some peaceful situation between them. At least that was her plan.

Lia turned to the ladies. "The tenants at Greenwood have finally moved out, and the remodeling and updating have begun in preparation for Sarah's arrival." A maid arrived with the beverage cart and over tea they spoke of the renovations to her mother's dower house that were now underway, and of the modern plumbing going into the home. The ladies ooh-ed and ahh-ed over the work being done, and even recommended several interior designers of their acquaintance.

"The proposition we have for you dears," Lia began, "is rather necessary and of the utmost importance."

"It seems His Grace does not wish for me to reside down in Surrey all alone until my husband returns from China in the spring," Sarah added. "He thinks I should have companions, and this is where you come in."

Sarah nodded to Lia who knew both ladies much better than she did. "You see, ladies, the future Countess Mackeever is expecting a happy event. We would love for you to accompany her to her home and stay with her until her husband returns at the very least…."

"Or for however long you wish," Sarah added, "as I would never presume to tell my husband he cannot captain his ships if that is what he desires."

The sisters both cried out in joy at the news, immediately exclaiming their complete and wholehearted agreement with the plan. Both widowed, the ladies lived together in a cottage on Haldenwood at the invitation of their godson, the duke.

"We accept this honor without hesitation, Your Grace," Lady Stone.

"Absolutely. Imagine," Lady Royce turned to her sister, "Eugenia, a baby! We'll be great-aunts."

"Why, this is simply wonderful news my dear," exclaimed Lady Stone. "We are so very, very pleased."

"That would explain the weight gain, my dear," said Lady Royce sagely. "Why when I carried my Edgar, God rest his soul, I must have gained three stone. Of course, after his birth, it disappeared, albeit slowly."

"Yes, dear, do not worry at all," offered Lady Stone. "All expectant mothers gain weight. You know, that's the *real* reason we retire to the country during our confinement. I shuddered at the thought of having had to appear in public while I was carrying. Why my fingers alone looked like little sausages."

Not to be outdone by her sister, Lady Royce chimed in. "And thank heaven for our long dresses! My legs were so swollen they looked like tree trunks."

Sarah wondered if this was what she had to look forward to for the rest of her confinement—legs the size of tree trunks and growing as big and round as the water fountain in the front drive. She thanked them both for their insight and well-wishes, then said, "I am certain Ian would love to have his favorite aunts in residence. He loves you both very much, you know. And our baby will have family around other than me."

"Only until a sibling comes along." Lady Royce winked at her sister, who agreed with her.

Sarah groaned inwardly as she smiled and nodded to her new relations. She just prayed to make it through this confinement safely. She certainly was not planning beyond that right now. Well, except for the invitation to her new grandfather, which she would send as soon as she was settled in her new home.

"Do you agree with my idea?" she asked.

"Obviously you both like the plan," Lia said. "It would relieve both my husband and myself of the worries we've had about Sarah's move down to Surrey."

"Absolutely."

"We would love to."

The approximate time line for moving was discussed, and it was decided that they'd all move down after the first of the year. This gave the contractors time to complete their jobs and Sarah the opportunity to spend Christmas at Haldenwood with the family. This would give her plenty of time to get comfortable in her home before the early April birth of her son or daughter.

One hour later, after the ladies had gone, Sarah turned to her sister-in-law. "That went over better than I'd expected."

"Why? The ladies are Ian's family as well as Ren's. They are both mothers and familiar with carrying and childbirth. They will know when to send for our physician."

"It was a truly inspired idea. Thank you." Sarah was thankful that Lia understood and even championed her case for living independently to her brother. When they were planning what to say to Ren, Lia had come up with the idea of asking Lady Royce and Lady Stone to be her companions. Her brother would only agree if she would take them and keep a hired security specialist among her household staff, as they did here and at Caversham House in Town.

"You're welcome. I'm full of wonderful ideas on occasion."

Sarah linked arms with Lia, and together they went up the stairs, Lia slowing her pace to keep up with Sarah's. "I feel so bloated, Lia. Everywhere."

"That's normal dear. Do not let Trudy tighten your stays. In fact, I'll let you in on a secret. I never wore a corset the entire time I was pregnant. With all three children. And I would advise you to do likewise, even though you think it helps you fit into a gown."

"Then I shall need a dressmaker to pay a visit, because I already cannot wear most of them." When they reached the landing, she turned to Lia. "You know, I've been wondering lately if there isn't more than one babe in here." She rubbed her belly. "It feels as though there is an entire litter of children playing inside me."

"Hmmm," Lia took in her appearance. She held Sarah's hands and felt how swollen they were, then she studied her ankles and face. "You are swollen. Perhaps we should call for Prescott to pay a visit. He might be retired, but I trust his opinion."

The very next morning, before her brother had a chance to leave the house, Sarah asked him for a meeting in his office. This was the second part of her plan: providing security to Ian and her child should anything happen to her while she gave birth.

"I would like to pay Ian's portion of the bank loan he took out to purchase the two boats. Could you find out which bank holds the note and arrange for this? Also, release my dowry into his name, leaving my inheritance to me and our child."

"Are you certain this is what you want? Even knowing it goes against Ian's wishes?" Ren asked.

His once coal-black hair was now peppered with gray, giving him a more distinguished appearance, if that was possible. As a child, she used to think he was frightening. Now she wondered why she ever thought that. He'd never raised a hand to her, nor his voice either, except when she deserved a lecture on her reckless behavior—a pattern of hers since her youth. There was also a time when she was very young that she thought Ren was her father, as she didn't remember her father or her mother. When she'd grown old enough to understand, Lia had explained as gently as she could the fact that her parents had passed away many years prior and that her brother had taken on the great responsibility of raising his two sisters as his father would have wished.

From that moment on, she worshipped her brother.

"Yes," Sarah replied. "There's more than enough money in my inheritance to pay for the refurbishing of Greenwood Manor, and for me to live on quite comfortably. Ian should receive the dowry as he would if this were a normal union."

"Did you know Greenwood is a part of the dowry? Do you want me to have that removed and replaced?"

"I didn't know that." She thought a moment, then replied, "Yes. I want Greenwood as part of my inheritance. I think you should replace the fair value of the property in the dowry with the equal amount in shares of that new rail company you bought into."

His gray eyes widened appreciatively. "Good choice."

She gave her brother a sly grin. "I guess I've learned a thing or two from you sitting at the same dinner table all these years."

"Good, I'll have my secretary make inquiries as to which bank holds his note and send for the banker. Then I'll have him send for Graham Davies for the legal contracts."

"I remember his name. Is he the new partner in Michael's firm? Would you recommend him?"

"Yes. He's been with the firm for years. I trust him with my own affairs."

"Then I shall use him for mine."

They were silent a moment, then Ren said, "I've always heard it was unwise for men to educate their women, for fear that one day they might want their independence. But I'm glad that you and Elise had an education beyond needlepoint and dancing. It makes me proud to know that as you go out into the world you will not be hoodwinked by bankers, brokers, or tradesmen because of your sex."

"Yes, my education was rather unconventional. Why, if a tradesman were to attempt such foolishness, I could shoot their toes off before they knew I held a gun in my pockets." One day she would have to thank him for the opportunities he gave her, allowing her to grow up as she did.

Ren laughed. "Not to mention chase him down whilst astride a horse with no saddle."

They laughed a moment, then stared at each other, Sarah with tears in her eyes. Her life was different now. She was no longer the girl of whom they spoke.

"I shall teach my own daughters the exact same skills you taught me. And if I need any assistance you'll just have to come and help me."

"You know I will, baby sister."

By late November, Sarah had been confined to her suite at Haldenwood. What made the confinement even worse for someone like her—someone who actually enjoyed a little solitude every so often—was the fact she now had around-the-clock companionship. She couldn't be alone even if she wanted solitude. She was the girl who could sail alone on their private lake for hours on end. She was the girl who could go on a walk or ride alone for hours and return reinvigorated and ready to take on the day's tasks.

A bed was moved into the adjoining dressing room, and Trudy now shared her suite. When her maid wasn't in the room with her, there was a constant stream of visitors. Her brother, her sister-in-law, the Ladies Royce and Stone, and her nieces. Of course, Dr. Prescott made his weekly trip up from London for his cherry tarts, and to check on her. As he was retired, he usually spent one night at Haldenwood then returned to Town the following day. Each week he pronounced her in good health for one her size given that she was carrying more than one child.

To keep herself busy, she did some sewing and embroidery. But as she'd never been good with a needle before, every attempt she made wound up looking like a child's first work. So she left the embroidery of the baby linens to ones with more nimble fingers.

She did a great deal of reading during this time as she found the belly a useful ledge on which to rest the book, though her arms did tire of remaining upright. Occasionally the moving babes would shake the book causing her to lose focus on the page. But she did manage to read nearly every romantic story in the house, even sending to London for newer titles. And as time slowly passed, she grew larger and rounder.

On the day after Christmas, Prescott confined her to the bed. To make matters even worse, she could not find one comfortable position to make bed rest any easier. She tried propping herself in every manner possible with a few pillows, then with quite a few more pillows, and also with no pillows. None of it made any difference.

In mid-February, a few days before Candlemas, Sarah didn't think she would make early April, when the babies were due. She very nearly was an invalid in that she could not manage to walk the few steps to her privy without assistance. One look in the hand mirror confirmed what she'd suspected, that she'd become a bloated caricature of her former self. It was enough to give a woman the dismals, except that she had a wonderful family supporting her.

As the weeks went by, she alternately cried because she missed Ian and laughed when she thought of his heartfelt speech about being thankful she wasn't with child yet. Ha! She wondered what he would think if he knew of the two gifts he'd given her.

One afternoon as she lay propped up against her headboard, she'd told Lia about the book, and her sister-in-law laughed. Sarah didn't tell her that she was now in possession of said manual. "I found it and read the entire book, cover to cover, while I was cooped up in the cabin. Ian never knew I'd read it." She felt the heat rushing to her cheeks. "It was rather arousing." Glancing down at her hands, she said, "Poor Ian. He never stood a chance once I'd decided to put to practice some of the lessons I read."

"Those manuals are produced more for their titillation factor than anything else," Lia said. "I'm sure there were drawings of positions and even color plates inside it."

Sarah nodded.

"Men are such base, primal creatures sometimes. If they only knew the way to a woman's heart is through her brain rather than her privates, they would be so much better off."

Sarah blushed, too embarrassed to admit that Ian had gotten to her heart by making her entire body feel good. Oh, he always spoke with her as though what she had to say were of significance and value. She supposed that was stimulating her brain. But he definitely stimulated her body first.

"What are you thinking?" Lia poured more tea. "You have an odd smile on your face."

"He spoke to me as an equal. And aside from the men in our family, there are few men I know who do not talk down to me." Sarah felt close to crying, but held back her tears. "It's one of the things I love about him. He's not like the rakes and dandies a lady meets socializing within our set. Ian's…different."

"Lucky says it's because he's American."

"He might be right, but I have no way of knowing as I've never met another American man." She nibbled a cracker. "I know his childhood was not as privileged as mine, but it has made him a man that I admire for his drive to accomplish his dreams. I just wish he'd realize that life doesn't always follow the time line you set for your goals. One cannot live by a timetable of planned events. Ian has his life mapped out. Having a wife and family was not something he wanted for several years yet—until he had the misfortune of crossing my path."

"Men are also obtuse creatures," Lia commiserated. "Sometimes they focus on this one path to a dream when, in fact, there are many paths to the same destination. Some of those paths are rocky and others more smooth. But even the rockiest path can be made easier when one has the love and support of family to help him along the way."

After Lia had left, Sarah thought about her sister-in-law's words. Ian may not have had that supportive family before, but he did now.

Her husband had been focused on the one path, waiting until his grandfather died, to reach for his destination—marriage and a family. Then Sarah had come along and taken him on a path other than that which he'd chosen. Thus, like a horse wearing blinders, he could not see his other options. He'd become frightened because it wasn't what he was familiar with, what he'd mapped out and planned.

So, she thought, if she were to continue using that analogy, she would remove the blinders from Ian's eyes and acclimate him to his new surroundings. She would show him there was nothing to fear by taking a different road so long as the destination was the same.

As long as he achieved his dreams.

This was the least she could do for him, because she was the one who'd interfered with his plans.

CHAPTER THIRTEEN

New Year's Eve, 1835, Port of Fuchow

"My men are all accounted for. Are we still thinking of leaving the day after tomorrow?" Lucky asked. "Or do you need more time?"

The sizable room was bustling with men from nearly every major country in the world, from the hundreds of ships that lay at anchor just off shore or in the harbor. Every one of them here trading wares and goods for what the locals called China Gold. Tea.

"No. All my men are present," Ian replied, "and supplies restocked. As far as I'm concerned we can leave on the morning tide." He lifted the mug and brought it to his lips, again wondering what Sarah was doing. It was something he did frequently to help him pass the time. He'd been counting the days since he'd last seen her, upset with himself for leaving her as he did, feeling deep remorse for upsetting her as he did. "Besides, you know how that old saying goes—both men and boats rot in port." He tipped it, downing the last of the nasty brew the Chinese bar-keep called English ale, then pushed the crude wooden mug aside, making a face as he swallowed. "Ugh." When he opened his eyes, he stared at his friend. "What was your final tonnage?"

"Nine hundred seventy-six thousand pounds. What'd you top out at?"

"Nine hundred ninety-two thousand. I've even got crates stowed in my cabin," Ian said.

"Why'd you do that?"

"I'm not using it. It was wasted space."

"Why are you not using your cabin?" Lucky asked.

"Because I'm more comfortable in a hammock." That wasn't the truth of it, and Lucky knew it. But Ian couldn't tell his friend the truth, that he saw Sarah everywhere on his own damned boat. Even the damned cat missed her, choosing to sleep by the cabin door, waiting for someone to let her in. Traces of Sarah's presence remained in every corner, nook, and cranny of the entire ship. Yet they lingered most in his private quarters, where her scent still resided in the pillows and blankets. The stain on the sheet, though it had been washed many times since that long ago evening, forced him to face her lost maidenhead each time he threw back his covers. And one evening he found the organization of his clothes press had irritated him so much that he'd spent nearly an hour mussing it up.

"You're a fool, my friend. Why don't you just admit you love her? And that you miss her? There's no shame in it."

Ian ignored Lucky, for to think about how he'd upset her hurt more than he wanted to acknowledge. "I've got an idea," he nearly shouted. "On our next trip here, let's bring real single malt and real ale to trade, instead of the usual textiles and such. These poor sots might pay a fortune for good Scotch and brew."

Lucky shook his head, his dark brown hair nearly as long as Ian's own. "Let's look into that. But I think you're avoiding the question."

It was only the two of them sitting at the table near the entrance, and Ian looked around them, then met his friend's brown-eyed stare. "I have been nothing but cruel to her. From the onset I said things. Things that hurt her. And... I've never apologized to her."

"Then make that the first thing you do when you get home because...." Lucky looked as though he wanted to say something but caught himself. Then he said, "Sarah loves you. Though God only knows why."

"She can't possibly," Ian said, remembering every cruel word he'd said to her. "That's impossible. I mean... she's never said as much."

Lucky looked as though he wanted to say something, but he held his tongue. Then he motioned to the servant as he passed them and asked the man for another glass. "You want another?"

"Why not?" Ian replied. "The stuff might taste like pond scum, but it's the only thing to be had that's tolerable."

After the old Chinaman returned with two more crudely carved wood mugs, Lucky's gaze became serious.

"She can't possibly hold any affection for me," Ian said. He stared out the window at the people walking on the raised wooded footpath, the muddy road below it nothing but a deep quagmire. Like his jumbled emotions. "I told her from the beginning that I have nothing to offer her. She accepted that."

Lucky turned his gaze away sharply, appearing disgusted with him. "I gave my word to her that I would not say anything, that I would keep out of your affairs, but I find I cannot keep that promise. Hopefully, one day she'll forgive me." Lucky didn't look at him as he spoke and the mug between his hands began to darken from his constant rubbing. "I keep thinking that if I were in your position, I would want to know. Especially since…."

"What are you talking about?"

Lucky took another swig of his Chinese ale. "When I went home before we sailed, I saw our family physician getting into his carriage. I thought nothing of it, and later asked my sister if everything was alright, and she said Sarah was not feeling up to snuff. Because I remembered she was sick in Liverpool, I went to see her for myself because I wanted to wish her well." Lucky's dark eyes met Ian's. The look bespoke a seriousness he'd rarely seen in Lucky—the depth of which unsettled him. "Ian, there's something you should know. You'll learn of it all when we return, so it might be better to use this trip to prepare yourself."

Lucky fell silent, frustrating Ian. "What on earth are you trying to say? Just spit it out, man."

"Sarah is carrying your child."

Suddenly the anguish on her face that night in Liverpool tore at him, and he felt no more than the lowliest insect that crawled the earth.

"No," Ian muttered. "She said she didn't believe…." Ian tried to process what Lucky had said and what he remembered seeing the two times he had seen her since arriving in Liverpool. She had been sick, but from the stomach illness, not from carrying his child. Sarah would have told him that!

Then he remembered what he'd said to her, and she confirmed that she wasn't carrying. So, could she have been telling him what she thought he wanted to hear? Very likely. That would be just like his Sarah.

Ian didn't take any more time to reflect on this new

information. He just downed the nearly full mug of bitter liquid in three chugs then slammed the thing on the table. He stood, swaying slightly. "I sail on the morning tide. Devil take it that it's New Year's Day." He stormed from the room without so much as a look back to his friend. When he reached his gig, the first thing he did before climbing aboard was heave the contents of the last two hours in that miserable hell hole the Chinese called a tavern.

He had to hurry home. He had to reach Sarah.

Ian pushed homeward hard, keeping *Revenge*'s masts at full sail for as much of the time as possible to catch as much of the wind as possible. He set and led the return course, following as close as possible to the open-sea route they'd taken coming to China. From Fuchow, they sailed to Manila, then Malaca, from Malaca to Ceylon, then to Madagascar, reaching Cape Town late in February. While rounding the Cape of Good Hope, he hit some stormy weather, lost both topgallants on the fore-mast and spent more time in port than he'd wanted replacing the canvas and rigging.

Ian felt guilty for the stress he'd put on his crew to get him home swiftly and let them have time in port in rotating shifts. This proved a critical mistake for he lost three good men, killed in a drunken brawl in which several Dutchmen had drawn pistols. In his investigation, no one could tell him what had precipitated the fight, and the authorities were unwilling to search for the men responsible. Now he was charged with relaying this tragic news to their expectant families. He decided to do so in person when he delivered their pay to the widows. News such as that should never come from a messenger, but from him because he was responsible for each man under his command.

As his repairs were near completed and he didn't want to spend any more time there than he had to, he scrambled to find replacements for his three dead crewmen and came up with two Norwegians, both of whom were veteran sailors. Just when he'd given up hope of finding a third man, a native approached him on the dock near where his ship sat moored. The man begged him to follow him partway into an alleyway and against his better judgment, Ian did, staying within sight of the boat.

"Good-sah," the young man said in coarse English, his eyes scanning the faces of the crowds moving around them. The man was tall, nearly six feet in height. He appeared healthy, lean and muscular, the dark skin of his shaved head shining in the sun. His feet were bare and his clothes too small.

"Yes?" With the way the man acted, watchful and skittish, Ian wondered if he was a runaway slave. He looked to make sure they weren't attracting attention.

"Need help, good-sah?"

"Do you want to sail? To work?"

"Yes." The man finally looked Ian in the eyes. He spoke slowly, as though trying to find the correct words in a language unfamiliar to him. "I work on ship for you, good-sah."

"How old are you?"

"Twenty summers, good-sah."

"Have you ever been on a ship?" At this, the man nodded his head. "The work is hard, but the pay is good."

He gave Ian a questioning look. "You pay gold?"

"Not gold, British pounds. I pay my men well. But I also demand loyalty in return." The man nodded again. He had an eager, expectant look in his dark eyes. But something more, something Ian couldn't quite put his finger on at that moment.

"Do you have family?" He shook his head, and Ian continued, "You would be gone for a year or more." The man agreed. "What is your name?"

"Tally, good-sah." He sneaked a quick peak around the corner of the alley, then turned a quick, expectant glance at Ian. "Tally."

"Tally." Ian wondered if the rest of the crew would accept a black man working with them. Right at that moment, the smell of spices and food cooking deeper in the alleyway caused his stomach to growl. Then an idea dawned on him. "Tally, can you cook?"

"Ah, Tally good cook," the man said suddenly animated and smiling. "Best cook in village! Best cook!"

Ian was sold. If the man said he could cook, he had a job. He did the mental sorting of his crew. He'd put Goran back on deck and have Tally in the kitchen with Seamus.

Too, Ian also wondered if this native were even a free man. He wasn't sure of the repercussions for taking another man's property, if in fact Tally was trying to run away, but the need for another pair of hands and a strong back on his already skeleton-staffed ship was crucial. "Tally, are you a free man?"

The man's eyes grew wide, then he shut them as he sighed. He visibly deflated as though all his hope had flown away on that breath. "Tally wants to be free man."

"I value honesty, Tally, thank you." Obviously Tally was a man desperate for freedom. It was something Ian had seen as a child growing up in Baltimore. "Let's get you on that ship, quickly." Ian turned and strode toward *Revenge.* When he looked back, the man had not moved. Ian motioned with his hands. "Come on, Tally!" And his new sailor stepped in close behind him.

Once on board, Ian led Tally down the companionway to his cabin. "Wait for me here." Then he returned to the deck and crew. He made clear that he expected no argument about his decision and if any man had a problem with it he was free to leave. When no man made a move to go, Ian clasped his hands behind his back. "Say nothing to no one. Once we clear this port, our new cook's helper will be a free man."

As he turned to go below, Ian saw a commotion develop on the dock as several men, both white and black, searched the area where he stood minutes earlier. He scowled at the men scattered around the deck. "If anyone comes aboard, say nothing."

"I ain't sayin' a thing, Cap'n," one sailor said. "I jus' hope he can cook somethin' other than gruel."

In the end, no one came aboard, and the next morning both ships pulled out of Cape Town, headed for St. Helena. From there, they sailed for the Verde Islands, then Lisbon, their last port before reaching London. He continued sailing hard, and when they reached Portugal, he surrendered to the fact that he needed to hire more men. While waiting on supplies, he went in search of two more crewmen and found them in the form of an old salt who swore he was handy in a galley and his son, who admitted he wasn't.

After sharing a meal and bottle of wine with them, he hired them and sent them to Nigel. Lucky too, hired several additional men, having come to the same conclusion. Both men's ships were running understaffed.

Ian and Lucky sat in the outdoor cafe on a small plaza near the docks, finishing their wine. "I'm thinking we'll need even more men," Ian said, "but I want to see what our profit is on this run. If we can, I'd like to add in the cost of more sailors in next year's budget."

Lucky nodded, then changed the topic by mentioning something Ian had thought of every moment of every day since he learned of it. "She would have had the babe by now," Lucky said. "Have you thought about what you're going to say to her?"

"Yes."

"Good." Lucky finished his wine, then asked, "Care to race home? I'll put up a bottle of Ren's best Scotch."

"You're on."

"What are you going to put up?"

"Nothing," Ian said through his smile. "I've already proven I can beat you."

It was one thing to race to get back home to beat your friend in a casual competition. But this was different. He couldn't wait to see his wife and their son or daughter. Ian needed to apologize to Sarah for his behavior before he'd left all those many months ago. He'd begun to think about the fact that he'd treated her callously before he left, and after eight months, he missed Sarah terribly. She also now had a babe. Their babe.

Later, the two men headed back to the boat and took a shortcut down a side street. Tall wooden shanties, residence lodgings they appeared to be, lined both sides of the path, blocking the sunshine. Several families seemed to be packed into each room, and children hung out the narrow windows. Laundry lines hung like spider webs overhead, and the sounds of women yelling and children crying, along with scents of rich, spicy meals as they cooked, filled the alley.

A young girl carrying a produce sack approached them from a recessed doorway. Her dark hair was matted to her head, and the skin of her face held a greenish-tint in areas, telling Ian she'd been beaten. Her jaw was swollen, and her nose looked to have been broken several times. She appeared no older than fifteen, a child really. His heart twisted at her plight.

She pushed the tied burlap sack into Ian's arms. She spoke quickly. Ian didn't understand a word of what she said. But she obviously wanted him to take the bag. Once he held the bag in his hands, the girl turned and ran down the alley in the opposite direction. He tried to follow sight of her as she wound her way into the crowd, but soon lost her.

"Did you understand what she just said?"

"She spoke so fast. I didn't catch it all either," Lucky replied. "But I did make one out one word, *levar*, which I think means *to take*. She obviously wants you to have the bag." He turned to continue down the street. "Are you coming?"

Curiosity filled him as he hefted the bag over his shoulder and followed Lucky. After a few steps, the contents began to move within the bag. At first, he thought the girl had given him a gift of food, maybe some bread. But she didn't look the type to have any extra when it came to food. Now he thought perhaps a few puppies or kittens as the thing began making noise.

"Damn! Lucky stop. I think this is alive. It's moving and making noises."

"You really have had the luck this trip, haven't you? First, you lose three good salts, then that African seeks you out over all the other ship captains in port and now...." Lucky's words died slowly as he saw what Ian lifted from the bag.

This was no puppy or litter of kittens. Squirming and mewling pathetically, the little bundle wore only the blanket and a rag covering its bottom. Both pieces of cloth were filthy and worn-through in areas from laundering. He moved the material covering the child's face and felt the breath slammed from his lungs. One look at the sunken eyes of indeterminate color, gray pallor, and bloated belly, and he began to curse a string of obscenities that would make an old salt cringe.

"Good God," Lucky shouted, causing the infant to make pathetic crying-like mewling sounds.

"Let's find the authorities...a church...someone...and turn it over. They can figure out what to do with it," Ian said, as Lucky stepped closer to inspect the babe. Ian's breath caught in his throat and he cursed. What in hell was the child thinking to hand over this babe to strangers? It couldn't possibly be hers because she didn't look to be more that a child herself.

"Hand it over," Lucky said. "Poor thing is half-starved."

Lucky took the infant from him, carrying it carefully and naturally. "How do you know this?"

"Long story," was all Lucky said, as Ian scanned the alleyway for an officer of some sort.

The two of them soon waited in a room in a shabby building not too far from the port. The local who led them here had said in broken English that this was an orphanage. The sounds coming from the infant were wearing on Ian. A part of him wanted to throttle the girl who'd dumped the baby on him, but the other part of him began to understand her intent, especially as he looked around him.

The girl had been hoping to give a better life to the child, whether hers or a sibling. That had to be it. Why else would she just give away an infant? Her circumstance didn't appear too healthy or comfortable, perhaps she wanted her offspring to have more.

A man of middle years, with a paunched belly and greased hair, entered the room, followed by a gray-haired woman, all in black, though not a nun. The woman made for Lucky who still held the child and extended her arms. He reluctantly handed the infant over.

After explaining to the man how the babe came to be in their custody, Ian watched as the woman carried it to a table in the corner of the room. She unwrapped the child's blanket and bottom cloth and held the squirming, crying infant up.

Ian and Lucky both watched as the woman lifted the naked babe who suddenly offered up a strong howl. The woman disappointedly shook her head.

"A girl," the older man stated, sounding as though the child wasn't worth the cloth she was wrapped in.

"Does that matter?" Ian asked, incensed at the attitude of the pair.

"A boy child can grow to be a worker. A girl child is worthless. No man wishes to marry an orphan, and Lisbon does not need another prostitute." He shook his head. "Perhaps you could try the church orphanage. See if they have room for another girl child." The woman re-bundled the babe in the same dirty linens and handed it back to Lucky.

"She's hungry," Lucky said. Ian wondered what his

friend was about. "We'll make a generous donation to your orphanage in return for some milk and a small goat."

"What are you thinking, Lucky?" Ian asked. "You're a single man. Do you think to bring the girl home and raise her as a daughter? Surely the church orphanage will take her if we make the same donation to them?"

"And have her grow to live a life of poverty and want? We can provide so much more for her. Lia will help me. I know she will. In fact, if I were to turn my back on this babe, Lia would be more disappointed in me than I would be in myself."

Two hours later, with a bottle of warm milk for the infant and leading a goat by a rope around the neck, they boarded *Avenger*. Ian chuckled at their odd luck. "We are a pair, you know. We cannot say no to people in need. Me with Tally, and you with…. What will you name her?"

Ian hoped the child survived the remainder of the voyage. If she did, she was going to have a much brighter future now that she was in Lucky's hands. Admittedly, Ian had a moment of doubt with regard to Lucky taking the child and keeping her, being he was a single gentleman without a home of his own either.

Then Ian saw the look on his friend's face as the old woman intimated that a girl child was worthless as naught but a future prostitute, and that's when he knew Lucky and his family would be the perfect home for the child. Lucky already had a strong fatherly instinct in him having been raised in such a large family with so many children around.

"I'll think of something. First we need to get her home and have Prescott take a look at her. If she survives, we shall christen her in the church. Perhaps alongside your son or daughter."

The men aboard the ship just shook their heads and went about their duties. Ian followed Lucky into his cabin and watched as he took a drawer, emptied the contents on the table and placed a pillow inside. Then he laid the baby on the table next to the makeshift cradle and unwrapped her.

"She smells like she needs a fresh napkin," Lucky said. "What do I do?"

"I haven't the slightest. Perhaps we can ask one of the crewmen if they have any experience with babies?"

"Good idea." Ian then went up to the main deck and began asking around. Most of the men gave him a bizarre look as they replied in the negative until one lad stepped forward.

"I used to care for my baby sister while mum worked when I was little. I can do it."

With the situation now well in hand, they left Lisbon harbor the next day on the afternoon tide, any thought of race between the two now long forgotten, though Ian continued sailing hard. This time his men were eager and anxious to be home, so they didn't complain at the pace he'd set. Ian and his crew arrived at the mouth of the Thames on the morning of April twenty-third, making him one day closer to seeing Sarah and meeting his new son or daughter.

Ian wondered how she was doing and hoped she might be at least somewhat happy to see him. He missed her terribly and cared for her deeply and didn't know how he was going to convey this to her. He didn't have the sensitivity in such situations as Lucky did. He needed to figure it out somehow, because he had to apologize to her for his earlier crass behavior.

During this entire journey to China and back, he had learned one thing—that he needed to be more of a gentle man, not just a gentleman. He needed to think not only of Sarah's wants and needs, but also her reactions before he acted.

While the stevedores and his crew unloaded the crates of tea from his boat, Ian went in search of the ledger he hadn't needed since the last tea run he'd made over a year ago. He thought about that run and this one and decided that the retrofitted lead plates on the keel had definitely made the boat easier to maneuver. Too, because of the reduced ballast, they were able to increase their capacity by nearly two hundred thousand pounds. While the first run had been profitable, and had paid for the upgrade and refurbishing, it had left very little after paying his crew and the bank.

This run, however, would make them a tidy sum. Enough to give his crew a bonus on top of their wages, pay the bank, and deposit a nice slice for him and Lucky each.

"Where's that bank ledger?" Ian muttered in his now-empty cabin, the tea crates having been removed earlier that day. "Damn it all. She organized the room almost a year ago, and I still can't find a thing." He remembered being thankful that she'd cleaned and organized the cabin at the time. But now? Something told him that he'd need to get her a home soon or she'd be rearranging his entire boat. Moving across the room to the bed, he pulled open the drawers one by one, pushed the contents aside and closed them when he didn't find what he sought. In the last drawer, his bank ledger rested on top of the stack of books. As Ian lifted the leather-bound book from its resting place, he saw a scrap of vellum sticking out from between two pages.

He lifted the folded sheet and opened it. As he began to read the elegant, feminine script, his heart fell to his gut. He hoped it wasn't what he feared, that Sarah regretted their marriage. He knew he was gruff with her at times, but he would work to change that part of his character because he wasn't going to lose her.

Ian,

Although I landed upon your ship quite accidentally. I will confess to you now I am not sorry I did so.

My time with you has meant more to me than you could know. Even though I fought the marriage in New York harbor, the voyage home showed me how very wrong I was in my initial assessment of your character. You are a caring, exemplary leader for your crew, and they respect you for it.

I have fallen in love with you. Because I feared your reaction to my words, I tried to show you through my actions how deep my feelings for you have grown. I had hoped that when we were together you would recognize my sentiments. As of this writing (the night before we arrive in Liverpool), I'm not sure you did.

Even so, I believe one day you will make a wonderful father. And if what I suspect is true, that blessing will occur before you arrive home from your tea run.

Godspeed my captain.
Yours, etc.,
S.

What did he do now? Sarah loved him. Or at least she loved him at the time of the writing of this note. She'd somehow fallen in love with him even after telling her he'd felt trapped into the marriage. And when she was upset over not carrying a babe, instead of consoling her he told her he was happy she wasn't.

How much more insensitive can a man be?

Not that she likely held any love for him now, he hoped when he arrived to Haldenwood he could make it up to her. He didn't deserve her love after the things he'd said. He just hoped if he came to her with his heart in his hands she would forgive him and want him back in her life. And if she said no, he'd remind her that they were already wed, then use his charm to force her to fall in love with him again.

He looked the note over once more. At the time she wrote this, she suspected she might be carrying his child. He sensed her hopeful longing in the letter. But something must have happened between this day and the next evening when he saw her in tears in her room in Liverpool. There she'd been upset thinking she was not. Several days later, she was still ill. He wondered how Lucky could say with certainty that Sarah was carrying.

If she was still carrying, she would have had the babe by now.

He wondered if he had a son or a daughter. Ian realized he would be happy whether Sarah had a child or did not. But there simply was no way of knowing yet.

And if there was a babe, he could only hope to live up to Sarah's expectations of him. She'd said he would make a fine father. Now he had to work hard just to be

LOVING SARAH

half the man she thought he was.

He'd didn't have any more time to think on that right then. There was a banker in town waiting for him and Lucky. He moved to set the note down on the bed and saw a post script on the back. Lifting the sheet, he read her final words.

Please forgive me for borrowing one of your instructional texts. I have been studying it intently since coming aboard. If you have a need for it again, please let me know and I shall return it—personally.

What instructional text could she mean? There were all manner of texts in the drawer, most remainders from his university days. Since they were all books he intended to incorporate into a library one day, he'd kept them. So he'd like to have it back, though it might be rather absurd for him to ask his wife to return it, as they'd soon be sharing the same library.

Curiosity got the better of him, and he wondered which topic had aroused her interest. After he returned from the bank, he'd have to see if he could figure it out. Perhaps if he presented her with a gift of another text in the same field of interest, she might be slightly more inclined to forgive him for the way he's treated her.

"I don't know what could be keeping my partner," Ian told the bank's manager, Mr. Chumworthy. "Normally, he's the one who's on time and I'm the one who runs late."

The portly, balding gentleman smiled behind his spectacles and rubbed his hands over the desktop. "We can give him a few more minutes. Beyond that, and we shall have to reschedule. I have another appointment in fifteen minutes."

"As do I, sir," Ian replied, knowing he still faced the unpleasant task of delivering the pay of his deceased crewmen to their widows before going in search of Sarah.

No sooner had he finished saying the words, than the banker's secretary knocked on the door and introduced the Conte di Lorenzo. Lucky strode in, the ledger for *Avenger* in his hand, and greeted the banker.

Lucky took a seat next to him, then leaned over and whispered, "When we are done here we must speak. It's very urgent."

"Now then, how may I be of assistance to you today, gentlemen?" Chumworthy said, politely ignoring the whispered conversation.

Ian spoke up. "We are here to pay you the annual payment plus interest on the boats and make a request."

"I'm sorry, Mr. Chumworthy," Lucky said. "My partner does not know of the developments that occurred while we were away. They were the reason I was detained."

Ian gave a half smile as he turned a curious, wide-eyed look at Lucky, then at Mr. Chumworthy. "What developments? Is there something I should be made aware of?"

"Mr. Ross-Mackeever," the banker said as he smiled at Ian, "the remaining balance on your half of the mortgage on your ships was paid in full several months back."

"What? There must be some mistake. According to my ledger, there is sixty percent on the principal, plus the accrued interest, remaining." He looked at Lucky. "We have six years left. Don't we?" After telling her brother to keep the monies in her name, Ren had gone and paid off his half of the mortgage on the two boats with Sarah's dowry. Ian wondered where he'd come up with the idea for that. It had to be Sarah's doing. She was the only person who knew how much these two ships meant to the start of his business, and she had the motive and capital to do it.

Damn her. These boats were his and Lucky's. His business and banking transactions were his affair and not her family's.

Mr. Chumworthy showed Ian and Lucky the contracts that his secretary had pulled prior to the meeting, and clearly both sets were marked paid in full.

Paid. He owed no more on his mortgage to the bank. But why did she do it? He told Sarah and Lucky, and later her brother and Lord Camden as well, that he wanted none of her money. Why did she go against his wishes?

Ian muttered a quiet curse. "What else has been done?"

"Nothing," said Chumworthy. "That was all. His Grace sent a legal representative with contracts, which had been signed and witnessed by that same representative and the Earl of Camden. After satisfying the balance, the remainder of your wife's dowry was placed in an account bearing your name." The banker passed him a small leather-bound ledger with his name embossed in gold leaf on the cover.

Ian grabbed the book, then stood and rather stiffly thanked the man before marching from his office. Instead of hiring a hack, he chose instead to walk to the docks. He needed the air. His head spun with the news. Damn her! He wondered how many people, aside from Mr. Chumworthy, now thought him an opportunist for marrying an heiress.

"Ian, wait!" Lucky called out from behind him.

Ian ignored him and kept his stride intent on his destination, which right then was away from any member of that damned family. Soon he heard running footfalls as his partner came up from behind.

"Stop. We must talk."

Ian kept on in the direction of the dock. He felt a hand on his shoulder, and it yanked him around.

Ian threw his hand off. "You were there. I told her brother I did not want the money. Silly me, I thought he understood." He tried to leave, but Lucky stepped in front of him. Ian stepped around him, unwilling to listen to anything he had to say regarding his wife just yet.

"You stupid American," Lucky hissed. "This is our way here! Ren did what he had to do to protect you, your children, and Sarah. And if you intend to upset her in any way, I'll not tell you where she is. Do you understand me? You self-centered, arrogant ass...." Lucky grabbed his arm, and the look he gave Ian made him stop in his tracks.

Ian felt the wind leave his sails. He knew the English customs and her brother, as guardian, had done nothing out of the ordinary. It was, as Lucky had said, custom here to dower the bridegroom. Marriages here were rarely love matches. More often than not, they were financial transactions in which the father of the marriageable-aged daughter sought the best title for what he could afford to dower.

He considered what Lucky had said. "You're right. I'm sorry. I guess I am often proud to the point of extreme."

"Damn right you are. But I wouldn't be your friend if I didn't understand you and forgive you."

"Thank you," he replied.

Lucky clapped him on the back. "Think nothing of it."

"So, is that why you were late? Does Sarah know we're home? How is she?"

"I went to Caversham House and turned the little one over into the capable hands of Mrs. Steen. No, Sarah's not here in London and I'm going to assume she does not know we are, as we've been here for less than twenty-four hours and I have not yet sent anyone out to notify the family of our return. They're still in the country."

"How is Sarah? Is our babe well?"

"No one would say. Though I was ordered to bring you without haste to Haldenwood."

Ian's heart sank into his belly as he worried about Sarah and the child. He closed his eyes and whispered a plea to the heavens. When he opened them, Lucky's face held no hint of his usual jovial manner. "I have an odd feeling. Something doesn't seem right to me, and I'd feel better if we got you to Haldenwood as soon as possible."

Chapter Fourteen

Ian followed his brother-in-law, the formidable Duke of Caversham, as he led him and Lucky into the study at Haldenwood. His Grace sat behind the broad, intricately carved, highly polished desk, and Lord Camden sat on the edge of it facing them.

"What took you so long?" Ren asked. "You arrived yesterday."

"Business," Lucky said. "We got here as quick as we could."

The atmosphere of the room weighed on Ian, and he knew intuitively something was not right. "Where's my wife?"

"Ian," Ren said, "we must talk before you see her."

"Is she well? Did she have the baby? Is it well?" Having been cooped up inside the coach for over five hours, he now paced the bare expanse of carpet before the chairs facing His Grace and Lord Camden. The odd reception in the home fed the nervous fear building inside him. Ian's heart began to race as he sensed tragedy hanging in the atmosphere of the entire home.

"Ian, have a seat," Michael said gently as he pointed to a chair, then waited until Ian sat before him. "There is no easy way to tell you this other than to come right out and say it. Sarah lost both babes. Twin boys."

"They were born prematurely, Ian. We are so very sorry," Ren said.

Ian just stared at his brother-in-law, unable to think as he attempted to digest the news. His heart twisted with pain for his wife. He cleared his throat, then swallowed back the knot of nerves that threatened. "Is Sarah well?" he asked, cursing the unusual hitch in his voice. "How did she handle the loss?"

"When she awoke, we told her," Michael said, "by then we had already buried the babes."

"Awoke?" He felt the color drain from his face, and his eyes began to burn uncharacteristically. "Awoke from what? What happened?"

"She'd lost a great deal of blood and was unconscious for over a week," Ren said.

"We're lucky she's alive," Michael added. "For a while there, we thought we might lose her, too."

"But that isn't the worst of it, Ian," Ren said solemnly. "Though Prescott has assured us that she is well, he doubts she can ever carry again."

"Oh, God." Ian dropped his head into his hands. He wanted to cry. He wanted to run from this nightmare. He felt responsible for all that had happened to Sarah. His beautiful, effervescent, charming Sarah who wanted nothing more than to be a mother.

"There's more, Ian," Michael said gently.

He twisted his body away from the two men, these bearers of tragic news, unable to think of anything other than how much Sarah had already gone through. He cleared his throat again. "How much more could there be? She's suffered so much already."

Michael shifted uncomfortably, as he sat on the

corner of Ren's desk. "Ian," Michael said, "Sarah doesn't remember you."

"What?" The thought was incredible. Oh, he'd heard stories of those who'd lost their memory, but never knew of a person first hand. Always it was the friend of a friend or someone's relative's relation, never someone he knew directly.

"She doesn't remember much of the last year," the earl continued. "She doesn't remember the sailing race at all. Thus, she has no recollection of your time together or of marrying you."

"Surely she knows she had to have been married in order to have been carrying a child," Ian said.

"She does. But she doesn't remember *you*. She realizes she miscarried but doesn't remember any of it."

"Can I see her?" he repeated. "Maybe seeing me will trigger her memory."

"Before you do, I have one question," Ren said. "As the heir to an earldom, you also will need heirs. It is unknown if she could ever provide those heirs. Does the fact that she may not bear you children change your feeling?"

"Of course not!" Ian couldn't believe what he was hearing. "Sarah is my *wife*," he stressed. "I decided before we reached China, before I ever learned she carried my child, that I needed to apologize for some of the things I said to her before I left. I realized what an ass I was and knew winning her affections again would take nothing less than a profound apology and vow of my affections." He studied the men across from him and knew they would understand when he said, "I missed her every day, and" —he swallowed hard, unused to emotion of this tender sort— "I…love her."

"Then you wish to remain wed?" Michael said. "Because if you don't, we had planned to tell Sarah at some point in the future that you had died and she was now a widow."

"You would add *that* sorrow for her to bear as well? You bastards," he hissed.

"I would do anything to protect my family," Ren snapped back. "And as you've made it clear that you didn't care about the earldom, I could provide substantial incentive for you to easily disappear and take up a new life elsewhere. Perhaps back in Baltimore."

"If children were going to be an issue for you, I had planned to assist you in a quiet annulment so that you might re-marry." Michael paused and looked to Ren, whose expression had already softened. "But as that is not the case now...."

Ian had heard his brothers-in-law were a ruthless pair—shrewd in business and protective toward the family. Never had he been witness to anything that would credit those rumors. Until now.

"She's my wife, damn you," Ian rose and began to pace the room. How could he get it across to them? How many times did he have to say that he was committed to Sarah? "I love *her*, not her ability to breed the heirs and do the social juggling and what-not that is so vital to your class."

"It's your class too, Ian," Lucky reminded him, as he stood and poured himself a drink. "And Sarah is my sister. I understand what Ren and Michael are saying. Their intent is only to protect her. Regardless of whether or not you are offended."

"Is this something you will be able to overcome, Ian?" Ren asked. "We need to know. She's had a horrible time these past months. She's just starting to smile again."

"We can work through this together," Ian said with more resolve than he ever thought he'd had. He followed Lucky to the sideboard and poured himself one of what Lucky was drinking. "She's not the frail china doll you think she is. She's got courage and spirit beyond what you know. I've seen it."

The room was uncomfortably quiet a moment, and when he turned back to them, the two men nodded, then Ren grew serious. "I'm sure you discovered the transactions I executed for Sarah while you were away. When she came to me and asked that I do this, I told her you weren't going to be happy about it. She insisted, and in the end, I supported her decision. But rest assured, neither Michael nor I influenced her in any way."

"I counseled her legally, and Ren financially, but all decisions were hers alone."

He nodded. "I'm sure she did what she thought was best after discovering her changed condition. I understand that now. It's just that I wanted to pay my own debts without her funds."

"I've told you before," Lucky said flatly, "we do things differently here. That money *is* yours."

Ian scowled at Lucky and the other men. "Yes, but now it can be said that I had to marry an heiress to fund my business venture. Do you know how humiliating that is to someone like me?"

Lucky smirked. "As Seamus would say, 'Ye daft American.'"

"Ian, rest assured that no one here believes you did that," Ren said.

"There are men in far more desperate straits than you who *do* marry simply for the money," added Michael.

"Like my own uncle, some are honorable men whose predecessors gambled away the family fortune and now they have extended families to support."

"There are other ways to get money than reaching for the girl who comes with the largest dowry." Ian should know. He'd gone from nothing to co-owning his own tea import company.

"Not all men have noble intentions," Ren said.

He was getting tired of this visit and wanted to see Sarah. "When can I see her?"

"Why don't I send word that you're here, and let's give Lia and Elise time to prepare Sarah." The Duke's look turned serious, "She's not as you remember her, Ian. She's emotionally fragile. And while we wait, we can have some luncheon."

Minutes later, the men entered the dining hall where a buffet had been laid for them. Ian was shocked to see the men serve themselves, piling their plates high with roasted ham and chicken, cucumber salad, and gravy potatoes. Ian's hands shook as he placed some of the same on his dish, unsure if the nervousness came from the fact that he would be seeing Sarah for the first time since that night in Liverpool or the events since. He'd changed so much in the last months, most of it in just the last hour when he'd learned what she'd gone through while he was away.

He hadn't lied when he'd said the decision to remain wed was made on the journey, before he'd even learned she carried his children. He'd driven himself and his crew hard the entire trip, because it was the only way he could sleep at night. He had to be so physically exhausted he could do nothing *but* sleep, and even then, his rest had been bothered by memories of Sarah.

His nights had been in living hell in which he never slept without dreaming of her. A day never passed where he didn't feel her spirit on his boat. She was the reason he couldn't sleep in his cabin any longer. It was the place where they'd loved—physically and emotionally. Once he realized this, he knew that he was incomplete without her in his life.

Now Sarah needed him, and he would not fail her. He was fortunate to be given a chance to start over with the woman he'd come to love. He had the opportunity to court her properly and make memories that would hopefully counter the ones from before—ones that were sure to hurt Sarah in ways she didn't deserve. Ian wished he could bring back the adventurous, witty, and perpetually happy young lady from the early days of the Atlantic race—from the time before his callous words had broken her heart.

Sarah paced the sitting room of her suite, twisting a linen handkerchief in her hands as she spoke with her sister and sister-in-law. She knew the day would come when the man who was her husband would arrive; she just hadn't expected it so soon. Try as she might, she could not recall him. She had no mental image of his face, no recollection of his personality, nor a single memory of their time together.

"Perhaps seeing Ian will help," Lia said. "Then you might remember the events of the year past."

"You said I loved him," Sarah began, wanting to know the truth as they knew it. "But did he love me?"

"We believe he did, though I don't know that he ever said the words to you," Elise said. "Lucky told Michael and Ren before he and Ian left for China that Ian's actions were always honorable toward you and he cared a great deal about you."

"Tell me again, how did we meet?" Sarah listened as they told her the story again. It did sound like something she would do, sneaking off and trying to stow away with Lucky. She remembered regretting not doing that same thing on his previous tea run to China and thinking she'd do just that on one of his future voyages.

So on this trip to New York, the man said they became intimate, which led to their hasty marriage there. This meant she became intimate with this man whom she barely knew. From what she remembered of herself before the race, that did not sound like something she would have done.

"Why couldn't we have waited to come home and marry?"

"Lucky did what he thought was the right thing after you had been compromised by sharing a cabin with him."

Sarah continued pacing. Worried now that with the loss of his children, this man who was her husband might wish to end their marriage. A man in his position needed heirs, and now that Prescott had ruled that possibility remote, her husband could quite readily seek, and receive, an annulment. If he did that, she would be shamed.

"I wonder...was he happy I carried his children?"

"He didn't know, Sarah," Lia said truthfully.

"I see." She stopped and looked from one sister to the next. She didn't fear her future *without* this man, but she did fear a future *with* him because she didn't remember him. "I don't remember him. And he quite possibly did not love me, especially if he was forced to marry me."

Sarah straightened and lifted her chin. "He should seek an annulment now. This way he can have his freedom to wed someone he *can* love and with whom he might have children, especially because he was likely forced into marrying me in the first place."

"Perhaps you should wait and see what your husband thinks," Elise said. "After all, you were preparing a home for him at Greenwood. The staff had been hired and remodeling completed. And you planned the same for your house in Mayfair."

"I agree, Sarah. Until the tragedy, you were committed to making the marriage work," Lia added.

Silence filled the cavernous suite as Sarah thought about a future with this man she couldn't remember. His name sounded familiar, as he was Lucky's business partner. But she could not put a face to his name. It was the most troubling thing about this episode of amnesia—not remembering her husband. Both Lia and Elise, in their attempts to comfort her, had both said it was a good thing that she didn't remember the event that caused the lapse in her memory because she was sure to be traumatized by it. It was also a blessing because she didn't have a strong bond with the babes causing her to mourn them.

It all sounded so bizarre. She'd obviously been intimate with her husband on at least one occasion. She couldn't recall, though she wished she could. There was an enormous part of her life that was missing in not having this memory of him—a part of her felt removed from the entire situation. There was a deep curiosity, but as she didn't know if she loved him, there wasn't much more emotion toward him than that. "You say he is here? Is he downstairs?"

"Yes, dear," Elise said. "Would you like to meet with him in the morning room or up here?"

"I shall see him in the morning room. It would be rather presumptuous of me, don't you think, to invite a... stranger into my bedroom?"

Elise and Lia smiled. "You are right, dear," Elise said.

Sarah took one last look into the mirror and realized she couldn't do much more to help her appearance. Never able to apply rouge to her skin because of the rash it gave her, she pinched her cheeks a few times and smoothed the skirt of her dove gray morning dress. Trudy had wanted her to wear her pearls, but she'd decided against it. Even though she was seeing her husband for the first time in her memory, she was still mourning the loss of her sons, and the wearing of any jewelry seemed distasteful.

She nodded to Lia and Elise, then followed behind them as they led the way to the morning salon. Several times she thought to turn around and return to her room, asking Ian to leave because she feared she might not be ready to see him. Sarah knew she had to face him eventually, to see if any memories were triggered or if any relationship stood a chance in the face of her new reality. She trembled as Lia stood before the door, a footman at the ready to turn the knob when she directed.

"Will you come in with me first?" Nerves twisted Sarah's insides. She hoped to high heaven she did not get sick in front of him. It would be the most humiliating thing to have happen. She closed her eyes and saw a privacy screen and chamber pot in a room she didn't remember ever seeing before. A floral pattern carpet in a color unfamiliar to her flashed before her, and when she opened her eyes, she knew this was the right thing for her to do. She took a deep breath before nodding to the footman. She smiled at Lia and Elise. "If all goes well, then you can leave us alone."

"I never planned to leave your side until you asked," Elise replied.

"I love you both. If I've never told you before, I want you to know that now."

The duchess nodded and signaled the footman to open the door. The three women entered the room, and Sarah smiled as she met Lucky's gaze, then Ren's and Michael's. The last man had to be Ian. Her husband.

He stood almost exactly as tall as her brother, but was broader of chest with arms that were nearly as thick as limbs on the ancient oaks outside. But it wasn't his size or musculature that she found intriguing or appealing. It was his rugged masculinity. The unspoken invitation, the invisible draw, and unmistakable sexuality of his mere presence that sent her insides to flutter uncontrollably.

She met his brown-green gaze, one that hinted of sadness and compassion, as she nodded and gave him as much of a smile as she could manage. Sarah tried valiantly to recall a memory of a time with him as he stepped toward her. His sun-kissed, thick blond hair fell onto her forehead when he bowed over her hand.

Her mind might not recall him, but her body certainly remembered him. Or at least his touch. She felt the heat rise to her cheeks as her knees went soft and her breath caught in her chest when this man lifted her hand and brushed his lips lightly across her knuckles. His fine, full lips lingered over long against her skin, and when she thought he would release her hand, he placed it against his warm cheek as he lifted his gaze to hers.

LOVING SARAH

The affection, the love, the concern, and even desire were all there in his warm hazel eyes.

"You cannot monopolize my sister, Ian," Lucky said. "I wish to greet her too, you know."

Pleasantries were exchanged all around. Lucky came over and hugged Sarah, giving her his sympathy for her loss. Before she could begin to cry, Elise made a great show of serving the tea that had just arrived.

Lucky and Ian discussed their voyage to China. While everyone chatted around them, Sarah sat quietly, praying that the sensation of comfort as she sat next to this man meant something positive. Her entire being felt at ease with this man, even though her brain didn't remember him. It felt almost as though she were two persons inside of her one body. She happily listened to everything Ian and Lucky said and at times felt as though she remembered certain sensations, but the visual memory didn't come to her.

When the conversation dwindled, Sarah looked up at Lia and realized she'd been under the magnifying glass during that entire conversation.

Elise and Lia smiled sympathetically. They recognized that she was processing thoughts and visions and emotions while they all spoke. When Sarah nodded to them, she was thankful they understood her silent plea. Lia asked her husband and brother to leave with her. Elise took Michael's hand and followed, leaving Sarah in the center of the great room, facing the husband she could not recognize with her mind, but whom her body remembered.

He gave her a shy smile. "I wish I could have been here…for you." Sarah could have sworn his eyes misted in commiseration for their loss.

Suddenly she felt her eyes burn. It was something she hadn't done since waking from her unconscious state. She'd seen her sister-in-law and sister weeping, even her maid and several of the female servants. And all these past weeks, she'd never been able to cry, and now all of the sudden, there were emotions. She didn't understand.

"I do not remember it at all." Sarah felt an odd sensation of tears choking her voice, and she turned away from Ian and went to the window. She feared if he touched her she might collapse into an incomprehensible mess. Something told her there was a flood of tears pent up within her because up until now she'd not cried. She felt enormously guilty for that, for not crying over the loss of her sons.

For some reason, she felt she could do it now. The void of emptiness was caving in, and she was drowning in emotion. Suddenly, the damn burst and Ian rushed forward and held her for several minutes, letting her pour it all out in his arms. It felt right and comfortable to share her sorrow with this man. Perhaps because her babes were his children as well. So she cried for their stillborn sons, the loss of their lives, and perhaps her inability to have others.

She also cried for Ian, who needed legitimate heirs to carry on the heritage of his ancestors. Lia and Elise said he hadn't known of her condition, and she'd wondered on more than one occasion if he would have been happy to have them.

She had her answer now. Felt it in the warmth of his embrace and the feeling of being safe and protected in his arms.

She sniffled and used the handkerchief to dry her eyes, then blew her nose in it. She knew she didn't cry prettily and likely looked a mess, but she could do nothing about that now.

"They tell me we had sons," she said. "I'm sure you are disappointed."

"I'm thankful you are alive. If we are meant to be parents, then children will come." He was silent a moment, and she wished she could read his mind. "Right now, we need to focus on getting you well."

She turned back to face him and sat in a wing chair before the window. He drew a chair opposite her and sat, their knees almost touching. "I *am* doing well," she said through a feigned smile. "I feel stronger every day and have had some tiny, irrelevant memories return. I remember wearing boy's trousers, but cannot possibly recall why." Her husband smiled, giving her the impression that *he* knew. She arched a curious brow.

"If I told you," he said, his tone serious yet light, "then you may stop trying to bring those memories back. If the last twenty minutes is any indication, I feel every bit of it will come back in time."

"Surely, you know that I have never been the patient sort."

"Yes, I know." His gaze grasped and held hers. "You are as beautiful as the day we met, Sarah. I've missed you greatly."

"You have been informed that I do not have any memories of you, my lord? I wish I did, for I am certain they were good ones." With the way he held her minutes earlier, and compassion he showed her thus far into their conversation, she was sure he was a gentle and kind man. These likely were the reasons she married him.

"For the most part, they were."

"Thank you for not lying to me. I appreciate that."

"I've never lied to you, Sarah, and I never will. Perhaps, in the past, I might have said things in frustration, or withheld my feeling and emotion, but from now on, I shall endeavor to be more open with you."

"Do you wish to remain married?" she said past the lump climbing her throat, "even though you have legal grounds for annulment?"

He nodded. "If we are meant to be parents," Ian said, brushing her loose tendrils from her disheveled hair behind her ears, his voice a sympathetic whisper, "then children will come. If not, we shall have each other as we grow old."

She took a deep breath. "Since you have thus far been honest with me, I feel I owe you the same respect. I do not know what I wish just yet. I want so very much to remember you, and on some deeper level, I already feel I do."

"That is understandable, considering what you have just gone through. I am a patient man, Sarah. I can wait."

"What do we do now? Where do we go from here?" Her need to know how to proceed was important. How was she going to rebuild a relationship without a stable foundation? A foundation that she felt needed to be rebuilt from nearly the beginning.

He took her hands and held them between his. "I want you to give me time to make you fall in love with me again, Sarah."

Her mouth grew dry at his words, and her heart began to beat a little faster. "You know I have no memory of you."

"Give it time, love."

"Did I love you?" She felt the physical attraction to

him from the moment she walked into the room, but love was about more than physical relations. And from the way he'd just held and supported her during her bout of tears, she was sure she got that from him as well.

"Yes. That is, you left me a note saying you loved me. But I took your love for granted. I'll not do so again."

"I wish I could remember." She looked up to him and gave him a shy smile, telling him that all was well. "Then I'd know whether I was angry with you or not for taking me for granted."

"So do I, Sarah."

She felt a growing sense of relief taking root. Suddenly, there was reason for optimism. "Where do you suggest we begin?"

"At the beginning," he said, his hazel eyes softening as he smiled. "We create new memories and pray the old ones return."

"You have a silken tongue, my lord. I think that is why I fell in love with you."

"And I fell in love with a courageous and spirited young woman who boldly came to me aboard my ship and said she could be of use to me as we sailed to New York during the race." He kept his gaze on her face as she processed that bit of information. "Do you remember that?"

"The words sound…familiar. But there are no mental images to match with them."

"They will return one day," he reassured her. "I have every faith you shall make a full recovery."

"And if they do not?" She wasn't trying to be a pessimist, but there was the possibility they would not come back according to Dr. Prescott.

"Then we will have the new ones, won't we?"

Sarah nodded, her decision made. For now, at least, she would remain Mrs. Ross-Mackeever, the future Countess Mackeever.

That evening, as the family finished dinner, Ian felt Sarah's grasp on his hand, and he met her worried gaze. He wondered what was going on in her mind. They'd spoken of so much earlier that day that she could be thinking of any one of a hundred things. Sitting next to him, she tightened her hold beneath the table, before setting her sorbet spoon down.

"I have something I would like to say," she began. The family all looked her way expectantly. "My husband and I would like to leave for London tomorrow. The Mayfair house has been ready for months now, and it is past time for me to carry on with living."

Ren stared hard at him, and Ian was sure the duke believed him to be behind his sister's declaration. What Ren didn't know was that Sarah herself had come up with the idea. She believed seeing the cabin aboard *Revenge* might trigger more memories for her, which she desperately wanted. To her way of thinking, if she could fill in the gaps in her mind, she might be able to move forward. Staying here triggered nothing for her.

Ian was relieved that the duchess agreed with Sarah as she explained her reasoning. But he could tell from the look on Ren's face that he was in for some serious questioning when the men retired for cigars and port. He didn't expect to get out of the home with his wife *without* being asked more about his intentions with Sarah.

LOVING SARAH

"I shall be headed back in the morning as well, as I have some business to attend to," Lucky said.

Ian wondered why Lucky had not yet spoken of the girl child he now had in his custody. He would ask him later and beg him not to mention the infant to his wife. At least not yet. Hopefully, if she regained some memory and dealt with the grieving for their twins, she would better handle the new member of the family, for Lucky wanted to raise the babe as his own.

"Good, then we three shall go down together." Sarah smiled at everyone at the table.

"I think," the duchess said, "that it is a good idea, provided you proceed with caution so as not to be overwhelmed."

"I agree with Lia, though I still worry for you. Try not to take it too fast, sister," Countess Camden cautioned.

"I promise to take things slowly," Sarah said. "Thus putting each memory and the emotions that accompany it in its proper place." She met her brother's gaze. "It's the only way forward for me."

Ren nodded, remaining silent during her declaration. As the footmen began to clear the dessert bowls, both brothers-in-law pushed back their chairs, a silent cue for Ian to do the same and follow them. Lucky must have read the unspoken invitation as Ian's alone, for he broke with convention and remained in the dining hall with the women.

Once he was in the duke's private study, a room that was fast becoming familiar to him, Ian took a seat across from his brothers-in-law and awaited interrogation. It wasn't long in coming.

"Did you place this idea into her head?" Ren asked.

"No." He was growing more than frustrated with the attitude of these two. Did they really think he would harm his wife? "Sarah told me what she wanted to do this afternoon when we walked in the garden. I agreed to support her."

"What if something happens," Michael said, "and she cannot handle it?"

"Then *I* shall be with her and will call her physician."

Ren sighed as he filled a glass with port and passed it to him. "Has she remembered anything since seeing you?"

"I think so. Several times she said that things or words sounded familiar, but no image came to mind. I asked her the last thing she remembered clearly, and she said traveling to Liverpool, the morning after attending some come-out ball."

"That would be the day before the race began," Michael said.

Ian nodded and sipped his port. It wasn't lost to him that her memories failed from the moment she met him at the home in Liverpool. All of the pain in her life occurred after meeting him. And he was likely responsible for most of it.

"As she is your wife and has said she wishes to remain so, I have no choice but to let her leave with you. But be careful of her. She's still recovering."

"You know I will."

Ian left the two men, intending to seek his bed after a long day of travel and revelations. Sarah had asked to return to London the very next day because of the immediate sensations she was starting to experience. They were not quite full memories she said, but sensations and snippets of familiarity.

Wanting to keep the flow of memories moving forward for her, Ian had agreed to return to London with her, Sarah wanted to "find her memory," she'd said and shared with Ian the hope she could find them in London.

He met Lucky on the landing going to his rooms. Because he and Sarah had decided earlier that Ian would keep a separate bed from her until she was ready, Ian was about to ask one of the footmen which room he was to occupy for the night when Lucky asked him to come into his for a moment.

Lucky asked for a ride into town with them, and Ian revealed his concerns for discussing the arrival of the child into the family during that ride.

"Oh, I agree. It's too soon," Lucky said. "We should wait until we see how she does for the next few days. Though, if Sarah were to come to Caversham House, it's likely I couldn't hide the babe from her. The entire neighborhood can hear her screaming down the rafters when she gets upset." Lucky leaned back with his glass of wine. "She'll learn about the child eventually, but I'd like to give her some time before we tell her."

"Thank you." Ian also told Lucky that he wanted to be there with her when she found out, just in case she became upset. Not that he expected it, but he didn't know with the type of memory loss she had if it would affect her in this way.

"You know, Ian, the babe's not newly born. I think she's well over one year old, except she's so malnourished her growth has been stunted."

"What makes you say that?"

"She has nearly a mouthful of teeth. And another two came through just on the trip from Portugal. That's why she was so cranky the entire time," Lucky replied through his troubled smile. "She was hungry and wanted to eat, but the poor thing's mouth was hurting. As I remember it, my nieces and nephews were all approximately one and a half when they had a mouth filled with teeth." Lucky closed his eyes and smiled. After taking a sip from his Spanish wine, he met Ian's gaze. "And she's trying to walk too. She pulls herself up but is afraid to let go the furniture."

"What do you do now?"

"Feed her," Lucky said, tossing back the remaining wine. "Get her healthy."

They discussed business for a while. Then Ian sought his bed, knowing that the next night, he would be sleeping in one of the two homes he and Sarah now shared. As a man who'd never owned a home before, it should definitely prove better than a twelve-by-twenty cabin in the stern of his three-masted Baltimore schooner.

Chapter Fifteen

Ian held his sleepy wife close to his side late the next afternoon as their coaches rolled into London. Lucky asked to be let off at Caversham House on the way into town. "I have some urgent business to attend to, and it really cannot wait." He nodded, knowing the *business* Lucky meant and hoping he came to a decision on what he would do now that they were back home. He mentioned last night when they were in the privacy of Lucky's sitting room that he missed the girl and had begun to call her Maura. They'd also discussed when to tell the rest of the family—especially Sarah.

"I understand," Sarah said, coming awake, preventing Ian from asking what Lucky's plans were for the child he now had.

"Ian, could you come around after you get settled? I should like you to be here for the meeting I'm about to schedule," Lucky added.

"Certainly." Ian looked down at Sarah, leaning into him, half-sleeping already, and smiled. "I shall go while you rest and you'll never even know I've been gone." She nodded, then closed her eyes and sighed as she curled into his side.

After leaving Lucky at the Upper Brook Street home, Ian and Sarah made their way toward their Mayfair home, just blocks away. Sarah looked up at Ian as she straightened from her nap. "I sent a messenger ahead last night to alert Mrs. Craggins of our arrival. She's our housekeeper, and her husband is our butler. Elise hired the staff at both houses, because I was bed-ridden at the time." A worried look crossed her delicate brow. "I wonder if it will ever come back to me, Ian."

"Don't worry, sweetheart. We're going to try jogging some of those memories and see what returns." He hoped beyond all hope she remembered nothing of certain things and everything of others. He prayed she lost those memories such as his accusation of her forcing him into a marriage, or when he told her he was glad she wasn't carrying a babe. But he wanted her to remember the good things, the days and nights of deeply passionate lovemaking that left them both spent and sated.

The vehicle moved slowly through the evening traffic, and Ian wondered at the meeting Lucky had arranged. Likely, he was having the physician come to check the babe over. That must be it, or perhaps he wanted help composing an advertisement for a nurse. He was soon to need one as well.

Their traveling coach pulled in front of their town home in Mayfair. The waiting butler sent the footman forward to open the door for them. Ian disembarked first, then turned and extended his hand to his wife.

"Thank you," his wife said to the young man holding the coach door. Ian helped her down, then she turned to the man standing at the base of the steps. "You must be Craggins," Sarah said.

"Yes, my lady." The butler turned and motioned to the woman standing at the top step of the entranceway. "And this is Mrs. Craggins."

"I am delighted to finally meet you both," Sarah said. "This is my husband, Mr. Ross-Mackeever." She looked up at the front stone facade of the home. "The home is lovelier than I remembered. I believe we shall be very happy here, Craggins."

"The entire staff certainly will do all we can to make that so, my lady."

They took a quick tour of the main level, so Ian could acquaint himself with the home, then soon they found themselves standing in Sarah's suite. She looked the room over, nodding at the personal effects her maid had arranged throughout. Decorated in her favorite yellow and blue, the room was both bright and cheerful, letting the afternoon sun in. It was a place void of memories for her, and he wondered if it was the right place for her at this time in her recovery. But she chose to come here, signaling to him that she was ready to move forward. He just had to be here if she needed him.

Ian crossed to the doorway adjoining and turned the glass knob. Their shared sitting room was nicely done in deep blues, burgundy, and gold tones, and through an open door straight before him he could see directly into his bedchamber. The enormous room was clearly twice the size of his cabin and the same color scheme carried into this room, except the furniture was heavier and much older.

"Yes, Mrs. Craggins?" Sarah said as the housekeeper entered the room.

"His lordship had no belongings sent over."

Ian came to stand next to Sarah. "I shall have my things sent over soon. I wanted you to see the cabin as it was during the journey to New York before I remove anything."

"Oh. I see. Then we shall go first thing in the morning. We can tour the remainder of our home after I rest," she told the housekeeper. "I'm tired from traveling."

"I understand. I shall send your maid up to assist you," the housekeeper said.

After the housekeeper left, Sarah inspected her room as Ian wandered back into his to do the same. He opened another door and saw a large dressing area with drawers and shelves built into one side of the wall and cedar cabinets on the other. On the other end of the long, narrow room was another door. He opened it, expecting to discover a study, and instead saw a bathing chamber with black, gold, and white tiles in an interwoven pattern on the floor and partway up the wall. An enormous cast-iron ceramic-lined tub sat raised upon a dais with steps leading into it. He looked at it, surprised at its size and modern plumbing accoutrement. Hot and cold water taps, both at the tub and in a deep porcelain wash basin, took away the need for servants to carry hot water. As he looked back into the dressing room, he noted the woodwork and pipes around the two rooms appeared new and concluded the chamber to be a recent addition done during the renovations.

The door from his wife's dressing room opened and she entered, smiling.

"Elise and Lia oversaw all of the renovations."

"I shall have to remember to thank them," Ian said as he studied the light sconces. "I just noticed…this entire house is set up for gas lighting. Amazing." He met his wife's gaze. "You'll have to tell me what their favorite beverages are, and I shall send them each a bottle."

"You can send them each a case if you'd like."

"It may take some time yet for me to get used to all of this."

"You will," his wife reminded him. He felt awkward standing there in a room that he'd never seen before that was now his. Not only that, the entire home was his and the servants were his. He was certain there might even be livery that was his as well.

A soft knock and then a door opening in her chamber alerted them to the maid's arrival. She took a few steps toward her room, then stopped to ask, "Will I see you for dinner?"

"Of course. Have a tray for two sent up and we shall dine here, in our sitting room."

He watched her walk away, thinking he'd just witnessed some of the old Sarah's personality. Either that or she was becoming more comfortable with him. Either way, tomorrow was sure to be interesting for them both. Still unsure if this was the right thing, he wondered if he shouldn't back out of taking her to *Revenge*. He could tell her there was an infestation of mice and that they needed to reschedule it for another day. But he knew he'd have to face the cabin, and the weeks aboard the boat at some point. If not now, then it would have to be later. Those weeks were the beginning of the time frame of the months she was missing. He didn't want to lose her if she remembered the hurtful things he'd said to her.

Ian traced a finger along the cool, smooth surface of the tub before quitting the room. He went in search of Craggins and asked him to have a horse sent around. After learning there were none as yet, he made a mental note to see to transportation for the household. He went onto the street and hailed a hackney driver and gave him the direction of Caversham House.

When he arrived, he was shown into the library,

where he found Lucky holding a crying baby while Dr. Prescott explained why the child cried.

"Her mouth hurts because she has two molars coming in at the same time," the elderly man explained. "Overall, I'd say she had a rough start. I see nothing physically wrong with the child, and I think with proper nutrition you should see a vast improvement in her health, including weight gain. But it has been my experience that infants who begin as she has never fully recover from the effects of the malnourishment."

"What problems will she have?" Lucky asked.

"For one, she may never reach normal height, as her growth will have been stunted. Then again, I could be wrong, only time will tell." He snapped his bag shut and looked at Ian, finally noticing his presence.

Lucky introduced him and the man gave his condolences on the loss of the twins, indicating that he was also Sarah's physician. Ian thanked him and Prescott turned back to Lucky. "She's a very fortunate little girl you have there, my lord. Very fortunate, indeed."

"Excuse me while I find Mrs. Steen. I'll be right back." Lucky left the room, carrying Maura.

"Doctor, may I have a word with you regarding my wife?" Ian wished he had more than just these few minutes. He was afraid with all of the questions he had that he'd never have the time to get them all answered. So he decided to ask the one that concerned him most.

"Certainly," the man said. "What would you like to know?"

"How is she? Really? Aside from her memory loss, is there anything...*physically* wrong with Sarah?"

The physician sighed and took a seat in the chair next

to the one Ian took across from the fireplace in the cavernous, book-filled library. "Your wife is doing far better than we expected at the time. I'm sure you were told the premature delivery was extremely difficult for her and we nearly lost her as well." Ian closed his eyes, thankful to still have Sarah, and nodded. The man continued. "There is nothing physically wrong with her that I can tell. We do not know if her memory loss is permanent or a temporary lapse. I've seen situations such as this where the person would recover the memory of the time lost and all is well. And I've seen cases where the memory was lost forever. Usually though, it falls somewhere in between."

"Will trying to trigger memories bring ill effects?" He had to know if he was making a mistake in trying to force the memories. He would rather have a wife with no memories of that time than one who might not handle the onslaught of emotions well. The thought of Sarah losing her mind completely terrified him, and if it were preventable, he'd never forgive himself.

"I doubt it. In fact, I feel safe saying it would do no harm. My advice would be to not try to rush the memories or bring too many on at one time. Go slowly and do not overwhelm her mind, as she may suffer a setback."

That's what he feared and said as much to the physician. The man reiterated taking things slowly. Ian agreed as his practical advice made sense to him. "I have one other question, though I don't know where to begin."

"Physical relations?" Dr. Prescott asked, seeming to know his mind. "There is nothing wrong with Lady Sarah to prevent you from being intimate. But you must know that she may or may not conceive again. We don't know. I want to believe that she miscarried because the babes were entirely too large for her petite frame. And there were two of them. Twins often come too early. If that is the case, she may deliver a babe in the future.

"Too, she may be the type of woman who miscarries each and every time she conceives. We do not know yet."

Ian was quiet as he digested the news. So forcing the memories might—or might not—pose a risk to Sarah's emotional state. And Sarah conceiving again might—or might not—pose a risk to her health again. Only he could decide if the risks were worth taking. "I thank you for your candor."

"Mr. Ross-Mackeever, I have known this family since His Grace was in knee pants. I've seen tragedy and triumph within the very walls of this home. And it never fails to amaze me the love and care they each have for one another." Prescott stood and lifted his bag as though to leave. "You have married into a unique family—one that is unlike other noble families."

"I see that already."

"Do not think they mean to be interfering. Right now, His Grace is learning to trust you with one of his own. Once you have his trust, you will have in him the strongest ally a man can have. He will stand by you for the duration."

Lucky re-entered the room. "Prescott, you're not leaving are you? I asked Mrs. Steen to have your favorite cherry tarts brought in."

The elderly man wobbled back to his chair and sat. "I haven't had cherry tarts in ages. Not since before Mrs. Prescott became ill." He became somewhat melancholy but caught himself, then forced a smile and looked at Ian. "No one made cherry tarts like my missus. Though these come very close."

After the sweets arrived and tea was served, Dr. Prescott turned to Lucky, who'd pulled up a chair to join them at the fire. "What are your plans for the child now that you've decided to adopt her?"

"I have Mrs. Steen looking for a nurse for her. She interviewed a woman this morning and has another applicant coming tomorrow. Hopefully before I sail again, I shall have her situated. And soon I shall have a home of my own. The reason I was late yesterday," Lucky said to Ian, "was because I met with my solicitor and asked him to begin hunting for some property. When I returned this afternoon, I found a letter from him stating he's heard of an estate for sale not too far from Oxfordshire. I replied for him to make an inquiry."

"Good," Prescott said. "I'm glad to see you're settling down." The older man seemed to want to say more, but kept silent. Ian wondered what the wizened doctor would have said.

"This is interesting news," Ian said, surprised at this development. Lucky had shown about as much interest as he in settling down, though he supposed it was getting to be about that time.

"I'm going to need a home eventually, so I might as well buy one now. No matter the medieval Italian title, my home is here. I should make it official and buy some land, as I'll never live in Italy."

"May I ask why?" Prescott asked. "I hear it is a beautiful country."

"Long story."

Ian shook his head in mock sadness. "That's his

answer for everything whenever he doesn't want to explain. I get that from him all of the time."

"My lords, I am not a nobleman, but merely an old man who's seen a great deal in his day. Could I perhaps make an observation and a suggestion?"

Ian and Lucky both nodded.

"You have no wife, and no home as yet," he said to Lucky. "You have a wife and a home," he said to Ian.

The tart and tea he'd just consumed threatened to reappear in a most humiliating manner. "I see where you are heading, doctor," Ian choked as he replied. "I don't think Sarah is ready...."

"But the baby is ready," the physician turned to Lucky and added, "for a mother."

Lucky stared at them both, speechless. The doctor settled deep into his chair. "You know that Mrs. Prescott, God rest her lovely soul, and I have six children." He met Ian's gaze head on. "What few people know is that only our eldest daughter, Georgianna, is our natural child. After she was born, Mrs. Prescott could not have any more, and she'd always wanted a large family.

"What began as saving one infant from an unwed, dying mother became the answer to my wife's prayers. And mine as well, for I only wanted her to be happy. That first infant grew to be our son Charles, and he is now a physician in practice near Cambridge. As a newborn, he came to us a few days after Mrs. Prescott had yet another miscarriage.

"So if you think that you must have perfect timing for your wife to accept a child into her heart, think again. A woman knows her calling in life, and though not all women make good mothers, I know a good mother when

LOVING SARAH

I see one. Lady Sarah will be a wonderful mother."

Ian listened with his heart, wondering if what Prescott suggested were possible. "How do you know this?"

"When your lady wife learned she carried twins, she did everything to minimize the risk of miscarriage. When I ordered her to bed at six months, she went without complaint. When I suggested a less than appetizing diet of organ meats, which would benefit her health and that of the babes, she consumed it. She chose names for the babies and happily planned their nursery and embroidered linens while on her sickbed.

"In all, I'd say she wanted to be a mother very much."

Ian felt the blood drain from his face. He rose abruptly and began to pace, something he did when upset. He couldn't take the babe from his best friend. Lucky had come to love this child. It was evident in his handling and care of her, in the way he smiled as he spoke of her.

Sarah would take the child in because she was a loving, giving person. But was handing the babe over to his wife who'd just suffered a great loss the right thing for her? Essentially, Prescott was suggesting masking the pain with a new focus. Was that such a good thing to do? Shouldn't she, and Ian too, mourn the loss of the twins before committing to raising another child?

Lucky sat frozen and unmoving, silently staring at his guests as they conversed. "But I've grown attached to her," he whispered. "I've even named her. Maura."

The doctor looked at Lucky. "Is there any reason why you cannot remain attached to her and love her as a niece, rather than a daughter that you are not prepared to care for?"

Ian came to Lucky's rescue. "Lucky, Dr. Prescott means no harm. He has simply given us something to think about."

"Not us, Ian! Me," Lucky went to the window and watched the traffic moving to and fro on Upper Brook. "I have fed her and changed her, held her and played with her. She's gnawed on my finger and has burped milk on me. But most of all, she smiles at me when I sing to her, and she falls asleep in my arms after having a bottle. You should see the look in her beautiful green eyes when she's content and the fire in them when she's not. She's strong enough now that she babbles, and I swear, what I hear is her calling me 'papa.'" He turned around and met his gaze, and Ian swore Lucky's deep brown eyes filled with tears. "But I know you are right in that I am not prepared to raise a child alone. I have a trip to America and Canada coming up. After that, we're both headed back to China in September for another tea run." He sighed before straightening his shoulders, then continued. "I'm always going to be gone. What good is having one parent, when that parent is never there? At least with you and Sarah as her parents, Sarah will be there for her when you and I are gone."

"Lucky, think on this for a while. You don't have to commit to anything right now," Ian said. "Then, if you're certain, we must plan how to broach the topic with Sarah."

Dr. Prescott stood and laid his napkin on his dessert plate. "I shall leave the two of you to discuss the matter, but trust that you shall both keep in mind the best interests of the little girl who's already missed out on so much in her short life."

As the two men watched the elderly physician leave,

Ian felt as if the outcome of Lucky's happiness rested in his hands. And he hated the feeling. "It was merely a suggestion, Lucky. We don't have to even consider his words."

"Yes, Ian, I do. And I had not thought of what he said until the old sneak planted the seed, which was more than likely his intent all along." Lucky poured himself two fingers of scotch, downed the first glass, then refilled it. "As I was not here when he examined Maura yesterday, he's had all night to think on this and plan what he would say. He's been our family's physician for as long as I can remember, and I cannot ever think of a time he was wrong in his judgment." He gave a half-hearted smile. "This takes a great weight off my shoulders. Little Maura will have my best friend and my sister as her parents."

"We'll have to see what Sarah thinks. I'm not so sure...."

"Sarah will be angry that we have kept Maura from her for so long already," Lucky interrupted. "She will accept her readily, love her greatly, and be a wonderful mother to her."

Sarah walked upon the deck of *Revenge*, Ian's schooner, the one he said she'd spent almost two months aboard. The smell of the vinegar and lemon concoction the crewmen used to polish the brightwork, the sounds of the boat creaking as it rode the anchor, all filled her senses, and the feel of the gentle rocking of deck beneath her feet brought to mind snippets of scenes. She wasn't sure if they were memories of actual events or imaginings of her mind. As she entered the companionway, she looked behind her and had a vision. Rain, hard driving sheets of it, and wind strong enough to push her backward down the steps. Waves rolling deep, one after another, causing the entire hull to rock violently.... The scenes all came rushing forward.

"Ian?" When he turned to her, she asked, "We traveled through a storm. Or I get the feeling we did, and something...something happened." In her mind, she saw Ian go overboard, saw the waves suck him below. Her entire body shook and her voice trembled. She'd never been so afraid in her entire life when she saw...tried to rush up to reach him but then...her head began to ache "You fell over." Tears burned her eyes. She forced them back, swallowed, and took a deep breath. "But you're here. I don't understand." What she saw should have killed him and still he was here, so strong, supporting her, leading her through this nightmare she'd lived once before and was doing so yet again. The memories...they were coming. Snippets. Scenes. Nothing to hold them together yet no matter how she tried.

Ian put his arms around her and held her as she started remembering. The feel of his strength supporting her gave her courage to draw more of the vision forward. "I fell and when I awoke, you were not there. But someone was. Who was it, Ian?"

"That was my sail maker and cook, Seamus."

She nodded. "I remember," she whispered. "He was kind to me."

"A crewman went over," Ian explained. "He was tethered, but unconscious after hitting his head, and unable to help himself back up. My line was attached, so I went over to retrieve him. After I caught his unconscious body, the crew pulled us back in."

"Did he survive?"

"Yes, he did."

He backed away from her and led her the rest of the way down to the cabin, taking the steps before her so he could assist her. Once inside, she scanned the room and found a cat lounging belly up on the bench in a beam of sunlight streaming through a porthole. "Mouser," she said as she smiled at Ian. "Is that right?"

"Yes." The look on his face told her he was pleased with her effort to recall the almost full year she'd missed.

A vision of a boot flying through the air at the corner of the room where a rodent had taken refuge between a clothes press and a wash stand came to mind. "There was a mouse in here one night as I tried to sleep, and you brought her in here."

"And ever since, she has wanted to sleep in here. I think she misses you."

Sarah sat next to the cat and rubbed its belly as she looked around the room from where she sat. "I cleaned the cabin. It was a mess."

"You made the mess. Don't you remember? You tore the room apart looking for the mouse."

"Vaguely." She began to sort the images as they came rushing to her, flooding her mind. A leather-bound text, a book of sonnets.... She remembered reading a book of sonnets. And Ian sitting next to her. She remembered he touched her bare foot, and Sarah felt herself blush as she relived that moment. Suddenly her gaze darted to the bed, her eyes wide. She licked her lips, her mouth suddenly dry. "I.... We...made love here."

She glanced back at Ian, and he gave her a grin.

"I remember, Ian," she said. "Not all of it, but some of it. I suppose I'm still frustrated that it isn't all making sense to me yet."

"I'm glad." He smiled as he gazed down upon her from his perch on the table.

"We were happy. Weren't we?" Even to her own ears she sounded frightened that he might say no. She wondered why he might say that, because he obviously cared a great deal about her if he was helping her with filling in the gaps of her memory.

"For the most part."

"What did we quarrel about?" She had to ask because she somehow knew that they had argued.

"We didn't quarrel. We discussed." He gave her a devilish grin and winked an eye. "And you always agreed."

"Somehow I find that hard to believe."

"Now, now… You're doing so well, I'd hate to spoil the mood." He stood and extended his hand.

Taking it, she let him lead her back up to the deck. They went forward into the bow, and Ian lifted the heavy wooden box lid hatch. The location, the sound, and sights did nothing for her.

"Take a look in the hold." He drew her forward. "Does this trigger anything?"

She looked into the darkness below the deck and saw only folded canvas. "It's very dark in there. I can't be sure."

He set the lid back in place when she stepped back. After the lid dropped down, she cried out. "I remember that, too!" Heat rose to her face as the sound triggered a memory and she remembered her actions. "I'm so sorry, Ian. I stowed away expecting this to be Lucky's boat and only realized after I'd been brought to you that I'd been left on the wrong ship." She placed her hands over her eyes and rubbed them. Sarah remembered the look on his face as he recognized who she was, and she burst out in an embarrassed giggle. "Oh my. You were so angry."

"My life was forever changed from that moment on," he said. "I had to assess the risk of returning to Liverpool and losing my position near the lead, as opposed to you losing your reputation." Sarah noticed his eyes lit up when he smiled. "I am, at heart, a greedy man."

"A greedy man who is too proud," she scoffed.

"I'll make no apologies for that," he replied.

The slight chop of waves on the river caused the boat to move under them, and Sarah glanced up at Ian. "I got rather banged up down there and couldn't take anymore, so I made my presence known."

Sarah grew quiet as she remembered more. She'd left her hair loose one evening and wore boy's trousers with no corset nor drawers. When she recalled this bit of information, she felt another blush creep up her cheek. She did this? What on earth could she have been thinking? Why had she done that? What did he think of her now? Turning away from him, she stepped down onto the main deck, wanting to hide from him. A vision of her lounging on the bench flooded her mind's eye. With her shirt unbuttoned partially, she'd enticed his touch, teasing him with her sexuality. She'd wanted him.

"What are you remembering? Talk to me Sarah."

She wanted to tell him, yet was concerned how he would react. She shook her head. "I don't know. The memories are jumbled together. It's hard to be certain if they're real or imagined. Since I cannot see myself behaving in that way, they must be false memories."

He bent down and brushed his lips against her temple and whispered, "If they are memories of us alone in my cabin, they aren't false."

His beautiful hazel-eyed stare drew the very breath from her lungs. And when a wicked grin spread across his sensuous lips, her knees practically became mush under her weight. "You remember." She'd never been frightened, upset, or ashamed at landing on Ian's ship. Never. Because somehow she'd known. All along, somehow, she'd known they would be together.

She turned away, embarrassed, if the memories were true. "I have never before behaved in such a manner. It could not possibly be an accurate memory. It seemed more a" —she struggled for the correct word— "fantasy." That's the only word to describe something that surely came out of a novel. A very sordid novel.

"It was," he replied tenderly. "It was my fantasy."

Unbelievable. It could not have possibly been her. Yet the sensations the images generated in her were…stimulating.

"I could not have possibly seduced you," she argued. "It's beyond my aptitude."

"Yet you did. And I enjoyed every minute of it."

She was silent a long while as she thought on what he'd said. Could it be he was telling the truth? If he'd been lying to her, then she would not have felt the truth of his words in her soul. And she did. Sarah got the impression that her husband was doing his best to repair her memory and make them a happy couple again.

"Oh, Ian. I *was* in love with you."

"I hope you still love me."

"I'm unsure," she replied honestly, feeling rattled by the nerves that came with wanting so much to make the right decision. "But I think I may."

"Then I could not ask for more." He wrapped his arms around her and led her back to the gangway. "Let's go home, wife. I think you've had enough for one day."

Chapter Sixteen

Ian and Sarah's new open carriage rolled through Hyde Park several days later on an unusually warm, sunny afternoon in early May, past the debutantes and their mamas eager to see and be seen and young bucks and rogues doing the same. Children played on the lawn with their nurses and governesses ever watchful from the sidelines. Ian felt the time was right to bring up the subject that had been on his mind for days. They'd spent the last week filling in the gaps as much as possible for Sarah, becoming familiar with each other again, learning likes and dislikes as all normal couples do while courting. They'd done some of this in the privacy of the cabin, but not much as they'd rushed head-long into an intimate relationship.

Sarah was still missing certain memories, the ones that would upset her a great deal if she remembered them. He wasn't proud of the things he'd said to her—the accusation he'd made and telling her he thought it was best that she was not carrying a child. Those words had devastated her, and Ian prayed daily that she never remembered them. If she did, he might lose the only thing that made his life worth living these days. Aside from his two aunts, Sarah was the only family he had, and he loved her. She accepted him for who he was and loved him in spite of it.

They'd received a few visitors, only the closest of Sarah's friends, all married young women who'd given their deepest condolences at their loss and best wishes for their future together. Time was now pressing upon him to find out if Sarah would be receptive to adopting Maura. Lucky wanted to leave for America and Canada the day after next, and he was finding it increasingly difficult to remain in the duke's home with the babe now that he'd decided Ian and Sarah would make ideal parents for the little girl.

But the subject was a delicate one and Ian feared his wife's rejection of the idea. He welcomed it though, thinking it a perfect solution, especially after hearing Dr. Prescott explain how his family had evolved and grown into a very normal one.

The warm sunny afternoon was pleasant, and Ian hoped her happy mood would make her more open to considering the idea he and Lucky had decided upon.

"Sarah, there's something I should like to ask you. It is very important to me that you give this matter your complete open-minded contemplation, as it affects someone I know and love dearly." He smiled down at her seated next to him. "Aside from yourself, of course."

"You should know that you can ask me anything. And since you have treated me fairly and with your complete honesty this past week, I will do the same."

Never one to skip around the bush, he asked her directly, hoping he was doing the right thing by taking the direct approach. "How do you feel about taking in children not your own?"

If the first expression to cross her face indicated her answer, he would assume she didn't think the idea a good one. He began to quickly think of another way to pose the question when her eyes narrowed. "Ian, are you suggesting I mother your...." She paused a moment, then asked, "Do you have any? Children that is? I don't remember you mentioning any. Or did you tell me about them and I lost that memory too?"

"No, Sarah-mine, I have no children. But I do know of an infant girl, not a newborn, who is in dire need of a mother's love."

She was silent a long while, and when she spoke it wasn't the reply he'd prepared for. "I hadn't considered it, but of course if there is a babe in need of a loving home, I would welcome her."

He smiled and exhaled, relief flooding through him. "This is not meant to be a replacement for the sons we lost. I would never have suggested it if you think that is what I meant." He slowed the horses and turned the carriage off the path and came to a stop, pulling the brake so he could face her as they talked. "You and I have much to offer as parents, and this is a baby whose circumstance was rather tragic."

"Ian, I love children and have always wanted a large family, having come from one. It is only natural and right that I open my heart as well as my home to babes not my own." Her blue eyes glistened with unshed tears. She was so very brave to be willing to do this, immediately without condition or reservation. His heart began to swell with pride. "Especially now, as it may be my only chance at motherhood."

"I was hoping you'd say that." He lifted her gloved hand to his lips and brushed them lightly across the knuckles.

She cleared her throat, her cheeks pinkening, as

affected by his touch as he was hers. "Where is this child? How did you learn of her?"

"It's a long story." Gad, but he was sounding like Lucky. "Though I should like to introduce you to her if you'd like? This way you can see for yourself what a charmer she is."

"Yes," she replied enthusiastically, her blue eyes aglow, and her smile genuine and full. "Take me to her now."

Releasing the brake, he cued the pair of horses back onto the path and turned toward Caversham House upon exiting the park. Hopefully Lucky would be home to help him answer Sarah's questions, because he knew his wife would be full of them.

A part of him ached for Lucky, at what he would likely go through, seeing the babe in his sister's arms, knowing he was giving the child he'd come to care for over to Ian and Sarah to raise.

Lucky would have to be Maura's godfather, the spiritual substitute parent in the eyes of the church. And in the case of their untimely demise, he'd make Lucky the babe's legal guardian. Ian smiled, feeling much better about the situation.

He drew the horses to a stop in front of the Upper Brook Street family home, and Sarah turned to him, a curious look on her face. "Why are we here?"

"Just come with me, Sarah." He handed over the carriage to the liveried groom who stepped forward, then assisted his wife from her seat.

"We may be a while," he said to the groom, "so you might want to bring it around back."

Sarah gave him a baffled look. "I thought we were going...."

"We are, sweetheart." He cut her off. "But we need stop here."

Ian had another purpose to not having the carriage on the street, one he didn't want to explain in such a public venue with all the foot traffic in front of the house. Should he and Sarah leave with the babe, he didn't want curious eyes to witness what should be their private affair. Those same people would surely spread rumors later, and he wanted to know all was well with Lucky and Sarah before news got out.

"Is Master Lucky in?" Ian asked as they handed their outerwear to the butler, who handed it off to a footman.

"He is in the library, my lord," the elderly butler replied. The man then turned to Sarah. "We are all so very thankful our prayers were answered and you are well, my lady."

"Thank you, Niles," Sarah replied as Ian grabbed her hand to drag her with him down the hall.

Sarah tugged on his hand, finally causing him to stop. "Ian, why are we here? Does Lucky know of the babe as well? Is he coming with us?" He didn't want to answer her barrage of questions out here when he knew they would all get answered soon enough in the privacy of the library. He resumed his long strides the remaining feet to the library, arriving as the footman opened the door.

Lucky worked at a desk at the far end of the room, and upon seeing Sarah and Ian, he asked the footman for a tea cart. He stood and came around the desk to hug his sister. Ian met his gaze over his wife's head, and he smiled at his friend.

"I hear you have memories returning. Is this so?"

"It is," Sarah said cheerfully. "Ever since the day Ian brought me to the ship, I have more and more coming back every day. Now I remember more than I'd forgotten, though there are still gaps in what I think are vital memories."

"Such as?" Lucky asked as he led Sarah to a chair before the hearth. Ian and Lucky both leaned against the mantle at opposite ends while they got the pleasantries over with.

His wife looked at him, then back to Lucky. "Well, it seems I cannot remember details of our wedding for one thing." Ian gave Sarah a supportive smile. "And a few other memories have yet to return as well, but I feel certain they shall come to me in time." The tea cart arrived, and Sarah poured after dismissing the footman. "Lucky, I've missed you of late and wondered why you have not come around for dinner. I've sent you invitations night after night."

"I've been occupied here." He motioned to his drawings. "What with my trip to America coming up. And other matters as well." Lucky pondered his tea nervously.

Ian set his cup and saucer down on the table, then looked at his friend. "Lucky, I've just mentioned to Sarah about Maura, and asked her if we might consider adopting her."

Sarah stared at the two of them, Ian seated next to her and Lucky across from her, as confusion played on her beautiful brow. He was sure she wondered what Lucky had to do with the matter.

"Do you know about her, too?"

Lucky nodded.

"When Ian asked me if I could love a babe that was not my own, I told him of course I could. Lucky, you know what kind of a family we are. There were always children tagging along behind us. First Ren and Lia's, then Elise and Michael's. Not to mention the children at Haldenwood and those in the village who were friends to us as we grew up."

"I know." A hollow timbre in Lucky's voice was the only clue to the true pain Ian knew Lucky was feeling. He turned his deep brown-eyed gaze to Sarah first, then to him. "That's why I think you will be the most perfect mother in the world for her."

"Lucky? What are you saying?" Sarah's eyes grew wide and round, and Ian read the confusion on her face. "Oh, God, Lucky, is she your...."

"No, Sarah...." Ian tried to stop his wife before she incorrectly assumed the same thing she did of him.

"It's not what you're thinking, Sarah," Lucky explained. "Not that at all."

Ian jumped in and began telling her the story of how he and Lucky came to be in possession of the baby girl, now named Maura.

"Oh God," Sarah whispered. The slight sound echoing in the vast book-filled room. She stood and headed for the door, firing questions at him as she walked. "Is she here now, Lucky? Where? I want to see her."

"Sarah," Ian called for his wife. "Please come back." He understood her desire to rush to the child, but this was more about Lucky's sacrifice right now than his wife's desire to embrace and nurture a babe in need of a mother.

Lucky stood and rang for a footman. When one arrived, he asked for the baby's nurse to bring her. Lucky then walked over to the French doors, which opened to the duchess's rose garden. "I will first tell you something about her, if I may." His voice was strained, and he visibly swallowed hard as he straightened his shoulders in an attempt to appear stronger than he likely felt. "I've been calling her Maura, because she has the same fighting spirit and will to live that I witnessed in my nurse when I was much younger. She died trying to save my life. Lia remembers the details more than I, for I was only a child. But my aunt was trying to kill me, and Maura, my *elderly* nurse, died when she was beaten after being caught trying to sneak food for me one night."

Ian had never heard this tale before, but he got the impression Sarah had. He never knew of the treachery his partner had survived.

"The baby Maura," Lucky continued, "has overcome a great ordeal. She is now gaining weight and growing. Though Prescott thinks she may have some lingering effects of her earlier malnutrition, he isn't certain and has tentatively proclaimed her healthy."

Ian heard the hitch in his friend's voice as Lucky took a deep breath to continue, and he knew his friend's heart was about to break when Lucky handed the babe over to Sarah and him.

"Her color is coming back to her skin, and her beautiful green eyes are not so sunken. They sparkle with happiness now. Her hair is beginning to grow back—so much of it had fallen out when we bathed her aboard the ship. It's dark brown with a slight curl at the baby-fine ends."

Ian didn't interrupt him and continued to listen, knowing how important this was for Lucky and for Sarah. "She smiles now, all the time. Ian? Do you remember that first day, when all she did was make that horrible mewling cry?" When Ian nodded, Lucky went on. "She has a beautiful smile, with a mouth full of teeth and another molar coming in right now. It bothers her sometimes, but aside from that, she's a happy baby, making noises and babbling all the time."

Ian glanced over at Sarah and saw tears streaming down her face as she understood how difficult this was for her brother.

"Lucky, you love her. Are you certain you want to give her to me?"

"There is no one I would entrust her to more than you and Ian. I know you will be the perfect parents for Maura. You will be a wonderful mother to her, and she needs a mother's love. Not that of a nurse or nanny, which is all I would be able to provide for her right now."

"Are you sure?" Ian saw tears welling in Sarah's eyes now. This was perfect for them all.

"I have never been more sure of anything. I've done some thinking these past few days. And I've come to the conclusion that I am simply not ready to be a father to her. I'm not prepared for it. I have no home, no wife, and nothing to offer her right now."

"Nothing besides your love." Sarah wiped her eyes.

In this entire transaction, Ian had never once thought about the fact that gaining custody of Maura would now make him a father. Sarah wasn't going to be the child's only parent; he was now going to be her father.

"You will fall in love with her too once you meet her." Lucky visibly relaxed, as though a great weight had been lifted from his shoulders. And Ian felt the transfer of responsibility as he willingly accepted Lucky's burden.

Minutes later, Sarah watched the young nanny enter the room with a squirming toddler in her arms. She came closer with the child and went to hand the babe over to Lucky, but he pointed to Sarah.

LOVING SARAH

"Let Mrs. Ross-Mackeever meet her new daughter, Penny," Lucky said.

Sarah suddenly became nervous, unsure if she would make an adequate mother. The girl brought the babe over, and Sarah felt her arms trembling as she realized this was now going to be her child. Lucky was entrusting this tiny life into her care, and Ian's as well, to raise and nurture into adulthood. It was an enormous responsibility, one she willingly accepted.

She looked into the bundle of blankets and saw the most serious, dark green eyes she'd ever seen. They overshadowed every other feature of the child's face. Darker than emeralds, they were so deep a green they were almost black. When the baby heard Lucky's voice, she smiled, then began to cry as the nanny handed her to Sarah and not Lucky. She wrapped her arms about the babe and began walking toward Lucky so Maura could see his face and reassure herself that all was well. Sarah's heart melted the moment the baby smiled upon seeing Lucky.

"She will come to recognize you soon. Do not worry." Lucky gently stroked baby Maura's cheek with a finger and stepped back. "Show her to Ian. He hasn't seen her in a few days. I swear she's gained two pounds this week." Sarah thought Lucky had to be in deep anguish because he was chattering while she held the babe he'd taken into his heart.

She went over to where Ian stood in front of the fireplace and presented the infant to her husband. "Isn't she beautiful, Ian?" Sarah stared down at the babe, in awe of her.

He made a sound of agreement as he stroked her dusky pink cheek. She watched her husband as he radiated joy when the babe grasped his finger and tried to put it in her mouth. He was so big and gruff, then at times he could be so gentle and caring. He was like a coin. There were two sides to him, but he was still the same man on the inside. And she loved him.

Lucky came toward them and said softly, "This is the right decision all around. As I said, I have nothing to offer her. I'm unprepared for fatherhood at this time. I'm not married, and I'm too young yet only five and twenty. Besides, it's not as though I'll never see her. After all, we *are* family."

Something in his words echoed in Sarah's mind as though she'd heard them before, but she shoved the thought aside as she cradled the baby in her arms. She'd never loved her husband nor her brother as much as she did right then. Ian, for his acceptance and willingness to be a parent to this child who wasn't his, even after learning of the loss of his two sons. And Lucky, for giving up this little girl he'd come to love so dearly. Her heart swelled with joy and hope.

"We shall name you godfather, Uncle Lucky," Sarah said to her brother. Then she began to cry again. A wave of guilt washed over her, guilt that she could love a babe other than the twins she'd miscarried. Even though Prescott had assured her that she'd done nothing to cause the loss of her pregnancy, she still felt that she should have done more to prevent it from happening.

She wanted so much to remember her twins, but Lia had told her that by the time she'd delivered them, she was unconscious, and the boys were already gone. In falling in love with Maura, she almost felt like a bad mother, as though she should be missing her twins more.

"Darling, why the tears?" Ian asked.

She considered her reply carefully, as she didn't want them to be alarmed at her misplaced guilt. In the end, she chose to keep her guilt to herself. "Because I'm happy, Ian." She turned and met Lucky's gold-flecked brown eyes, swimming with unshed tears of his own. "I am so very happy," she repeated as she stroked the infant's head feeling the downy-softness of her baby hair.

Within hours, Sarah and Ian's Mayfair home was descended upon by Elise and Michael, who'd arrived at their Hanover Square home that morning for the opening of the Parliamentary session the following week. Sarah sent a note to her sister telling her she needed her help but not what for, and almost immediately, her sister and brother-in-law were in the drawing room. Ian had kept them company until she could come down with her new daughter.

"What did she need me for?" Elise asked. "Perhaps I should go up and see if she's...."

"I am fine, Aunt Elise," Sarah said as she crossed the threshold. "But my daughter will need baby clothing immediately," she said as he entered the room with her sleeping bundle. The surprise that crossed her sister's face was priceless. Sarah handed Maura to her sister, as once again Ian explained how the child came to be in his and Lucky's charge and the condition of her health.

"Do you mean to tell me that Lucky's been hiding this babe in the house for a week? And Mrs. Steen assisted him?" Elise appeared surprised that the elderly family housekeeper would have been party to something so desperate, yet wonderful. "Where is he? I want to wring his neck and kiss him at the same time."

"He remained at Upper Brook Street to allow us some time to get to know our new daughter," Sarah said softly, as she cradled the sleeping infant. "The babe's nanny came with us to help me learn Maura's routine, and I believe she'll stay on."

"Don't be angry with Lucky. He didn't want to tell anyone because of what Sarah had been through," Ian defended Lucky's decision. "And he wanted to wait until the time was right before we mentioned her to Sarah, and discussed possibility of adopting her." Neither he nor Sarah felt it necessary to mention that Lucky had fallen in love with the infant in the short time he'd been caring for her and that his heart was in tatters over his decision to allow them to adopt her.

"Is that what you're naming her?" Elise asked. "How'd you arrive at that?"

"Lucky named her," Ian replied, "and we've decided it suits her."

The discussion turned to the legalities of adopting the infant, with Michael promising to make all of the necessary arrangements for the paperwork. "It shouldn't be too difficult as the woman who gave her to you is in another country and willingly handed her over to you in front of a witness."

"I don't think she cared that there was a witness," Ian said. "If you had seen the desperation on her face and the way she just shoved the sack into my hands and ran off, you would know she wanted the babe to have a better life than what she could provide."

"I wonder why she chose to give the babe to you, instead of to Lucky?"

"I've asked myself that over and over. The only thing

I can think of is that because I am fair-haired and light-eyed, she assumed I was from another country. Lucky, being dark-haired and dark-eyed, could have been Portuguese for all she knew, even though he dresses better than I and exudes wealth much more so than I."

"It doesn't matter to me why she did what she did," Sarah said, so happy at that very moment her heart could burst with joy. "Right now I could hug her for this precious gift."

"Have you sent Lia a note yet? She'll want to come see her as quickly as possible."

"Yes." The tea cart arrived, and Sarah poured a cup for Elise and set it in front of her and handed one to Ian and the other to Michael before pouring one for herself. "And we have decided that, since Maura is named after Lia and Lucky's deceased nurse, they and Ren should be her godparents." She met her sister's gaze, then added, "I hope you don't mind. You can be godparents for our next child."

Ian felt the most hope that he had since learning of the miscarriage the week before. Sarah was starting to regain her memory, and they were beginning to rebuild what he'd once thought a doomed relationship. And his wife was starting to be optimistic about the future and the possibility of more children.

"Of course we don't mind," Michael said.

"As long as you don't forget," said Elise, cradling the sleeping infant in one arm and sipping her tea with her free hand.

"If I did," Sarah replied, "I'm sure you would remind me."

"I wouldn't be the conscientious older sister if I didn't."

Later that evening, after Sarah had put the baby down for the night, Ian knocked on the door of her rooms. He'd worried the last few hours over asking her if she would be fine if he decided to go to Scotland, Canada, and America with Lucky. Though not imperative that he go, he felt strongly that he should because the new ships were partly his. Something as important as interviewing the shipbuilders should be a shared obligation. Ian and Lucky had conceived and sketched these ships, the designs were his, and he wanted to make certain the shipbuilder understood and agreed to his drawings. Lucky could negotiate the costs. The business aspect had always been his area of expertise, whereas Ian was a naval architect, a ship designer at heart.

When she invited him to enter, he opened the door and found her seated on the floor before a chest at the foot of her bed. In her hand were embroidered linens and spread on the Persian rug around her were infant gowns, woven blankets, and tiny, fur-trimmed, hooded baby coats. He watched as she fingered the embroidered lettering on the napkins and caught the sheen of tears glistening in her eyes.

Perhaps it wasn't a good time to bring up leaving just yet. He didn't know what to say to her. Should he hold her? Is that what she needed? Did she need to cry for the twins again? Or could these be happy tears?

Then his heart sank into his gut. Were her tears because she remembered his words to her the night before he left her in Liverpool? How on earth would he explain that?

Just how did he approach her or break the silence?

She took care of that for him. "It took me one entire day to sew one tiny baby napkin," she said as she held one out to him, "but I made these all myself."

"They're perfect," he said, not sure what to say. If he could just discern what she needed from him, he would give it. He didn't know what else to do, never having had a lady in his life on a daily basis before now. He had his aunts, but he'd never lived with them. His mother died when he was a boy, so he had little memory of her. And the various mistresses he'd had over the years were no comparison to his lady wife.

"No. They're not. I do horrible needlework. Even a blind woman can embroider better than I can."

He sat on the rug next to her and gave the stitching a closer inspection. "You know," he said, hoping he could lighten her mood, "you're right. But when you think about what part of the body these cover and what they're intended for, who cares what the initials look like?"

She laughed. "I suppose I do sound a bit silly, don't I?"

He shrugged. "You're entitled to a little lapse in reason. Just for tonight, mind you. Tomorrow you must be completely rational again. Our daughter depends on it."

The linen she held fell to her lap as she sighed. "Oh, Ian. I had given up hope of ever becoming a mother, and now this miracle has come to me. Do you have any idea how truly blessed I feel right now?"

"I think I have some idea." He hoped she understood that he, too, felt truly happy at the prospect of fatherhood. The fact that this baby wasn't of his seed meant nothing to him. She was a beautiful infant in need of loving parents. He and Sarah were now Maura's mother and father.

Sarah turned serious. "There is a cloud over my happiness, and it isn't because of the twins."

"What is it then?" Dear God, don't let it be those memories. He could take just about anything but that right now.

She wiped a stray tear and took a deep, reinforcing breath. "That my brother is hurting because of the gift he's given us. He bonded with Maura before he knew I'd lost the twins. And I know Lucky as well as you. He would have raised Maura as his own daughter. His words this morning were his way of convincing himself he was doing what he thought was right for the child. It wasn't for my benefit. He was trying to ease his own pain.

"He has given me the greatest gift one human could give another, aside from laying down his life. He's given *us* this gift, Ian. She's *our* daughter, not just mine."

Ian thought a moment before replying. She was right. Lucky had bonded with the baby girl the entire trip home from Portugal. He'd turned his cabin into a nursery for her and fed the child himself when he was not at the wheel. Lucky had immediately made whatever changes were necessary to his life to raise Maura. And when he discovered Sarah had lost her babes, and that it was unlikely she would ever have children again, his best friend willingly cut out his own heart to give it to his sister. "Then we shall do our best to make certain that Lucky is always a big part of Maura's life."

"Yes," she said, "we should. He needs it. Maura won't remember these events, but Lucky will."

He stared at his wife, noticing for the first time that she wore a diaphanous robe over an equally enticing gown. He felt a familiar stirring, but his wife was likely not ready for lovemaking yet. "Are you ready for bed?"

She folded the last linen and placed it on top of the stack, then gave him her attention. "Did you want to ask me something? Why did you come?"

"For no reason," he said, fingering the fringe on the edge of the rug. "I wanted to see if you were still happy." He needed to tell her about his travel plans, but it just wasn't the right time to burden her with the fact that he'd be leaving again.

She gave him a knowing little grin. "I think I know why you've come, and you don't have to ask my permission to go. I'll be fine while you're gone. Elise is here in town, and soon Lia will be here as well."

"How did you know?"

"Because as I sat in that chair in the library holding our new daughter, I overheard you and Lucky discussing the fact that you really should go, but you didn't think it appropriate just yet." She began to remove more baby items, setting them on the floor in front of the chest. "You shouldn't think you need my permission to do your job. It's your business, Ian. Please don't let it suffer because of me."

Something inside him swelled with pride at having this woman by his side. Not just in physical proximity, but as a mate and partner in life. He loved her. He may not have loved her the night he was forced to marry her, but by God, he did now. And he wanted her to know it.

"Are you certain? Lucky and I decided in the interest of time, that we should divide the list. He will go to Halifax and Baltimore, and I will go to Aberdeen only. I should only be gone about three weeks, four at most," he said.

"I overheard Lucky say he will be gone two months," his wife said.

"If we were together it would be three months or more that both of us are gone, and that puts us back just in time to prepare for departure to China. It would give you and me very little time together." He really did not wish to be gone that long. Not when he and Sarah were happy again and they had Maura.

Sarah sat back on her heels and continued to lift clothing out of the trunk. "He is probably being nice to you because we are new parents."

"Probably," Ian mused, wondering if he should even leave at all knowing she hadn't fully recovered her memory yet.

"I was joking, Ian," she said. After glancing up at him, concern crossed her brow. "Ian, your business is sailing and bringing that highly desired beverage home to the English consumer. These will be your boats. Yours and Lucky's. We both know you want to go. And Baltimore is near your childhood home, is it not?"

He nodded. It *was* his childhood home, though there was nothing or no one left for him there since his father's death. He watched her sort more baby clothing as she continued chattering.

"If you go to Aberdeen only," she said, "will you make a stop in Edinburgh to visit your grandfather? Your aunts wrote and said he had very much recovered from his illness, though Aunt Royce says he is still grieving the loss of his good friend, Lieutenant Morgan who passed the week prior to the onset of his heart malaise. I am sure it is difficult to lose such a close friend of so many years. Especially after going through so much together as they did. Why, I didn't know...."

LOVING SARAH

As Sarah chattered on about his grandfather, all he could think of was how much of a shame it was that the old bastard had not cocked his toes up and died as well as his lover. Eight years ago, his grandfather had sent his thugs to intimidate Ian into silence. Ian hadn't said of word to anyone of what he'd seen, because he was too repulsed to think of it, let alone speak it. Later he sent a letter to his grandfather informing the old man that if anything happened to him, an affidavit would be sent to the admiralty of the events Ian had witnessed that long-ago day in his grandfather's office. That handwritten note had sufficed to put a stop to the men following him.

"Husband, if you wish to remain with me, I would love to have you at home with us. But I think this might be a perfect opportunity for you to make peace with your grandfather. You both deserve it after all these years. It has weighed heavily on you for just the short time I've known you."

"It can never happen, sweetheart. He will never agree to it."

They stared at each other for a moment. He brought her hand to his lips and kissed the open palm. He heard her intake of breath and knew she felt that same burst of heat he'd felt upon touching her. "I have missed you, Sarah. I will not be gone long."

She lifted her hand to his cheek and rested it there. "Now that I remember you, husband, I will miss you each time you sail."

Ian leaned forward and brought his lips to hers gently, sweetly. Afraid of hurting her, he didn't pressure her. Even though every inch of him screamed to make love to this woman, his fear of being too rough after all these months without her won over, and he held himself in check. He broke the kiss and rested his forehead against hers as he stroked her arm under the bell sleeve of her robe. Her skin so soft and her scent so tempting.

"Dr. Prescott says I'm well now, Ian," she whispered.

"It's been a long time, Sarah, and I…I'm afraid I might hurt you."

"It's been equally long for me, and I need you."

"Are you sure?" Even as he said the words, he was afraid of hurting her. How on earth was he supposed to temper his emotion? This woman had no idea what she did to him physically. One look, one word of invitation from her, and his cock was as hard as a lad about to bed his first lassie. He also feared getting her with child and possibly losing her the next time. His father never recovered after losing his mother. Ian didn't want to imagine that pain.

Instead of replying to his question, she led him to the bed. "I was sure this morning after remembering how good this was between us."

"Now, here's the woman I fell in love with."

Chapter Seventeen

"The candles...." Sarah said as she moved to stop the flow of gas to the sconces on the wall. She couldn't bear for him to see her with the flame lit, surely he'd find her body repulsive now.

"Oh, no." A wicked grin spread across his handsome face when he took her hand and pulled her back to him. "I want to see you, sweetheart.

"I'm not as you remember," she whispered as her head fell onto his chest. "I've changed."

"How so?"

She had to tell him, for he would surely notice. "Aside from this...memory problem, there are...physical changes. To my body, Ian."

Sarah feared his revulsion when he saw the marks on her belly and breasts. Marks from her skin stretching while she was pregnant with the two babies. Lia had told her they would fade with time, but in the almost five months since her miscarriage, they'd not diminished as much as she'd liked.

He leaned back slightly and tilted her chin so she might see his face. "Do you think that I might find you less desirable because of it?"

She closed her eyes and nodded. She didn't think she could stand to see that look in his eyes when he realized for the first time how truly hideous she'd become underneath her corset and fine dresses.

"Sarah, love, you're wrong."

His hands untied the ribbon beneath her throat holding the robe together and gently parted the filmy material. He let it fall silently to the floor at their feet. He bent his head and traced tiny kisses over her bare shoulders, sending shivers racing over her entire body and a clenching sensation in the vicinity of her barren womb. She choked down her tears before they interfered with their loving. Now was not the time to think of her sorrow, not now, when they had a future together—one that included their new daughter.

The ribbon-thin straps of her nightdress fell down her arms as Ian murmured, "You are more beautiful now than the first time we made love." His thumbs raked across her nipples. "That night you captivated me with your delectable" —the gown slid over her hips and pooled atop the robe— "and very distracting charms."

His hands caressed her curves, more pronounced now than before. She wondered if he really didn't object to them or find them as unattractive as she did. "So soft and perfect." His hot, moist breath over chilled skin heated her blood and caused her heart to pound a little faster. His fingers sliding up and down her thighs and hips caused a rippling effect over her entire body, and she suddenly felt herself grow moist with readiness for his loving. He bent and lifted her naked body and laid her gently in the center of her turned-down bed. She grabbed a pillow and hugged it to her body as he stepped away to divest himself of his own clothing.

"Think of this…." He kicked off his shoes. "When the great masters painted the female nude, did any of them ever paint a thin, half-starved form? I don't think they did." As he unbuttoned the last button on his shirt, it fell where he stood, and he began to unbutton his trousers. "And why do you think that is? Could it be perhaps that what a man thinks is the ideal female form differs from what a woman believes it to be? You are a woman with a woman's body. No longer a girl with the body of a girl. You are now soft and gently rounded where you should be. And yet, you worry over whether I will be repulsed by the lines that mar the skin on your breasts and belly." After undoing the last of the buttons, Ian kicked the trousers off, sending them across the room. Sarah got a glimpse of his erection and closed her eyes, suddenly remembering how he felt and how he tasted. She turned into the pillow, choking down her tears. She was not going to cry over his beautiful words. He was making her feel desired. And loved.

"You couldn't be more wrong, Sarah-love. I see them as a symbol of your womanhood. Your body held our children. Not one, but two! Though we were not blessed with having them live, you did your best to care for them. I know this fact if I know nothing else of you. You loved our children as you now love Maura and as you will love our future children as well. I *know* this."

He slid onto the bed next to her and pulled her close to him. He took the pillow she held and tossed it off the bed, continuing to touch and soothe her—something she very much appreciated and needed, especially this first time.

"The marks are ugly," she whispered. "But as long as you say those things to me, I don't think of the scars, for you make me feel as beautiful as you did on the boat."

"Let me pose another question to you. If I were a

soldier and had come home from war missing a limb or disfigured in some other way, would that affect your love for me?"

"Of course not. What I feel for you goes beyond...." She understood now what he was saying. His love for her went deeper than the marks on her fuller body.

"I see you finally get my meaning, woman. What I feel for you goes far beyond what people outside of this room could perceive. Our sons may not have survived, but Sarah, I am thankful to God that you did and are still with me, because I don't want to think of a future without you in it."

She swiped at the tears that began to pool in her eyes, forcing herself to stop. He loved her. She was over-the-moon happy because she needed to know that he still wanted her and loved her, even though she might never be able to provide him with the heir he would need.

He rolled her onto her back and began to trace his fingers over and around her hardened nipples. Her breath caught in her throat. She closed her eyes as she concentrated solely on the exquisite sensations he caused by his mere touch. When she moaned, Ian chuckled then raised himself over her and began loving her with his mouth, tracing kisses from her forehead, temple, and cheek, down her shoulder, breasts, and even lower still, dipping into her navel before continuing down even farther.

"Ian, no!" This wasn't proper! Even as her mind fought the idea of what he was doing, her body gave in to his intimate touch. He seemed so familiar with her body that likely they had done this before. And she hoped it was on more than one occasion! "Oh, Ian."

He raised his wicked gaze to meet hers. "Oh, Sarah,

yes." His fingers delved into her wetness and parted her before his tongue darted out to touch her.

He *had* done this before, she remembered. As she relaxed, she let herself fall into the most intense vortex of pleasure she'd ever known, letting herself be carried away on a wave of pure sensual ecstasy. She sighed with pleasure as a tight coil began to wrap even tighter within her as he relentlessly drove her closer and closer to breaking. Shattering.

Then she did. Her very soul fragmented into millions of tiny pieces of being, only to be united when this man, her husband, slid over her and entered her.

Ian forced himself to go slowly, holding himself back so as not to hurt her. He wanted so much to just drive into her hard and fast and lose himself in her welcoming heat. But he couldn't. After what she'd gone through, if he acted upon his baser instinct he'd perhaps harm her, then she could possibly fear lovemaking. He remembered the physician's words and knew the man had been correct. This was probably the most important act of manhood, making love to a woman after she'd suffered the loss of a child, and, in their case, children. He had to take his time. And for her, he *would*.

Once fully inside, he held himself still until she relaxed her muscles, which had tightened in anticipation. She sighed and shifted beneath him, and as she tilted upward to meet him, he began to move, gently, thoroughly, yet ever so slowly. He brought his lips down on hers and whispered tender endearments and encouraging love words in between deep, soul-stirring kisses.

Before tonight, he'd never wanted to hold back his passion once he'd started on the quest for release. But now he wanted to. He wanted to give her more memories, new memories to erase the old, those that he wasn't proud of. He wanted these to be what she'd always remember when she thought about their lovemaking.

The moment he'd realized he loved her, everything changed for him and his life became less about what he wanted and more about what they could achieve together. He had known this before Lucky told him she was carrying his child. It came to him during the long hours alone with his thoughts as he stood at the wheel or lay in his hammock trying to sleep.

Ian was on the verge of losing himself within her. He felt Sarah nearing her climax as her body tightened around him and her breathing became shallow and labored. Several slow, deep thrusts later, he led her over the edge and they dove over together, and nothing ever felt more right.

Moments later, he eased himself off and lay on his side next to her, pulling her languorous form into the curve of his body. He held her close, her head resting on his upper arm, and her feet entwined with his.

"Was it always this good between us?" Sarah rolled onto her side and watched his expression.

He decided now was not the time to tell her all the details of their intimacy. Even though he might have said some insensitive things to her in the past, their loving was always this good. "Yes. It was."

"I thought so. That was so…wonderful." She mumbled something unintelligible in her half-slumber.

"I didn't understand a word of what you said, but know that I will miss you while I am away, wife."

She sighed, then said softly, "I said, maybe that will

entice you to hurry home."

Her husband sailed to Aberdeen two weeks later, just days after seeing Lucky off on his trip to Halifax and Baltimore. The first few days Ian was gone passed slowly for Sarah, even with her new daughter occupying her time. Already a few weeks into the Season, and she felt out of place in town for the first time ever. What few invitations she did receive were from connections to both of her sisters, as she noticed that her friends from the past few years had, as Ian once predicted, distanced themselves. This was when she decided she wanted to go to Greenwood, the home she'd inherited from her mother, because she had no desire to remain in London for now.

So she began instructing the servants to make arrangements for their transfer to Surrey. Ian could hardly argue that the country air was not more beneficial to Maura. When he returned from Aberdeen, they would go together to their new home in the country.

On the morning of the fourth day, she had the most marvelous idea and sat at her *secretaire* to compose a letter to the Earl Mackeever, inviting him to stay the summer with her and his great-granddaughter at Greenwood beginning at his earliest convenience. She didn't tell him that his grandson, her husband, would also be in attendance. And she would not tell Ian of the Earl's arrival either, for he'd likely find an excuse to be away.

Sarah thought it was long past time for their feud to come to an end, and she was making it her mission to see it happen.

She knew she couldn't keep Ian tied to her side and had accepted the fact that his life was building his company. She loved him, and as his partner in this marriage, she determined her position was to support him in his endeavors. Sarah had to suffer through his absences so that one day he'd not have to leave the family. It was what her brother had done early on, though later he'd stayed home with his wife, managing his business interests from his London office.

A lump grew in her throat at the thought of his leaving her alone. She loved him and wanted to be with him always. With all of the meetings he'd had with his solicitors before leaving, Sarah hadn't the opportunity to tell him. Of course, she'd have to wait until the time was right before she revealed to him these newly discovered feelings.

Most days, she had her sister, sister-in-law, and nieces close by to help her with all of the decisions thrust upon her by the arrival of Maura Luchina Ross-Mackeever. A few close friends came to wish her well and visit the new arrival to the family. But it seemed to Sarah that every matron, and even the young married women, were more reserved in their congratulations than she'd seen in the past. She wondered if it was because news of her miscarriage had spread through the ton or if they felt sorry for her presuming she was now unable to give Ian the heir he needed for the continuation of the title.

While this upset her for a short while, Sarah soon forgot about them as she played with her new daughter. Maura was like sunshine to a flower. No one could stay in a down mood around her. She would naturally draw Sarah into her imaginary toddler games and the entire world could cease to exist outside the walls of her nursery. Her daughter was such a happy, curious child—unless she was hungry and a meal was not within easy reach. According to Lia and Elise, this was much like Sarah had been as an infant and small child.

"I haven't grown out of it either," Sarah confessed. "I *still* get irritable when I'm hungry and cannot get my hands on something to hold me until dinner."

"I don't know how you ever managed to remain so tiny with that enormous appetite you've always had," Elise replied as she poured them some tea one afternoon after laying the baby down for her nap. The three of them sat in the morning room in the Mayfair house, awaiting the arrival of her new interior designer to show her his sketches of her daughter's room that she was having redone.

Elise clarified, "According to the ladies, you got that from your mother. She was petite as well, with an enormous appetite."

"Speaking of the ladies," Sarah said, as Lia took the vacant seat next to her on the settee, "I received a reply from them yesterday, stating they are both eager to join me for the summer at Greenwood. It will be good to get away from town for a while."

"I know you are sad because of the lack of visits from among your group of friends, but they likely do not know how to approach someone after such a tragic event." Lia was doing her best to be reassuring, and Sarah loved her all the more for it. "I do believe things will all smooth over in time. Besides most people do not even know the truth of what has taken place. The ones who do know are the ones who matter to you and our family. And we are all thrilled that you and Ian now have Maura. So you have nothing to fear."

"The other day Lady Burton came to see me about two riding horses for herself and her daughter. She said she heard your good news about Maura, then she mentioned something you might be interested in hearing."

Sarah and Lia both turned curious looks to Elise.

"Lady Burton said that she had a friend many years ago who had difficulty conceiving, and after many years of trying, she and her husband had adopted an infant girl from an orphanage. Well, the new babe had been in their home less than one year before her friend became with child. So after all those years, her friend had finally delivered her husband an heir."

Sarah wanted to cry, even though her situation was not completely similar. It wasn't that she had trouble conceiving. Her problem had been carrying through to delivery. She said as much to her sisters.

"But, dear, don't you see?" Lia patted her hand as the two sat side-by-side on the settee. "There is always hope. Do not be discouraged."

"Yes," Elise said, "Prescott said the only reason he saw for your miscarrying was the fact that you carried twins, and you are so very petite." She hugged Sarah. "He said there was nothing physically preventing you from having more children. Perhaps another pregnancy will result in a healthy child."

"As women, it's all we pray for," Sarah said.

"I've always said that stressful situations during pregnancy should be avoided at all costs," Lia said. "And remember the amount of stress you had when you were pregnant…what with wondering if Ian would accept a babe after saying he didn't want children."

"That reminds me of something I wanted to ask," Elise began, and when she lifted her gaze to Sarah's, she paused.

Sarah finally recovered enough to say through the tears knotting her throat, "He didn't want children." She choked, the memory flooding back. Her head began to hurt, and her chest felt as though it were in a tightening vise. Air. She needed air.

"Sarah, what is it?" Lia asked. "You've gone pale."

"Is it another memory?" Elise asked.

She inhaled deeply, as though starved for breath. Through the rush of emotion flooding her she choked out, "He didn't want to marry to me. He'd gotten drunk. And they forced him to marry me. Then at the end of the race, after I thought we'd settled into what I assumed was a companionable relationship, he said he did not want children."

"That blackguard," Elise said, wrapping her arms around her little sister.

"Elise," Lia scolded, as she came to Sarah's side. "Take a slow, deep breath, Sarah. Calm down. All is well now, as Ian obviously loves you."

"He hasn't *said* he loves me. And he will one day be Earl and will need heirs," Sarah whispered through a clenched throat, "of his own blood." She desperately fought for a breath of air, and once she was able, she choked out, "I cannot give him that."

"You cannot be certain that he plans anything of the sort," Lia stated. "The man I saw return from China was a far different Ian than the one you describe."

Sarah nodded. "That is why I do not understand. Why his change of heart?" She brought her hands to her face to wipe her cheeks. If they only knew how kind and gentle he'd been when he loved her just days ago, how he held her so tenderly afterward when he'd told her he would miss her. If they only saw the way he looked when he held Maura and how he beamed with pride when the baby extended her arms out for him to lift her from the cradle.

What had changed? He left for China the year before not knowing of her condition and after telling her he did not care to have children.

She suddenly felt sick to her stomach and fled the room.

Three days later, she and all of the necessary staff left for Greenwood Manor, as it would now be her home. Sarah left specific instruction for the remaining staff at the Mayfair house: they were not to inform his lordship as to her location. Craggins, though saddened by the turn of events, agreed.

Lia and Elise had agreed with her decision to leave town more for the solitude afforded by the country. Lia agreed to stay behind in London to await Ian, while Elise accompanied Sarah to Greenwood for a few days to help her get settled into her new home.

Their procession of coaches pulled through the gates of Greenwood, and Sarah wrapped the baby's light blanket around her daughter. "We're here," she cooed to the infant. "This is our new home."

She managed a smile for the benefit of her sister as they rolled to a stop in front of the impressive limestone facade of her new home. They both commented on how much better the house looked than it had the last time they'd seen it—before the renovations were begun the year prior.

Loving Sarah

Several footmen descended upon their coaches and began opening the doors for them. Others came forward and began unloading their baggage and assisting both women from their seats. It was an impressive sight to see—four coaches all lined up along the macadamized drive, their inhabitants disembarking.

Sarah lifted her emerald-eyed bundle and went up the wide stone steps to the front landing and looked up at the facade of her new home. "This will be our home, sweetheart. Yours and mine. I will teach you to sail and ride, and we shall fill our stables with only the finest horses, courtesy of your Aunt Elise. And we shall have grand adventures each and every day." The door opened, and as she stepped inside, she continued talking to her daughter. "Then, when the day comes and you wish to marry, we shall consider men only from the most noble of families. And the young man will have to be very handsome, for I will not allow my beautiful daughter to marry a toad." She handed Maura over to her nurse and greeted the staff, thanking them all for having everything in readiness for their arrival.

Her sister helped to see her settled into her new home, but wanted to get back to her children and husband. Elise left the morning after the arrival of the two agents from the security firm Ren used. Sarah did as instructed and placed them among her staff to protect her.

The days turned into weeks, and it wasn't long before Sarah suspected that she carried Ian's child again. She immediately sent a note to Lia, and another to Elise, both still in London, asking them to come to Surrey.

Two days later, over dinner, Sarah said, "Believe me, I am ecstatic to be carrying again. You know how desperately I want more children. But what is to happen if he learns of my condition?"

"You worry for nothing," Lia said. "Ian will be thrilled. You just have to reconcile that last memory with him. And ask him to clarify. Does he, or does he not, want to remain married and have children."

"He should be back any day now," she reminded them.

Elise paced the long carpet in front of her settee where she rested. "Though I agree with Lia that you may be worried for nothing, I think I would like to speak with him before we send him out here. We must first learn what Ian's intentions are once he finds out you have remembered everything."

"The only way to find out is to ask him," Lia said. "So I will leave a note for him at your Mayfair house asking him to come see me upon his return."

Chapter Eighteen

The first days at sea drew on forever. At least they did until they reached Aberdeen. From there, the voyage would be homeward bound, and he couldn't wait to see his wife and daughter again. Perhaps it was his good mood, or the fact he'd had, thus far, a very enlightening journey. An architect at one of the two shipyards he'd visited thought his drawings had some merit and even asked if Ian minded his copying one of the designs for further study. But most of the people he'd talked with, both ship builders and naval architects, wanted to push their own designs. One builder had shown him some very interesting drawings for the clipper he was wanting to build, but as of yet had no buyer. Ian wasn't certain about the viability of his design and told the man he'd consider his proposal. In reality, that man had only wanted another opinion on his own design. So Ian went to visit a third shipbuilder and a fourth one after that. All of the yards and designers were in the forefront of their fields, and a couple actually merited second visits with his partner.

He wondered how Lucky fared in Halifax and Baltimore, and if he'd met with Mr. Pook as Ian had suggested or gone to Indian Point to meet with Mr. Watkins, the man his father had worked with. Both men were very respected in their fields of ship design and construction, and he and Lucky would do well with boats coming from the shipyards in Baltimore, as they were Ian's preference—and not only because he was familiar with the designs.

On the return trip from Scotland, Ian counted the hours till he was home again. He found himself wondering how long he was going to continue to sail. Certainly now that they were making money, they could afford to hire another captain. They'd need several more in two years anyway once they had their new ships, and he thought it was something worth considering now, especially as he found himself missing Sarah and Maura. They were not just his family, they were his home now.

And that was another change he'd noticed in himself. He didn't know when it happened, but suddenly he had a sense of home, where he hadn't really had one since his father died. He'd lived on the ship since leaving university, his cabin the only private quarters he needed as he desired little in the way of material possessions.

He'd heard love had a way of upending one's life and he was now living proof. What had been normal before—the free and unencumbered lifestyle he'd been living the past three years—now seemed inadequate in light of his recent change of heart.

That was when he had realized that loving Sarah had changed him completely. Perhaps that was what was meant by the term "becoming a man." Because what he'd thought he wanted before in terms of an unencumbered lifestyle now seemed so insignificant and irrelevant. He longed for the responsibilities of home and hearth, of caring for his family and growing old with a woman.

One woman. But not just any woman.

LOVING SARAH

Sarah.

So as he made his way up the Thames to London, he sighed. Relieved to finally be here. Even for what little time he had before they sailed again. This time to China.

The weather in the southern hemisphere dictated when they had to round the cape, thus mandating their departure before mid-September or else they would never make the return around the tip of South Africa before their winter set in. The journey to Fuchow and back was easily nine months, and that was if luck was favoring them and they had no emergencies requiring docking to make repairs for any length of time.

The more he thought about how long he would be gone from Sarah, and Maura, the more he dreaded making the run. But he decided he was not going to let that cloud of gloom mar his reunion with his wife and daughter. Once they docked, he immediately sent word of his return to their home. And in the note, he told his wife how much he looked forward to seeing her that evening.

Ian pocketed his mother's ring, having decided it was time to give it to his wife. He then made quick work of leaving orders for Mr. Johnson and quickly went to the Mayfair home he shared with Sarah. Upon entering the foyer of the house, he sensed a change had taken place in his absence. Dread washed over him as he envisioned the worst scenarios imaginable. Craggins, their normally unruffled butler, would not meet his gaze and stood stiffer than usual.

"What's happened?" Ian looked around the house at the servants who were peeking from around corners and behind doors. "Where's my wife?" He immediately began taking the carpeted stairs two at a time, and when he reached the landing, he turned to the butler who followed behind him as fast as his elderly legs would carry him. "Craggins, is my wife home?" The butler shook his head. Ian hated that he could hear the weakness and fear in his own voice when he asked, "Where is she?"

"We are not at liberty to say, sir. We have been instructed by Her Grace and the Countess not to reveal the lady's location."

Ian knew then he'd lost her. She'd remembered everything and had now chosen to leave him.

He'd known all along it was only a matter of time. But he'd hoped to have more time to give her newer, better memories before the old, harsh ones returned. It had been a chance he'd been willing to take at the time, and now he'd come out on the losing end.

The footman opened the door to his rooms, and he entered, expecting to find a note from her, something to explain why and where she might be.

Then he saw it. On his desk in their shared sitting room. Folded parched vellum. And as he drew nearer, the wax seal. When he lifted it, he noticed it wasn't Sarah's seal, but that of the duchess. He ran a finger under the fold, opened the note, and read:

Mr. Mackeever,

Our sister is safe. It is in the best interest of her health that you not see her just yet. We must first know what your intention is toward her now that her complete memory has returned.

If you would like to see her, then you will need our

assistance. Please call upon us immediately on your return.

*Sincerely,
Your Sisters-in-Laws*

At five minutes after eight, Ian ran up the steps of the home of the Duke and Duchess of Caversham. He reached for the knocker, but the massive wooden door opened on its well-oiled hinges, a sign that they waited for him. Upon asking for the duchess, he was led to the library where a footman opened the door and motioned him into the room. He saw the duchess seated behind a lady's desk and the countess standing next to her.

He strode toward them, intent on dragging the information he needed from them. "Where is my wife?"

"Good evening to you, too, Mr. Mackeever," Elise said.

Lia stood and motioned for him to be seated in the chair opposite them. "She is in a very safe place, awaiting our report of this evening's discussion."

"Where is she?" he repeated, ignoring the invitation to sit.

"We will not divulge her location just yet," Elise said. "Her condition is fragile, and she does not need added worry or stress from a confrontation with you."

"I would never do anything to cause my wife undue anxiety. And why is her condition *fragile*? Aside from having her full memory return, she is in good health, is she not?"

"Please sit down, Ian," Lia stated firmly. Frustrated at being made to wait to see his wife—when she was likely above stairs at that very minute—was upsetting. And only when he sat in the chair opposite her at the desk did she continue. "Yes, she is in good health. But her continued good health depends on what your plans are now that you know she's remembered everything."

"Her heart is breaking because you accused her of trapping you," Elise lashed out, almost coming out of her chair. "She did not intentionally land upon your ship, Captain. So there was no trap."

"But after you did marry, she said you began to come to a comfortable arrangement on the return voyage." Lia glared at him disapprovingly. "Until you told her you were glad she was not carrying a child, the day she was feeling ill in Liverpool."

"That was morning sickness you dolt," Sarah's sister railed. "She was already with child."

"How could you, Ian?" This lash was from Lia. He'd sensed she was more likely to pity him than Elise. "She loved you," her voice trailed off, obviously heartbroken for her sister-in-law over his actions. He'd said those things, and he regretted them now, had from almost the moment the words left his mouth.

"I hope she still does." Ian shoulders slumped, and he fell back into the chair, the bluster blown out of his sails. "Because I love her."

"Why haven't you told her?" Elise asked.

Ian thought over his reply and said, "I don't know." He couldn't speak past the pain in his throat. He swallowed again and tried to finish. "I am afraid…of losing her. And I did try to show her how deeply I cared by protecting her from what I knew were sure to be painful memories. *These* specific memories."

"Then is it your intent," asked Elise, "to now

apologize and reconcile with our sister?"

"Of course it is," he replied honestly. "I have missed her and our daughter."

The two women exchanged a glance.

"Then we suggest you find a way to win her over," continued Sarah's sister, "as she's convinced you were only being kind to her after learning she miscarried the twins."

"What can I do? How can I prove to her that I don't want to lose her?"

"You can start by telling her you love her," Elise replied.

"But whatever you decide to do," added Lia, "you must hurry if you intend to leave for China next month with my brother."

The mid-August afternoon held a little chill, and Sarah tucked the blanket around Maura's body more snuggly as the baby rested in the pram. In an attempt to get more exercise, she'd begun walking through Greenwood's extensive gardens each day, pushing the baby's carriage herself, with Maura's nurse and a guard following behind.

But on this afternoon, Sarah strolled along the gravel path without the nurse, just she and her daughter, with her ever-present footman. She thought about Lia's note, which she'd found on her bedside table when she awoke.

Ian had paid them a visit last night and insisted on seeing her. They had given him their blessing and her location, and as yet he had not arrived. Even on a slow horse, it was less than a five-hour ride from doorstep to doorstep.

According to Lia and Elise, their impression was that he was remorseful for not clarifying his feelings for her. He'd said he was hoping she would not remember his accusation before their marriage, his harsh words, and careless sentiments that evening in Liverpool.

He went on to say that by not mentioning these things to her, he was hoping to spare her from upset.

How did he think that lying to her—even lies of omission—would spare her from hurt? Especially because he knew her memories had been slowly returning and that she would eventually remember all. Perhaps he'd hoped to buy some time, making her fall more in love with him, by omitting the full details of their relationship.

And that was what bothered her. She wanted to know his reasons for not telling her. She wanted to know what he had hoped to gain by pretending to be the happy husband, concerned for her well-being. He hadn't cared a smidgen about how she felt that last evening at the rented house in Liverpool. His only thought was of his own joy to discover that she was not with child.

He didn't give her an opportunity to share her being upset or to cry on his shoulder—things she believed most husbands did. She had needed him that night, and he was trying to convince her she should be happy as well.

All of that had indeed been very stressful on her, and she was sure it had had a negative effect on her condition at the time. But she was stronger now.

She had so much more to smile and laugh about these days. She had Maura—the only bright spot in her currently troubled mind. And except for this last bit of troubling memories, her life really was idyllic. She reminded herself of this daily because she really believed it was better for her mind and thus her physical health, to help her carry this child to full term before delivery.

She smiled to herself as she thought about what Ian would say when he learned she carried again. According to Lia and Elise, they were sure all would be well now, and since reading their letter, she felt sure about it too.

But there was one more issue that her husband knew nothing about, and she was unsure how he was now going to react to what she'd done. His grandfather, the Earl Mackeever, and his widowed daughters, Lady Royce and Lady Stone, had arrived two days prior.

Having known both ladies her entire life, she knew they were a delight at the dinner table and in private. But the earl was a conundrum she'd yet to figure out.

With a straight back and head held high, the aged earl still carried himself as a very proud naval officer. Sarah could tell that he'd once been a strapping big man, just like her husband, but during the last few years, his condition and his age had stolen the heft off his frame. His gait was stilted as well because he walked with a prosthetic and a cane, but his presence commanded that he not be judged any less a man because of it.

Sarah knew upon meeting him what a kind soul he was. She'd heard the story of the commander, a much-loved national hero, saving the lives of his crew as his ship sank during the American war—an act for which he'd been given the navy's highest honors and an earldom from the old King George. Now the earl was aged and infirm, with not many days left ahead of him, and he had risked those remaining days to travel to Greenwood for this chance to speak with his grandson.

He'd also welcomed the chance to come south, he'd said, to enjoy the warmer climes, and to meet her especially after everything his daughters had said about her. "My last days are upon me, I acknowledge that. It is my hope to mend the fence with the man about to take my title. I do not dispute that there are issues to resolve, misunderstandings to clear up, and an apology to make on my part. But it is time, and seeing as he will not come north, I accepted your invitation in hopes you might aid me in this last quest."

Sarah was going to make it happen—for him, and for her husband.

Rounding the bend to enter the summer garden which was in full bloom. Sarah caught a glimpse of an elegant and well-dressed gentleman as he descended the steps onto the lawn. She knew it could not possibly be Ian, for he always wore casual clothing due to the nature of his chosen profession. He also was more than a bit of a miser, and this man's clothing appeared tailor-made to fit his tall, muscular form. Likely he was the courier, sent by her brother with papers for her to sign.

But as the man drew closer, she realized he was not the usual messenger from Ren's solicitor's offices. Placing her hand over her eyes to block the glare, she squinted in an attempt to distinguish who else it might be. His hair was of an undetermined light color and combed back neatly. And Ian, though always clean and well-groomed, had a more rugged appearance. His hair was always just a bit shaggy, and he usually had a short growth of stubble because he hated shaving. She'd once told him that he wouldn't have to do it himself if he'd hired a valet. His reply had been that one needed the income to support servants if one wanted to have them.

Loving Sarah

She squinted hard into the sun and finally recognized one thing about him, her husband's intent, purposeful stride. It could be no other man.

He had come. Her heart leaped in her chest, and her body quivered where she stood.

She caught herself before she ran to him. Turning the pram she walked in the opposite direction from him while she tried to figure out what he'd done. He appeared so different. So...gentlemanly. Modern. Normal. Where was *her* Ian? The man she'd fallen in love with? The man whose shirtsleeves were usually rolled to his elbow, who never wore a waistcoat—and scandalous though it was, often not even a coat in summer. Where was the man whose trousers were old but serviceable and whose boot leather was never polished to the shine this man's had?

If she didn't know any better, she'd say it was *not* her husband, but someone else masquerading as her captain. She wanted the man she'd fallen in love with aboard *Revenge*. The man who was rough around the edges and relaxed in her presence. The man whose heart was tarnished because of neglect, but whose pride was often too rigid to allow her to love him.

When he drew close, his eyes grew soft and he smiled. It was the same man without a doubt. His left cheek dimpled slightly when he gave a genuine smile. And this was as unfeigned a smile as she'd ever seen.

As her heart began to melt at his nearness, Sarah had to remind herself she was still angry with him. He'd lied to her. Well, perhaps not outright lied, but lying by omission was still lying. Wasn't it?

"You are a vision, Sarah-mine. You grow more beautiful each time I see you." He kissed her cheek, and the warmth of his lips sent a tingle through her body.

She was supposed to be angry, she told herself. Angry women do *not* melt inside when a man uses an endearment.

"I remember it all, Ian." The words slipped from her lips. She really didn't want to start off on this foot. It would cause nothing but discord, and that wasn't what she intended.

"I know." He appeared chagrined.

"What do we do now? Where do we go from here?"

She was the most beautiful woman he'd ever seen. She'd always had a fire to her eyes when she was mad at him, and he remembered dousing those flames with kisses. They were some of his fondest memories. He wondered if that would work now.

Just as he moved in to try, Maura began squealing and kicking inside the pram.

"You've awakened her." Sarah sounded miffed.

"So I have," he replied as he bent over the carriage and caressed his daughter's cheek. "I see my girl would like a hug from her papa. She's got her arms outstretched for me."

"Don't flatter yourself," she said. "She just wants out of her carriage so she can toddle off and make us chase her."

Ian watched as his wife clutched the carriage handle as though his throat were in her grasp. He hoped kissing her anger away would work one more time. He leaned closer, until he felt her warm breath on his cheek. But before his lips could touch hers, an annoyed cry from within the carriage stole her attention from him. Sarah backed away from the conveyance, and Ian lifted his daughter.

"Do you crawl now, Maura?" he asked as he lifted her up and held her in the crook of his arm. He looked at his wife and said, "She's grown so much while I was away."

"She's walking, Ian," Sarah replied with more than a hint of pride. "She's catching up with her age markers just as the doctor said she would." This broke the ice wall she'd constructed around her. Sarah softened slightly and he knew this was the route into her heart. "She's growing so much and so fast. It's hard to remember the little darling as she was when I first saw her six weeks ago. She stands in her crib and tries to climb out. And where she'd only had the one molar she now has all four."

Maura kept reaching down for his watch chain, so finally he removed the thing and handed it to his daughter who studied the closed watch case. "What has Prescott said of her?"

Sarah rescued the watch before it went into their daughter's mouth. She smiled at Ian. "That she is thriving. He is also optimistic that she should bear no long-term effects of her previous condition."

"Good. Very good." He met her gaze over the infant's head. "And what has he said of your health?"

Sarah's dark blue eyes grew wide with surprise. Then she blinked and when her eyes reopened again, it seemed as though a shutter had closed on her emotion. "Nothing at all. Why would he say anything about me?"

She was hiding something. Instinct told him now wasn't the time to question her, but he would before the day was done. "No reason in particular. I was curious how my wife fared, that's all."

Sarah turned from him and made busy rearranging

the baby's blanket within the pram. "I am well," she said. "Very well, in fact, now that my memory has completely returned."

"I knew it would, eventually."

"Did you?" She pushed the empty baby carriage as Ian fell in step beside her with his squirming daughter in his arms. "Is that why you pretended to be the concerned, devoted husband? Because you *knew* my memory would return? No, I think you were hoping it would not. Although I haven't figured out yet why, except for the benefit of my family since you are in business with my brother."

"You have it all wrong, Sarah." If she didn't believe him in this, he didn't know what to do to change her mind. "Everything I said and did when I returned from China was genuine. I truly missed you and was deeply saddened by the loss of our sons, but so very thankful that you were alive.

"After Lucky informed me of your expectant state, I pushed my men hard and made for home as quick as we could possibly get here."

A female servant, perhaps the child's nurse, arrived and held her arms out for Maura, and she placed the toddler in the carriage and pushed it back toward the house, leaving the two of them alone. Sarah dismissed the guard as Ian glanced around the gardens. Spying a side entrance to the house, he directed Sarah up the two steps and into an orangery.

Sarah removed her cloak. The white dress she wore under it complemented her pink cheeks and up-swept golden hair. Ian knew that he'd never tire of looking at her. Sunlight through the mullioned windows shot beams of color onto the crushed stone walkway and her skirts.

LOVING SARAH

He followed her to a bench, making sure no one was in the conservatory with them.

"We need to discuss a few things, and I would rather do it free from prying eyes and accidental eavesdroppers." Once he was certain they were alone, he leaned against a trellis post and smiled. He felt like a nervous schoolboy, happy that she nodded and waited for whatever came from his lips next. "Motherhood suits you, my darling. If it is at all possible, I'd say you are even more beautiful, though I cannot pinpoint exactly what it is about you that looks so different. You're radiant and…something more."

At first she blushed, then she took a deep breath and sat on the wooden bench. "Your flattery is not desired right at this moment. As you said we have much to discuss."

"You are right," he replied. "Where shall we start?"

"The beginning is always a good place." Sarah folded her hands primly and settled them in her lap, setting lips in an equally straight-laced fashion.

He'd never seen Sarah nervous like this. She flattened imaginary creases in her day dress with her fingers and would not meet his gaze. He wondered how far back she wanted to go. It was of no use to go as far back as their time on the *Revenge*, so he chose to begin with his arrival after the tea run.

"When we returned from China, I made for the bank to deposit funds, as we do after each voyage, and make the note payment on the boats. Imagine my surprise to learn that you had already paid my portion of the debt in full. I was angry, but by this time I had resolved myself with the fact that you Brits do things differently," he scoffed. "Lucky has often accused me of being a thick-headed American, but I'd like to think of myself as proud. Perhaps even to a fault." How did he get across to her the feeling of inadequacy he felt whenever he thought about the fact that her money was funding his half of the business? He just didn't think it was something she could understand. "I did not want to be known as the impoverished nobleman who needed his wife's dowry to fund his business venture. I'd told you before, it was a point of honor with me that I do this on my own."

"Why, Ian? What is it you're trying to prove? And to whom? Certainly not me. Not to other members of our class, because they do this sort of thing all the time. Men choose which bride to take quite frequently based on the size of her dowry, her connection to certain families, or both. It's a social and financial arrangement. Sometimes affection will grow between them, but even if it doesn't, they still marry, produce heirs, and continue to live their lives."

"That's not what I wanted. I wanted more. I wanted what my parents had. My father loved my mother and mourned her until his own death. It also certainly doesn't appear to be the way you were raised either. Love is the core that holds your family together. Though my father loved me, when he looked at me he saw my dead mother. It was hard for him to show affection, but I loved him anyway. He was my father." Ian remembered the day his father told him he'd have to go to Scotland without him. He'd argued at first, and in the end cried, because he was a child who didn't want to go to the place where he knew he was not going to be loved and wanted as he was with his father. "When I turned twelve, he sent me to live with my grandfather so

I could receive what he called a *proper* education, as I was going to inherit my grandfather's title one day. After I'd gone, my father was dead within the year."

He pushed away from the post and began to pace the gravel walk in front of where she sat, upset that in her desire to get answers to her questions she'd brought him to the point of frustration and anger. "You asked me once what drives me. I'll tell you. It's the fact that my grandfather disowned my father for loving the daughter of a servant. My father probably added fuel to that fire by marrying my mother, but he loved her very much. I witnessed their affection and his mourning.

"I was a small boy when my mother died. When she did, father sent letters to her family and to his, informing them of his loss." Ian stopped in front of Sarah and looked her in the eye. "Mother's family sent their condolences. But do you know what his own father did?" Her eyes grew wide and frightened. "He sent the letter back unopened, making the cut permanently irrevocable.

"This society in which you live places more value on status than on love. My father loved my mother, but his father refused to acknowledge their union. They were forced to leave rather than be a constant humiliating reminder to his father.

"When I took possession of Father's belongings, I found among them a letter from my grandfather. In it, he stated we were no longer his kin." In Ian's opinion, there was no repairing a tie that no longer existed.

"He was angry, Ian. Your father is no longer alive, and the man who wrote that letter no longer exists. You do not know each other."

"That doesn't matter, because the damage has been

done. From that moment, I have been determined to be successful in my own way. I was forced to come here, will be forced to accept a title I'd rather not have. After studying the courses he chose for me to study, I wanted to go into trade. So I did. He sent a letter to me, through my Aunt Royce, in which he railed at me for not taking the post he'd arranged for me with the naval command designing war ships. The same post he wanted my father to take before he left for America." Ian closed his eyes and shook his head, surprised to this very day at the audacity of the man he had to call grandfather. "The irony was not lost on me." Ian dropped his head as he rest against the post. He squeezed the bridge of his nose between his thumb and forefinger, wishing the past didn't have the influence it still did in his life. "Yes. I wanted to hurt him, for the pain he caused my father and mother, for the cruel things he said to me as a child. And I did that by doing the exact opposite of what he expected of me."

Sarah's expression softened, and when she spoke, her voice held all of the compassion he'd never received from any relative he'd ever had. "You have both done your best to hurt the other it seems. Now you must let go of that pain, my love, or it will consume you until you're as bitter and angry as he was."

"She's right, you know."

Ian's head snapped up, and he searched the long, narrow room for the owner of the familiar voice he still heard in his nightmares.

Chapter Nineteen

Sarah rose and went to the man she hoped her husband would forgive for his past cruelties and abuses toward Ian and his family. Holding out an arm, she supported him as she led him to the bench she'd just vacated.

The man hobbled slowly. He was frail, his skin had a translucent gray pallor. Frankly, he'd seen dead men who looked better than his grandfather at that moment. His oft-repaired serviceable clothing appeared far too large for his skeletal frame, and with the wheezing sounds he made, Sarah wondered if he'd even live to see another week.

This truly was his last wish, just as he'd said when he'd arrived.

"What is he doing here?" Her husband's voice was filled with venomous hatred that had been stewing inside him for many years. His rigid stance showed no compassion. Sarah was surprised at Ian's vitriol toward his grandfather, even after seeing his morbid condition.

"I invited him to stay the summer with us." She would have to set the ground rules now for them both. "Your grandfather is a guest in our home, Ian, and you *will* be kind to him."

"You're named after me you know." The old man sat

on the bench. "Ian Alexander. I might have been angry with your father for marrying beneath him, but I knew all along he'd be the son to give me the first heir to the title." The old man held Ian's attention. "Your uncle and I were similarly afflicted, you see."

Sarah didn't know what his affliction was, but the most important thing she wanted to have happen right now was to get Ian to see the old earl was harmless and held none of the control over his life that Ian had imagined.

"Then it's no wonder my father left the home," Ian spewed. "He likely feared catching your 'affliction' as well."

"Ian!" Sarah felt her cheeks flame for her husband's rude behavior. "My lord, I am sorry…."

"Bah!" The old earl brushed off Ian's words. "I deserve some of his hostility, but he'll have to hear me out now because I'm going nowhere until he does." He then looked up at Ian who still leaned against the post. "Take the gloves off lad, come on. I am old, near death, and cannot do you a bit of harm."

"Sarah," —she lifted her gaze to Ian— "if I promise not to kill him, will you leave us?" The only reason she might consider it was because Ian's stance was less defensive now and more guarded.

"I will do what your grandfather wishes."

The old man gave a slight, almost imperceptible, nod of agreement. "You might not wish to hear it all, lass."

"Ian, do not hurt him," His wife whispered harshly to him as he held her elbow and escorted her down the finely graveled path to the glass doors that opened to an interior hallway of the home he'd yet to see. "He's your grandfather and he wants to reconcile with you before he

LOVING SARAH

dies. It is his final wish. Do not disrespect him."

He wanted to choke on that. Sweet, innocent Sarah had no idea what a cruel man her grandfather could be. Ian needed to hear him out and do whatever was necessary to get him out of this house.

After the door was firmly closed behind her, he walked back to where the old man sat upon the bench. He'd grown dramatically thinner and much older in the ten years since Ian had last seen him. Ian was willing to even acknowledge that the man might, indeed, be ill. If that was the case, then he did likely risk his health traveling here.

He returned to the post and leaned against it again, rather than sit next to the old man. "Did my father know of your *affliction*, as you call it? Because I'm trying to imagine the agony he felt knowing he was dying and that the only male family member he had to send his only child to was a sodomite."

His grandfather slumped forward onto his cane, which he'd placed between his knee and his prosthetic. The old man sighed heavily as though he were Atlas and the weight of the world was finally rolling off his shoulders. "He did not know. My two wives did not know either. I found out about Trahern a few years after his death when his *friend* began to blackmail me. He was going to tell the entire naval command about your uncle. At first, I feared he knew about me as well, but found out later he did not.

"After many years of giving this blackguard every penny I could squeeze out of my estate, my lifelong...friend, Morgan, put an end to it for me. He used his connections to discover who the blackmailer was, and the man was finally stopped."

Ian didn't know whether to believe him. There were many questions he still had. "Is that why you quit paying for my education? Do you know what a burden that placed on my aunts? Your own daughters?"

"I know you think it was because I was angry when you'd arrived early and witnessed…what you did. But, God's truth, by this time I had nothing left." The man broke into a fit of coughing, and when he got it under control, he continued. "You saw the condition of the home that day. There were no servants except those who were unable to find work elsewhere."

"You're thugs…."

"On my honor, I swear they were there to protect you. You were *always* protected until the day you left your studies." The old man sounded sincere.

"Why didn't you say so? Why let me fear them?"

"Perhaps I was wrong to do it as I did, but those men were loyal to me and would have died to protect you, my sole heir."

Ian spent most of his life hating this man for his actions, and now here this man was, near death and begging for understanding and forgiveness. How could Ian believe this man after all of the bullying and horrible things he'd said about Ian's parents?

"You said things about my mother—things I would have called you out for had I been older. She loved my father and he adored her."

"Second son or no, he should never have married against my wishes. Your mother was beneath him. I stand by that." Ian was about to interrupt him when his grandfather stopped him. "When I was enamored of the bottle, I perhaps said many cruel things, all of which I ask your forgiveness. I knew no other way to raise a young man than to make him a hardened, battle-ready officer. It's how I was raised. I thought I was doing what was right."

The old man wheezed and took a moment to collect his breath before he could continue. "I need to know that you forgive me before I die, because I will likely not make the return to Edinburgh."

Ian didn't know what to think. Everything he had thought was true was not, and the man he had thought despised him actually cared for him. What was he to do now?

"Morgan died last year." His grandfather's emotions caused him to choke on his words. "I miss him terribly. He was…the best friend a man could have for over sixty years. What you walked in on that day was not shameful or abominable. It was the two of us showing our love for each other. You never should have seen it, as I had no warning that you would arrive early."

The two men were silent a long time. Ian wondered how he could ever resolve the image in his head of that day as anything close to loving. It wasn't what he imagined when he thought of love and making love with Sarah. That was abhorrent and….

"I can see you are still having issues resolving that in your mind," the earl said. "But know that I never loved anyone as much as Morgan, and you are the only person alive to know this."

Sarah paced the hallway just outside the orangery, waiting for either one of them to come out first. She assumed it would be her husband. She didn't expect to see them both, the earl hanging on to her husband's arm.

The sight brought tears to her eyes. She couldn't imagine her husband not forgiving a dying man, because she knew at his core Ian was a good person, no matter his previous hardships. Somewhere in his past he'd learned compassion.

She smiled at them both and let them pass by her as she followed them into the foyer, where the earl had two servants waiting to carry him up the steps in his sedan chair.

When the earl was at the top of the landing, Ian strode out of the front doors so quickly she had a difficult time catching up to him.

"Ian stop, please," Sarah called out as she ran after him. He did not turn around, so lost was he in his pain that he likely could not hear her calling. He'd gone so far down the drive that he almost reached a back gate that led to a field. When he finally did stop, Sarah was winded and leaned against the nearest tree, doubled over trying to catch her breath.

"Why didn't you call for me?" He came to her and led her a few feet into the woods. Finding a fallen tree, he then sat upon it and brought her down onto his lap.

Sarah attempted to slow her racing heart and her heaving breath. "I did. Several...times."

"I should be very angry with you, springing him upon me as you did." Even though his voice was stern, he cradled her in his arms protectively.

She met his warm gaze and knew his heart was confused. Rather than defend her actions, she said, "When we spoke yesterday, after he recovered somewhat from his travels, he told me his last wish was to ask for your forgiveness. He admitted he did not deserve it, but he wanted to apologize and explain.

"He readily admits he made mistakes. But he would like a clear conscience and lighter burden to carry as he passes from this world to the next."

Her husband turned his head away as he collected his emotions.

"Ian, you can forgive him or not, that's between you and God. But he deserves your compassion, if not your respect."

He was silent for a while, then nodded. "It will just take me a while to get used to not hating him. That's all I have known. None of the things I believed about him were as I thought. And I'm trying to...sort out how I feel about it all now."

"Sort quickly because he does not have long."

He lifted her from him, and she took his seat on the fallen tree and watched as he paced a path before her.

"Why did you really leave London? What was it you were upset about? Was it because of the memories?" He didn't sound accusatory, but like a desperate man in need of answers.

"After you left for Aberdeen, I remembered the night in my room in Liverpool. You said you didn't want children. And here we now had a daughter, which you seemed to love, and I didn't understand. We made love several times before you left, knowing full well it might lead to another child." She gave him a satisfied smile. "And it did."

He started to speak, but Sarah stopped his interruption with a barely perceptible lift of her hand. Despite his look of stunned happiness, she wanted to finish while she had the answer formed in her mind.

"Neither of us knows if I will carry the full nine months, nor even if, at the end of that term, I can give birth to a healthy child. But I know one thing, Ian. I love you. I lusted for you during the race to New York, and fell in love with you somewhere along the return voyage. Then to have you tell me that you didn't care for children as I was in the throes of morning sickness felt like a slap in my face."

"Can you ever forgive me? It was thoughtless of me," Ian said.

"I will forgive you because you are my husband, I love you, and we are a family. I also truly believe you are a better man now than you were then."

He stared at her for a moment until he realized what she'd said. She loved him. She could see realization dawning in his hazel eyes. He closed his eyes and bowed his head, the stress of years of fighting something invisible flowing out of him.

"I have loved you for a while now." His hand reached into his pocket. "I just did not know how to say it." He took his hand from the pocket and held it out to her and opened it. Her breath froze in her chest as she looked down at the ring she had tried on that first day in his cabin.

The oval ruby solitaire was set in a white gold band with four prongs holding it in place. She held out her hand, knowing he'd never be able to get the ring on but unwilling to tell him how she knew this.

"It was my mothers, and it appears we shall have to have the band stretched," he said.

"It's beautiful, Ian," her voice cracked, disappointed that she was unable to get it over her knuckle.

"Both times I was away from you," he began, "I missed you terribly. I missed your ready smile, your infectious laughter, and your giving spirit. I missed being with you, the way you smelled, the way you tasted. I missed talking with you, walking on deck with you" —he reached out and lifted a lock of her hair— "and watching you use a pitcher of water to wash all that glorious hair. I missed your presence in my bed and at the table in the evening." He tilted her chin up to meet his gaze. "I knew I loved you, Sarah, before I even knew you carried my sons."

Her breath caught. Then she gave a shaky sigh as she fought tears.

"I want you, Sarah," he said, his voice as filled with emotion as she was. "I want you as my wife, and Maura as our daughter. And I want as many children you want, but if the physician says you should not, then I will not surrender you for the sake of a child. Because, in the end, I love you and cannot live without you in my life."

The sun was moving lower in the sky, and Sarah shivered, having forgotten her pelisse on the dash out the door to follow him. Ian removed his coat and placed it over her shoulders. She was surrounded by his scent—a combination of him and faint traces of the soap he'd used. It was what home smelled like to her. Home was where ever this man was, whether it was a cabin aboard a ship or home in London, Surrey, or Scotland.

She nodded and he extended his hand. She placed her trembling one in his, and he helped her to stand, then wrapped his arms around her, holding her close.

There was no better feeling in the world for her than being in Ian's arms, and second was being wrapped in his warm coat. She savored his masculinity and needed his strength.

"We should be going back," she said. "Dinner will be in a few hours."

Later that night, his fingers stroked her cheek and she stared into the green-brown depths of his soul and knew he spoke the truth. He loved her. Desire sparked between them, and he fanned the ember when he brought his lips down to hers in a single, searing kiss. She opened for him, and his tongue swept across the ridges of her teeth, then mated with hers. She grabbed onto him as though a woman drowning, and he her only lifeline.

She met his passion with equal enthusiasm, telling him with her body that she'd wanted him as much as he wanted her, and missed him just as much as he had missed her. When he broke the kiss, she pressed her face into his chest and groaned as she struggled to catch her breath.

His amorous intent was obvious, but she had to stop him—hopefully only for now. "Ian, I'm not sure I can just yet. I sent a note asking, and I'm still waiting to hear if it's safe."

He backed away and held her gaze, a tender smile on his face. "I apologize. You must think me a lecherous sort." He sat up. "If Prescott says you shouldn't, then we won't."

She didn't think it important to tell him that it wasn't Prescott she'd asked, but her sister-in-law. The doctor would likely say she shouldn't, where Lia was a woman and a mother three times over. She was also incredibly knowledgeable in areas such as this.

Ian rose from the bed and pulled on his banyan, tying it loosely around his hips.

"Where are you going?"

"I thought to sleep in my bed so as not to disturb you."

"I want you with me," she whispered. "Please?"

He slipped off the banyan again, then slid between the sheets until he was behind her holding her against him again, cradling her in his arms. Sarah took his hand and placed it over her softly rounded belly, and he nuzzled the back of her neck, sending warm shivers throughout her body.

"Stop wiggling your bottom against me," he whispered. "It's unfair."

"I'm sorry. I'll try not to again." She shifted again, trying to get comfortable in his arms.

"This is why I should sleep in my own bed," he grumbled into the dark.

Shortly before sunrise, Sarah stirred when she heard Trudy place a salver atop her nightstand. One eye crept open, then she slid from the cocoon of Ian's embrace, hoping she did not rouse him. Throwing her wrap over her arm, she took the note and went into the connecting sitting room.

Bringing the note over to the chair next to the hearth, she took a tinder and lit the pair of candles on the end table. She eagerly broke the seal and began to read, her sister-in-law's words bringing first a frown, then a smile to her lips.

Dearest,

You are completely forgiven for rousing me from my husband's bed. I cannot tell you what a fright I had when my maid brought me your note. Thankfully, I had the forethought to open and read your missive before sending Ghita to call for the coach and pack my trunk.

In response to your question, I have one of my own.

How do you feel? In my opinion, if you are feeling well, then, by all means, proceed.

L.

Sarah smiled in the dim light of the sitting room. Glancing back at the open doorway to her chamber, she rose and blew out the candles before re-joining her husband.

Even though there was a late summer chill in the room, she slid the wrap from her shoulders and dropped it as she walked, then lifted the hem of her night dress and pulled it over her head. At the edge of the bed, she parted the curtain and folded back the covers before climbing upon the thick down mattress. She dropped her slippers then slid in next to Ian's naked warmth.

It took a fraction of a moment for him to realize what she was about as she ever so slowly traced a finger down his bare chest. Just when she was about to reach his shaft, he placed a hand over hers. "Stop now," he said, "or I'll not be able to."

"I don't want you to stop," she whispered.

"Are you sure?"

"Absolutely," she replied as she nuzzled and lightly kissed her way over the strong curve of his jaw and wrapped her fingers around his rising erection.

"I don't want to hurt you."

"You won't."

"The babe…?"

"Will be fine."

Her words were all the assurance he needed as he moved over her, holding his weight from her so as not to harm their child. He caressed the curve of her breasts with his lips, marveling at their fullness before leaning forward to worship them thoroughly with his mouth. And only when she lay beneath him, quivering with a need as deep and sure as his own, did he gently come to her, filling her completely, giving her everything he was, everything he would ever be. He gave not only his heart, but his very soul, into her safe keeping, to nurture as she did their unborn child. And only after she'd reached her climax did he take his own release.

For the next two weeks, while Ian was in Surrey, he spent time with the old earl, getting to know him as a man, and not his former guardian. One afternoon, Sarah and Ian sat with him in his rooms as he was describing the Siege at Charleston for Ian.

"I remember nothing after that until I awoke on the *Jersey*. It was after I returned from that last battle, missing my leg, but with most of my crew alive, that North petitioned the king to elevate me from a mere Baron to the Earl Mackeever. You will be the second Earl Mackeever. There is no entail, no wealth, just a title awarded for...bravery."

Sarah placed a hand on Ian's arm to get his attention. "Perhaps we should let him rest."

"I'll have eternity to rest," the old man said. "I have one more request before I go though."

Ian nodded, and the earl closed his eyes and smiled. "See to it that Seamus Black is cared for. He has been where I wanted to be these past four years, sailing by your side. He says you've a fine hand on the wheel, and that I should be proud." The earl coughed a bit and struggled with his breathing. Once it settled, he added, "I just wanted you to know that I am."

Two days later, Ian and Sarah, along with his aunts, buried the first Earl Mackeever in the parish cemetery on Greenwood.

Epilogue

Ian dumped the contents of the drawer onto the bed. The books he had kept from his days at university, and the few he'd bought or had been given since fell onto the woolen blanket. He lifted first one, then another, and another, scanning the titles, wondering which one was of interest to Sarah. No, he thought, she kept the one that interested her.

So which title in his paltry collection did she take? It was difficult to tell. It had been so long since he'd taken a book out to read. He looked over all of the volumes spread out on the bed and concluded he'd never figure it out. The one book on poetry he had was still here, and it was the only book he remembered her reading while she was aboard.

Heavy-booted footfalls in the narrow gangway alerted him to Lucky's arrival. Since Ian had arrived after dark, he'd spent the previous night at the house in Mayfair and notified Lucky of his arrival in the morning, asking Lucky to meet him aboard the boat. Lucky entered the cabin looking as though he hadn't slept, and Ian wondered which of his friend's vices he'd been up to the night before.

"Was it a woman or a good game?"

"Baccarat at Vinton's," his friend replied, walking

over to gaze at the disheveled heap of books on the mattress, "and I just barely came out ahead."

He pushed a few books aside, gazing at the titles. "I need to find a bed, and as this one is piled high with the contents of your entire library, you'd best hurry before I fall over where I stand. What did you call me here for?"

"I've decided not to go to China."

"Good call, my lord," his friend said, as he thumbed through a book on maritime law. "I hated this class," he said, tossing the heavy volume aside and lifting another before sitting on the edge of the mattress. "I'm assuming you've already sent word to Nigel."

Ian nodded.

"He's fully qualified to take the helm y'know. And I'll bet he's ready for it." Lucky leaned against the table and continued flipping pages.

Ian agreed, then added, "But that's not the only reason I asked you here. I need to know what subjects interest Sarah. I want to surprise her with a gift for her birthday. After much thought, I remembered that a while back she left me this cryptic note saying she was 'borrowing' one of my books but didn't say which title she took. I thought that if I could figure out what it was that interested her, then I'd get her another book or two of the same subject."

Lucky looked at the collection on the bed and shook his head. "I know she reads a lot of those romantic novels. She likes poetry, history, and mythology. I'm not sure what else." He flipped over a book, read the title, then did the same with another leather-bound tome. "Did you keep that book I gave you for your birthday back when we were in school?"

"What book was that?"

LOVING SARAH

"The one with all those erotic color plates and explanations and drawings of various positions?"

Ian scratched his head and thought a moment. "Surely I wouldn't have given *that* book to a lending library. It had an inscription inside where you'd written my name." He pushed aside title after title and didn't find anything that looked the least familiar. "I thought I kept it." He looked in the other drawers under the bed and found nothing. "Of all the embarrassing things to put into circulation...."

All of a sudden, he felt as though a lead anvil crashed into his gut when, coincidentally, raucous laughter welled up in his friend. And Ian knew then, that he and Lucky had arrived at the same conclusion. "She didn't," he said more to himself than Lucky. "She wouldn't...."

"Oh, I'll just bet she did." Lucky's laughter grew louder as he said, "In fact, I'm willing to put money on it my friend."

After lifting the lids to the bench seats along the bulkhead and coming up, empty-handed, he stared at Lucky and burst out laughing himself. When they'd settled down and caught their breaths, Ian said, "It would explain so much if she did." Ian straightened and stared at Lucky, kicking himself that he'd left it where an uninitiated miss could so readily find it.

Taking a deep breath, he surrendered to the inevitable. "That's the book she took."

Lucky stood and clapped him on the back. "Ian, my friend, I should have warned you about Sarah a long time ago." At Ian's look of puzzlement, Lucky added, "She's never been a typical girl." He shook his head and went to the door. "No, sir. She's always been far too curious and adventurous for her own good." He opened the door, and before he left, he added, "I think you now know the subject that interested her so much. All you have to do is find her a copy of something similar. Might I suggest the *Ovid's Amores*? I have it in Italian. You can have Sarah can read it to you. She's fluent you know."

THE END

Author's Note

Putting our work out there makes most artists feel vulnerable. But for a few of us, there is nothing in the world we would rather be doing than creating stories that touch the heart, no matter the fear of scrutiny. I hope you enjoyed reading about Ian and Sarah as much as I enjoyed writing their story. If you did, please leave a rating or review at the vendor where you purchased this book. I truly believe all constructive criticism helps writers better themselves at this craft we love so much.

Lucky's Lady

Sandy Raven

Now please enjoy the first chapter preview of LUCKY'S LADY, which will be coming soon!

Chapter One

Curtis Bay, Maryland, Late June 1836

Lucky Gualtiero strode through the bustling Watkins Shipyard and watched as a hundred or more men and boys left their work stations as the day drew to an end. He knew from the position of the sun that it was nearing six-thirty, and as he scanned the yard area, he smacked the leather folio against his thigh. In it were the specifications and drawings compiled by his partner Ian Ross-Mackeever, now the second Earl Mackeever, and some notes Lucky had compiled over the past few weeks while visiting other shipyards, as well as the letter from their creditor bank in London guaranteeing the mortgage for two new clippers.

This was the last stop of the three North American shipyards and Ian's builder of choice; his father had worked for Mr. Watkins before Mr. Ross's death twelve years ago. Lucky made his way through the dry dock, looking for their offices, while scrutinizing several new vessels under construction, all at different stages. One appeared near finished and was floating, and another was just a hull up on blocks, still in the early stages of interior construction. Others were in various stages between.

For Lucky, watching the building process was enlightening, because he could clearly recognize the quality of workmanship at different stages in the construction. So far, it appeared that Watkins built a very fine hull. The floated boat had three solid masts, where one of the boats on blocks nearest him awaited cladding, the copper sheeting used to prevent shipworm and saltwater from damaging the wood. All of the wood used for hulls appeared to be solid cypress. The rudder was about to be placed on the hull in dry dock, which would be interesting to watch if he were still here in a day or two. The inner post and stern post were already affixed and the rudder—a typical gunstock shape—lay on blocks on the ground waiting for the hinge apparatus to be joined to it. Once that was done, the whole unit would be lifted into place.

He turned and kept walking toward what he thought were the company offices, a brick two-story building, and was stopped by what appeared to be a lad as he neared the door.

"Can I help you?"

Lucky turned to look at the most amazing thing he'd seen in his life: a young female garbed for working in a shipyard with the voice and diction of an educated woman.

His momentary shock faded, and he met the golden brown-eyed gaze of a young woman with straight auburn hair tied back and bound in netting and golden-red-brown eyebrows arched delicately over an expressive, curious gaze. A sprinkling of freckles spread across her cheeks, over the bridge of her nose, and up to her forehead. She stood near chin-height to him and wore charcoal-gray breeches and a dove-gray, lightweight, short-sleeved jacket that fell over the hip. Under that, a white blouse buttoned up to the chin to protect her modesty. She had a pretty face, even though her eyes appeared tired, and her smile looked almost forced.

"May I help you?" Now she sounded a tad annoyed out that he'd kept her waiting for his reply. Her wide-brimmed straw hat dangled by its tied strings from her fingers while she removed the writing pad from under her arm and a pencil from her jacket pocket.

He shook his head to clear his thoughts. "I'm looking for Mr. Spenser Watkins."

"My husband has gone for the day." She fumbled with the pad, pencil, hat, and jacket while she waited for him to reply.

Damnation. The first intriguing woman he'd met in a long time and she was married. But it was his experience that married women quite frequently made the best lovers. She was so interesting and attractive and…different that he'd have to see how married she was. Perhaps he might get—God, he hated when his friends said it—but perhaps he might get lucky.

"My name is Lucky Gualtiero. My partner and I currently sail two one-hundred-and-twenty-foot clippers and are looking to expand our tea import business by adding two more ships to our fleet. We are in the market to have some custom work done and your shipyard came highly recommended."

Her eyebrows rose and she smiled a crooked smile at him. "Oh? Your partner knows of our work?"

"Yes. My partner is Ian Ross."

She pursed her lips and squinted, apparently deep in thought as she seemed to search her recollections. "Ian Ross. Why does that name sound familiar? Likely he's had work done here before."

"No. His father worked for…" Lucky paused, unsure about the age difference, then speculated, "your father-in-law perhaps?"

"That's right." Recognition registered on her face and she smiled. "Ian is Hamish's son. No, Hamish Ross worked *with* my husband. They were partners. Mr. Watkins still speaks of his dear friend often."

Lucky followed Mrs. Watkins. She held the door for him and he entered, waiting for his eyes to adjust to the dim light of the entrance hall. He paused just inside the door and waited for her. Then it struck him.

Had he lost all manners? *She* held the door open for *him*, and obedient lamb that he was, he had followed her. She had to be no older than twenty-two or twenty-four, and she was married to Spenser Watkins? He'd gotten the impression from Ian that Watkins was an elderly man. And what was even more disconcerting than the age difference was the fact that she was so…so…comfortable in her position, her clothing even. She didn't fluster or get nervous as a young woman at home would have upon meeting a gentleman while she was alone. Alone and awkwardly dressed.

Oh, there was no lack of modesty for she was covered from chin to toe even in this sticky heat. He was sure her baggy breeches, light jacket, and tall leather boots served the purpose for working in a shipyard. That big straw hat did an excellent job of keeping the sun off her face because while she was not as milky-fair as the young ladies at home, she bore the healthy glow of someone who enjoyed the outdoors, much like his sisters.

Lucky appreciated the sway of her bottom as he

followed her up the stairs, then through a narrow corridor toward a great, open ante-chamber, with a bank of open doors where she motioned him in. He wondered at her position in the business as he met the gaze of one gentleman standing at a drafting table who nodded a simple greeting. The man worked on making copies of the architectural print spread before him, while two other men in rolled-up shirt sleeves worked in offices with doors open to the main antechamber. This, he was certain, was to aid in the circulation of air for, as he was quickly learning, summer in Baltimore was a hot and muggy season indeed.

Mrs. Watkins opened yet another door, one marked Spenser Watkins in black lettering on the frosted glass pane, and left this door wide open as she went into the room. His eyes followed her trouser-and-jacket-clad form as she moved behind the desk. She unbuttoned and removed her loose jacket, revealing her sleeveless white high-necked blouse underneath and exposing her bare arms. Lucky's mouth suddenly felt as dry as the desert in Africa. Not only was she beautiful to look upon, the woman was lithe, graceful, and, in his opinion, perfectly formed. What in heaven's name was she doing working in a shipyard? And the men in the antechamber behaved as though her presence was normal and accepted.

"Please. Have a seat." She motioned to a chair and put her hat on the rack with her jacket, then took a seat herself behind the large, masculine desk. She began to rifle through the drawers in search of something, then lifted out a fresh sheet of paper and a sharpened pencil.

Lucky didn't know how to say what he'd wanted to say, and instead asked, "Will your husband be in the office tomorrow?"

The look on her face quickly changed from warm and friendly to business-like and reserved.

"Yes," she replied. "He doesn't tolerate the mid-day heat very well at his age so he keeps morning hours, returning home around noon. If you would rather speak directly with him, he is usually here around seven a.m. We tend to get more work done in the office early in the day when it is cooler. In the afternoon, you can usually find me out in the yard where the breeze off the bay makes the outdoors more bearable."

Lucky nodded. He cleared his throat, nervous that his next words might offend her, but he'd never encountered a woman—a young woman—in such a position of leadership in a male-dominated business such as this. "Mrs. Watkins, I'll be frank with you. I have never done business of this magnitude with a woman."

"Not many men have," she said setting aside the pencil and lifting her tired gaze to his. She must have recognized his hesitation to do business with her. "And you are not the first to have this reaction, but I assure you I am quite competent in what I do." She pointed at the wall of windows beside them. "Each one of those ships out there in that yard was designed by me and built by the men who work for my husband's shipyard. There are twenty-eight vessels of my design currently sailing the world. I might be relatively young, but I am more current in the mechanic arts as it applies to naval architecture and the engineering of composite materials than most men currently designing clippers. If you would like references, I can give you the names of boats and their owners. Some of whom still do not know a woman designed their ship."

Lucky felt surely he was gaping at her, unaccustomed

to such dialog coming from a woman. He didn't want to be rude to the woman, but even she admitted this situation was quite unusual.

She lifted the pencil again and rolled it between her hands. "Now, what is it you are looking for, Captain? You mentioned custom work."

"Yes." He cleared his throat and noticed a spark of interest rise in her expression when she glanced up at him. "My partner and I are looking for custom work—new builds. Two of them."

She smiled. "That is my specialty. If it relieves your concerns, all business related to the transfer of funds and signing of contracts will be handled through my husband, our firm's legal counsel, and our accountant here at Watkins Shipyard."

"Good," he replied, relieved he'd not offended her.

She was very professional and all business as she said, "I'd like to know what you need. What do you want in a boat? What size, type, number of masts, cargo hold, guns, cabins, construction? I engineer the design according to what your needs and desires are." Astonished at hearing her speak, Lucky did not interrupt her. He was eager to hear what she had to say.

Mrs. Watkins confidently leaned back in her too-big chair, her elbows resting on the armrests that pulled the material of her shirt tight across her slight bosom. "Here at Watkins, we craft solid wood hulls of oak, cedar, or cypress, all of which are prevalent in these parts. We then sheath the hull in a fifty-fifty copper and zinc alloy to reduce the speed of erosion. We clad on top a layer of tar one-quarter of an inch thick. The plate is up to twenty-four inches above the load waterline at aft and amid, graduating up to thirty-six inches above at the bow. All logs are milled and treated here on site. We have our own loggers, blacksmiths, fitters, and coopers."

His mouth went dry and he was unable to peel his gaze away from her face as she spoke. This fascinating woman was talking to him of ship construction. At home, talk of this sort was usually left for the company of men. How on earth had she received the education necessary to do something only the brightest of men in the world could do? Still dumbfounded, he shook his head. "I'm going to admit to being knocked off kilter with your questions. I hadn't prepared myself to discuss these things with a…a woman, and" —he felt a bit sheepish, and uncomfortable— "I don't mean to offend you."

She smiled at him again. A full, true smile. Her teeth were white and mostly straight, and she had two dimples, not just the adorable one on the left. She was truly enchanting and alive, not milky white or rouged. This vibrant young woman had a healthy glow that caused his heart to skip a beat, maybe two, even though she was married. "None taken, I assure you. If it would make you feel better, I can have my draftsman, Andrew, come in and take notes with us."

"No," he began, then cleared his throat, still a bit nervous as he glanced out to the drafting table beyond the open door. "This is fine." Lucky reached into the file folder and handed Mrs. Watkins their specification sheet. "The top half" —he motioned to the upper portion of the sheet— "has our requirements. Where this section" —he pointed below that— "is a wish list of sorts. If they are possible, we'd like to see them done also." He pushed the page across the desktop to her.

Mrs. Watkins scanned the page and began to make

notes. "We can do single tree masts, though I recommend composite." She looked up at him with luminous, golden-brown eyes and his tongue stuck to the roof of his mouth, preventing him from replying. He had to get over this fascination with her, especially if they were to conduct business. He didn't want to offend the woman's husband. "But we can discuss that later," she added through her smile before turning her attention back to the sheet in front of her and continuing to scribble notes. She looked up at him again. "One hundred eighty-five feet is lengthy," she said. "Depending on how she's sparred, it could appear too long or visually unbalanced. What's your cargo?"

"Tea," he replied. "And perhaps other cargo, eventually."

"Human cargo?" Their eyes met and he understood her meaning.

"Never." He tried not to sound too judgmental. He knew slavery was an accepted practice in the States. Even though he didn't agree with it, he didn't want to offend the potential shipbuilder for his business.

She exhaled a deeply held breath and relaxed her shoulders, which told Lucky exactly where she stood on the issue.

"Good. I don't think my conscience would allow me to build for the slave trade," she replied and continued asking him questions and making notes. "What is your time line for delivery? We are about to have a slot open for a new build. Though only one right now, as we're soon to have *Carolina* floated. *Ajax* is the nearly completed boat at the dock. Her owner is expected at the first of the month for transfer of ownership. At the moment, construction is running ten to twelve months, and I don't foresee it getting any faster as my yard is at capacity right now."

Lucky could only nod his head in agreement, still a bit unbalanced by the whole discourse. They continued their discussion on specifications and requested items, closing with Mrs. Watkins asking for a few days to sketch something he might like. Lucky, again, could only agree, so dumbstruck and fascinated by this intelligent wisp of a young woman was he.

"Please come by tomorrow morning, say, around eight. I shall make sure Mr. Watkins is here. I'm certain he would love to hear how Hamish's son fares." She backed the chair away and stood. When she reached out with her ungloved right hand, intending for him to shake it, Lucky stared at it for a moment. At home, a lady was never so forward as to offer her hand to a gentleman she did not know, much less an ungloved hand. It felt as though he'd entered a strange land with strange customs and courtesies. But rather than offend her, as she might be designing his and Ian's new tea clippers, he reached out and took it, holding it lightly between his thumb and fingers.

The heat radiating through his fingers from her skin jolted him. His body was reacting in ways he'd never experienced. He'd been with women intimately, but this was a feeling beyond anything he'd ever known or felt. A warm tremor moved through him, finally settling low in his abdomen.

Before meeting Mrs. Watkins, the married women he'd had affairs with never interested him long enough to want anything beyond a quick, mutually satisfying romp in the sheets. He could barely tolerate conversing with them. He perfected early on the skill of politely listening as they droned on about their day, their shopping, or the latest gossip. He'd never visited courtesans, though he had kept a mistress who taught him well, before he began sailing regularly.

But never had any of these women ever touched that emotional depth inside his heart that made him care. Made him crave.

He looked down at her hand in his, which was far easier than looking into the depths of her amber-colored eyes or focusing on her luscious pink lips. And he *craved*.

He thanked her for her time and promised to return in the morning. He felt the room closing in on them, and he realized that he'd completely forgotten that there was another man in the antechamber and at least two others in offices nearby. She'd made him forget the world outside this room so much that he could have easily reached down and kissed another man's wife.

It wasn't as though he'd never bedded a married woman, because he'd enjoyed the favors of many willing wives over the years. But he always had to know beforehand if the woman was in a certain type of relationship with her husband. The last thing he wanted was some lovesick spouse calling him out.

The only line he would never cross was dallying with the wives of friends, and he hoped to hell Watkins wasn't a likable chap. Lucky definitely had to watch himself where Mrs. Watkins was concerned, because he wanted the red-headed beauty in the worst way. Right now he felt the need for a cold swim, and because water cold enough to subdue his rising ardor wasn't likely to be found around here, a confessional and penance might do the trick.

Once he exited the building, he walked briskly toward town intending to find a confessor.

Mary-Michael closed the door to her husband's office and plopped into his leather chair. Her nerves still rattled from the man's touch. How had she maintained her calm business-like demeanor when all she wanted was to melt into a puddle of muck at the man's feet? Thinking on it, she decided that the way he held himself, the way he spoke, dressed, and walked all contributed to the air of confidence that intrigued and aroused her. All of it together made him so…captivating.

And then he touched her. Yes, she'd held her hand out first to shake his, so theoretically, she'd encouraged his touch, but oh, heaven—Mary-Michael smiled in the empty room. *That* was forward!

At one point, she had felt as though she might lose his interest, just as she had on many occasions when a potential customer discovered M. Michael Watkins was not a male, but she quickly touted her credentials and areas of study she'd focused on when learning this trade, all so as not to lose this potential sale. Mr. Watkins would be proud.

Laying her head on her crossed arms on top of the desk, she heaved a deep, trembling sigh. God help her. This was not good. What was his name again, this friend of Ian Ross? He had a British accent, but his surname wasn't English. Was it Spanish or Italian? Portuguese perhaps? She sighed as she recalled his image. He had an exotic appearance, with a swarthy, olive-skinned complexion and head full of shaggy, wavy hair. His strong square jawline and chin bore a smattering of stubble, as though he'd not shaved recently. Instead of making him appear unkempt and disgusting, it had the opposite effect on her. He appeared rakishly handsome in his finely tailored and starched white shirt, form-fitting buff-colored breeches, and high black leather boots polished to a near mirror-shine—unlike her scuffed black work boots. The man wore no coat, likely because of the unseasonably warm weather, but she felt sure that if he had it would have been of the same superior quality as his breeches and linen shirt. And under all that fine clothing, he looked to be well-muscled and very fit, telling Mary-Michael that he spent his days working right alongside his crew.

She sat up and stared out the open windows into the shipyard and recalled the full lips that had captured her gaze more than once. Mary-Michael had had to force herself not to let it linger there, for he could easily have suspected she was a woman of loose morals had he caught her. This business was hard enough for a man, the only credibility she had—and she fully recognized this—was in her marriage to her husband, one of the finest shipbuilders on the eastern seaboard. Mary-Michael only had a short time to establish herself before he passed away and would be left on her own, which was why she could never have her reputation called into question. Ever.

Though she might not remember the man's name, she certainly remembered his look. And the one time he smiled fully, she got a glimpse of even white upper teeth, with the lower ones just slightly, endearingly, crooked. It didn't detract from his looks at all and was perhaps the tiniest of imperfections in the most perfect specimen of man she'd ever seen. Oh, and his eyes....

Surely his dark brown eyes could see into her soul, witnessing all of the conflicted emotion his presence created within her. Something that had never existed until he arrived. The man was unnerving and quite simply beautiful. She could think of no other word to describe the man but *beautiful*.

Suddenly, the project her husband mentioned a few days earlier was now forefront in her mind. Mary-Michael now had to reconcile the morality of it, against the reality. She was a married woman with a husband who couldn't give her what she so desperately wanted, because that wasn't the kind of marriage they had.

Flustered and unable to think clearly about work, Mary-Michael stood and collected her light jacket, ready to call an end to the long day. As she left the office, she said goodnight to Andrew, asking him to lock up on his way out. She walked through the long hallway, lined with framed drawings of the most prominent vessels her husband's shipyard had built over the thirty years he'd been in business. She wanted to draw something on par with *Olympia* or *Mermaid* for this client, a vessel sleek and fast, able to cut through the waves and fly with wind.

Wending her way into the shipyard stable, she saw her driver hammering a shoe to the horse's hoof and changed her mind. "Victor, I think I shall walk home this evening. I could use the exercise." Not to mention the time to think on what she'd now tell her husband about the visitor and what he wanted. She also needed to reconcile these errant emotions, which were sure to get her into trouble if anyone noticed.

"It's not safe for a young woman such as yourself to go walkin' through these streets near the docks." Victor, Mr. Watkins's servant for longer than she's been alive, started his usual rant about her walking. "One never knows what mischief lies around a corner out there nowadays." He set the horse's foot down and looked at the four to check them for balance. "Time jus' got away from me, Miz Watkins. If you'd give me a few minutes, I'll have the ol' girl between the shafts in no time and get ya home safe soon enough."

Mary-Michael leaned against a post and watched as he picked the hoof up again and removed the temporary nail holding the shoe, took the file from his back pocket, and began to rasp more hoof away.

"It's okay, Victor. It's almost time for dinner. Besides, you know walking helps me clear my head after a busy day. We have a potential new client, and I want to think about some designs from the notes I took during the meeting. He's coming back tomorrow to meet with Mr. Watkins."

"At least get one of the lads from that Dutchy's crew to walk with ya."

Mary-Michael began the trek through the yard toward the street, calling back at Victor, "I'm fine. See you at the house."

Once through the yard, it was only a short eight blocks to the house she shared with Mr. Watkins and their servants, Sally and Victor. She could run the distance in less than ten minutes, but a nice leisurely walk through the wharf business area wasn't as bad as people often thought it was. For certain there were the shady types, the drunken rogues who hung around the alleyways near the pubs waiting for their doors to open, though the constable kept most of them in line. But for the most part, people down here were hard-working, church-going people. She should know. This was where she'd grown up. Every day either on foot or in the buggy, she passed the dry goods store she'd lived above as a child before the fever took her parents, leaving her and her brother, George, orphaned. This was her home. She'd never left Harbor Village in her life except to visit Mr. Watkins's farm several times a year. It wasn't as bad as Victor always made it out to be.

The houses on Washington Street weren't like the houses farther in town with a lot of extra rooms for visitors. Most of these modest homes belonged to tradesmen and their families and, thus, were on the small side. Though their home was one of the larger of these, it wasn't by much. Mr. Watkins had added on to the house when his first wife, Abigail, had been with child, so this house had three bedrooms, where most had two. He'd also turned one of the two downstairs sitting rooms into an office for himself not long after that first wife passed away trying to deliver their babe.

Mary-Michael crossed her front porch, relishing the bit of evening breeze they caught up here on the slight knoll overlooking the bay. She pushed open the screen door. "I'm home, Sally," she called out as she went down the hallway looking for Mr. Watkins in his study. She tossed her jacket on the banister rail and heard Sally acknowledge her from out in the kitchen. "I walked, so Victor will be along soon. He was nailing a shoe on Buttercup when I left. She must have lost it when Victor brought Mr. Watkins home at noon." She knocked softly on the door to her husband's office but heard no reply. She thought perhaps he was asleep. Cautiously pushing the door open, she discovered she was right. He sat in his favorite wing chair in the corner, holding the evening paper.

His rheumy eyes opened and he smiled. "Ah, Mary, my girl. A man couldn't have a better companion."

"I'm also your wife, Mr. Watkins." She poured herself a glass of water and took a seat across from him on the settee.

"Just on paper. But that's all that matters, eh?"

"Yes, sir."

"What's Sally cooking for dinner?" Mr. Watkins made a great show of raising his paper and snapping the wrinkles from it.

"I don't know, sir, but it smells delicious."

"She doesn't cook a thing that isn't, my girl." Her dear, yet wizened, husband began to peruse the inside pages. "So how is everything at the office?"

"It got interesting after you left," Mary-Michael said.

The elderly man lowered his paper enough to meet her gaze. "How so?"

"We had a visitor. An Englishman. He said he is the partner of a Mr. Ian Ross, formerly of Indian Point." She awaited his recognition of the name, and when he smiled, she knew he'd remembered. "He said Ian is soon to inherit his uncle's title. He will be the Earl of Something, Mr. Watkins. Your old friend's son will be a nobleman, and the two men are partners in a tea-importing company."

Her husband folded the paper and nodded his nearly bald head. "It's why Hamish sent his only child to live with that old...." He cut off what he was going to call the man, likely so as not to offend her. "What did he want, this visitor. Was Ian with him?"

"No, sir, he was not." Mary-Michael tempered her excitement and continued. "This gentleman said he admired the vessels under construction as he walked through our yard."

Her husband's eyes danced with merriment. "Did you tell him they were all your designs?"

"Yes, though you know I am uncomfortable doing so. We only spoke for a few minutes. The man said he and his partner are looking at the expansion of their business. They are in need of *two* new clippers." When her husband's eyes grew wide with interest, she went on. "They are in need of boats that can compete in the tea trade. They're currently sailing a pair of twenty-one-year-old clippers from none other than Jorgensen's yard up in Halifax."

Mr. Watkins continued to nod acknowledging their competitor who'd shown interest in buying them out, and she went on.

"They have one hundred and twenty footers now, and he's looking at one hundred and eighty or eighty-five feet. With that, I can increase his cargo capacity by sixty to eighty percent *and* get him where he needs to go faster, but I didn't tell him that." Mary-Michael couldn't stop the grin from spreading across her face.

"Why not?"

Mary-Michael considered her words. "Well, like most men, he didn't seem comfortable discussing business with a woman. In fact, I think he'd rather deal directly with you. And secondly, I wouldn't want to promise any percentage increase in his profit until I knew exactly what he wanted in accommodations and trim."

Her husband chuckled. "I taught you well, my dear."

Sally walked in with a fresh pitcher of water with sliced lemon and two glasses with big cut pieces of ice.

She poured their drinks and said, "Dinner will be served in ten minutes, Miz Watkins."

"Thank you, Sally."

Her husband swallowed deeply from his cold drink and held it as he stared at her in an odd way. "I want to know if you've given any thought to what we discussed the other day, Mrs. Watkins."

"Regarding what, sir?" she asked, though she knew exactly what topic he meant to revisit.

"Regarding your heart's desire."

Mary-Michael sighed and turned to stare out the window at the lengthening shadows of the trees on the bricked streets. "I'm not sure I can do it."

"You could if you met the right person, lass." He sipped from his glass again. "We will need to find you this right man soon. I never know when I lay my head down at night if I'll be picking it up the next morning. If you want your babe to carry my name, you should do something about it soon, Mrs. Watkins."

He saw her slowness to reply as a need for more time to think on the subject. What her dear mentor and husband could not know was that she'd already begun to consider his plan during her walk home. First, she wondered if she could do it at all. And second, there was this unexplainable attraction she felt with this man. If this was what her friend Molly had meant when she said Mary-Michael would know it when she felt it, then she was certainly feeling it. And *that* was the only reason she might consider doing it.

She wondered what it would be like to create her babe with this man, the one whose name she did not remember.

"I would never push you to do this," Mr. Watkins said, "except I've heard you cry at night and know my days are numbered."

She wiped at a single tear, unwilling to cry over this again. "Sometimes I feel this desire for a babe has me so envious of my own friends that I avoid them. I know they sense me distancing myself from them, too. It's not that I'm not happy for them, because you know I am." She wiped again. "It's just that I'm so jealous of their happiness I've thrown myself into my work even more and given up their company so as not to feel my own pain. It's a self-centered jealousy that I fight, sir, and I'm not sure that those emotions are good to feel if one wants to be a good mother."

"You are the least selfish woman I know, Mary Watkins, and you deserve this child of your heart." He sat back and closed his eyes.

"But what I have to do to get this child of my dreams means committing a grievous sin." She could never take a sin as enormous as this into the confessional—at least not in Harbor Village—both priests knew her personally. She'd have to go into Baltimore. And after? Even after confessing, for the rest of her life, while she enjoyed the beauty of motherhood—if she were so blessed—she would always know in her heart that she'd sinned to create her little miracle.

"Is it a sin when I am willing it? Did not Sarah give her maid, Hagar, to Abraham to conceive his children?"

"Yes, and it broke Hagar's heart to give over her son to Sarah after his birth."

"You will not have that issue if the father of your child is someone who isn't from here," her husband countered. "We can go to New York, Washington, or Richmond if someone from Baltimore is too near for you to choose." She wiped her eyes, thinking about the gift her husband was giving her to allow this. "I will help you all I can Mrs. Watkins, but I must know you want my help."

Through her tears, she nodded. "I may not have to go that far, sir. You can tell me if you approve of Ian Ross's partner tomorrow, for he is someone I might consider."

He smiled finally. "Well, I hope he is a handsome and intelligent specimen, for I cannot have a son or daughter of mine be anything less than both!"

Mary-Michael gave her husband a nervous laugh. Mr. Watkins was sure to find fault with the English captain whose name she couldn't remember, but whose touch still burned her hand. She would just have to remind her husband that he told her she was the one to do the choosing, not he. And she chose the dark-haired, dark-eyed Englishman who stirred up a whirlwind of confusing feelings in her.

After dinner, she discussed with her husband all of the items she'd written down from her conversation with the Englishman regarding the two new builds the man had requested. Mary-Michael thought to sketch out some rough designs for their meeting the next morning, so she excused herself from the table, telling her husband she would like to have something to show their potential client when they met.

She went up to her room and took a seat at her dressing table, then untied her hairnet and let her braid drop down her back. Lifting her fingers to her throat, she unbuttoned the top three buttons of her blouse. The room's two windows were wide open, but because there was hardly a breeze moving outdoors, none moved in the house. The heat caused a sheen of perspiration all over her body. She parted her bodice. The ivory-handled fan that one of her husband's customers had given her from his voyages in the pacific lay on the table. She picked it up and fanned her chest and neck.

If it was this hot in June, God alone knew how hot it would be in August.

Moving to her desk, she set up her paper and graphite pencils and began to think on what to sketch for this friend of Mr. Ian Ross. Two more clippers would be good for business, giving her crews steady work for the next year and a half, not that there was any lack of business. In fact, just the opposite. Watkins Shipbuilding was currently running one year for delivery, even though she'd promised the Englishman ten to twelve months. She'd have to put the word out for more qualified tradesmen because she really wanted to build these two boats before Mr. Watkins could no longer assist her in managing the yard. Or, heaven forbid, he decided to sell it, which was something they'd discussed a few times.

Mary-Michael went over and over the conversation with the Englishman, and she kept coming to the same conclusion. She was certain she did not mistake his desire for speed and efficiency, and given the specifications from Mr. Ross, she knew they were of one mind when it came to design. For the past six years, she'd been giving the customers what they wanted in their new builds, but she got the impression the Englishman and Mr. Ross were willing to consider *her* ideas and plans.

Her passion was designing clippers. Ships that had sleeker, faster hull designs with sail plans that would best use the wind. She loved dreaming up composite material design to reduce weight and allow for more cargo. *That* was her life's work.

There were only a handful of shipyards in the area that specialized in cargo-carrying clippers, though it seemed each year one or two more began to build them, especially because the demand for clippers was increasing almost daily. The only other shipyard out on the point with them, Barlowe Marine, focused solely on military-type vessels, heavy and armed from aft to jib, as the owner had a previous career with the government as a naval architect. Though well-constructed and of different design, they were military ships and not true clippers.

Watkins specialized in cargo carriers, where the amount of goods transported and the speed in which the cargo arrived to the owner determined how much money was made. Speed. It was important, but not the primary consideration in her designs. Optimizing the cargo space and making the loading and unloading of cargo easier and more efficient was as vital to turnaround time and profitability as speed.

Safety, speed, optimization of space. That's what she wanted to give this client. And hopefully he would give her a babe in return. She smiled and placed her hand over her womb and imagined the possibility of having a child growing within her soon.

Mary-Michael returned her attention to the drawing and tried to remember everything the Englishman had said. She began to draw a hull, a bell bow, the headworks, keel, keelson, stern. Her pencil flew across the sheet as she added deckwork and masts and rails. Spanker to flying jib, she gave her new creation full sail. She marked the hull for copper sheathing, and for drama, she added waves and clouds against a stormy sky. The deck arrangement was a basic deck house with rear cabins; she was still unsure of which actual layout he'd prefer. He'd mentioned two full cabins on each as a preference, but Mary-Michael didn't know if he wanted them separated or side by side.

She stared at her creation, her heart swelling with pride. She loved drawing ships under full sail. For her, they came alive on the page. When she began drawing ships as a child, she could imagine herself standing on the fo'c'sle deck looking out into the ocean and watching the waves as they parted under her bow. Even now, she could almost feel the wind in her hair and the spray on her face as the bow sluiced through the water.

She could imagine it, just as much as she could imagine a babe in her arms this time next year. And both this drawing and that child of her dreams might become reality if Mr. Watkins sold the deal to the Englishman.

About The Author

Sandy Raven has a husband who spoils her rotten and kids who are just a hair's breadth away from perfect. She's addicted to *House Hunters International* and has *never* missed an episode, though she acknowledges that she could never live in most of those countries because the houses are just too small. She is also addicted to Starbucks' chai latte and never passes up an opportunity to have one.

Sandy grew up on the Texas Gulf Coast with sand between her toes and perpetually frizzy hair, which is why she now lives in the middle-of-nowhere Virginia in a place with minimal to moderate humidity (for perfect, non-frizzy curls), rolling hills, and farmed forests. The only downside to living where there are no lines on the paved roads is having to drive at least one hour to get herself a chai latte.

Her home is a renovated old farmhouse she shares with her hero husband in the foothills of the Blue Ridge Mountains, where she's owned by more cats, dogs, and horses than she cares to admit. She's a long-time member of the Romance Writers of America and a member of the Virginia Romance Writers and the Beau Monde. Second to writing is her love for her horses. She practices natural horsemanship and loves to ride her barefoot Tennessee Walkers on the trails and in the woods around her home.

You can visit Sandy on her website at www.SandyRaven.com, or on Facebook at www.facebook.com/SandyRavenAuthor.

Printed in Great Britain
by Amazon.co.uk, Ltd.,
Marston Gate.